EMPTY MILE

EMPTY MILE

Matthew Stokoe

ISBN-13: 9798638523305

www.matthewstokoe.com

For my son, Zane.
You were in my thoughts through all the long writing of this book.

CHAPTER ONE

Eight years. And now I was back. Back on my street. Back in my town. The house was still two hundred yards away, but I pulled over and killed the engine. From London to San Francisco, from San Francisco to this basin-shaped valley in the foothills of the Sierra Nevada mountains, the anxiety of my return had grown like some ravening tumor until now, with so little left between me and my past, I could no longer stand the tightening cage of the pickup's cabin.

I got out and started walking. Fast along the sidewalk. Past houses I had seen a thousand times before. But it wasn't enough. This last distance, this final minute between me and my homecoming, was a pain that threatened to blow apart my soul. So I ran. I ran with my arms pumping and my head thrown back. If I had had the breath I would have screamed.

Finally, in front of the house. Finally. Panting, pushing through the low gate, running the short path to the front door, and the front door opening, opening as I approached, swinging back into the house and Stan standing there, shaking his hands and running on the spot in his excitement. My brother Stan, eight years older and bigger, but still everything I remembered.

"Johnny!"

My name leaping from him like it was alive.

"Johnny!"

In that one word, in that snapshot frame of him shaking and running in the doorway, there was everything I needed to tell me that what I had done in leaving Oakridge was irredeemably, indisputably, wrong.

He danced backwards in front of me all the way along the hall, lunging in to hug me over and over, hanging on so tight we almost fell, yelling questions a million miles an hour, faster and faster, gulping for breath until the things he wanted to say outstripped his mouth and all he could manage was "Johnny, Johnny, Johnny, Johnny...." clapping his hands and smiling so hard I thought his lips would tear.

And then he stepped close and held me, hung on with his arms and pressed his forehead against the side of my neck...and in doing so tore open the memory by which I was most haunted - Stan in my room on the night I left Oakridge all those years ago, his face pressed against my chest as I hugged him goodbye, the silence drawing out around us, around my awful inability to make my leaving even slightly less catastrophic an event for him, hating the pain I was causing and hating myself because of it.

And the sound that had echoed through all my days afterwards, the only sound he had made against me - a single dreadful sob, bitten down on as soon as it was out. And as we stepped back from each other, seeing that he had forced himself not to cry so that I might not feel any worse than I already did. So that I could go and do what I had to do without the weight of his unhappiness holding me back.

Now, Stan pulled away and he was smiling.

"Hey, I want to see who's tallest."

We stood back-to-back and he ran the flat of his hand across his head to feel where it hit mine. He was much taller than he had been and his body, which had begun to soften in the years after his accident, had grown bulky and curved. I wanted him to be small again, to be the boy I towered over and my arms fit around, but he outweighed me now by forty pounds.

"You're still bigger than me, Johnny, but I'm almost there."

It seemed to me that morning that so much needed to be explained to him, to be made right, to be excused. But all I could do was say lamely, "I'm sorry I stayed away so long."

Stan laughed. "But you're back now! Dad'll be here tonight."

"He couldn't take time off?"

Stan shrugged. "Do you have a car?"

"A pickup."

"I'm not allowed to drive. Look, I'm wearing your jacket."

In my early twenties I'd lived in a black leather biker jacket. I'd given it to him as a going-away present. At twenty-three it fit him now, though tightly. Under it he wore a pale blue bowling shirt with his name embroidered on the left breast. With his dark hair slicked back and his square black-framed glasses he looked like some chubby '50s garage attendant.

"I like the look, Stan."

"Yeah, it's sharp."

We went out into the back garden. It was long and narrow and from our position on the northern slope of the Oakridge basin it gave a view back across the town. Beds of flowers and small shrubs had been newly planted against the enclosing wooden fence. They were tidy and well cared for. Stan saw me looking at them and puffed up.

"I do the garden."

"Really?"

"I've got green fingers."

He fluttered his fingers in front of my face and began to point out his work.

"These are blue pearl. They flower in spring and summer and they like the sun. This one here is a peace lily, you have to give it a lot of water."

"How do you know all this stuff?"

Stan tried to hold it in but couldn't. "It's my job."

"You got a job?"

"At the garden center. I catch the bus. I've been working all year."

"Why didn't you tell me?"

"So it was a surprise."

Below us, on the floor of the valley, Old Town - Oakridge's original Gold Rush heart of 1800s wooden buildings - glowed whitely at the center of town. In the distance, further south, a thin curve of the Swallow River glittered.

"Stan, do you ever see Marla around?"

"Sure."

"How does she look?"

"She looks good."

"Does she ever say anything about me?"

"Of course she does, Johnny. She always asks how you are."

Later, I walked up the street and showed Stan my pickup and moved it closer to the house. I carried my things inside and went upstairs. I'd been traveling solidly for a day and a half and I was tired.

Despite the sunlight that fell dustily through the windows, my bedroom was cold. When I was twenty-one I'd moved out of the house to live with Marla and my father had stripped it bare. It had been empty ever since and on the day of my return all I could find of the time I had spent there was a set of grubby outlines on the cream walls where my posters had been. A single bed had been placed under one of the windows and there was a small table beside it. There was nothing else.

I had not expected a magically reconstructed teenage cocoon, but the barrenness of the room was dispiriting. Like my father not being there to meet me.

I sat on the edge of the bed. Outside, I could hear a bird singing and further away the occasional distant grinding of an engine as someone drove up the slope from town. The scent of the carpet, the walls, the dusty air.... All of it closed about me and for a moment I was able to force a sense of belonging. But it wouldn't hold and I was left with what the room most meant to me - sitting, like this, every night when I was eighteen and nineteen and twenty, staring at nothing, wishing that I had not left Stan alone the day we went up to Tunney Lake.

I lay down on the bed and after a while I fell asleep.

CHAPTER TWO

In the late afternoon I went downstairs and my father was home. There was a smell of Chinese food in the house and in the dining room the table was set with plates and chopsticks and cartons of take-out. My father had just finished lighting a single candle on a cake that had the words *Welcome Home John* iced across it.

Stan made a trumpeting sound when he saw me and clapped his hands and yelled, "Heeeeere's Johnny!"

My father hugged me and made a big show of me being home, but I could hear his throat constrict as he told me how good it was to see me again.

I had memories of him being loving, of being swung up onto his shoulders and spun around. But that was a long way back when I was a child and still too young to demand much of his emotions. What I remembered more was his withdrawal of affection as I'd grown older, how the small badges of encouragement and pride and worth had disappeared one by one.

Later, no doubt, there were reasons for him to be disappointed. I worked only when I felt like it, I drank too much. And, of course, there was Stan and Tunney Lake. But before this, what can a boy in the first years of adolescence do that turns his father away from him? It took me until I was an adult and had had time to observe him with other people to realize this distance between us stemmed not from any transgression I was guilty of but rather from the fact that he was simply incapable of being close to *anyone*.

The day of my return, though, we sat and ate and talked, and it felt good to be with him and Stan again, to be in that house, to be part of the small bedrock pleasures that bind a family - food, conversation, sharing time....

After dinner, Stan went into the living room to watch a Spider-Man DVD and my father stood over the sink in the kitchen with his sleeves rolled and washed the dishes. He wouldn't let me help, so I sat at the kitchen table and watched him - a man in his late fifties wearing office clothes, working his way through a chore that in most other families someone else would be doing.

He spoke as he worked, about conditions at the office, the state of the housing market, various properties he was pushing. This was one of the few subjects he ever showed much interest in and to me it had always seemed faintly hilarious. Oakridge was a town that had seen constant growth. He sold real estate. Any other man in his position would have grown rich, but our family had only ever just scraped by and it had taken a small life insurance payout when my mother died to get anywhere close to paying off the house.

"Stanley has a job now, you know."

"Yeah, he told me."

"Makes him feel worthwhile."

"I think he feels that way anyhow, Dad."

"I mean in a community sense. Work is the oil that allows the wheels of life to turn, John. What are your plans, now that you're back?"

"To spend time with Stan. And you. I haven't thought beyond that."

"And a job? I can't support you, you know."

"I'll be okay for a while. I saved some money in the UK. I want to see Marla too."

My father frowned. "Do you think that's a good idea?"

"Why not?"

"You've been away a long time."

"Well, I have to at least say hello, don't you think? I'm bound to run into her sooner or later."

"Have you considered that it might be better for her if you didn't go stirring up the past? You need to be careful not to be too selfish, John."

Stan ran into the kitchen then, smelling of toothpaste, wearing pajamas with pictures of Batman on them. He hugged me tightly.

"Sorry, Johnny, I was going to come back in but I forgot because of the TV. Can you drive me to work in your car tomorrow?"

"Sure."

"Awesome. All right, pardner, I gotta hit the hay."

He turned abruptly and galloped from the room. At the foot of the stairs he yelled "Yee har!" then thundered on up to bed.

My father made small-talk after he'd gone, papering over the cracks of our last exchange. But both of us, I think, were saddened by the fact that after so long apart it seemed that nothing had changed between us. In the end, he went into the living room to watch the late news.

When I got up the next day I found Stan pacing quickly back and forth along the upstairs landing. He was wearing a full Superman costume and was trying to get the cape to billow out behind him.

"Hiya, Johnny. Dad already went to work."

"Nice suit."

Stan stopped and looked down at himself. He ran his hands over the blue material that covered his bulging stomach.

"Dad doesn't like them.... But I paid with money from my job, so it's okay. I'm not allowed to wear them outside, though. One of the neighbors saw me in the backyard and told Dad I was weird."

"Them?"

Stan beckoned me into his bedroom at the far end of the landing. He slid open the door of a large built-in wardrobe, reached into a rack of hanging clothes, and pulled out a black and gray outfit.

"Batman."

He put it back and pulled out another.

"Captain America. Sometimes it's good to be someone different."

"Tell me about it."

"You can feel the power more too."

"Superhero power?"

Stan looked a little at a loss and shrugged.

Later that morning I drove him to work. The road took us through Back Town, Oakridge's business and commercial district, and as we passed the shops there Stan stared dreamily out of the window.

"You think it would be fun having a shop, Johnny? Or a business? Doing stuff around town?"

"Be better than working for someone else, that's for sure."

"I think it would be great. People would come and ask you things and you'd tell them what was right and what they should have. And they'd know you were the guy for what they wanted."

Bill Prentice's garden center was a ten-minute drive along the Oakridge Loop once you got out of town. It was a large fieldstone building built high off the ground and set fifty yards back from the road. It had a lovely view over the Swallow River and one side of it had been converted into a café. A large pressed-metal warehouse connected to the rear of the building and out front there was an ornamental garden with a birdbath and a fountain. A hundred yards to the east there was another, smaller warehouse that looked unused.

I parked in a white gravel lot on the café side of the building. As Stan and I got out of the pickup he pointed to a silver-blue BMW SUV.

"That's Bill's. He's a businessman. I'm going to introduce you."

Inside the garden center Stan put on a full-length apron and left me in the café while he went to find Bill Prentice. I ordered an espresso and wandered over to a window that looked down into the parking lot. An old Jeep Cherokee had parked next to my pickup. Several spaces further along, a man crouched beside the front wheel of Bill Prentice's SUV, pressing something against its tire. While I watched he lurched forward slightly as whatever he had in his hand punctured the rubber sidewall.

The man stood and looked quickly around. As he did so, his gaze passed across the café window. For a moment his eyes held mine without recognition, then a grin spread across his face and he waved rapidly and pointed several times to the Jeep. I turned away from the window and went back into the garden center.

Stan was beside a display of potted plants, talking to a thin woman in her mid-fifties. She was well-dressed and smoking a cigarette despite a sign on the wall. When Stan saw me he hustled over, grabbed my arm, and dragged me to meet her.

"Sorry, Johnny, I was looking for Bill but then Pat came in and we had to have a chat. Pat, this is my brother, Johnny."

We said hi and made small talk for a minute or two. I knew who she was. If you were married to Bill Prentice you would have to be a recluse not to attract at least a small measure of attention from the town. And on two occasions back when I was living in Oakridge she'd attracted a little more than that. She'd used a different method each time. First, she'd tried to cut her wrists, then a couple of years later she'd tried pills. The outcome had been the same each time - an ambulance ride to the medical center in town and a quick save by the staff there.

These suicide attempts weren't splashed across the front of the local paper, in fact they weren't reported at all. But word gets around when the person involved is married to a town councilor and is also, independently, the richest woman in town. I didn't know if she'd made any more attempts while I was away, but from the flat look in her eyes and the deep lines across her forehead I wouldn't have bet much money that her emotional state had improved over the last eight years

Toward the end of our brief exchange Bill Prentice appeared. He was a fit-looking man around the same age as his wife with prematurely white hair and a square, ruddy face. He'd been a man around town ever since I was old enough to know what that meant, and after he'd secured his place on the town council he'd made a name for himself as a proponent of growth through investment in infrastructure. Less publicly trumpeted were the rumors that he was a bit of a pervert.

He clapped Stan on the shoulder. "Stan the man! This the brother?"

Pat whispered "Jesus" just loud enough for him to hear.

Bill looked tiredly at his wife. "I didn't know you were coming in."

Pat held up the butt of her cigarette. "Don't you have any fucking ashtrays in this place?"

Stan looked wide-eyed at me and tried to pull his head into his shoulders. Bill took the cigarette and put it out in an empty flowerpot, then he held his hand out and we shook. As he let go, he ran his eyes over me and I had the uncomfortable feeling he was assessing my sexual potential. For a moment there was silence between us, then he thought of something to say.

"Stan's doing very well here. We're lucky to have him working with us."

Pat's lighter snapped as she lit another cigarette. Bill looked irritated and fanned the smoke away.

"Do you need to see me?" When she didn't answer he stepped close to her and put his hand on her forearm. "I'm not busy."

"Since when did that make a difference?" For a moment she looked emptily at him, then sighed and shook her head and said, "I'll see you tonight."

Bill watched her as she left the garden center, then turned and walked into the warehouse without saying anything else.

Stan led me out to the front steps. Pat had just turned onto the Oakridge Loop. She was in an olive Mercedes and she drove with her forearms against the steering wheel, leaning forward in her seat like she didn't have the strength to hold herself upright. She was still smoking.

The day was warm and the display garden hummed in the sunshine. The mix of fragrances from the flowers made the air feel clean. Stan took a deep breath and let it out in a rush.

"Pat says plants know we're here. They've done tests on them and everything. Like if you go to cut their leaves off they get scared, and they like it when you talk to them."

I was about to leave when he grabbed my sleeve.

"Oh, Johnny, I forgot. I finish early on Tuesdays. Can you take me to my dance lesson?"

"Dance lesson?"

"Yeah, dance lesson. Be here at two o'clock, okay?"

I promised I'd be there, then walked around the corner of the building to the parking lot where the man who had once been my best friend waited for me.

CHAPTER THREE

Gareth was a tall, slim guy with red-blond hair and pale skin that looked as though it had a layer of rust underneath trying to get to the surface. He had a habit of putting his hands on his hips and when he walked he strutted like a peacock.

We met in a bar when I was eighteen and he was a year older. He'd recently moved to Oakridge from Sacramento, the last in a string of relocations that had started when he was twelve and his mother ran off with another man. Gareth's father was a car mechanic and had bought a small garage in town that the two of them ran by themselves.

At first it was fun hanging out with him - we were into cars, we liked the same music, we got drunk on beer. As I got to know him better, though, I found that there were other aspects of his personality which were not quite so carefree.

His mother's abandonment and his father's failing life-long struggle for financial security had left Gareth with a lasting sense of insignificance. It wasn't that he thought he was inferior to other people, because he certainly did not. He had simply come to believe that the universe had no interest in his existence. Because of this, he tended to treat people as mirrors in which to reassure himself of his own identity - a view of others which made friendship with him repetitive and draining. It also, on one occasion at least, translated into some pretty spectacular violence.

There was a small bar in Back Town where we used to play pool. I'd been in there one night, shooting pockets by myself, waiting for Gareth to turn up so we could head over to Burton and see a band.

Two guys on vacation from somewhere on the coast thought it bad form that I was using a table to practice on when they wanted a real game. Things got heated and eventually I figured it was safer to surrender the table and catch up with Gareth at his place instead. But that wasn't good enough for them and when I left the bar they followed.

My car was parked a few hundred yards along the street in a kind of no-man's-land between Back Town and the Oakridge commercial precinct. It was darker here and the road was lined with scrub-filled lots that had been pegged out to service Back Town's creeping expansion. The two guys figured it was a perfect place to hammer an uppity local.

They were big men and they were liquored up and after they'd knocked me down a few times the action and the booze combined to kick their poolroom anger into overdrive. One of them held me and the other took out a clasp knife and was preparing to cut his initials into my chest when a major disadvantage of that location, for them at least, made its presence known. The street was one of the ways you could get to the bar from Gareth's place.

They didn't realize he was there at first because he didn't yell out or tell them to stop. He just walked up with a wrench and hit the guy with the knife hard enough across the side of the head to knock him out. The guy who was holding me threw me to one side and stepped forward. He was about the same height as Gareth but fifty pounds heavier. The extra muscle, though, didn't make any difference. Gareth smashed the side of his face in with the wrench then kicked him in the ribs until something in the guy's chest snapped.

That was the night I learned my friend had the potential to be a very dangerous man, and even though he'd saved my life I never felt entirely comfortable with him again - something, I guess, which spared me a little angst a couple of years later.

Gareth first saw Marla when she took her car into his father's auto shop. She was an orphan who'd wound up in Oakridge at seventeen when her third set of foster parents took a job as caretakers at one of the campgrounds. After a childhood and adolescence spent in the harsh concrete of L.A., largely unloved and unhappy, Oakridge for Marla was a cool green refuge of the spirit, a haven from her past that she had no intention of ever leaving.

So, two years later, when her foster parents decided to return to the city, she stayed on alone, working as a waitress in a series of Oakridge's cafés and restaurants. She'd been supporting herself like this for three years when she and Gareth began their relationship.

For Marla, he was a sanctuary from the emotional rootlessness of her earlier life. For Gareth, any attractive woman who agreed to live with him would have been useful, would have satisfied his need to believe that he meant something to the world. But he found more in Marla than that. Bizarrely, for someone so obsessed with himself, he found a woman to fall in love with.

They lived together in a small apartment over his father's garage. When he and I were alone together he spoke about her constantly. It was a pairing which might have led to marriage, growing old together, children...except that I was in love with Marla too. And eventually she fell in love with me.

When it happened, when I took her away from him, it killed our friendship. He broke all contact with me, refused even to look in my direction when we passed one another on the street. This anger, this heartbroken enmity, had not lessened one degree by the time I left Oakridge a year later, so to find him now, waiting for me in the parking lot of the garden center, made me immediately wary.

He pushed himself off the Jeep and stuck his hand out.

"Johnboy. Been a long time, dude."

"Gareth."

We shook hands and pretended to be old friends glad to see each other again. Gareth must have sensed my uncertainty, though, because when the reunion was done he cleared his throat and stuck his hands in his pockets.

"This is an amazing coincidence, Johnny. When I heard you were coming back to town I hoped like hell we'd meet up, and now we have. I've been waiting for this a long time, man."

"Really?"

"What happened was fucked up. Losing Marla was a blow, I can't say it wasn't, but after you left and she and I didn't get magically back together I realized it was just one of those things. I felt like such a prick, you know? We were buddies. What happened with her shouldn't have changed that."

"Well, it was a long time ago."

"Yeah, but I promised myself if I ever got the chance I was going to make it right."

Gareth took his hands out of his pockets and raised his shoulders.

"I'd sure like to be friends again."

I had enough to deal with in Oakridge without subjecting myself to Gareth's particular brand of friendship, but with him there in front of me, holding out an olive branch, I didn't feel I had much option. And, of course, there was the fact that he'd saved my life hovering in the background.

"Okay."

"Awesome, man. Awesome! This is like such a huge fucking weight off my mind."

We made nice for a bit longer, then I got my keys out and turned toward my pickup. Gareth was suddenly aghast.

"Dude, what are you doing?"

"Going home."

"I thought.... Look, you don't know anything about my life now. Why don't you come out to my place? We don't have the garage anymore. You'll get a kick out of it, I promise."

"I don't know...."

"Johnboy, come on! Follow me in your truck. An hour out of your day. Jesus, man, this is an event!"

We left the garden center and turned right on the Loop, following the wide curve of the Oakridge basin northeast. The country along our route was mostly light forest, but occasionally there were driveways leading into the gardens of large homestead-style houses. I had the windows down and warm air that smelled of pine needles and hot tarmac blew across me. For a little way we ran parallel to a stretch of the Swallow River and the trees that lined the road broke its metal glint into a pattern of backlit leaves and smashed silver water.

It was only when the scattered houses disappeared and the forest became denser that I began to suspect where we were going. I could have turned back, of course, I could have U-turned and raced for the safety of town. But I knew that sooner or later my time in Oakridge had to involve a return to this place, that it would be impossible for me to reconcile my past without it.

And so I followed Gareth when he turned into an unpaved, deeply rutted series of cutbacks that had originally been gouged into the hillside by Conservation Corps workers back in the Depression. It took us five minutes of scrabbling up the steep grade before the track leveled out and gave onto a place every Oakridge local knew well enough, but which for me was burned like a brand across the soft tissue of memory. A place I had not been since I was eighteen.

Tunney Lake was oval in shape, about four hundred yards by a hundred and fifty. It was fronted on its long side by a beach of coarse sand that was bordered to the right of where the trail came out by solid forest, and to the left by cleared land. There was no shoreline on the far side of the lake. Instead, a cliff of pockmarked rock rose fifty feet, straight from the water. Above this, the trees continued, giving the lake the appearance of a giant soap dish chiseled into the side of the hill.

On the beach, a scatter of people sunbathed on towels or played in the dark water. For the most part, though, the place was deserted. Late morning on a weekday the locals were at work and the tourists, not having the incentive of knowing how beautiful the place was, were almost always turned back by the difficulty of the road.

The track we were on ran almost the whole length of the beach and ended in a dirt parking lot which had a small set of public toilets in one corner. Beyond this there was a bungalow with a barn out back, and a collection of rundown weatherboard huts in a row along the last of the land by the beach. A wooden jetty cut into the water here. At the end of it, a small rowboat lay upturned, the white paint of its hull flaking in the sun.

Gareth and I parked in the lot and got out of our cars. He walked a few yards toward the bungalow then turned back to me with his arms spread.

"Here it is, Johnny, the brave new venture."

Like the trail, the bungalow and its row of huts had been built by the Conservation Corps in the 1930s. They'd used them as their barracks while they cut hiking trails through much of the hill country around the Oakridge basin. When they were banged together their projected lifespan had probably been two or three years, but their frames and foundations had been well-made and they'd ended up standing for more than seventy. Much of their cladding, though, was now not original and the roofs were patchworks of replaced tin.

As long as I could remember the place had been run as a low-rent motel serving the few tourists who hung tough on the road, or the occasional party of locals who got too drunk at their barbecues to make it back down the hill. It had had a string of different owners, but when I was last at the lake it had been one of Bill Prentice's satellite concerns, a poor relation to his successful garden center.

The front of the bungalow had a red and white neon *Reception* sign in the window and had been made over into an office that faced the lake. I couldn't see clearly through the grimy net curtains, but it didn't look like anyone was in there waiting for business to show up.

Gareth led me through the front door. In the office there was an unmanned white Formica desk littered with scraps of paper and empty coffee cups. Behind the desk a doorway gave access to the rest of the house. We went through it and along a corridor. The rooms we passed were shadowed and dim and there was a smell of old cooked grease and stale urine in the air.

The hallway ended in a large combination kitchen/living room. Set into the rear wall of this was a wide door and a window which showed a short view of the barn and the forest beyond it. In the living area of the room the floor was covered with dusty, worn-through carpet on which a ragged lounge set had been untidily arranged. There was a brick fireplace that had old ashes in the grate and, beside it, a scarred card table with bits of some mechanism strewn across it

"As you can see, we've moved up in the world."

"You run the cabins?"

As we were speaking a man in a wheelchair pushed open the back door and rolled into the room. He caught what we were saying and grunted, "When anyone can get up that fucking road."

I knew who he was but he was very much changed from the last time I'd seen him. Then, David, Gareth's father, had been a physically tough man of medium height who, if you asked him, would tell you he worked damn hard three hundred and sixty days of the year. Now his legs were withered, his face was dried out and leathery, and he had some kind of scar running around the front of his neck. And he was in a wheelchair.

He rolled over to me and looked hard into my face.

"Which is hardly fucking ever. I remember you." He stuck his hand out and we shook, then he rolled away, over to the card table, and called over his shoulder. "You know what this is? It's supposed to be a fucking toaster. Only, the fucking Japs make 'em with parts that are so fucking weak, twelve months after you buy it it stops being a toaster and turns into a nice compact piece of scrap metal instead."

Gareth looked sadly across at him. "You need anything, Dad?"

"Pair of legs and a lucky streak."

Gareth tried to smile but it didn't work. He moved to the kitchen, took two beers out of the fridge and motioned me through the back door to a patch of grass behind the house. We sat in the sun on plastic garden chairs.

"What happened to your father?"

"This place. Five years ago he sold the garage and bought it figuring he'd finally found something that was going to bring in the bucks."

"Really?"

"It sounds stupid now, but it didn't then. The only thing that stops this place being a goldmine is the road - too difficult for the tourists. But the way the deal was put to the old man, it sounded like the road was going to get fixed. Know who he bought it from?"

"It belonged to Bill Prentice when I was here."

"Right. About a year before Dad got involved, Prentice was made Resource and Development Manager for the council - gets to say what bridges need to be built, do we need another set of traffic lights, etcetera. And, of course, what roads need to be built. The council has to vote on it but he pulls a lot of weight, so if he's behind something it's got a good chance of going through. Anyhow, time passes and old Bill strikes a cash flow problem, decides to sell the cabins. His wife's worth ten times what he is and could easily have fixed him up, but apparently she keeps her money very separate indeed from his little enterprises. So Bill needs a buyer, but the place is a fucking dump and no one bites. Until Dad. And what made him stupider than everyone else? Bill let slip accidentally on purpose that the council was planning to build a proper road up here. Bingo. Tons of tourists, tons of money. Dad was hooked."

"If it was that certain, why didn't Prentice hang on to it himself?"

"Oh, he had an answer for that. Know what it was? The council couldn't build the road while one of their councilors stood to benefit from it. Not bad, huh?"

"But the road never happened."

"The council changed their minds, decided it wasn't the right time for that kind of expenditure or some other bullshit. Bill swore blind he thought the road was a done deal. Said he was really sorry. But of course he didn't want to buy the place back and we were stuck with a property that couldn't pay for itself."

"And the wheelchair?"

"After a couple of years trying to keep it going Dad started to suffer from depression. They put him on some pills but they didn't do any good. What he needed was a shitload of cash. Anyhow, along with the depression he couldn't sleep. I didn't know it at the time, but in some people who have bad depression taking sleeping pills can lead to a preoccupation with suicide. So the doctors wouldn't give him anything. What he does, then, is call up some biker whose Harley he used to work on when he had the shop. Next thing you know he's got a pile of benzos. Sure enough, a month or so later he jumped off the barn with a rope around his neck. He would have died for sure except the strut he tied it to was rotten and snapped when the rope maxed out. Dad hit the ground feet first and broke his back."

"Hence Bill Prentice's tire today?"

"Petty, I know, but sometimes I just can't help myself."

The cabins were set a little further back from the lake than the bungalow and from where we sat we could see along the front of the row. They looked largely unoccupied, but as Gareth finished speaking two girls in their early twenties, wearing tight swimsuits and oversized sunglasses, walked down the path from the parking lot, unlocked the end cabin, and went inside. I raised my eyebrows at Gareth.

"You do get some customers, then?"

"They're what you'd call an external source of income."

"Huh?"

"They're hookers, Johnboy. We have a mutually beneficial relationship. I set up their tricks and give them a place to stay, they give me thirty percent."

"You're kidding."

"Nope. Oakridge has changed while you've been gone. All those rich people up on the Slopes? They're used to being able to buy whatever they want, and what some of them want to buy is sex. So far it's meant the difference between this place going under and just scraping by."

"They come all the way up here?"

"No way. House calls only. A guy who can shell out three hundred for a girl isn't going to risk the Porsche on Lake Trail. It's a niche market but there's plenty of business, believe me."

Gareth was quiet then for a moment and there was a calculating glitter to his eyes. When he spoke, though, he sounded genuine enough.

"Maybe you can help me out. You're not working, right?"

"No."

"I need a delivery man sometimes, someone to take the girls to their gigs and bring them home again when they're done."

"Like a pimp?"

"Like a driver. I'm the pimp."

"I don't think that's something I want to get involved in."

Gareth looked at me like he was trying to figure out if I was retarded. Then his face brightened.

"Marla."

"What?"

"Marla. You think hanging out with hookers might not be the smart thing to do if you want to get back together with her."

"Who says I'm going to do that?"

"But you are, aren't you?"

"I don't know what I'm going to do."

"Dude, no skin off my ass. Get back with her, don't get back with her. Way too late to make any difference to me. But think about the driving thing, okay? I don't like leaving Dad here by himself at night. It'd really help me out and it'd be easy money for you."

While we were talking David rolled out of the house and into the barn and began working on something with a lathe. The screech of metal on metal killed the rest of whatever conversation Gareth and I might have had. Gareth stood and beckoned me into the barn. He said close to my ear, "Pretend you're interested."

All the benches and the various pieces of power machinery in the barn had been set at a level low enough for David to reach from his wheelchair. When he realized we were watching him he stopped the lathe and held up a cylindrical piece of metal.

"Lamp base. Got an order for two hundred. Take a look. Now that's quality work."

He spent a minute or two pointing out its merits and Gareth explained that his father did custom piecework for a company of architects in San Francisco. The fittings he made were top-end limited runs and couldn't be bought in stores. I made some appropriately impressed noises but I'd had enough of Gareth by then and I leveraged this interruption into an opportunity to leave, saying I had to pick Stan up.

Gareth walked me back through the bungalow and at the front door made me give him my cell phone number.

"We gotta stay in touch now, Johnny. Hey, take a photo of me. Today is a special day. We need a record."

I had no interest in recording anything to do with him, but I snapped a picture with my phone because it was quicker than arguing about it.

After he'd gone back into the house I walked through the parking lot, past my pickup, and over the grass bank that separated the road from the beach. I took my shoes off and walked along the edge of the lake.

Marla and Gareth had been together almost a year when she and I knew that we would end up with each other. I was often at their apartment and I'd seen the meals she made, the cleaning and washing she took care of, the standard endearments she sprinkled over him. But I'd seen too, as time passed, that she was not in love with him. So I started going to the coffee shop where she worked and in her breaks we'd sit and talk. She was his partner, I was his friend. Both of us knew what was happening but neither of us could stop it.

And of course the time came when we were given our chance to do more than talk. A tailor-made day: unusually warm, Marla rostered off work, and Gareth away with his father in Sacramento buying car parts. Stan was eleven years old and on summer break and he wanted to go swimming. How natural then, how innocuous, that on such a hot day Marla should come with us to the lake. What else could you do in heat like that but swim?

If we had been somewhere else, somewhere with good roads and plenty of ice cream, the lake's beach would have been packed. As it was, by Oakridge standards it was still pretty busy. We found a spot at the southern end of the lake, twenty yards or so short of where the beach ended in a sprawl of rocks that merged, further on, with solid forest. We spread out our towels and hit the water

I have an image of us that day. Flashes of moments in the water jolting before me like sun through the windows of a moving train. And sun there is. It is bright around everything. It catches the spray we send into the air, it coats the surface of the lake in long scallops and bows, it makes the wet skin of our bodies tight and alive and beautiful. I see the sheen of it on Stan's dark wet hair, how it picks out the white of his teeth and makes diamonds in the drops of water on his lashes as he leaps up and down, waist deep, throwing scoops of water into the air, watching the liquid break apart into a fall of heavy drops that hold all the colors of the world as he laughs and shouts, "Hey, Johnny! Hey, Johnny! Look at me!"

Of these remembered images I wish that that was all there was. I wish some part of me had been good enough to hold on to just these. But there is another image which overlays itself on this glittering cavalcade, which my gaze was drawn to over and over during that last careless playtime we had together - that of Marla's back. Flat and smooth, pliant as it twists about the axis of her spine, the clasp of her bra, the elastic of her briefs squeezing a gentle line about her hips as she jumps from the water, splashing Stan. And me, watching behind her, thrilling with the knowledge which has just that instant become a certainty - that my hands *will* press against her body, that I will undo that clasp, that my thumbs will hook the elastic of her briefs away from her waist, dragging down over hips and thighs....

The question the two of us pose closes at that instant and there is really nothing more to do but wait.

Ah, that image...that knowing. It should have been a sun-spangled confection of memory, an Olympic torch of the heart burning down the long tunnel of the past. But to me now and for all the years after that day, the image of Marla from behind has become less a capturing of her beauty and my desire for it, than a portrait of my own horrific selfishness.

Afterwards we lay in the sun, stretched straight in a row, soaking up heat like cells in some giant organic battery. The outside of my thigh rested against Marla's and our blood pressed at the barrier of our skins until we could no longer ignore what we had gone there to do.

I told Stan that Marla and I were going for a walk in the forest. He wanted to come, of course, and when I said he had to stay and guard our things he gave a resigned snort. But he seemed happy enough and rolled onto his stomach and pulled a book out of his bag. Before I left, I looked down at his skinny back. Stan was a smart kid, smart enough to be a grade ahead of his age at school, and his superior IQ allowed him to excel at most things his world presented, but he was a poor swimmer and though he loved the water he could do no more than an uncertain dog paddle.

"You need some sunscreen."

"Okay, in a minute."

"And remember, don't go in the water, okay?"

"Sure."

"Promise?"

"Yeah, Johnny, I got it. Don't go in the water."

Marla and I walked casually across the sand, but as soon as the forest closed behind us she put her hand in mine and we started to run. We didn't have any idea where we were going but we knew what we needed. Between the trees the ground was soft with long grass and there were patches of light where the sun fell through holes in the canopy of leaves; outside these glowing islands the forest was cool and shadowed and the grass was cold against our legs.

A couple of hundred yards back from the lake we found a swale of grass in a cone of sunlight. We stopped at its center and the noise of our dash died suddenly around us. We stood panting, face to face, smiling. Light and dark. A heartbeat of stillness. Out there, out in the splashing, picnicking world, there were reasons to hesitate, to question what we were doing, but in this wooded sanctuary there was only us and what we wanted from each other. I felt the sun sizzling in my cells and my eyes, even in the strands of my hair.

The grass we lay on slid against our bodies as though it had been polished. It bruised and tore beneath us as we moved, leaving a pale wash of green on knees and elbows and shoulders. The moment was not lingered over, it was stolen time and could not be wasted on the languors that arpeggiate love. It was everything at once, as much as we could cram into a handful of minutes. Afterwards, as we lay beside each other, the scent of the grass we had broken rose about us.

Who knows what plans we might have made then? What resolutions to join our lives, what fretting there might have been about the hurt we would inflict on Gareth? But these turmoils were not to be, not that day. Sounds from the lake carried to where we were. They were baffled by the trees but if you listened you could guess at their meaning - the willowy scale of laughter, the short barking of a complaining child, the calling of a mother, two or three notes, over and over, like an instrument being tuned....

We had not heard these sounds, of course, as we strained at each other. But now, as our bodies quieted, they began to fall upon us. And as they fell they changed, from a collection of commonplaces to a harsh blatting that lanced the warm cocoon Marla and I had drawn about ourselves. For a moment I lay listening, trying to decode their meaning. And then I was pulling on my shorts and running, running, running....

Because the sounds I could hear were panic and danger and alarm. And I knew what was causing them.

Out of the forest. Into the sun. Our towels and bags were still at the edge of the lake. Stan's book, too. But as much as I willed the image, as much as I screamed for it to be so, he was not there reading it. A few yards further on, a group of people were crowding over something.

I ran through them, shouldering bodies out of the way, and stopped abruptly. A man was kneeling, driving his locked arms rapidly up and down. The jeans and shirt he wore were soaking wet, and beneath his pumping hands the body of my brother was dreadfully pale and dreadfully still.

As I dropped to my knees opposite the man, I felt a sudden desperate need to explain that I was the one here to whom this terrible event was most terrible, to confess my part in this tragedy to the ring of faces peering down at me.

"He's my brother," was the only thing I could force past my lips.

The man grabbed my hands, putting them where his had been, locking my elbows, showing me how to do it.

"When I stop blowing, pump."

For several seconds the back of his head hid Stan's face. I felt the narrow chest rise and fall but there was no elasticity to it, no willful drawing in or pushing out of air. His flesh, too, was dense beneath my palms, as though muscle and tissue had become somehow compacted.

I was moaning. I could hear the sound, but I couldn't stop it.

"Pump! Pump!"

I hammered down on Stan's chest.

People in the crowd started to bead together what they had seen into small strings of explanation.

"He was out by himself. I saw him go in - he looked okay."

"We thought he was playing. We couldn't tell he was in trouble."

"Jared saw him go under."

"Yeah, he was way out, but I knew something was wrong."

The man kneeling opposite me touched my shoulder and I stopped pumping while he blew another series of breaths into Stan.

When I started again, he spoke in rapid sentences around his own gasps for air.

"He was under a long time. My kids saw it happen, but I couldn't find him."

I knew all of this without being told, of course. Without the blinding caul of my lust, that this would happen was just so fucking obvious. Don't leave a child alone by water - a primal understanding. I should have been looking after him. I should have been with him. But being with Marla had been more important.

As I massaged Stan's heart the utter clarity of my guilt, the knowledge that I alone was responsible for the stillness of his body, took from me part of myself, stole away that quality most humans assume to be the bedrock of who they are - the quality of believing oneself to be a good person.

After that day I would never think that about myself again.

When Stan choked and spluttered back to life, when his eyelids fluttered open and he gazed past me into the blue sky, I thought I would faint with relief. As he sucked in great sobbing lungfuls of air I held him close, shouting to the crowd, "He's alive! He's alive!" And as they clapped and cheered I promised myself that I had learned my lesson, that I would never again be careless with another human being. I had no idea, in those moments of jubilation, that my lessons were only just starting.

The paramedics arrived while I still had Stan in my arms. They had lumbered their vehicle up Lake Trail in response to a cell phone call from one of the crowd. There were two of them and they pried Stan away from me, strapped him to a backboard, and carried him across the sand to their truck. I trotted beside them, repeating to Stan that he was going to be all right. He'd been looking around him as though enraptured by what he saw. When his eyes came to rest on me, though, he stared blankly for a moment and I felt the tendrils of a new fear tighten around me.

"It's Johnny. Are you okay, Stan? It's Johnny."

He smiled and closed his eyes. "Johnny...."

Then his head lolled sideways and we were climbing into the ambulance.

Before they closed the doors, I saw Marla. She must have been following us but I had not noticed her, had not even thought of her. She was standing still, watching me, and as our eyes met we both knew that what we had started in the forest that day was going to stay buried there for a long, long time.

The paramedics took Stan fifty miles to the hospital in Burton on radioed instructions from Oakridge's own emergency clinic. I remember the time as a strip-lit nightmare of recriminations from my father and my own worry for Stan. My father tried, I think, to keep his anger in check, but there were times when it was just too much for him.

Through the battering storm of doctors and tests and waiting rooms and not knowing, a word began to surface, a wicked piece of flotsam that weighted our lives forever after and tore from me any hope that Stan's near-drowning might ever become forgivable.

Hypoxia. A brain starved of oxygen longer than three minutes begins to die. Like never leave a child alone near water it is something we all know. But which parts will die, what trajectory of sacrifice the brain will plot and its effect on the individual, are never known until after the fact. Likewise the extent of recovery varies unpredictably.

A doctor, trying to give us something to hope for, said, "There is no certainty of interpretation in brain trauma. In the way the brain interprets it, I mean."

He only wanted to help, but it was wasted on us. We could see for ourselves that Stan's brain had interpreted its trauma pretty fucking severely.

There was a transition phase in the weeks and months that followed. There was rehab and therapy, rapid improvement in motor skills - a sloping graph against the axes of time and damage. After three months Stan had pretty much gotten as good as he was going to get.

The doctors said it could have been much worse. They neglected to mention that it could just as easily have been much better.

Stan was more than functional. He did not come out of it a slavering vegetable, he was not paralyzed down one side or deprived of the use of language. He suffered neither ataxia nor aphasia. But he was changed, there was no doubt about that. Gone was the diamond-bright focus he had directed at the world, gone was the goal-oriented overachiever, gone was the IQ that set him apart. He was Stan number two and he was never going to revert to what he'd been before, never going to heal beyond this particular threshold of resurrection.

And it was all my fault.

Now, twelve years later, standing on that beach again, I felt my guilt no less keenly. I'd left a kid who couldn't swim alone near water and all the time that had passed since then, all my years of isolation in London, all my blind-eye-turning, had not made the slightest difference to what I thought of myself.

I walked across the sand to the parking lot and got into my pick-up. It was not until I had begun the treacherous descent down Lake Trail that I realized Gareth must have known what my reaction to being at the lake again would be.

CHAPTER FOUR

When I got to the garden center, Stan was waiting outside for me. He bounced into the pickup.

"Hey, Johnny, I thought of something today. I thought of an idea to have a business."

"Lay it on me."

"A man came in and bought a whole load of indoor plants - weeping figs and dracaenas and yuccas. He wanted them for his office. But he didn't know how to look after them. He didn't know anything about plants. And that's when I got my idea. What about a business that rents out plants to offices and stores and places like that and then goes out and looks after them?"

"That's a great idea, but people already do that. We used to have it where I worked in England."

"Yeah, but nobody does it here in Oakridge. I asked Bill."

"Are you sure?"

"Absolutely. And he'd know, he's like king of this place."

"Well, keep it in mind, then."

"Yeah. Yeah, I'll do that. I'll keep it in mind 'cause, Johnny, I think it'd be good to be a businessman. It'd make me part of everyone again."

I started the pickup and we headed into town. For a while I was able to stay quiet, but eventually my visit to the lake got the better of me.

"Do you go up to the lake much, Stan?"

"I can't swim. I like the woods near our place better."

"Are you scared to go up there?"

"You shouldn't think about the lake, Johnny."

"Don't you?"

"Sometimes."

"I think about it a lot."

"You know something I think about? When I was on the sand and I woke up, I remember how bright the sun was and how good it felt to look up into the sky and it was like I could feel everything all around me. And then I felt your hands on my chest and I could see you and I could see the sun and the sky and I felt good, Johnny. That's what I remember, I felt good. I didn't always feel good later, but when I felt bad, when I couldn't understand something or when the kids were teasing me, I remembered that - the sun and feeling everything all around me."

Stan's dance lesson was in a clapboard community hall that stood alongside a church in a residential street north of Back Town. The hall had a concrete area out front for parking that was about two-thirds full of small cars. Several old people were tottering across it toward a set of open double doors.

Stan wanted me to come in and watch him but my visit to the lake had jarred loose too many memories and there was something else I wanted to do. He sulked a little until I promised I'd come back before he finished.

The Channon was southeast back over the Swallow River and was about as far away from Old Town as you could get and still say you lived in Oakridge. It was an area of light forest that held a scatter of small, widely spaced houses. A place where the rents were low and people kept to themselves.

Marla's house was a two-bedroom wooden bungalow a few minutes drive into the area. It was screened from the road by a hedge and separated from its closest neighbor by twenty yards of trees. I drove slowly past it. A driveway ran down the left side of the house and from what I could see through the gap it made in the hedge, it didn't look like anyone was home. There was no car out front and the glass of the windows was flat and dark.

I parked the pickup a hundred yards further on and walked back along the road, my hand tight around a set of keys I carried in my pocket. These keys had been with me through all my time in London - two for my father's house, one for the wooden bungalow I was now approaching.

The front of the house had not changed. When Marla and I had found the place the window frames and the front door with its pebbled glass window had been white, but on our second day there we'd painted them red to mark the exuberance we felt at finally making our home together. I was twenty-one and Marla had just left Gareth for me - scratch one friend, gain one lover.

I wasn't sure if she still lived there. I'd written to her after I left Oakridge and she'd replied for a while, but her letters had been full of accusations and sadness and after a year she'd stopped writing back. Since then the only news I'd had of her had come in the rare letters or e-mails my father and I exchanged. Even the letter I'd sent telling her I was coming back to Oakridge had gone unanswered. But somehow it didn't seem possible that I would not have known if she'd moved. It was reassuring that the window frames and the door were still red.

I walked quietly down the side of the house, looked through what had been our bedroom window, and saw immediately that I'd been right - this was still Marla's house. The room was still a bedroom, it even held the same bed and dresser. And on the dresser, a framed snapshot of Marla and me posing at some picnic spot on the Swallow River.

I went back to the front of the house. I knocked on the door and waited a long time and knocked again but no one answered. I looked around me. None of the other houses in the street could see into Marla's front yard. So I took her key out of my pocket and pushed it into the lock and turned it and opened the door. I stood on the threshold for a full minute, listening, then I stepped through and closed the door quietly behind me.

Memory drove into me like a truck - the polished wooden floor of the hallway, the two bedrooms on the left, the living room on the right, kitchen and bathroom at the back. Even the smell of the place carried signatures of my time there - hot wood, air heated through glass. This house and the relationship that went with it had been one of the landmark abandonings of my exit from Oakridge.

The past reached out to me from every room - from shelves I had assembled and screwed to a wall, from hooks I had put in the backs of doors, from a hinge I had clumsily fixed with a nail.... The house was not a morgue for our time together, though. My ghost was there, but it was buried under eight years of her own living and showed through only in small patches, as though in painting on the layers of the present, time had missed a bit here and there.

I tried to guess what her life had been like since I'd been gone. It was obvious she had not become wealthy or even comfortable - there was not the accumulation of new possessions that would indicate eight years of stable finances. Had she found another man? I looked for signs and to my relief found none. There was, however, one change to the house I could not decipher.

We had always used the second bedroom as a storage room, had rarely ever gone into it. Now it was empty of household junk and held instead a double bed made up with dark blue sheets and a quilt. At first, I thought Marla must have taken a boarder, but there was too little in the room to point to regular occupancy. Apart from the bed there was only a small dresser and a wall mirror. But still, there was a fragrance of use here, a sensory mark that made me think the bed was sometimes used, that the mirror was occasionally looked into.

I pulled back the covers of the bed. They had not been recently washed and the smell of sex rose from them. Dusty smears of dried semen stood out against the dark material. I opened the drawers of the dresser. The top one held a set of lacy black woman's underwear and a bottle of personal lubricant. The other two were empty.

I was closing the drawers when I heard a car pull into the yard out front. If it was Marla I didn't want our first meeting to be like this. If it was anyone else I doubly didn't want to be found in the house. I bolted from the room, down the short hall to the kitchen. There was a back door there that opened onto a small garden. I unlatched it and stood waiting, ready to run. The size of the house meant that to have any chance of escaping undetected I'd have to wait until whoever had just arrived opened the front door and stepped inside. The moment they did this I'd race down the side of the house and out onto the road. And hope that whoever it was didn't look out of any windows while I was doing it.

A minute passed and I didn't hear steps on the porch or the scrape of a key in the lock. It occurred to me then that the driver of the car may well have just been using Marla's driveway to make a turn.

I pulled the back door shut, cursing myself for this insane act of unlawful entry. I left the kitchen and crept along the hall to the living room. There, mercifully, the curtains were half drawn and by staying close to the wall I was able to work my way around the room and look through the window at an angle that showed most of the area in front of the house without exposing myself.

The noise I had heard had not been that of a turning car. Sitting smoking a cigarette in her olive Mercedes was the woman I had met at the nursery that morning - Patricia Prentice, the jittery, unhappy-looking wife of Stan's boss. As I stood watching her, a second car pulled into the yard and parked.

My mother died in a car wreck when I was sixteen and from then until I left Oakridge I'd never known my father to be with another woman. He had loved my mother in his distant, battened-down way and I always figured his sense of what was right had prevented him from looking for anyone else. But it seemed that eight more years of being without a woman had eroded this sense of rightness just a little, because the second car was his and he was standing now, holding Patricia, cupping her breast and running his other hand down her back to her buttocks.

It was shocking to watch him touch another person so intimately. It was so far beyond my frame of reference for him that by witnessing it I felt I was stealing something from him, some charged emotional possession that should have been his alone to know about.

I didn't have long enough to really start feeling bad about it, though, because the kiss and the touching ended and Patricia and my father headed toward the porch. I crept along the hall to the kitchen and stood by the back door until I heard a key turn and footsteps cross the threshold. And then I ran, crouching low, out into the back garden, around the corner, and along the side of the house. I stopped for a moment at the edge of the front yard, scanning the place where the cars were parked, but it was clear, my father and Patricia were in the house and the door was closed behind them. I walked quickly out to the road and back along it to my truck.

As I drove away I suffered the unsettling realization that the semen I had seen on the dark sheets of the bed in the spare room must have been my father's.

The hall where Stan was dancing was a pretty basic affair - a stretch of bare floorboards, a curtainless stage at one end, a piano and several stacks of orange plastic chairs pushed into a corner. Almost all the people there appeared to be in their sixties or seventies and I couldn't help wondering if this gathering was less a lesson than some sort of community program organized to allow pensioners to socialize.

I stood in the doorway and watched the last dance of the afternoon. A portable stereo on top of the piano played an upbeat rhythm with a Latin feel and I guessed the class was practicing the cha-cha. For most of them, practicing was the operative word. They moved uncertainly through the steps and often stopped to confer with each other about what move came next. But Stan and his partner were in a different league entirely.

He was dancing with a girl about his age wearing a faded pink shift and a pair of old running shoes. She had dark straight shoulder-length hair that looked dull and unwashed and a lot of the time she kept her eyes on the floor. They were the youngest there by far, but they moved with confidence through the whole of the dance.

This was something of Stan I had not seen before - my bouncing, stampeding brother was suddenly graceful. It seemed that in this controlled world of set moves he was able to feel sure of himself again, certain of his abilities. That he was able to claw back some of what he had lost at the lake.

When the lesson was over Stan and I walked out to the parking lot. The girl he'd been dancing with had beaten us outside and was standing by an old orange Datsun. She had her keys in her hand but she hadn't opened the car. Stan waved to her. The girl didn't meet his eyes but she lifted her hand and smiled.

As we pulled out onto the road Stan turned his head to keep her in sight. Then he straightened and let out a breath.

"What do you think, Johnny?"

"You were great. You're far too good for the rest of them. I had no idea you could dance like that."

"What about Rosie?"

"The girl you were with? She was good too."

"I like dancing with her."

"You dog!"

Stan laughed, embarrassed but pleased at this man talk. "Have you asked her out yet?"

"Nah...."

"Are you going to?"

"She might not want to."

"What are you talking about?"

Stan shrugged and looked out his window. "I don't know...."

"Looks like she likes you."

Stan turned back from the window and smiled quietly to himself. "Yeah."

We were silent for a while. Then, as we drove through Old Town, Stan spoke again.

"Johnny, did you think about my idea?"

"The plant thing?"

"Yeah. I thought of a name for it. Plantasaurus. What do you think?"

"Like a dinosaur?"

"Yeah."

"Like it's some kind of plant-eating dinosaur?"

"You don't get it, do you? Planta-saur-us. Planters are us. Planters are us! We could be the Godzilla of the plant industry." He pointed out the window. "Look at all the stores. There are so many places that'd like plants, I bet. Don't you think it'd work?"

"Plenty of stores have plants already."

"But not proper ones. Not displayed all nice and looked after. People don't know how to, Johnny. They don't have time. We could deliver them, set them up in planters, and every week come around and water them and clean them and replace them when they needed it. Rich people might even want them in their houses."

"So, all we have do is buy a van, buy the planters, find a supplier to get the plants from, do some advertising so people will know about us, and find an office to work out of."

I'd run through this list as a joke to try to make him see things in a more practical light, but by the time I'd finished I felt bad for stamping on his idea so hard. To my surprise, though, he didn't seem fazed.

"Yeah, and we'll need a place to store our plants. Like a warehouse or something."

"You're serious about this?"

"Serious as a heart attack. Don't you think it's a good idea?"

"I think it's a lot to think about. You can't just start doing something like that."

"Why not?"

"You've got to arrange things, put things in place. Think it all through."

"All you gotta do, Johnny, is start doing it."

"Stan-"

"What are we driving?"

"A car."

"A pickup. So we don't need a van. There's a place in Burton we can buy planters from, and I can ask Bill where to buy plants. We don't need an office, but we do have to have a place to keep the plants and Bill has that other warehouse he doesn't use. He'd let us use it, I bet he would."

"He'd let us rent it, you mean."

Stan rolled his eyes like I was splitting hairs.

"No, Stan, it's important. All this stuff has to be paid for. It isn't free, you know."

"I know that, Johnny. I've been saving all my pay, Dad told me I had to. I've got almost nine thousand dollars."

"You're joking."

"That's what I've got."

"I don't know if it'd be enough to start a business."

"But you've got money too, don't you?"

"Yeah, a few grand."

"So we could put it together. We could be businessmen. Come on, Johnny. Please? I want to be someone people say hi to on the street. Please, Johnny. If I'm a businessman people won't think I'm so dumb."

"You're not dumb, don't say that."

"Johnny!"

"Okay, okay.... Let me think about it for a while. It's a good idea, but I need to think about it some more."

Stan smiled and punched the air. "Yes!"

In bed that night I turned the problem over. It didn't seem possible to me that a business could simply come into being the way Stan thought it could. Businesses, I assumed, needed detailed planning, market research, the raising of capital, prolonged evaluation of particular strategies....

In a way, though, the mechanics of starting a business weren't the issue. Stan believed that being a "businessman" would compensate for his reduced mental capacity, that it would place him on a more equal footing with the rest of society. If that was so, if there was a chance that his life could be made better or happier this way, then however naïve the attempt might be, I owed it to him to do all I could to make it happen.

It would consume our savings, and our lack of experience would probably doom the business from the start, but I had caused him to be as he was and this was my opportunity to make some small payment toward the debt of my past.

Later that night, while I was still awake, my door opened and Stan poked his head into the room.

"Did you think about it yet? I couldn't get to sleep, I'm too excited. Did you think about Plantasaurus?"

"Yeah, I thought about it. Count me in, dude."

Stan gasped. For a moment he was frozen, then he started running on the spot, shaking his hands in front of him.

"You mean it, Johnny? Really? Really?"

"But I don't want to tell Dad about it just yet, okay? We have to be certain about things first. And before we can do anything we have to sort out that warehouse with Bill."

"You bet, Johnny. Oh boy, my head's spinning round!"

CHAPTER FIVE

When I was twenty-two I was drinking too much and had already dipped my feet into the murky waters of entry-level crime, stealing cigarettes and liquor from the back rooms of stores at the edge of town and selling them to small-time hoods over in Burton.

Eventually there was an incident, a line drawn across the flow of time beyond which, for a single clear moment, I could see the future. And what I saw was the stereotypical small-town boy gone bad - cars and booze and brawls and petty crimes...all of it leading straight to some bigger crime that got me caught and sent to jail.

It was not a terrible thing that I did, not in the catalog of crimes available to human beings. But it was bad, and it was enough. I got drunk one night and stole a car from in front of someone's house. I drove it out of town and into the forest and a mile down a fire trail I punctured its gas tank with a screwdriver and set it on fire. I watched it burn with my jaw set tight in a selfish fury at a world that had maneuvered me into hating myself so much.

When the flames died I curled up beside the wreck and listened to it tick and crack until I fell asleep. I was drunk enough to feel, before I lost consciousness, a self-righteous satisfaction at the small revenge I had wrought.

But it was different in the morning. The charred stink of the car's remains woke me and I saw what I had done. What I had really done. The booze-fueled justice of my vandalism had been replaced while I slept with a reality that was mean and vicious and petty. I had stolen someone's car. Chances were that it was the only one they owned, that it was their largest purchase, scrimped and saved for. Chances were that it was not insured and that it would take my unknown victim months to replace.

When I told Marla what I was going to do, what I had to do to have any chance of finding some sort of pathway through life, she begged me not to go. She promised me everything she could think of - counseling, support, the dedication of her life to mine....

But I knew none of it would be enough, and within a month I was gone from Oakridge, leaving Marla with a broken heart and her dream of a safe and normal relationship in ruins.

The second time I went around to Marla's house after my return to Oakridge it was seven o'clock in the morning on my third day back. My father had told me she'd left waitressing and worked now for the town council, so I was pretty sure she'd be at home. I could have called first, but I was too frightened she would tell me not to come.

I knocked on the door. I could hear a radio playing inside and it crossed my mind that she might be listening to it with someone. I'd seen no evidence of a lover on my previous visit, and when I'd thought about her during my years away I'd taken it for granted that she would always be available. But it struck me now that I really had no reason to think this, that I might be about to enter a scene that could turn out to be very awkward indeed. But then, even the best-case scenario that morning was going to be anything but easy.

The radio dropped in volume. There was time to draw a breath, time to feel my blood fizzing with adrenaline, time for the pressure of an unbearable anxiety to stretch my heart. Time for me to realize I didn't have a clue what I was going to say to her. Then the door opened.

And she was there in front of me, slim, short, her dark hair long and tied back in a ponytail. She was dressed in office clothes, but her blouse was not fully buttoned and she was wearing tired-looking Ugg boots on her feet. When she saw me her hand flew to her mouth.

A second later she reached out and took a handful of my shirt and pulled me against her.

"I wondered how long it would take you to get around to me."

She looked closely at my face, my eyes, then stepped away and walked back down the hall, calling over her shoulder for me to come in.

In the kitchen the air smelled of toast and coffee. She took a cup from beside the sink and filled it and handed it to me, then stood leaning against the counter, examining me coolly.

"You're going gray."

"Yeah."

"You've got lines too."

"Still me underneath."

"The old you? Not after eight years, Johnny. I'm not the old me."

We were silent for a long time, neither of us knowing how to swing open the great barrier of time that stood between us. Eventually I said the only thing I thought might have meaning for her.

"I'm sorry."

A look of disbelief crossed her face. "What?"

"I know I hurt you when I left-"

"Do you know how pathetic that is? Hurt? I wasn't hurt, I was fucking destroyed."

"You know why I had to go. We talked about it-"

"You asshole. Don't you dare make it sound like we had some sort of discussion. The 'talking' was you whining about how unhappy you were and me trying to tell you how much I loved you so you wouldn't go. And what good did it do? Did it fix all your problems? Did it make Stan better? Did it make everything all right again?"

"No."

"What? I didn't hear."

"No, it didn't. It was a huge fucking mistake."

Marla took a breath and let it out slowly. "Do you know how many nights I cried over you? Do you have any idea how empty I felt?"

I put my arms around her. She kept hers by her sides but she rested her head against my chest and spoke quietly.

"I knew you'd do this. Just turn up one day.... Jesus Christ, I feel like I'm coming apart."

"Do you want me to go?"

She was silent for a while. When she spoke again there was such a note of defeat in her voice that I felt dirty.

"No."

I kissed her. For a moment she responded, pressing herself against me, then she pushed away.

"Enough, Johnny! Jesus! We're going to have to take some time about this, don't you think?"

We sat at a small wooden table that stood against one wall of the kitchen and drank coffee and sidestepped the misery that boiled in our pasts by talking about the plain surface of our lives.

Marla told me about keeping the house on after I left, how she'd had some bad times but had turned things around a year ago when she'd landed her job as an administrative assistant for the town council. I told her about London. Twenty minutes later, as she was making her final preparations for work, I raised the subject of my father and Patricia Prentice.

"I drove by yesterday."

"Really?"

"In the afternoon. I saw a couple of people come in here. Into the house. Their cars were parked in the driveway."

"You aren't the only person I know."

"You know who they were, then?"

Marla dropped her house keys into her bag. "Just some friends."

"Friends, huh?"

"All right. Jesus. You saw who they were."

"You can't blame me for being curious about what my father was doing here."

"Why don't you ask him?"

"As if I could ever ask him anything like that."

"He wouldn't want me to tell you."

"So what?"

Marla sighed. "I rent them a room."

"What would they want a room for? Our house is way big."

"A room to fuck in. Okay?"

"Really?"

"Really."

"They don't like doing it in motels?"

"It's more discreet here."

"And being she's who she is, discretion would be important."

"You know her?"

"I met her at Stan's work."

Marla shrugged. "I've known your dad a long time. Patricia's kind of a friend. When he asked, I couldn't really say no. They only use it when I'm out at work."

"How long has this been going on?"

"Six months."

"Wow, good for him."

"I suppose."

"You don't approve?"

"Pat's not well. You see them together and you just get this feeling of desperation on her part, like he's something she's grabbing onto, trying stay afloat."

We left the house. As Marla got into her car I put my hand on her arm.

"I could come back this evening, after you finish work."

She looked at me for a moment, then shook her head slowly.

"You're a smart guy, Johnny, but sometimes you can be fucking dumb. I have a lot of stuff to think about. When I'm done I'll call you; until then don't come around, okay?"

She kissed me, then she drove away.

At lunchtime I went out to the garden center and Stan and I had a short meeting with Bill Prentice about leasing his unused warehouse. He said he'd think about it and get back to us in a few days.

CHAPTER SIX

That Saturday we had a family outing. My father drove Stan and me out of Oakridge and into the hills. The forest was sparser here and ran down into gullies and small valleys. It was a hot day and the air had the dusty smell of dry pine and thirsty soil.

We parked in a clearing that was already full of 4x4s and pickups. A walking track led downhill and, carrying gold pans, a shovel, and a backpack of food, we followed it for ten minutes through land that was as much a wilderness as it had been two or three hundred years before.

Halfway along the trail Stan stopped by a fir tree and leaned against it. He reached his arms around as much of the trunk as he could and took a long slow breath through his nose.

"Stan, what are you doing?"

The annoyance in my father's voice came more, I think, from his discomfort at Stan's display of intimacy than from any delay to our progress. Stan didn't answer him. He had his eyes closed.

"I can feel it, Johnny."

"What?"

"The power. Sometimes trees can bring it across."

I looked at my father for an explanation but he just gave an irritated shake of the head and carried on along the trail.

I said to Stan, "Native Americans used to hug trees for energy when they were tired."

"I know that." Stan turned his head and smiled at me. "Everyone knows that."

The Forty-Niners, after they had made the trek across the continent by wagon train, or sailed into San Francisco and then hiked to the rivers and streams inland and had at last washed their first payable amount of gold, would write to family back home that they had "seen the elephant."

It was a description crazy enough to suit the desperate men they were and it suited the members of the Oakridge Elephant Society just as well. If you wanted a laugh, if you wanted to see the kind of whackos and crackpots that people in big cities make jokes about, then the Society was a good place to start.

Oakridge had begun life in 1849 as a placer mining encampment on the banks of the Swallow River and this group of gold-prospecting enthusiasts couldn't shake the heritage. They suffered a common addiction to the notion that somewhere, in some creek or stretch of river, there was still enough gold dust to make a man rich. All the history books said Northern California had been mined out a hundred and fifty years ago, but the members of the Elephant Society didn't always believe what they read.

They met each week in a hall above a drugstore in Back Town. They held jobs and raised families, but on weekends they took their pans and shovels and drove out to the hills to someplace they were certain the Gold Rush had missed.

They did find gold sometimes, what they called "color" as it lay mixed with black magnetic sands at the bottom of their pans, but most of the time it was only enough to refine and seal in a glass vial and pass around as an object of interest at Society meetings.

My father had his own collection of these vials, accumulated over twenty years. They stood in a line on a shelf in our living room, a tantalizing hint of American wealth, wealth which had never yet come his way. And it was to bolster himself against a declining belief that he would ever hit the financial mother lode, I think, that he'd joined the Society a couple of years before I left Oakridge. It was a place where the dreams of others could support his own.

The recreation area the Elephant Society had chosen for its annual summer picnic bordered a level stretch of river bank that had been, as most picnic destinations around Oakridge were, the site of a Gold Rush diggings. The place was too far from town to see much use and the grass had grown long and there were small yellow flowers scattered through it.

Membership of the Society was not high and with kids and wives thrown in there were only about a hundred and fifty people in the clearing. They were grouped in separate family units but they waved to each other and went over and said hi and tossed cans of beer around. It was friendly without being invasive. I could see how a man like my father, who was anything but a social animal, could find it bearable.

He greeted several of the families as we passed them and people stood up and shook hands with him. He seemed genuinely pleased with the contact and there was something touching about the way he laughed and spoke, something a little shy and holding back, as though he felt like an impostor doing it. It made me see how thoroughly lonely he must have been, this man who had to do battle with himself each day to force the emotional responses most others took for granted.

We spread our picnic rug out and sat and ate and talked about times in the past. My father could have had any number of reasons for taking us there that day, but I saw in the anecdotes and the paper plates of food an expression of his need to reach back to the memories of other picnics, other outings like this when we had been more of a family. When life had not yet done its dirty work. What he wanted, what the three of us wanted, was confirmation that there had indeed been a shared happiness in our pasts. At least at some point.

While we were eating, Bill Prentice turned up on a quad bike he must have trailered to the parking area. He wasn't a member of the Elephant Society, but he was on the town council and council members were elected, so smart council members made friends in every social and business organization they could. Bill had brought several crates of beer with him. After he'd unloaded them and called out for people to help themselves, he started giving kids rides on the back of his bike. My father did his best to appear disinterested.

After Stan had run over and taken a turn on the bike, the three of us went panning. Many of the adults were already ranged along the edge of the river. We found a spot among them and crouched over our pans, throwing in sand then sluicing in a little water and gently rolling the mixture, over and over, until the lighter sediment had spilled off, leaving a curve of fine sand that could be made to reveal.... But there was no gold in this river anymore and the Elephant Society was panning only to express its identity.

Stan and I had been panning many times with my father when we were boys, so today was nothing new for us and knowing there was no chance of finding anything in this impoverished riverbed made it a pointless exercise for me. But I stayed at it, squatting there beside my father, swirling dirt and water around in a circle, because this quiet crouching together, this time that did not need too many words, was the closest we could get to each other.

Stan gave up after ten minutes and sat with his bare feet in the shallows of the river. His pan held nothing but water and he tilted it in a slow rhythm, side to side, so that its unbroken surface caught the light and threw it back across his face in a bright pulse. He was dazzling himself with the reflection and behind his glasses his eyes were unfocused and wide.

Behind us, Bill Prentice now had a girl at the end of her teens with him on the bike. She wore a tight T-shirt and a short tartan tennis skirt which flapped back over tanned thighs.

Twenty minutes later my father stopped panning and stood up. The movement snapped Stan out of his daydream.

"Can me and Johnny go exploring in the woods?"

"If John wants to; it's too dangerous by yourself."

Stan and I walked away from the river, back through the picnic area toward the bordering forest. The quad bike stood riderless and quiet now beneath a tree. On the other side of the grassed area my father lay down on the rug and tented a paperback novel over his face. One or two of the families were packing up to go home.

A number of narrow trails led away from the recreation area. Stan and I took the first one we came to.

"Here we go, Johnny. Lock and load."

"Lock and load?"

"Danger lurks everywhere."

"Really?"

Stan made a face like I was an idiot. "It's TV, Johnny. Boy, I wish I had a costume."

Almost immediately, the forest closed about us. Stan leaped about on the trail like he was on a Special Forces mission. When he stopped to catch his breath I asked him what he'd meant by "power" when he'd hugged the tree earlier that afternoon.

He shrugged. "Just power."

"Yeah, but electrical power, gas turbine power, what?"

"It's everywhere, Johnny. It's behind things. We can't reach through to it, but it's there and it comes across, like it's just on the other side of everything we can see."

"How'd you come up with that?"

"When I drowned. When I woke up I just knew it."

We followed the trail for about ten minutes. It sloped gradually down into a gully then turned to the right behind an outcrop of rock. Beyond this, it continued along the bed of the gully and lost itself in thickening trees that looked gloomy and vaguely threatening. What held my attention, though, as we made the turn, was not the sinister nature of the trees, but Bill Prentice's naked buttocks, luminous in the middle of the trail about twenty yards further along. Crouched in front of him, her face hidden by his ass, was the slim girl in the tartan skirt.

Stan gave a short gasp of amazement and quickly clamped his hand over his mouth. The obvious course of action was to turn around before they realized we were there and go quietly back the way we'd come. I was just starting to do this when Stan jerked my arm sharply and pointed to the opposite slope of the gully where a black bear was padding its way between the trees. It wasn't a large animal, about three and a half feet from foot to shoulder, but out there in the woods with no bars to keep it at a distance and make it cute it was an extraordinarily frightening sight.

The bear had seen Bill and the girl and was moving slowly down the slope toward them. For a moment Stan and I did nothing, frozen in a crazy moment where it was impossible to tell what the right thing to do was. Should we yell a warning and risk spooking the bear into attacking? Or should we stay quiet and hope it turned back into the forest?

The girl solved the dilemma for us. The black shape lolling through the trees must have tweaked her peripheral vision because she jerked her head away from Bill's crotch and shrieked like she was in a horror movie. Bill jumped backwards, grabbing at his pants, looking wildly about for what he must have thought was the arrival of some angry parent. When he saw Stan and me he seemed puzzled, as though he couldn't match the severity of the girl's reaction to our presence. By then she was on her feet and racing up the trail. As she passed me she twisted her head over her shoulder and screamed one word, "Bear!"

Bill saw the animal then. He backed into a hollow of trees at the side of the trail and grabbed a fallen branch, holding it out in front of him like some sort of leafy broom. The bear was ten yards away from him now and had only a small patch of ground and the trail to cross. I started picking up rocks to use as ammunition. Stan stared at the bear as if he was trying to calculate its weight.

When I straightened again the bear had come to a stop in front of Bill, just a few feet beyond the reach of his branch. Bill's face was drained of color but he did not look weak standing there with his puny weapon. He hadn't crumbled.

The bear wrinkled its snout and sniffed the air, moving its head through a swinging half-circle. It sat back on its haunches and raised its front paws.

The first rock I threw hit it on its flank, the second bounced off its shoulder. The animal stretched its neck forward and made a hoarse braying noise, then fell forward on all fours again. I could see the canine teeth of its lower jaw. Bill shouted at me, "Stop! You're pissing it off."

"It looks pretty pissed off already."

"We've got to scare it away, not make it so mad it attacks. Get a branch. Three of us should be too much for it."

Stan and I found a couple of long sticks at the side of the trail. For a moment I stood wondering if it was really such a good idea to go charging at an angry bear, but Stan didn't hesitate. As soon as he had his weapon, he went careening down the hill screaming and yelling and waving his arms, 200 pounds of stout heart and soft flesh and greased-back black hair. With him on his way, I had no choice but to follow.

The bear half turned to meet us, but Stan did not stop. He ran to within five feet of the animal and stood his ground, whipping his stick wildly about and shouting "Git!" and "Yah!" and "Go away, bear!" The bear, faced now with an enemy on two fronts, swung back and forth, rocking on the large pads of its forefeet, baying its anger at this sudden outnumbering. Bill, seeing the animal's attention was split, stepped out of his hollow and began yelling and thrashing his branch about as wildly as Stan.

For a moment I thought the bear might pick one of us to attack out of sheer frustration, but after swiping once or twice at the leaves flicking in front of its face, it turned abruptly and bounded off a few paces. It stopped once to look back at us over its shoulder, then loped away into the trees and disappeared up the far side of the gully.

Bill dropped his branch and without a word stepped forward and hugged both of us.

"Well, that was something."

Stan made a face of exaggerated horror. "I thought you were a goner, Bill."

"If it hadn't been for you guys, I would have been for sure."

The three of us headed back along the trail, sharing a kind of survivor camaraderie, rehashing the event and commenting how lucky we all were to have escaped unhurt.

At one point Bill clapped us both on the back. "Well, I guess you know what answer I'm going to give you on the warehouse."

Stan yelped. "Really, Bill, do you mean it? Really?"

"How could I say no to a fellow bear fighter?"

Stan looked suddenly serious. "I won't be able to work at the garden center anymore once our business gets going."

"You just stay on as long as it's convenient."

Stan was anxious to tell my father about his adventure and ran on ahead. After he'd gone Bill said he'd have some lease papers for the warehouse drawn up and that he'd give us a discount on the market rate.

"And the, er, thing with Nicola, that girl, we can be discreet?"

"It's none of my business what you do. I'll tell Stan not to say anything."

"Good, good.... We understand each other. It's crazy, I know. I love my wife very much, but sex.... I'm not like other men and for me, when it rears its head, it's like going mad, something I just can't control."

Bill looked like he was set to continue sharing, but just then three of the men from the picnic met us on the trail. They were carrying an assortment of makeshift weapons and when they saw us they looked visibly relieved. Nicola had raised the alarm and the Elephant Society members who hadn't yet gone home had sent their finest. Bill was in his element answering questions and describing how close to death we had all come.

When we got back to the picnic ground he got to do it all over again. Among the people who gathered around to ooh and ah at the drama I noticed a tall man and a blond woman with their arms around Nicola's shoulders. They watched Bill with a little more scrutiny than the others and I couldn't help imagining that a small part of them was puzzling over the exact nature of their daughter's excursion into the woods.

My father was not among Bill's audience. He had fallen asleep beneath the pages of his paperback and since he was on the far side of the picnic ground Nicola's panicked cries had not disturbed him. Stan woke him and told him about the bear, all energized and proud of himself, wanting to impress him with this feat that surpassed what might have been expected of even a normal person. He was surprised, I think, when my father drew him close and held him tightly for a long time without saying a word.

Later, as we were heading back to the car, my father told me I was never to take Stan into the woods again.

CHAPTER SEVEN

Around eight o'clock in the evening, several days after the Elephant Society picnic, Gareth called me on my cell and asked if I could do him a favor. A job for one of his hookers had come in but he had a date and needed someone else to drive her. I wasn't desperate for the fifty dollars he offered, but I wanted an excuse to get out of the house, to do something that didn't involve Stan or my father. So I said I'd do it. If nothing else it was a distraction from worrying about whether or not Marla was ever going to call.

The drive up to the lake in the dark was brutal and I was glad when I pulled into the parking area and saw the lighted windows of Gareth's bungalow. I went into the office and found him sitting behind the desk, wearing a dark suit and drinking a can of beer.

"Thanks for helping out, dude. I do not want to blow it with this woman." He handed me a business card. "Her address. When you're finished tonight come over, I want you to meet her."

I read the card. It had her name, *Vivian Gelhardt*, her address, and, at the bottom, the title *Environmental Friend*.

"Environmental Friend?"

Gareth rolled his eyes. "No one's perfect. She'll tell you all about it if you ask her."

"I'll see how I'm feeling."

"Sure. Here's the place for the girl."

He handed me a scrap of paper with the scrawled address for a house on the Slopes.

"Just drive her up there, make sure she gets inside okay, wait in the car till she's finished, then drive her back here again. Shouldn't be more than an hour. Here's your dough." As he passed me the money he held my eyes and said, "We're going to be good friends again, Johnny. You'll see. I bet in a while we'll be spending a whole lot more time together."

We went outside and Gareth pointed down the line of cabins.

"She's in the last one. I'll see you at Vivian's."

He walked off toward his Jeep.

The girl was waiting when I knocked on her door. We said hello but not much else. She spent most of the trip puckering her lips at herself in the rearview mirror.

The Slopes sat high above town on the north face of the Oakridge basin. Between them and the residential areas behind Back Town there was a wide, steeply climbing belt of Bureau of Land Management forest through which a long, narrow road had been cut, connecting Oakridge's richest residents with the common folk below. Once we'd passed through town and entered the forest, the dark wrapped itself around us like a blanket and there was nothing to see from the road except a solid black wall of trees and the occasional entrance to a fire trail.

The house I took the girl to was built to look like it had been made out of mud bricks. It had a five-car garage and a garden that was separated from the street by an adobe wall. The plants in the grounds were lit here and there by gentle baby-spots. I watched as the girl was buzzed through the gate and made sure she got up the driveway and into the house. Then I just sat and waited and an hour later she came out again and I took her back to Tunney Lake.

I didn't really have any great desire to spend time with Gareth, but I didn't feel like going home either. Plus I was vaguely interested in seeing what type of woman could bear to be with him. So I checked Vivian's address on her card and made my way across Oakridge and back up to the Slopes again.

The house was on the first cross street at the top of the road through the forest. It was a two-story log cabin the size of a large suburban house, made from pale wood that had been stripped of bark and varnished. Over the front door there was a semicircular panel of stained glass that threw a fan of blotchy colored light onto the fieldstone path leading across the lawn from the street.

Gareth answered the door when I knocked. He had a drink in his hand and looked relaxed and at home in surroundings that were very much more salubrious than those of his own home. He led me through a foyer of bare wood and hanging Indian blankets that gave directly onto a large open living area. The décor here was Rustic Frontier - rough-woven rugs on the floor, two long couches in earthy, natural fabric facing each other over a chunky coffee table.

Gareth raised his eyebrows and whispered, "Not bad, huh? I'll tell you a secret, Johnny. I'm in love with this woman."

I looked at him, thinking he had to be joking, but his expression was perfectly serious. A woman with a glass of white wine in her hand entered from a door at the far end of the room. She folded herself onto one of the couches.

"Vivian, this is my friend Johnny."

We said hi and Gareth got me a drink and then sat next to Vivian. I sat across from them on the other couch.

Vivian was about ten years older than Gareth. She had sharp features and dark blond hair. Her gaze was direct and her voice had the harsh edges of a German accent. She spoke before I was properly settled in my seat.

"Gareth tells me you stole his girlfriend."

"That was a long time ago."

"But these things hurt just the same, no?"

"I suppose so."

"Something always remains, some piece of emotional grit that you can never quite get rid of, I think."

Gareth gave an embarrassed laugh.

"Viv, give him a break."

She took his hand and kissed it.

"If you wish, my broken one."

If Gareth really was in love with this woman then it looked to me like it was a one-sided relationship. She seemed fond of him, but it was pretty obvious she knew he wasn't what she needed.

In an effort to prevent the conversation from revisiting my part in Gareth's past, I asked her about herself.

"What's an Environmental Friend? Some sort of Greenpeace organization?"

Vivian changed gears abruptly. Her eyes lit up like she had a fever and I realized I was almost certainly going to regret the question.

"An organization? Bah! I am not one for organizations. It is a state of mind. An approach to life. It is one of the things I am."

"Cool."

"Yes, it is very cool. After university I left Germany. I vowed I would never go back and I have kept that vow. You cannot imagine the claustrophobia of Europe, the catastrophic rate at which the so-called cultured countries are covering themselves with concrete."

"I lived in London for a long time."

"Ach, what a pigsty. You know what I mean, then. I met my ex-husband in San Francisco and lived there with him for a long time. You cannot stay in that city without becoming passionate about the environment. No European can, at least. The harbor, the fog, the hills, the coast. So much beauty, so big and so wild. But what did I see? The same destruction I had witnessed in Europe. So I made a commitment to myself that I would not accept it like everyone else. And that is why I call myself an Environmental Friend. Because I am not blind to environmental concerns."

"Do you work in the community, that sort of thing?"

"I have done." She waved dismissively. "But that was another life. After I divorced my husband I moved here, and in Oakridge there is less to fight against. I struggle now in smaller ways, in the philosophy of what I consume, in the letters I write to the town council."

"You don't like the council?"

"They are not wholly bad, they can be persuaded in certain things - the glass recycling bins you see around town are my doing. But they are like every other commercial entity. They believe that to survive you must keep getting bigger, that you must expand and expand. It does not dawn on them to put their energies into devising a sustainable status quo."

Gareth, who had grown a little uncomfortable during Vivian's speech, stretched and asked no one in particular what time it was.

Vivian looked at him with disapproval. "Gareth, I think, does not see the world in terms of its beauty. For instance, he would support the council if they were to build a road to his cabins."

Gareth gave a bemused smile and lifted his hands. "Of course I would, Viv. Jesus...."

"Money, ach! That lake is a jewel. It should be protected. First a road, then a thousand people a day, then hot dog stands and the damn Coca-Cola logo. Let's have a Starbucks too! No, a road would ruin it."

She stood up abruptly and held her hand out to Gareth.

"It's time you took me to bed. I'm tired of talking about myself. Goodnight, Johnny. Please lock up on your way out."

Gareth winked at me.

"I'll call you, dude. Thanks for tonight."

After Vivian and Gareth had gone upstairs I sat for a moment feeling the big room around me, listening to the silence and to the short bursts of muffled laughter from Vivian's bedroom. Then I got up and went out to my pickup.

It was cold outside now and on the drive home I felt empty and alone. It seemed everyone that night had the solace of a warm body next to them, even if it was mercenary, like Gareth's hooker and her john, or as mismatched as the pairing of Gareth and Vivian. I fiddled with the controls of the heater, but it wouldn't work, so I zipped up my jacket and drove faster than I should have to get home.

CHAPTER EIGHT

I saw Marla the following Saturday. It was a hot day and she'd phoned and suggested going to the lake for a swim. Tunney Lake was not the first place I would have picked to continue our reunion but I was so relieved she'd finally called I would have said yes to anything.

When I picked her up she was wearing a tight white T-shirt and denim cutoffs and as she slid into the passenger seat I was suddenly aware of how dreadfully alone I would be if I failed at working her back into my life.

She seemed preoccupied during the drive and spent most of it staring through the side window and picking at the frayed hem of her shorts. It wasn't the best of signs for reestablishing a relationship but when we got to the lake and parked and were walking away from the pickup she put her hand in mine and squeezed it.

We went down to the southern end of the beach where there were fewer kids running around, stripped down to swimsuits, and stretched out. I could feel the heat of the coarse sand through the cotton of my towel. I rolled onto my side and looked at Marla. She was wearing a plain red bikini and I noticed that she had put on a little weight. Her breasts were fuller than I remembered and her waist no longer lay flat between the bones of her pelvis. She saw me looking and sat up and drew her knees up in front of her.

"You're very pale, Johnny."

"Yeah."

"Did you think about me in England?"

"I thought about everyone and everything. It got so I thought I'd go crazy with it."

I saw from her face that this wasn't the answer she wanted.

"Yes, I thought about you a lot."

She looked out across the lake. "I used to come up here after you left. Until the water made me think of you on the other side of the world. Then I stopped."

Her arms were folded on her knees. She turned her head and rested it on them and closed her eyes.

"You know, Johnny, if the past was a forest I'd burn it down."

She stayed that way for a while, cradling her head in her arms. The air was hot and heavy around us and I thought she might be falling asleep. I watched her face, the dark lashes that lay against her skin, and wondered why she would say something like that.

"Were things that bad? I don't mean me not being here, but life generally."

She lifted her head and blinked. "Life generally? Yeah, life generally sucked."

"How?

Marla lay down facing me and sighed. "I don't want to get into it today, Johnny."

She glanced past me and I turned to see what she was looking at. Back up the beach Bill Prentice was sitting on the grassy bank between the sand and the parking area. He was facing our way and though he was busily drinking from a can of soda I was certain that he had been watching us a moment before. I turned back to Marla.

"Tell me about your job."

She shrugged. "The admin side's okay. I take minutes. I organize filing, make appointments, set up meetings, that kind of thing. But I also get to research stuff and that can be cool. Like I'll have to find out the history of a particular building, or some old fact about the Gold Rush. That's the part I like most. If I hadn't gotten this job I honestly don't know how healthy I'd be now. Mentally, I mean. I have to take a piss."

She stood and walked quickly away toward the parking area and the small cinder-block set of public toilets. I watched her as she went. The day was not going quite as I'd hoped. I'd pictured us sunbathing in each other's arms by now. I rolled onto my back and closed my eyes.

Marla came back after a while and sat down beside me full of jittery energy and comic disbelief. She jerked her head toward the parking area. Bill Prentice was still there, but now he was standing with his hands in his pockets, looking straight at us.

"You know what he asked me?"

"Bill Prentice?"

"Yeah." She laughed like it was the biggest joke, but it was a brittle sound and I could tell that she was nervous. "He wanted to-" She stopped herself and shook her head. "It's too ridiculous."

"What?"

"He wants to pay to watch us have sex."

"You're kidding."

"That's what he said."

"You're kidding."

"You know about him, don't you?"

"I've seen him in action."

"What?"

"Stan and I saved him from a bear at an Elephant Society picnic the other day. He was getting blown by a cheerleader at the time."

"A bear? Wow."

Marla made me tell her about the episode, but before I was halfway through she interrupted me.

"You think doing something like that would be gross?"

"Having someone watch? I don't know. Right place, right time, right person to do it with. Might be interesting."

We'd been treating it as a joke but when I said this things suddenly became serious. Marla looked at me and I held my breath. After a long moment she shrugged.

"I guess we've got to start somewhere."

And I, of course, figured that all my Christmases had come at once

"Where would we do it?"

"He knows a place back in the forest. He wants it to be outdoors."

"What did you say to him?"

"I said I'd ask you. He said he'd pay two hundred dollars. But you know we totally don't have to do it if you don't want to."

The air in the forest was so humid it seemed to push back at me and the buzzing of cicadas made my head swim. What we were doing was crazy, but I couldn't stop myself. The heat and the insect noise and the throb of sexual desire had joined in a kind of fever that made me want to race through the trees, to be wherever it was we were going right then, that second. To be inside Marla.

The place Bill led us to wasn't far into the forest, but it was well screened and it was unlikely any nature-loving hiker would stumble across us. Behind a large boulder on which some delinquent teenager had splashed red paint, there was a shallow dish-shaped hollow that was shielded around three-quarters of its circumference by a wall of trees and shrubs. As we entered it I was aware we were probably only a few minutes away from the place Marla and I had first made love.

Marla avoided looking at Bill or me. We had brought our things from the lake and she rolled out a towel in the center of the hollow. Bill sat a few feet away. I did my best to pretend he wasn't there.

When Marla had finished with the towel she stood beside it, her arms straight at her sides as though she had no desire to make any further movement. I realized that she was scared.

Bill watched us like nothing else existed. His hand was between his legs, squeezing his crotch.

"Do you want us to, like, just start?"

Bill nodded. "Yes, please. And take all your clothes off."

I stepped close to Marla and held her. For a moment she didn't respond, then she lifted her head and looked at me sadly and whispered, "This shouldn't have been our first time."

I kissed her. And with that kiss I tried to pull us into a dark co-coon that would hide us from the man who sat watching. For a moment it worked, for a moment we were lost in each other. But then his voice came again.

"Take her clothes off."

I knew, even as I began undoing her bikini top, that I should stop this, that she was uncomfortable, unhappy, that the honorable thing to do would be to just give Bill his money back and tell him we'd changed our minds. But I didn't. I couldn't let go of this opportunity. I wanted sex, there was no doubt about that, but what drove me more to peel away Marla's swimsuit was a raging emotional greed, the need to be close enough to her again to begin fixing the piece of my past that belonged to her.

We got down to it, there in that warm hollow that like a lens seemed to capture the heat and concentrate it about us. When I entered her, despite being watched, despite the tawdry circumstances of the act, I felt an immediate and overpowering sense of relief. She had let me close to her. And if she could do that then surely there could be no further barrier to becoming a couple again. In Marla, too, I sensed a relaxation of spirit, as though she had wanted to clear this hurdle every bit as much as I.

This letting-go of hers, though, didn't last long. At some point she shifted under me and I saw that she was looking over my shoulder at Bill. I turned my head. He was standing, pants around his ankles, masturbating as he watched us. It didn't surprise me. In fact I had assumed he'd do exactly that, but it seemed to disgust Marla and she went stiff and kept her eyes closed until we were finished.

Bill left as soon as it was over, just buttoned his pants and walked away. I thought about yelling after him to look out for bears, but I didn't. Marla and I sat there silent and naked and watched him go. When he was out of sight I turned to her and forced a laugh.

"Well...."

I wanted her to laugh too, but she stayed quiet.

We got dressed and made our way back through the forest holding hands and not saying anything.

In the parking lot Bill Prentice was waiting beside his SUV. He waved for me to come over. Marla let go of my hand and went to wait by the pickup. Bill had the lease papers for the warehouse ready for me to sign - one year with the option to renew for two more, a reasonable yearly fee, three months up front, the rest in monthly installments. I signed them against the metal of the car's hood and prayed that this venture with Stan would not turn out to be too disastrous.

CHAPTER NINE

I stayed the rest of the weekend at Marla's place and by the end of it she had agreed to a permanent relationship again. Even though our exhibition in the forest had played a role in this reconnection Marla seemed haunted by the episode.

"Sometimes, I can't believe what we're capable of. The things we do...it seems like we're programmed to destroy ourselves."

"Forget about it. It was a crazy afternoon, that's all. We've got to leave the past behind us."

Marla looked at me skeptically. "I really don't think you're made that way, Johnny. But what choice do we have? You want to be with me and I can't live without you. We'll have to go through it until it all falls apart again."

"It's not going to fall apart. There's nothing to say we can't have a great life together."

She smiled sadly. "We'll see."

About eleven o'clock on Monday morning I got home to find Stan sitting at the table in the kitchen, eating a large bowl of cereal and reading a comic book.

"How come you're not at work?"

"'Cause Dad wants to take us somewhere. He said it was a big surprise. I called Bill, it's okay."

"What sort of surprise?"

"I don't know, Johnny, that's why it's a surprise."

Stan pushed the cereal box toward me.

"Have some breakfast. Nutrition's important. And guess what? Bill's leaving the key to the warehouse with the girls at the counter. Can we go check it out after?"

"Sure, you bet."

"Awesome!"

Stan got up and stared shunting around the room like a train, chanting, "Business-man, business-man, business-man...."

Half an hour later my father came home. He was carrying a flat package wrapped in brown paper. We followed him into the living room and watched as he tore open the wrapping and lifted out a framed black-and-white photograph about two feet long. He set it on the back of the couch so that it leaned against the wall.

Stan bent forward and examined it.

"Is it around here?"

"Yes, not far."

It was an aerial photo of forested land. The dark line of a river curved in from the right of the frame and made a pronounced bulge around what looked to be some sort of rock spur. Trees lined both sides of it. In the upper half of the photo they were unbroken, but below the river there was a patch of cleared land. On the bottom right-hand corner of the picture a serial number was imprinted and the image itself looked slightly grainy, as though it had been blown up from a smaller print.

"Did you go up in a plane and take it, Dad?"

My father laughed. "Not me, Stan."

"Are you going to put it on the wall?" Stan sounded dubious.

"I was planning to."

"You should have gotten something with colors."

"This is a special picture. What do you notice about it?"

Stan squinted hard at it, then stepped back and blinked his eyes rapidly.

"Whew, that made me dizzy. It's just a river, Dad. Is it the Swallow River?"

"Well done. See anything else?"

"Yikes, you're going to make my head spin round. I can't see anything. Ask Johnny."

"It's just trees and a river to me too."

My father smiled and looked at the photo and shook his head as though he couldn't believe his luck.

"Come on. We're going for a drive."

We left the house and got into my father's car. As we rolled out of the driveway Stan put on a pair of mirrored aviator shades and tied a patterned silk handkerchief around his neck.

The place my father took us to was called Empty Mile. Once we were out of Oakridge it was about a twenty-minute drive, the last few miles of it along a single winding lane of blacktop known only as Rural Route 12. Along the side of this road, dusty wooden poles supported an old electricity feed that served isolated dwellings erected over the years by a handful of families who preferred a more reclusive lifestyle.

Neither tourists nor townsfolk had any reason to come out this way - there was nothing to see here that couldn't be seen closer to town or in more scenic surroundings. The only sign that the area was inhabited came from occasional boards, hand-painted with family names, that marked the entrances to unpaved trails.

At one of these my father turned off the road and onto a track that was just two tire furrows worn in the earth. We drove along this through sparse forest until we emerged at the top of a wide meadow of deep grass that sloped downhill for several hundred yards. My father stopped the car and we got out.

The trees we'd passed through were behind us, and to the left and ahead of us also the meadow was bordered by forest. On our right the land rose in a steep rock wall about seventy feet high.

In the top left corner of the meadow there was an old wooden house that needed paint. It was set off the ground and had a short flight of steps leading up to a roofed veranda. A beaten-up orange Datsun was parked beside it and in an unfenced garden washing hung on a line.

On the opposite side of the meadow from this house, about half-way down the slope, there was a much newer log cabin. This too had a stoop along its front and there was a large rainwater tank and a small shed out back.

Stan lay down on the grass. He rolled over a couple of times, then stood up and brushed himself off. My father was wearing a suit as he almost always did. He had his hands in his pants pockets, his jacket hooked back behind his wrists

"What do you think, boys?"

Stan looked perplexed, trying to figure out what answer my father wanted. "It's not any good for rolling."

"What about you, Johnny."

"Nice spot. Are you marketing it?"

"I own it."

"Really?"

"Closed the deal today."

"The whole field?"

"Most of the meadow and on down through those trees at the bottom. The Swallow River runs on the other side of them and that's where the property ends. That log cabin comes with it too, but the house over there is on a separate title."

Stan ran his hands nervously through his hair.

"Oh boy, Dad. Oh boy."

"What's the matter, Stan?"

"Are we moving here?"

"No, we're not moving."

"But you bought a place with a cabin."

"We're not moving, Stanley. Don't worry."

Although I didn't share Stan's nervousness about moving to a new house I could understand his confusion. The piece of land my father had bought appeared to have no other use than as a place to relocate to. It had nothing going for it as an investment. It was too far from town and too isolated to subdivide and sell off in property lots. And as something to do with the tourist trade it was also a washout. Pretty and peaceful as it was, it had nothing that anyone would spend time traveling to see.

My father strode off across the deep grass. He swung his arms as he went and there was a jauntiness to his step that seemed put on, as though this man who had so much difficulty with his feelings was making a deliberate attempt to communicate his happiness to us.

We entered the trees that lined the bottom of the meadow. They grew thickly at first and there was grass underfoot, but after about ten yards the ground became dusty and the trees weaker and thinner and more widely spaced. My father stopped here and looked around as though he had no interest in continuing to the river. He scuffed at the dry earth with the toe of his shoe then walked a few yards to his left to a small hole someone had dug in the ground.

Stan and I waited for him to start moving again but he seemed lost in a daydream, looking at the hole and nodding to himself. Stan cupped his hands and raised them to his mouth. He made a noise like static on a radio.

"Earth to Dad. Come in."

My father lifted his head and chuckled and started walking again. Twenty yards further on, the trees ended and we stepped out onto the bank of the Swallow River.

After the Swallow passed under the bridge at the southern end of Oakridge it ran through ranks of quartz-bearing hills until it joined the middle fork of the Yuba. It was nowhere near the size of famous Gold Rush rivers like the American or the Feather, but it had been well known as a river that was consistently rich along its length. We stood now on the inner curve of a bend in its path where the water ran shallow and wide. To our right, looking upstream, I could see the ragged end of the meadow's rock wall sloping down through the trees to the edge of the riverbank.

Stan looked knowingly back and forth along the river.

"I know where we are, Dad. This is your photo, isn't it? This is the river in that photo."

"Correct, Stan."

"I thought so! Cool."

I knew my father didn't have the kind of money to go around buying land for the heck of it and it crossed my mind that after a lifetime of financial failure, of looking after Stan single-handedly, he might finally have succumbed to some sort of mental illness.

"What are you going to do with this place, raise crops?"

My father tapped the side of his nose. "You'll see, John. You'll see." He took a deep breath and clapped his hands. "Remember this day, boys."

We followed him back through the trees and up the meadow to where we'd left the car. As we came level with the wooden house I heard Stan draw his breath in sharply. Two people were sitting on the stoop in the afternoon sun. One of them was the girl from his dance class. He tugged my sleeve and whispered, "It's Rosie!"

The girl saw Stan and lifted her hand in a weak wave.

"You better go over, dude."

"But what am I going to say?"

"You talk to her at dance lessons, don't you?"

"Yeah."

"Well?"

"Will you come with me?"

My father was a little way ahead of us. He turned when he heard our conversation.

"You two go over for a few minutes, if you want. I'll wait in the car."

The boards that made the steps up to the stoop were bare and worn soft with age. In the sun they gave out a faint papery fragrance that dried the back of the throat. Rosie was standing now. Beside her in a bent-wood chair was a thin woman of about seventy. Her gray hair was long and held by a pencil in a slowly collapsing bun and though her skin was sun-singed and deeply wrinkled, her eyes still held a sharp brightness and it was not hard to see that she had been good-looking in her youth. A light crocheted shawl lay across her knees and her fingers pushed a small collection of crystals absently back and forth across it.

Rosie rocked gently from side to side and watched Stan. She was barefoot and there was dirt between her toes. She wore the same faded pink shift as she had when I saw her last.

The woman smiled at us and said hello. Stan coughed uncertainly.

"Um, I'm Stan. I go to dance lessons with Rosie."

The woman nodded. "Yes, Rosie's told me about you. I'm Millicent Jeffries, Rosie's grandmother."

Stan raised his hand quickly at Rosie.

"Hiya, Rosie."

Rosie shifted on her feet as though she was tired and said, "Did you come specially?"

"I didn't know you lived here."

Millicent squinted across the meadow.

"Is that your father over there?"

Stan nodded. "Yeah, he just bought the land."

"I know him a little. Why, he should have come and said hello."

Rosie held her hand out to Stan. "You can come inside if you want."

"Is it okay, Johnny?"

"Sure, not too long, though."

Stan and Rosie went into the house and Millicent gestured for me to sit on the chair next to her.

She picked a small glass ball from her lap. Its surface had been cut with triangular facets and as it rested on the flat of her palm small rainbows quivered against the dry skin of her wrist and across the woolen shawl that covered her knees. She moved her hand a little and smiled as the rainbows danced.

"Look at that. You'd never think there was all that color just waiting inside light, would you? And all you have to do is look at it a certain way. Beautiful, don't you think? My Rosie mentioned your brother. She likes dancing with him. Is he a little slow?"

"He had an accident when he was young, but he isn't slow."

"A little...different? Rosie is a little different, too. Only it wasn't any accident that did it to her. Life just knocked her around until she couldn't see any joy in it anymore. She's lived with me since she was nine. She supports herself now cleaning people's houses."

"What happened to her parents?"

"Her mother was a heroin addict. In the evenings, after she'd had her fix, she liked to sit on the windowsill to catch the breeze. They lived in an apartment building and one night she just fell out. Rosie saw it happen. Her father wasn't the sort of man who could see through to the other side of things, so he started drinking and about six months later got in his car and never came back."

She set her crystals and her shawl on a small table beside her chair and stood up.

"Some folks might have reservations about someone like Stan and someone like Rosie starting up a friendship. They might say it's bound to end unhappily. But you get to my age and it seems like happiness is only ever temporary anyhow. So if they can pretend for a little while that they aren't so different from everyone else, I'm just going to be happy for them."

She went into the house and a couple of minutes later Stan and Rosie came out.

"Rosie put the stereo on and we practiced a dance."

Stan looked flushed and excited. Rosie leaned against the railing that ran along the outside of the stoop and stared out at the meadow. She sighed and her eyelids drooped a little.

"Can you hear the wind in the trees? I can hear it. Sometimes I wish it would blow through my head like that, then all my thoughts would be untangled. Like ribbons."

Stan looked uncertain. "I gotta go now, Rosie."

She turned from the view and kissed him on the cheek and wandered back into the house. Stan called goodbye as the screen door bounced against its frame.

We climbed down off the stoop and started back toward the car. Stan was quiet and I wondered if the whole thing had been too much for him.

"Everything go okay? You still like her?"

"You bet. I hope she doesn't think I'm a dumb-o."

"Didn't look that way when she said goodbye."

"Yeah, I know! And in the house, when we were dancing, she kissed me on the lips. It made my head spin round."

My father dropped us back at the house and went into town to finish off his working day. Stan and I took the pickup over to the garden center to check out the warehouse we'd just leased. Bill Prentice wasn't there when we arrived, but the manager, Rachel, had a set of keys for us and a business card for a plant wholesaler in Sacramento.

The warehouse stood to the side of the garden center at the end of a short white-gravel driveway. It was made of pressed steel and had a row of corrugated fiberglass skylights down each side of its roof. From its front entrance the view was as beautiful as that from the garden center - a sweep of meadow, a line of trees, the river on the other side of the road, and then forested hills marching back into the distance.

Stan and I unlocked the sliding door that formed part of the front wall and went inside. The layout was simple - a single open space with a small office built into the back left corner. The concrete floor was dusty and the air in the place was hot and stale. The fiberglass panels let in a diffuse light that made the place feel vaguely churchlike.

"Wow, Johnny, this is it! This is the beginning of everything. I can't believe it."

"Believe it, man. The papers are signed, no one can take it away from us, not even Bill if he changes his mind."

"I'm going to be something, Johnny. Something!"

We poked around for a bit, talking through what the best way to arrange the place would be, how we were going to kick off the business.

"I got a great idea for that, Johnny. What we'll do is get a whole lot of leaflets and put them in all the stores' letter boxes and all the rich people's houses. Advertising is essential. We better call those plant people too. And we have to tell Dad."

"Yeah, I know."

"He's going to feel a lot better about me now."

I wasn't sure that my father would see things in exactly the same light as Stan. I could already hear how it would waste Stan's hard-earned money, how it was irresponsible of me to enable this fantasy, how it was a lousy idea....

"Listen, Stan, let me tell him, okay? I want to make sure he doesn't get the wrong idea about what we're doing."

Stan shrugged. "Okay, Johnny, if you want."

We locked up the warehouse and headed back to the pickup. On the way we dropped into the garden center so Stan could grab a Coke. While we were there Rachel asked us if we could take a couple of flowering plants around to Bill's house. He was working from his office in the town hall and wouldn't be coming into the garden center. He wanted them delivered to his wife that day.

Bill and Patricia Prentice lived a half mile north of the garden center on a plot that was almost the size of a playing field. The house was a large white single-story Californian with green shutters and a brick driveway that made an S from the road up to the front door. Patricia's olive Mercedes was parked carelessly under a tree in front of the house.

There was no answer when I rang the bell. From inside the house I could hear the babble of a talk radio show. I rang a couple more times, but no one answered.

"Maybe we should just leave the plants out front."

"But she's got to be here, Johnny. Her car's here. She just can't hear us because of the radio. I don't want Bill to get mad because we didn't do what he said."

I tried the door. It was unlocked and swung open to show a foyer tiled in white stone. We could have left then, it would have been easy enough to do. We were only dropping off a couple of plants, after all. But there was a feeling about the house that didn't seem right to me. A car out front, a radio on, someone who should have been home....

Stan and I stepped through the doorway. After the heat outside, the house felt cool. From the foyer I could see into a sunroom on my right and, directly ahead, a large living room. It was from there that the radio noise was coming. The blinds in both rooms were down and the light in the house was muted and didn't fully dilute the shadows that pooled in corners and under furniture. Air conditioning whispered through vents near the ceiling. There was no one in either of the rooms.

Stan shouted nervously, "Mrs. Prentice, it's Stan! We've got some plants!"

When no one answered, we put the plants beside the door and, with Stan glancing about apprehensively and holding onto my sleeve, walked through the living room and turned right into a long hall that followed the rear wall of the house. On our left, there were windows that must have looked out onto a back garden, but these were shuttered and I could see only thin strips of sunshine around the inside of the frames. On our right, there were three doors. Two of them were closed, but the last was open and it was through this that we found Patricia Prentice in what was obviously the master bedroom.

There were curtained French doors at one end of the room and a large bed with a white cover and a wide space of pale carpet. Against one of the walls there was a writing desk and a chair, and against another a wide-screen TV made a sound like surf, its screen effervescent with static.

Patricia Prentice lay on top of the covers of the bed. She was wearing clothes similar to those she'd been wearing the day I'd seen her with my father - a knee-length skirt, a peach-colored blouse, black patent leather sandals, one of which had fallen from her foot. It looked like she'd gotten up that morning and dressed to look nice.

Perhaps when she lay down on the bed she had composed herself, positioned herself elegantly on her back, her arms folded across her breasts, legs crossed at the ankles. Perhaps.... She looked anything but composed now. She was curled on her side and her clothes were twisted about her body as though she had slept through a fever. Her tongue was swollen and dark and stuck obscenely through lips that were drawn back over her teeth. A blot of milky vomit had collected around her neck and the lower half of her face. The back of her skirt was wet.

On a nightstand beside the bed there was a collection of empty Halcion blister packs and an empty half-bottle of whiskey. Beneath the bottle there was a slip of notepaper with a single line of writing: *I waited as long as I could.*

When my mother died in her, car my father had insisted on a closed coffin to spare Stan and me the sight of her injuries. So I had never seen a dead body before, but I could have told anyone who asked that Patricia Prentice was dead beyond any hope of resuscitation. Even so, I checked for a pulse in her neck. Her flesh was too cold and too solid and I had to steel myself against its touch.

"Should we do mouth-to-mouth, Johnny?" Stan was rubbing his hands rapidly back and forth across his chest and his voice trembled.

"She's dead. It wouldn't do any good."

"She killed herself."

"Looks like it. The pills and everything."

"Poor thing." Stan's voice broke and he wiped his nose with the back of his hand. "Bill's going to be so upset."

We were silent for a moment while I worked up the nerve to start calling people. As I was about to reach for the phone Stan groaned and put his hands over his ears.

"That TV noise is freaking me out."

There were two remotes on the floor by the side of the bed. I picked them both up and hit the power button on one of them. The tray in a DVD player beneath the TV slid out. The hissing electron jumble on the screen went black and quiet. I pressed power on the second remote and turned the TV off.

"Thanks, Johnny. My head was going crazy. She must have been watching a movie."

Wondering what someone might watch while they killed themselves I checked the disk that sat in the player's tray, but it had been burned on a computer and there was nothing on its surface to identify it beyond a small smiley-face sticker. I left it where it was.

"Can I go outside, Johnny?"

"Yeah, go wait out front. I'll be along soon."

I picked up the phone, called the garden center, got Bill's cell phone number from them, and called that. When he answered I did it as well as I could, but there was nothing I could say that would make anything any easier for him. He cried out and dropped the phone. I waited a long time but I didn't hear anything else, so I hung up and called the police.

After that, I went outside and sat with Stan on a large ornamental rock at the edge of the driveway. He looked pale and stunned. I put my arm around his shoulders.

"I don't understand how anyone could do that, Johnny. I can't think how it would even be possible."

"She must have been very unhappy."

"Can we go home?"

"Not yet, we have to wait."

Stan leaned into me and put his head on my shoulder. A few minutes later Bill's SUV skidded to a halt in front of us. He threw himself out of the car and ran for the house. His face was set and he was shouting as he passed us.

"Where is she? Where is she?"

But he didn't stop for me to answer and ran on through the front doorway as though by his speed he could somehow turn back what had happened. I let him have five minutes alone, then I went inside to check on him.

As I walked along the corridor to the bedroom it seemed to me that the air was not as silent as it had been, that there was an ambience to it, a sense of space, as though the outdoors could be heard inside.

The door to the bedroom was almost closed now. I knocked, not wanting to walk in without warning. Bill shrieked an obscenity and I heard him move across the floor. The sound in the air stopped.

I wasn't sure what to do, but I felt obliged to at least offer some sort of support. After hesitating a moment I pushed the door open and went into the room.

I thought I might find Bill with his head bowed over his wife, broken, crying, on the point of collapse. But he was nothing of the sort. He was standing near the TV holding the remotes. His light windbreaker, which had been open as he ran from his car, was now zipped closed. I glanced at the DVD player. The disk with the smiley sticker was gone.

Bill's face twisted when he saw me and he began screaming. The torrent of abuse shocked me, but the man's wife had just killed herself so I put it down to grief. I took a step forward, intending to comfort him, but he raised his fist and told me to fuck off. It was obvious that he was beyond comfort, at least any I could offer, and, figuring that maybe I was doing more harm than good by being there, I backed out of the room and left him alone.

An ambulance was pulling into the driveway as I joined Stan outside again. A cruiser from the Oakridge police department had already arrived and two uniformed cops were climbing out of it.

They both had mustaches and one of them wore yellow-lensed sunglasses. They asked us briefly where in the house Pat was and how we came to be there, then the one with the sunglasses and the two ambulance men, who'd just pulled a gurney from the back of their wagon, went inside. The other cop got out a pad and took our details and asked more questions and wrote down our answers.

In a little while, the ambulance guys came back out and told the cop there was no chance of resuscitation. They got into their truck and started the engine for the air conditioning and sat in the cab making notes on a clipboard. The cop said he wanted us to walk him through exactly what we'd done inside and took us back into the house.

When we got to the bedroom, the cop in the yellow glasses was standing with Bill by the writing desk and it looked like they were just finishing up. Bill's anger seemed to have dissipated and he was reasonably composed, but as I entered the room he shot me a quick hateful glance which neither of the cops caught. Stan and I reenacted what we'd done. When I mentioned turning the DVD player off, the cop with the glasses went over and looked at the machine. When he saw there was no disk, he asked me what I'd done with it.

Bill spoke before I could answer.

"I took it out of the machine. I'm sorry, I didn't think it was important."

"What did you do with it?"

The cop's tone was only one of mild inquiry. We hadn't been rushed or cross-examined during their inquiry, and as far as I could tell no one here was treating the scene as suspicious.

"I put it on the pile."

"What was it?"

Bill looked blank for a moment.

"I can't remember."

"That's okay, don't worry about it. Was it this one here?"

There was a stack of DVDs on a cabinet beside the TV. The cop took the one off the top and held it up.

"This it?"

Bill nodded. "It must be. I didn't look at it."

The cop nodded to himself. "Barefoot in the Park. I like that movie."

The DVD was a commercially recorded rental and certainly not the disk I had seen when Stan and I first found Patricia. Bill was lying. I was pretty sure he had the real disk concealed under his windbreaker. But what difference did it make? If Pat had been watching

83

something more personal than a Hollywood love story - a family vid-eo of happier times, perhaps - who was I to interfere if Bill wanted to keep part of this horrible event private?

So I said nothing. And Stan, who had paid no attention to the DVD beyond wanting the TV to be quiet, had no idea that there was anything to say nothing about.

Stan and I went outside again, but Bill stayed in the bedroom with his dead wife. We spent another half hour making formal statements which the cops typed into a computer in their car; after that they told us we could go.

When we got home, Stan put on his Captain America suit, jammed his glasses on over the mask, and settled himself in front of the TV. I made him the peanut butter sandwiches he asked for and he sat and munched and focused his attention on some Japanese action cartoon.

"How come you put the costume on?"

"Huh?"

"The costume. Why?"

Stan looked down at himself and smoothed the red, white and blue material over his belly. He turned his attention back to the TV and said without looking at me, "Protection."

He didn't answer when I tried to talk to him further, so I went into the kitchen and called my father and told him about Pat. The conversation was not long. I outlined what had happened, he asked for details and then he was silent. He cleared his throat a couple of times but was unable to say anything else. Eventually he thanked me and we hung up.

I went upstairs to my room and lay down on the bed and called Marla on my cell and gave her the same news. After we'd arranged to meet the next day I put the phone down and turned on my side and closed my eyes. The windows were open and a hot, slow breeze moved over me.

I woke to Stan shaking my shoulder. It was dark outside but the light was on in the room and moths pestered the bulb. Stan was still in his Captain America suit.

"Dad's downstairs. Something's wrong."

"What time is it?"

"He came in and went into the kitchen and when I said hi he wouldn't lift his head up. He just kept staring at the table. He's got a bottle of booze."

"Booze, huh?"

"Yeah, booze."

"He'll be all right, don't worry. I'll go check on him. You go to bed."

"Shouldn't I come down with you?"

"No, just let me talk to him."

"Okay, Johnny."

I walked Stan along the landing to his room. He climbed under the covers of his bed and took off his glasses and mask.

"Aren't you going to get rid of the costume?"

Stan shook his head.

"Are you okay about Pat?"

"Yeah. You don't have to worry about me, Johnny."

He nestled against his pillow and for a moment I saw him as a young boy again and was freshly overcome with a sense of loss for all the time that had passed while we were not together.

I turned out the light and went downstairs to see my father. He was sitting at the kitchen table in his suit. His tie was loose at his throat and his hair was mussed. There was a half-full glass and a bottle of whiskey on the table in front of him. He looked up as I came into the room and smiled weakly. He was a man who rarely drank and he seemed embarrassed at himself.

"I'm afraid I'm a little drunk."

"Are you okay?"

"Just had a few at the office after work."

"Dad, I know you were seeing Patricia Prentice. Marla told me about the room."

"Oh.... I see."

He nodded slowly. Everything about him was heavy - the words he pushed from himself into the over-bright kitchen air, his head on his shoulders, his arms bent on the table. His gaze would not hold mine and slid constantly to his hands. He seemed a man monumentally overwhelmed by the weight of being alive.

He lifted his glass and drank from it like a child forcing down medicine, then coughed and wiped his eyes.

"Pat was a person who needed emotional support. Her mistake was looking for it in me." He shook his head disgustedly. "I couldn't give her what she wanted. It wasn't that I didn't want to. I did. I just didn't have it in me."

"I don't think there was much you could have done either way. She was a sick woman."

My father poured another drink and swallowed it. He was very drunk. His words were beginning to slur.

"What sickens me is that I always had it in the back of my head that if I stayed with her long enough some of her money might rub off on me. And all the time I was thinking about money, she was thinking about killing herself."

He slumped forward on the table and put his head in his arms. I waited for several minutes until I thought he must have fallen asleep. I was going to rouse him and try and get him up to bed, but when I shook him he lifted his head and told me to leave him where he was. There wasn't much else I could do, so I put a glass of water on the table next to him and headed out of the room. As I reached the doorway he called to me.

"Johnny, that friend you used to have - Gareth."

"What about him?"

"He isn't the sort of man you want to be mixed up with."

He pointed his finger at me. His face was swollen and loose and his eyes were bleary.

"You hear me?"

"Yeah."

"Good...."

He dropped his head into his arms again and his breath came out in a sob.

The room felt abandoned, as though everywhere outside was empty and gone. The electric clock on the stove ratcheted painfully through the minutes and the light from the ceiling bulb made things dirty around the edges. I felt terribly sad standing there watching my father. It seemed to me, at that moment, that the world was nothing more than a place where lives fell apart.

CHAPTER TEN

Stan asked me to drive him to work the next day. Bill Prentice was unlikely to be in and Stan wanted to be there to help out as much as he could. After I'd dropped him off, I headed into Back Town to meet Marla. She worked in a modern-looking annex the council had built for its administrative staff a block away from the town hall itself. We went to a café called the Black Cat opposite her building. It was a basic place with plain tables and hard chairs and had been around long before gold town nostalgia became the obligatory decorative motif for eateries in Oakridge.

At breakfast and lunch the place was busy with workers from neighboring businesses but midmorning it was almost empty and Marla and I had our pick of the tables. We sat at the front of the place by one of the large plate-glass windows. Around us sunlight picked out dust motes in the air and the occasional chink of plates from back in the kitchen seemed somehow to point up the loneliness of this in-between time

Marla looked efficient in her office clothes but under her lipstick and eyeliner she was pale and her eyes were tired.

We talked about Pat dying. When I told her it looked like an overdose of sleeping pills she tensed and began twisting a napkin between her hands.

"What sort of sleeping pills?"

"Halcion."

"Oh Jesus...." For a moment she closed her eyes. "I gave them to her."

"What?"

"I gave her the pills."

"To kill herself with?"

"No! For fucksake, Johnny. She couldn't sleep, she wanted something. I was going to get her some grass, but when I asked Gareth all he had was pills."

"Hang on, why are you asking Gareth anything?"

"He's the only guy I know for that kind of thing."

"So you're what, in touch with him on a regular basis?"

"Jesus Christ! Didn't you hear what I said? I'm telling you she got the pills off me, and all you're worried about is if I'm seeing Gareth."

"Are you?"

"Fuck." Marla let out a breath and worked at not being angry. She reached across the table and took my hand. "Why would I be seeing Gareth?"

She looked at me levelly until I gave in.

"Okay.... Okay, I'm sorry. Were you close...with Pat?"

"She'd come around sometimes without Ray and we'd talk. I liked her but we weren't girlfriends or anything."

"Why didn't she get her own pills?"

"Her doctor wouldn't give them to her, I don't know why."

"Was she taking antidepressants?"

"Of course, she'd been on them for years."

We finished our coffee and went outside and stood in the sunshine in front of the café while Marla smoked a cigarette.

"Do you think the thing with my father and Pat would have gone anywhere?"

Marla shook her head. "She would never have left Bill. He treated her like shit, fucked anything that moved, but she loved him. She had this dream that one day everything was going to come right between them. And Ray always seemed really uncomfortable with the whole affair thing."

Marla rubbed the butt of her cigarette against the wall of the café and took a few steps along the sidewalk to a trash can. I watched her until movement a block away on the other side of the road caught my eye.

Bill Prentice, alone and wearing a dark suit, was running down the short flight of stone steps in front of the town hall, toward us. From the expression on his face it looked like he was reprising the anger he'd exhibited toward me in his wife's bedroom.

Marla stepped back from the trash can and stood close to me. Bill didn't slow when he got to the sidewalk on our side and as I opened my mouth to make some sort of greeting he raised his fist and hit me hard enough on the side of the face to knock me down. I struggled to my feet as fast as I could, expecting further blows. But they didn't come.

Bill stood before us, quivering, arms straight at his sides and rigid, his head turning in a narrow arc between Marla and me as though he couldn't decide who to settle on. The tension in him was so great he seemed unable to speak, and in those silent moments I saw a dreadful sadness replace his anger and I knew I was looking at a man for whom the world had become incomprehensible.

When he finally spoke his voice was strangled. "Why did you do it?"

"We just found her. We didn't do anything."

Bill looked around him as though he didn't know where he was, then stared hard at me again and screamed, "I don't understand!"

Marla moved forward a little. There was a tremor in her voice when she spoke. "Bill, you've had a terrible shock. You should be at home. Do you want me to take you?"

"You bitch! You fucking evil bitch! Do you know what you've done to me? What did I do to you? What did I do? I paid you. I didn't touch you, I just watched. What did I do wrong?"

Marla looked uncertainly at me. I felt out of my depth. I didn't understand his anger and I didn't know how to help him.

"Bill, come on, man-"

"Fuck you! Fuck you!"

He broke down then, sobbing, clenching his fists in front of his chest. A couple of people on the sidewalk stopped to watch and one of the security guys from the town hall came over. He recognized Bill and stepped between us.

I felt Marla pulling me, dragging me away. It didn't feel right to leave him like this, crying and so obviously broken, but she pulled harder and we walked away and left him there collapsed in the arms of the guard.

We went back to where I'd parked the pickup. We were both shaken and we locked the doors after we got in. Marla shuddered.

"He was talking about what we did at the lake."

"Yeah."

"Jesus Christ."

She groaned. I put my hand on her arm but she jerked away angrily.

"Don't touch me!"

"He's just feeling guilty. It's not our fault if he feels bad about it now. We're just someone he can take it out on."

But Marla wasn't listening. Without warning she twisted in her seat and slapped me across the face. The blow wasn't hard but it caught me on the same side as Bill's punch and it stung.

"What the fuck!"

"Why did you have to leave me? Why the fuck couldn't you have stayed? Look what you turned me into! Someone who can fuck in front of another man. I'm disgusting. We could have bought a house and had a kid. We would have been normal and clean. We would have been fucking happy."

She put her face in her hands and fell against me and sobbed.

"Jesus, Johnny, Jesus...."

I held her and let her cry and stared blankly through the windshield. The town bustled about its business, people walked along the sidewalk, cars drove down the street, but I saw nothing through the glass except the cold shine of my own guilt. Later, when Marla had quieted, she went back to work and I drove fast along country roads for a long time with all the windows open and the air rushing in.

CHAPTER ELEVEN

The day they buried Patricia Prentice my father was almost killed. And because I'd accepted his offer to drive into town with him and have breakfast before he started work, I was almost killed too.

Earlier, I'd tried to talk to him about Patricia Prentice but when I raised the subject his conversation became monosyllabic and guarded and he avoided saying anything except that he was okay and I shouldn't worry about him. I didn't press the point, I knew from experience that any coming to terms he had to do he'd do deep down inside, in that hidden part of himself where his emotions were sealed.

The end of our street joined a long road that ran downhill. As my father turned the car into it I saw him frown a little.

"Brakes are a bit soft."

He shrugged and wound down his window. We gathered speed and he took an exaggerated breath of the air coming in.

"I like this time of morning. Before everything starts." He frowned again. "These brakes really don't feel right."

There was very little traffic about at this time of day and going downhill we'd reached a speed of about fifty miles an hour. A hundred yards ahead of us, the road curved sharply to the left where it crossed a culvert, before flattening out against the floor of the basin. We needed to slow quickly to make the turn but the car continued to pick up speed. I looked across at my father. He was staring through the windshield, gripping the wheel so hard his knuckles showed white beneath the tan of his hands. His right foot pumped rapidly on the brake pedal. He shouted, "The brakes have gone. Hold on!"

He yanked the emergency brake and the scream of the locking rear tires added to the cacophony of sound that had suddenly engulfed us - the engine of the car, the rush of our passage through air and over tarmac, the thudding of our hearts and the roar of our blood, our shouts in the last sickening second as we entered the turn, my father wrenching the wheel around, fighting the weight of the car.

"Cover your face, John!"

And then the howl of the wheels losing their grip and the sideways drift of the car, beyond any hope of control now, out across the angle of the curve as though it floated on oil, the white beams of the guardrail across the edge of the culvert suddenly at my window. And then our impact, a single explosive bang and a hail of shattered glass, the final slewing through a quarter turn, the lurching drop as the back of the car went through the guardrail and over the concrete edge of the culvert, the shriek of metal being scraped from the bottom of the car. And then silence.

For a moment, after it all stopped, neither of us moved or spoke, sure that we must be hideously injured and that movement of any kind would reveal to us the terrible nature of our wounds. But the seconds passed and we did not find ourselves dying or drenched with blood and we peeled ourselves away from the positions into which we'd been thrown.

"Are you all right, John? Are you hurt?"

I flexed my legs and arms. I'd hit the side of my head on the doorframe and I had small cuts on the backs of my hands, but I was uninjured.

"No, I'm okay. I'm not hurt. Are you?"

My father moved a little in his seat and then smiled like he didn't believe it. "You know, I think I'm all right."

"You're bleeding a little."

He had a small cut on his cheekbone and a drop of blood had run halfway down the side of his face. I pointed to it and he took a handkerchief out of his pocket and dabbed it away. He held the handkerchief in front of him and looked at the small red mark his blood had made. He turned it so I could see it. And we both began to laugh at the insanity of surviving such violence and noise and danger with nothing more than a few drops of blood to show for it. For a long time we couldn't stop, but eventually the tension left us and we climbed out of the car.

The impact with the guardrail had buckled the panels along the entire right-hand side of the car. Although the back wheels had gone over the edge the car was stable on its belly and didn't shift as we both got out through the driver's door. Six feet below us a small creek entered the mouth of a tunnel which allowed it to pass beneath the road. On either side of the culvert there was a margin of woodland and then houses. In the garden of one of these a middle-aged couple stood watching us anxiously. They were holding hands and they waved at us.

The police turned up ten minutes later and my father answered questions for their report. They figured the only thing that had saved us was hitting the guardrail side-on. If we'd ploughed straight through it, they said, we would have gone nose-first into the culvert and the impact would have killed us for sure. A couple of people who'd come out to look at the damage nodded and made agreeing noises and said how amazing it was we weren't dead. The police radioed a garage to come out and tow the car, then they gave us a lift into town

By the time we got there it was late in the morning and my father couldn't do breakfast anymore. I arranged to come in and pick him up after work, then I wandered around town by myself for half an hour and bought an espresso.

I was about to get a cab from the small taxi stand in Old Town when two dark vehicles caught my attention. A hearse and a town car, both bearing the name of a funeral home in gold lettering on their sides. The hearse carried a pale brown coffin and the town car had only one passenger, a man in a dark suit with a rosebud pinned to his lapel. He sat in the back of the car looking straight ahead.

I had not expected that Bill Prentice would be alone for this occasion. He was well known and gregarious and he'd been that way for a long time. When I thought of the kind of funeral procession that might attend his wife I thought of a long train of cars, elaborate wreaths, parties of people for whom he had done favors or been in business with. I thought of an event.

But there was nothing of this about the two lonely cars that passed me. They seemed closed and inward-facing, as though the thing they carried was not to be shared and they wished to pass from view as quickly as possible. I watched them as they moved along the road, their brake lights occasionally flicking red as they slowed for traffic or waited at signals. And then they turned a corner and were gone.

I hadn't been at home long when Rachel, the manager of the garden center, dropped Stan off in front of the house. He came down the hall and into the kitchen all breathless and full of news.

"Bill closed the garden center."

"Yeah, I think it was Pat's funeral today."

"No, I mean forever. When I got in Rachel was giving everyone their last paychecks and telling us not to come back. Bill's so sad he's not going to open it again. He's not even going to live at his house anymore. He's gone up to his cabin in the mountains. Rachel said he sold all his furniture."

"Ah, man, your job...."

"No, Johnny, it's good. Now we can go full power on Plantasaurus. And guess what? Rachel told me that Bill said I could take all the big plants to help me start, and all the sacks of potting mix too. It's a reward for the bear."

Stan went to the refrigerator and got a can of Coke.

"You should cut down on that stuff. It isn't good for you."

"What are you talking about, Johnny? It powers you up."

"It's full of sugar."

"Of course it is." He took a big swallow of the drink and made a growling noise. "Powerin' up for Plantasaurus!"

Drinking so fast made his eyes water. He blinked rapidly and burped.

I told him about the crash that morning. He went wide-eyed at the story of our narrow escape and then seemed to withdraw into himself. Later, he went upstairs to his room and put on his Batman costume and sat down at his desk with his comic books and his drawing things.

Stan and I met my father at the garage in town. Oakridge had three of these places but, by chance, the Ford had been taken to the one that used to belong to Gareth's father. The place had been bought and expanded by a nationwide chain and was now run as a franchise by staff who all wore matching uniforms. A short, fat mechanic carrying a clipboard joined us in the workshop. He moved slowly, as though the weight of the fat dragging at his body exhausted him.

"She's up there."

He jerked his head at a hydraulic hoist, then took a flashlight out of his pocket and shone it on the underside of my father's car. The damage was extensive. The exhaust system had been torn away and the drive shaft was no longer connected to the differential. The base of the car itself was scraped and gouged and marked in places with powdered concrete.

"Brake failure."

Using the flashlight beam he traced a thin metal pipe that came out from somewhere in the engine and ran along its base before splitting out to feed the brakes on each side of the car. Where the pipe bent to curve around the engine it looked discolored and corroded.

"Someone hold the flashlight."

I took it from him and held it trained on the spot while he went to work with a pair of wire cutters. When he was done he stepped out from under the car and held his hand out to us. A six-inch section of the pipe rested on his palm. The metal on one side of it had rotted away leaving a hole in the pipe wall about two inches long. My father took it and examined it closely. His face was tight with anger and he shook his head slowly.

"Unbelievable."

The mechanic snorted derisively. "Yeah, it's pretty poor. Looks like some sort of metal fatigue."

"But these things aren't supposed to corrode."

"What can I say? You got a defective part. This is a reasonably old car."

"It's only a '93."

"Yeah."

My father passed the pipe to me. I passed it on to Stan who muttered under his breath, "Unbelievable."

The mechanic picked up his clipboard and ran his finger down a list of handwritten entries on the top sheet of a pad of printed yellow forms.

"Your car's written off. Rear axle, diff, drive shaft, all, er, shafted. Chassis out of true. Panel damage down the entire right-hand side. Not worth repairing in a car this age."

"It's sixteen years old."

"Yeah."

The mechanic signed his name carefully at the bottom of the form then tore off the sheet and handed it to my father.

"You'll need that for your insurance company."

On the way home my father was pensive and didn't speak much. I tried to make conversation once or twice but each time, when he responded, it was as though I had dragged him into the present from someplace far away. In the end, I left him alone and listened to the radio instead.

That night at dinner, when my father wasn't looking, Stan kicked me under the table and silently mouthed, *Plantasaurus*. The warehouse was costing us money each day and good business sense dictated that we begin our operation as soon as possible, so I really couldn't put off telling my father about the scheme much longer.

But right then, with the crash and Pat's death still so close about him, it didn't seem the best of times to tell him something I was certain he was going to object to. So I shook my head at Stan, and he and I ate silently and watched my father pick distractedly at the food on his plate.

CHAPTER TWELVE

A week later, when we officially started work on Plantasaurus, I still hadn't told my father about it. Stan and I went over to the garden center midmorning and found the place full of men in coveralls loading everything that could be moved into trucks outside. Rachel showed us the plants Bill had said Stan could have. There were forty assorted centerpiece shrubs around six feet high - dracaenas, weeping figs, kentia palms, etc. - ten large trays of smaller subtropical plants, and a pallet of potting mix.

It took us two hours to lug the plants and the soil over to our warehouse. When we were done we drove to a copy shop in Oakridge. Earlier that morning we'd sketched out a design for the fliers that were to be our principal means of advertising - I'd written a description of our services and above this Stan had drawn a smiling, cartoon-style brontosaurus holding a big flower in its mouth. We talked through the design with the copy guy and ordered five thousand fliers.

After that, we hit the road for Burton. There was a plastic-molding business there that had the kind of containers we needed as planters for the displays Stan had in mind.

The hour-long drive felt like an adventure - the day was beautiful and we were on a mission, out in the world actively pursuing the dream of self-employment. Stan was twitching with excitement.

"Hey, Johnny, you think we should get the truck painted too?"

"With a dinosaur?"

"Yeah, and the name, so people will know as soon as they see us."

"This truck?"

"It'd look cool."

"Would we have to have the flower as well?"

Stan laughed. "Hey, Johnny, you know what? I'm stoked."

Burton was twice the size of Oakridge and it took us a while to find the molding factory. When we did, we bought what the pickup would carry of the models we wanted - cylindrical drums and long rectangular troughs - and placed a wholesale order for more to be delivered the next day.

It was early afternoon when we got back to our warehouse. The workmen had gone from the garden center and the complex was closed and locked and already had an air of abandonment about it. After we'd carried our planters inside Stan showed me how to build a display.

I followed his instructions on how high to fill the planters with soil and what plants to use and where to place them so that they looked good and gave a balanced effect. The drums were simple. A layer of pumice stones, several inches of potting mix, remove the black plastic wrapping from the root mass of a single palm or dracaena, center it in the pot, and fill it up with potting mix.

After we'd done a few of these we moved on and prepared a couple of troughs. Stan called these "display planters" and they took more time since a selection of plants had to be used to create a sym-metrical display that rose gradually from the ends of the box toward a high point in the center.

It was pleasant being there like that. The scent of the dark moist earth and the green humidity of the plants made the work seem clean and real and good, and for the two hours we spent at it there was no need to think too deeply about things.

Even so, I couldn't help moments of vague unease. I'd had to pay Bill Prentice the first three months of the lease up front and even though he'd given us a good price, that and the deal we'd just done for the planters had taken more than half my savings. We still had Stan's money, but there would be more plants and soil to buy, and there would be bills too - electricity, insurance, the cost of running the pickup....

Toward mid-afternoon, while we were still working, I heard a car pull up. Shortly afterwards, faintly, beyond the tin walls of our warehouse, it seemed to me that someone was walking around the outside of the garden center. I assumed it was someone who'd come to buy garden supplies and that they'd go away when they finally figured out the place had gone out of business. But when there were still noises five minutes later Stan and I went outside to take a look.

Midway between the garden center and our warehouse a man stood looking carefully at the section of land. Though he could not have failed to notice us he gave no immediate indication of it. Instead, his gaze continued to wander over the buildings as though he was taking an inventory. Beyond him, in the parking lot, a red convertible E-type Jaguar bounced sun off its paintwork.

When he'd finished his inspection the man walked over to where we were. For an instant, as he looked at me, an expression of hatred rippled across his face, then he smiled and it was gone and he stuck out his hand.

"Jeremy Tripp. You're Johnny Richardson. And you're Stan."

Stan made a surprised noise. "Wow, how'd you know?"

Jeremy Tripp waved his hand dismissively. "A man moves into a new town, he does his homework." He gazed toward the trees that lined the road. "This is a very nice spot."

There were two wooden benches in front of the warehouse, put there to add a little rustic charm to the metal shed. Jeremy Tripp sat down on one, leaned back comfortably, and gazed at us. He was in his late forties and a few inches under average height. He had brown hair that had been highlighted and a body that, while not overweight, was more padded by fat than muscle. He looked like a man who was used to dealing with people. He waved at the other bench.

"Sit down, it's a beautiful day."

I found his proprietary air offensive but as we were just starting a business it seemed sensible not to be offensive back. Stan and I sat and I forced myself to make conversation.

"So you're new in town?"

"Mmm, arrived yesterday. Got a place on the Slopes."

"What brings you to Oakridge?"

He looked levelly at me and took some time to reply. "I'm thinking about building a small hotel here."

"Oh? Whereabouts?"

"I'm not certain yet, though I have a possibility in mind."

"Is that what you do, build hotels?"

"I ran a telecommunications company. I'm taking a leave of absence. I was getting flaccid. The challenges in that world are really not so interesting. The boardroom is bullshit. What I'm interested in is something real. We're like children, John, always children. We have to keep pushing at the walls of our playpens. Without that there isn't a whole lot else to do."

"I guess."

"You don't sound as though you know your own mind. You should watch that. The mind is the most powerful thing we have. A big, strong guy can beat someone up. But a smart guy can destroy a whole life."

"If he wanted to."

"If the person deserved it, it would be satisfying, don't you think? Manipulating events to get that result."

Despite the dictates of good business sense, I was thinking of getting up and leaving him to pontificate to himself, but he laughed and shook his head.

"Don't pay any attention to me. I get these crazy ideas and I blurt them out. I don't mean a word I say. What do you do, John?"

Stan chirped up before I could answer. "We're starting a business."

"Really, Stanley? Tell me about it, I'm all ears."

"We're going to put plants into stores and people's houses."

"I know the sort of thing."

"Hey, you could be our first customer. Is your house big?"

"Yes, it is."

"I bet it would look better with some plants in it."

"It might. How are you structured? A one-off start-up fee and a monthly maintenance charge?"

Stan looked nervously across at me and I pretended I had at least some idea of what I was doing and answered Jeremy Tripp with a firm "Yes."

Stan took him into the warehouse and showed him the displays we'd assembled. When they came out again Tripp told us how many planters he wanted, then he shook Stan's hand and sat back down.

"Done deal."

I thought Stan would burst with happiness. "Boy, this is incredible! Hey, Mr. Tripp, can I go look at your car?"

"That's not a car. That's a VI2 E-type Jaguar. Yes, you can look at it."

"Wow, thanks!"

Stan bounded off to the parking lot. Jeremy Tripp watched him go.

"Your brother appears to be quite invested in this plant venture."

"Yes."

"For the money? Because he doesn't really seem like the money type. Tell me, is he challenged?"

"He had an accident when he was young."

"And this is his chance to feel like he's part of the normal world?"

"I don't know."

Tripp smiled knowingly. "Did you research your market?"

"What's to research? No one else in Oakridge does it."

"Even so, I'd be surprised if the town could sustain this kind of business. You'll get customers, of course. The question is will you get enough of them? You have to pay for your stock, cover your operating costs, and generate sufficient profit to make the whole thing worthwhile. Juggling income and expenses can be tricky, John. I should know."

"Well, we're going to give it a shot."

"How do you think your brother will react if that shot fails?"

"I guess he'll come to terms with it."

"Really?"

Stan came back from the parking lot then. "Cool car, um, Jaguar, I mean."

Tripp's face brightened. "Just the man! How would you feel if your plant business didn't make it, Stan?"

Stan looked at him in surprise. His mouth trembled and he glanced at me then back at Tripp. "Don't you want plants anymore?"

"Oh, I want them, don't worry about that. But what if no one else does? What if no one ever leases plants from you?"

"Well, I.... I...." Stan couldn't form an answer and I saw tears start in his eyes.

I stood up and clapped my hands together and made a show of being the upbeat, busy guy who really just had to get on with his work. "Well, we've got a lot to do here. We can come out tomorrow with your displays, if that's convenient."

Jeremy Tripp just sat and smiled at me for a moment. Then he stood up. "That would be dandy." As he turned to go back to his car he put his head close to mine and whispered, "Doesn't look like he'd come to terms with it to me."

After he'd gone Stan looked at me unhappily. "He's weird, Johnny."

"You can say that again. But guess what? We got our first customer."

Stan made a superhero noise and raised his fists in the air. "Yeah! Plantasaurus lives!"

And though it was an exciting event, and I high-fived and clowned around with Stan, I couldn't help wondering how the hell Jeremy Tripp had known our names and where to find us. And what he really wanted, because I was sure he had no interest in our plants at all.

My father came home that evening with presents for us. In the past his choice of birthday and Christmas gifts had been a family joke. Although he never missed these occasions the things he bought seemed either to have come from some bargain basement bin, or otherwise had no relevance to the person for whom they were intended.

As an adult I had tried to understand this seeming incompetence. He was an intelligent man, so it wasn't that he didn't have the ability to make appropriate choices. He was not a wealthy man, but neither was he so strapped for cash that he was prevented from buying something reasonable. What I came to suspect was that he felt the choosing of a gift that would delight its recipient, that required thinking about and searching for, was an action that would betray too much emotional involvement on his part.

And so he chose instead to give gifts that were empty of meaning and maintained the barriers to engagement that seemed so necessary to him. But this evening, when he came home in a white Ford Taurus rental, his presents were nothing like that.

We sat around the table in the kitchen. The back door and the windows were open and the scent of the garden came lightly in, as though its essence had been dried and powdered and was suspended now about us, whispering of all the things summer could be. The sun was low against the rim of the Oakridge basin and the sky above the trees had turned rose with the warm dust of evening.

My father was pale beneath his sallow skin and looked tired, but it seemed that whatever had made him tired had also loosened his usual restraint because he spoke easily and his movements were open and unthought. It was a magical time. One of so few across the stretch of my life where he let fall the armor of fatherhood and allowed himself to become equal to his children.

The three of us talked for a while about nothing in particular. My father told the small stories that accrete about every family, the domestic occurrences that for some reason or other take a wrong turn and become, with the passage of time, a trove of intimate humor. They were part of Stan and me, they were part of my father, and the three of us laughed at ourselves in them. They would have seemed boring to anyone else. To us, though, their meaning was not in their content but in their ability to make us remember that we were father and son and brother.

In one of the lulls between conversation my father cleared his throat and, looking quite embarrassed, took two gift wrapped presents from the pocket of his jacket and put them on the table before us.

"I, ah, wanted to give you both something."

Stan clapped his hands then frowned. "It's not birthday time, Dad."

"I know, but I just wanted you two to know how much you mean to me."

He spoke haltingly and I could almost feel him squirming inside.

"I've been something of a...peculiar father and I haven't done or said everything that perhaps I should have. So I wanted you to have something you could keep in case...well, in case you were ever in any doubt about how I feel."

Stan and I sat looking at him without speaking. We were dumbfounded. I think in a way we were almost scared. Surely this kind of speech was something we'd only hear as a prelude to catastrophe - an impending earthquake, perhaps, or a recently pronounced sentence of death.

We opened the gifts. Mine was a Tag Heuer watch, engraved on the back with *To John, from Dad*. It was by far the most expensive thing he had ever given me, and more than that, it was tastefully chosen. On the other side of the table Stan drew a gold chain from its torn packet of wrapping paper. He held it up to the light.

"It's beautiful, Dad. Look, Johnny." Stan fastened the chain around his neck and stroked it. "I love it."

My father laughed uncomfortably. "I'm glad you like it, Stan. Do you like your watch, John?"

"It's fantastic, Dad, thanks."

"It should last you a lifetime."

"It must have been expensive."

"Don't worry about that. I just wanted you to have something to help you remember that despite how I might seem sometimes I am very fond of you."

We avoided looking at each other for a moment and I felt a cold sadness trickle through me. I knew his emotion was genuine, that he did feel the way he said he did. It was just that what he felt didn't run deep enough. On that magic, memorable night I caught sight of a dreadful truth - that even at his most intimate, even when he was trying his hardest to make some statement of his affection for me, he could not cast aside that final portion of reservation that would allow him to say "love" instead of "fond," that part of himself which still blamed me for what had happened to Stan.

Despite this defective statement of his feelings, though, I figured there probably wouldn't be a better time to tell him about Plantasaurus.

"Um, Dad, you know how the garden center closed down and Stan doesn't have a job anymore?"

"Yes, it's a terrible shame."

"Well, we're thinking about going into business together. In fact, we already have."

"Really?"

Stan and I told him all about Plantasaurus, about the plans we had for it and the steps we were taking. When we were finished, instead of the torrent of criticism I'd expected, instead of the lecture on how foolish and inappropriate it was to involve Stan in a business venture, he just nodded to himself and said gently, "Well, that sounds like a great idea. You boys should follow your dreams. I hope it's a big success."

Stan didn't watch TV after dinner but stayed with us at the table and babbled about how cool it would be to be a businessman. Later, when he got sleepy, he kissed us both and went upstairs to bed. He held his chain out from his chest and tried to look at it as he walked.

My father took some papers from his jacket and laid them out in a businesslike way in front of me.

"I had an appointment with my accountant today, just to go over a few things, and we talked about the Empty Mile land. He suggested that it might be better if I put it in the name of a family member. There's some sort of a tax penalty if you own a house and another piece of property. Capital gains or something. I didn't quite follow the ins and outs of it, but he says it will save a fair amount of money. So I wondered if you'd mind if I put it in your name."

"The land?"

"And the cabin. All of it. It's all paid for, you're not liable for anything. It's just a matter of bookkeeping."

"You really want to put it in my name?"

"There isn't anyone else I can trust with it. All you need to do is put your name on a piece of paper. Nothing else. I'll still take care of everything. My lawyer drew this up. It's a standard transfer of title."

My father flipped through the pages. My name had been typed below several signature spaces. This was way out of left field, but it was such an expression of his trust in me that I didn't want to disappoint him. And if it was going to help him with his taxes I could hardly say no.

"All right, Dad."

He handed me his fountain pen, but for a moment he held on to it. "There's just one thing you have to promise me, John, and it's very, very important. If there's ever a time when I'm not around, for whatever reason at all, and there's some question of what to do about the land, you cannot sell it. Okay? If I'm not here to make the decision you've got to hold on to it no matter what. Do you understand?"

"Sure, Dad, I promise. I won't sell the land."

"Good boy."

And so I signed the papers and then my father signed them as well. There were two copies and he told me I should keep one in a safe place and that he'd lodge the other with his lawyer.

CHAPTER THIRTEEN

Jeremy Tripp lived on the downhill side of Eyrie. I recognized the street immediately. It was the first of those that ran off the steep forest road after you hit the Slopes, and it was the same street on which Vivian, Gareth's woman friend, lived.

His house was a two-story piece of modern architecture with flat off-white walls and dark smoked-glass windows that looked violently out of place against the surrounding natural beauty. A tall, precisely clipped hedge ran more than halfway across the front of the property from right to left. Tripp's driveway led behind this and made a sharp left at the side of the house into an open garage in which his E-type Jaguar gleamed softly.

The front door was open and when we rang the bell Tripp's distant voice shouted for us to enter. Inside, there was a wide foyer that rose the full height of the building. Ahead of us a flight of stairs led to the second story, and to our right and left corridors disappeared into the two opposing wings of the house. The whole space was covered with polished white stone and the ceiling was dotted with small inset lights that glowed golden and made the stone shine. Stan turned around in a circle, wide-eyed.

"Wow, Johnny! It's like Disneyland."

Tripp yelled again and we followed the corridor on our right till we found our way out onto a deck at the back of the house that held a large Jacuzzi and scattered wooden outdoor furniture. The deck looked across a gently sloping expanse of lawn that ended in a wall of forest. There was an archery target set up in front of the trees and

Jeremy Tripp was loosing arrows at it from a longbow. He was a good shot and his arrows were all clustered inside its two central rings.

Stan stood off to one side and announced formally that we were ready to begin our installation. Jeremy Tripp didn't seem particularly interested and told us to just bring the plants inside and put them wherever we wanted. His voice was brusque and I could tell Stan was a little hurt.

We went back out to the truck and manhandled the planters into the foyer one by one. While Stan fussed with the positioning of two trough displays in the foyer, I hauled several of the single-shrub drum planters upstairs and looked for places to put them.

Most of the rooms I checked were unfurnished, but in the master bedroom there was a large unmade bed, several pieces of blond-wood furniture, and an open built-in wardrobe showing a rack of expensive men's clothes. As I was positioning one of the planters in a corner of this room, a louvered door beside the wardrobe opened and Vivian stepped out of a bathroom, wrapped in a towel and wet from a shower.

She seemed perfectly relaxed.

"Johnny, how nice to see you again."

I pointed at the plant. "My new business."

"Very enterprising."

I couldn't think of anything else to say so I turned to leave.

"Johnny."

"Yes?"

"Whatever you do is your own business, of course, but Gareth is very young. In the way his mind works."

"I'm not going to say anything."

"He would be upset."

"I think he'd be very upset."

I went back downstairs and Stan and I left the house without seeing Jeremy Tripp again. As I was about to pull out of the driveway an old orange Datsun stopped in front of the house and Rosie got out and started loading herself with buckets and mops and other cleaning equipment. Stan jumped out of the pickup and they spent a couple of minutes speaking hesitantly to each other. When they were done Stan kissed her awkwardly on the cheek. Back in the pickup he told me she'd been hired by Jeremy Tripp to clean his house once a week.

We'd done our first installation and Stan was ecstatic. On our way down from the Slopes he babbled about his plans for moving forward - distributing fliers, visiting every business in Oakridge, ordering plants from the wholesaler in Sacramento....

We spent the remainder of the day back at our warehouse and then headed home. On our way through town Stan said he wanted to celebrate, so we picked up Chinese food for a surprise dinner with my father.

At the house we set out plates in the dining room and put the food in the oven to keep warm. We sat in the kitchen and waited for my father. But my father didn't come home.

When it was past seven I called his office but it was closed and I got the machine. There was no answer from his cell phone. It was unlikely, but still possible, that he was out late showing a property, so we kept on waiting. After a while Stan went off and watched TV and at eight we took the food out of the oven and the two of us ate a quiet dinner in the kitchen. Stan put on a brave face but I knew he was worried.

An hour later I called the Oakridge police. I got put through to a detective who told me they had no reports of recent car wrecks or any other incidents that might have accounted for my father's absence. He said he'd check with the medical center in town and the hospital in Burton and call back. In the meantime he wanted me to call my father's friends and the people he worked with in case they knew anything.

My father's boss was Rolf Kortekas. I found him in the phone book and called him at home. All he could tell me was that my father had left the office around six as usual and that he hadn't said anything about showing a property after hours. Kortekas assumed he'd headed straight home.

After that, who was there? My father had no close friends and the woman he'd been seeing had been buried two days ago. The only other person I could think of was Marla. I figured he might have gone around to her place to commiserate about Pat. I called her house and her cell phone. There was no answer at either.

When the detective called back he had nothing to report. No one of my father's name or description had been admitted to the medical center or to the Burton hospital. He said he'd put the word out to the patrol cars and that if my father hadn't turned up by morning some-one would come around to the house. Before he hung up he told me not to worry too much, in his experience ninety percent of these cases turned out to be nothing more serious than someone sleeping off a drinking binge in a motel room.

I wasn't convinced. Drinking binges weren't something my father did. But we seemed now to be in the grip of the police machine and all its iron procedures. In an attempt to feel like we weren't just wait-ing around, that we were in fact doing something, rather than out of any real hope that he would actually be there, I suggested to Stan that we check the only other place I could think of that had any con-nection to my father - the cabin on the piece of land at Empty Mile.

The drive out there in the dark felt as though it was mandated to end in some episode of domestic tragedy. The roads were unlit and the tunnel our headlights cut into the night served only to point up all the uncounted horrors that could befall a human being. The meadow, though, when we pulled off Rural Route 12, was peaceful. Under the starlight the long grass held a sheen of silver and when I parked in front of the cabin and turned the pickup's engine off the silence of the place seemed to fall like some heavy curtain about us.

The cabin was dark. No flashlight or lamp or burning candle gave away my bivouacking or binge-drunk father and when we entered through the unlocked door it took us less than a minute to confirm that the place was empty, that indeed it bore no sign my father had ever been there.

Across the meadow there was light in some of the windows of Millicent and Rosie's house. On our way back I stopped and asked them if they had seen my father at Empty Mile that day. They had not.

My father was still absent when we returned to our house and the anxiety that had been riding Stan all evening rose to a physical agitation that had him pacing the hallway and shaking his hands, asking me over and over what could have happened and what we were going to do. It took me half an hour to calm him enough to get him into bed and even then he lay staring at the ceiling, wide-eyed with apprehension.

Afterwards, I stayed up, sitting alone in the kitchen, calling both of Marla's phones every half hour. I was worried about my father, of course, but the fact that Marla didn't seem to be at home added a streak of jealousy to the mix. There weren't too many encouraging scenarios I could come up with for her not being there at that time of night. When she still hadn't answered half an hour after midnight I gave up and went to bed.

Stan and I were both awake early the next morning. Neither of us had slept well and around dawn we got up and sat in the kitchen. I made coffee and Stan drank hot chocolate. He looked haunted and drawn and he sat hunched in his chair. My father had not come home during the night and we both knew something was very wrong.

Around seven a.m. I called Marla's landline. She answered on the second ring.

"Who is it?"

"It's me."

"Johnny?"

"Yeah. Are you all right? You sound weird."

"I'm okay. I just woke up, that's all. I was going to call you today. I miss you. Is everything okay?"

"My father's disappeared."

"Disappeared? What do you mean?"

"He didn't come home last night. We don't know where he is."

"Oh no."

"You haven't seen him?"

"No. Why would I see him?"

"I thought because of Pat and everything he might have come around."

"No. I haven't seen him since before she died."

"But you were there all night? You would have known if he came around? I called you till about twelve and there was no answer."

"I had a killer day at work. When I got home I just turned off the phones and crashed out. I'm sorry, you must have needed someone to talk to. Have you called the police?"

"Yeah, last night. They're sending someone over."

"Are they going to do an investigation?"

"Well, I'd think so, wouldn't you?"

"Oh, Jesus, Johnny, I really don't want to get dragged into it."

"Why would you?"

"Because of the room. They're obviously going to ask you if he was seeing anyone. And then they'll come here."

"Is that a problem?"

"Of course! I'm renting a fuck pad to a woman who just killed herself, whose husband's a big noise on the council, and whose lover has just disappeared. Not to mention I gave her those fucking pills."

"Did anyone else know about the room?"

"No one. No one knew anything. Can you please keep me out of it? Please."

"Okay.... If it comes up I won't say anything about the room. Okay?"

Marla sounded relieved. "Thank you, Johnny. Thanks."

Detective Patterson turned up midmorning with a uniformed officer and a laptop. Patterson was about fifty. He was not a tall man and he was thick around the middle. He wore a dark suit and his hair was held in place with some sort of product that smelled faintly of mint.

Stan and I and the two cops went into the kitchen. Patterson put his laptop on the table and faced us with his hands slightly raised, as though he wanted to make absolutely sure we understood what he was going to say.

"All right. The news so far is that we have not found your father. Neither do we have any information about his movements last night. What one of our cars did find in the last hour, though, was a white Ford Taurus parked in the lot behind Jerry's Gas."

He handed me a sheet of paper that bore the logo of a car rental company. My father's signature was at the bottom.

"Your father's rental agreement. We've checked with the car people and there's no question - the car we found is the one he rented. No one at Jerry's knows anything about how it got there. Unfortunately they don't have camera coverage in the lot. The car was unlocked and the key was in the ignition."

Stan let out a small moan.

"We've checked it out pretty thoroughly and we haven't found anything to indicate that he might have come to harm - no damage to the bodywork, no marks on the interior."

For the next half hour Patterson asked about what my father did, where he worked, how long we'd lived in Oakridge, what happened to my mother...obviously compiling background to help him in his search. He typed all our answers into his laptop without looking at the keys.

"How long ago was it that your mother died?"

"Fourteen years."

Stan was sitting beside me. Patterson was opposite us across the table and I saw him glance at my brother.

"So there were just you two boys and your father after that?"

"For a while. I went to live in London eight years ago. I only got back recently."

"Do you think your father found it difficult, working and being Mr. Mom all those years? Particularly after you left?"

"I guess."

"Was he bitter about it, do you think?"

"I think he was...frustrated that he didn't have the money to make it easier."

"Mmm." Patterson frowned and nodded to himself. "Would you call him a happy man?"

"He wasn't suicidal, if that's what you're driving at."

"I was thinking more along the lines of depression. Was he unhappy with the state of his life? Would that describe him? Was he on medication? Antidepressants?"

"No, no medication, no antidepressants. He wasn't a happy man but he wasn't clinically depressed, either. He was unfulfilled. He always wanted to be more successful."

"Okay. See, where his car was found, that lot, that's a pickup stop for the Greyhound that runs up to Burton and on to Nevada, and back the other way to San Francisco. Several people got on the San Francisco bus last night."

"Was he one of them?"

"We don't know. We spoke to the driver by phone. All he remembers is that out of the people who got on there were a couple of men. They weren't together and they paid for their tickets with cash - no credit card ID. He couldn't give a description beyond that they were white and middle-aged. We'll e-mail him a photo, but I don't know how much we'll get out of him. All we know is that all the passengers went through to San Francisco, no one got off along the way. I'll need your father's bank details, by the way, so we can put a trace on his cards."

Stan had been listening to all of this, rubbing his hands together as though they were hurting him. He spoke up now and his voice was angry. "My dad wouldn't go away like that. You're talking crazy."

Patterson looked at him uncertainly for a moment and I knew he was trying to gauge the boundaries of Stan's ability to understand the situation. To his credit he didn't start speaking like a grade school teacher.

"No, you're right. It seems unlikely. But I have to consider every possible scenario. And, unfortunately, it is a possibility."

"Stan's right, though. My father isn't that sort of man."

"I hear what you're saying, but it's a fact that in many, many missing persons cases the person, I don't know..." Patterson looked around the room as though he might find some other way of putting it, then gave up and continued, "...just kind of snaps."

Stan had tears in his eyes. He shouted at Patterson, "My dad didn't snap! Something happened to him!"

Patterson nodded gently. "That, again unfortunately, is also a possibility and we will absolutely follow that line of inquiry as well. Listen, Stan, I wonder if you'd go into the front room with this officer here. He has a form we need you to fill out to start an official missing persons case."

The uniformed officer rose. After hesitating a moment Stan got up too and followed him out of the room. Patterson looked at me carefully.

"Your brother...."

"There was an accident when he was eleven. He was underwater for a long time, he suffered some damage."

Patterson made another entry on his laptop. "Must have made it doubly difficult for your dad bringing him up."

"I can see where you're going, but honestly it's impossible for me to imagine my father just running away."

"Was he seeing anyone?"

"How do you mean?"

"How do you think I mean?"

"Well, I don't-"

"Johnny, this is not the time to get creative. Being discreet won't help him or us."

"A couple of weeks ago he told me he was having an affair with Patricia Prentice. I really don't know any more than that, my father didn't like to talk about anything personal."

Patterson raised his eyebrows. "The Patricia Prentice who recently committed suicide?"

I nodded.

"How long had they been seeing each other?"

"Six months, apparently."

"Did her husband know?"

"As far as I know, no."

Patterson winced. He asked a few more questions then had me fill out a formal missing persons report. By the time we were done Stan and the officer were back in the kitchen. Patterson packed his laptop away and shook our hands and told us someone would be in touch every day and that the minute they knew anything, we would. He stopped in front of Stan before he left and put his hand on his shoulder.

"We're going to do everything we can to find your dad. I promise."

After he'd gone Stan walked around the kitchen running his hands through his hair.

"Oh boy, Johnny, oh boy.... What's happened to Dad?"

"I don't know."

"What did he mean about the car when he said marks?"

"Just anything that was a clue, I guess."

Stan shook his head solemnly. "He was talking about blood."

"I don't think he was talking about blood, but anyway he said they didn't see any."

"Do you think he got on the bus? Do you think inside he always wanted to go somewhere else?"

"No, I don't. Do you?"

Stan looked at me miserably and shook his head. "I have to put a costume on, Johnny, I don't have enough power."

"Stan, listen, calm down. What we have to do is wait and let the police do their stuff and try not to freak out before we know anything solid, okay?"

But although that's what we did, and although Patterson was genuine and diligent and the Oakridge police combined forces with the larger Burton department, nothing came of it

During the two weeks following my father's disappearance, the police interviewed the people he worked with and the one or two acquaintances who were the closest thing he had to friends. None of them had any idea what might have happened to him. Police patrols covered all the roads that ran through the hills around Oakridge and the forestry service did the same with the fire trails. Neither found any trace of him.

His bank and credit card accounts were monitored but they remained unused and a photo of my father, e-mailed to the driver of the San Francisco bus that had picked up at Jerry's Gas, brought forth no excited cry of recognition. A story about my father's disappearance in the Oakridge Banner was similarly unproductive.

At one point Patterson showed us a video from a security camera in the San Francisco bus terminal. He asked us to look for anyone who might be our father. It was black-and-white and shot from high up. We watched it twice but we didn't see him and I got the feeling that Patterson wasn't seriously considering the bus scenario anymore.

It seemed, briefly, that Stan and I may have become suspects because Burton sent over a forensics team to go through our house. But the fact that there was nothing to find and that my father, although he carried home and car policies, had only minimal life insurance, turned the investigation back out toward the world again.

Bill Prentice, too, had his fifteen minutes of institutional scrutiny. As the husband of my father's lover the notion that he might have exacted a fatal revenge was not something the police could ignore. It turned out almost immediately, though, that the day after Pat's funeral, Bill had taken his BMW and headed down to Los Angeles to visit his mother. While down there, grief over his wife's death had driven him to the bottle and on the evening and night of my father's disappearance he had the cast-iron alibi of having been locked up in Santa Monica while he was processed for DUI.

Patterson came around to our house for the last time a month after my father vanished. He told me the police had run out of ways to approach the case. Stan was up in his room at the time and Patterson asked me not to call him down. We went out into the back garden and sat in the shadow of the house.

"Truthfully, we have no indication as to what might have happened to him. We've listed him as missing but I have to tell you, those details have been available to the California law enforcement community since the start of the investigation and nationally for the last two weeks and we haven't had a bite. The length of time is very much a negative factor. On the other hand, we have nothing concrete to say he isn't alive and well - no items of clothing, no blood, nothing. The case will stay open of course, and we'll keep doing what we can, but we're off that part of the curve now where we could expect any sort of timely resolution. I'm sorry. Basically, all we can do is hope he makes contact with you, or..."

He shrugged, and didn't say any more, but it was plain enough he meant: '...or the body turns up'.

After Patterson had gone I went upstairs to Stan's room. He was sitting on the corner of his bed, crying quietly. His head was bowed and he didn't look up when I came in. I sat beside him and put my arm around his shoulders. After a long time he cried himself out and his breath shuddered through his heavy body.

"I saw him through the window. I didn't want to come down."

"It's okay."

I told him what the detective had said. When I'd finished he said solemnly, "Dad's dead."

"Yes, I think he must be."

"Does it feel weird to you, Johnny? That there's just you and me now? It feels like we're in the sea and there's nothing holding us in the right place anymore. Like everything around us is empty."

"Yeah, it's weird."

"Remember that night at the beach, when you were showing me the stars?"

When I had just turned sixteen and Stan was nine our parents took us on a short summer vacation to Santa Barbara. One warm night Stan and I lay on the beach after dark and looked up into the sky and I pointed out the few constellations I knew and told him how a planet didn't twinkle and how sometimes you could see satellites moving against the backdrop of stars. And Stan had been lost in thoughts of infinity and dreams of what might be out there, and I felt his wonder and shared it, and in sharing had been drawn so close to him that it seemed we became for those moments almost part of each other, seeing with the same eyes, feeling together the vastness of the universe passing through us....

"Yes, I remember."

"I wish we could be back there."

Stan's voice slowed and a little while later he started to drowse. I laid him on the bed and pulled the covers over him even though the sun was still high outside and the room was warm. I went downstairs and made a cup of coffee and sat at the kitchen table and thought about that night in Santa Barbara.

It was a memory I had cherished through all my years apart from Stan. My mother and father had both been alive then, Stan had not yet slipped beneath the dark waters of Tunney Lake, and I had still to spiral from my own good graces. It seemed a memory like that should have led to a better life for Stan and me, should have been part of a lifetime of events that were equally as cherished. In the kitchen that day I felt that I had thrown something away, that I had been granted some magic opportunity but had chosen to waste it

In the evening the phone rang. I knew it would be Marla but I didn't answer it. Stan slept without waking until the following morning and I was left alone with my own terrible thoughts.

CHAPTER FOURTEEN

B etween my father's disappearance and Patterson's last visit there had been days where Stan and I did nothing more than sit in the house waiting for news.

But there had been days, too, when we could not bear to be alone with our thoughts. On these days we either went into town and walked ourselves to exhaustion delivering Plantasaurus fliers, or to the warehouse to tend to our stock of plants. And once each week we drove to the Slopes to maintain the displays at Jeremy Tripp's house. In this way we put Plantasaurus into a holding pattern while we absorbed the absence of our father.

But the news that the police had reached the end of their inquiries was a turning point for us. We did not discuss it. We did not sit down and try to figure out what the right thing to do was. We simply started work in earnest the day after Patterson's visit.

We got to our warehouse around ten that morning. We'd had around twenty responses to our fliers so far and I started calling people back and making appointments to see them. We took a guess at how many plants we might need over the coming month, on top of those that Bill had given Stan, and placed our first order with the wholesaler in Sacramento. In the afternoon we went into Oakridge and closed deals with three of the stores I'd contacted, then we went back to the warehouse and made up displays. It was a good day. We were occupied enough not to think too much and we had made definite progress with Plantasaurus.

In the evening Marla came to our house. She'd been over a number of times in the past weeks to cook for us and be supportive. That night she brought a bottle of wine and the three of us had dinner at the kitchen table with the back door open and the warm evening air drifting in. There were moths above us, softly battering themselves against the frosted glass of the ceiling light. Stan looked at them often as we ate

"There's a lot of moths, Johnny."

"It's the light."

"I know, but there's more than usual."

"Do you think so?"

"I think it's a message."

"Really?"

"Because of Dad and Plantasaurus and everything."

"What are you talking about?"

"We need power, Johnny, to make sure Plantasaurus works. They might be here to bring it across for us."

"Dude, you're freaking me out."

"They might be magnets for power."

"Stan-"

"They might be, Johnny, you don't know."

"They're not magnets, they're moths. They're insects."

Stan ignored me and lifted his hand toward the light. One of the moths, in the process of making a longer than usual loop, touched down on his finger and clung there for a second before continuing its mad orbit. For a long moment after that Stan looked as though he had discovered a wondrous secret.

That night he wore his Superman suit to bed. He made me open his windows and leave the light on.

"I wish there was a Mothman, Johnny, with moth powers and stuff. I could have one of his costumes."

"What sort of powers would he have?"

"Walk upside down on the ceiling? Be able to fly?"

"Be a bit of a pain, though. Every time you went past a light you'd have to run into it."

Stan rolled his eyes. On the way out of the room I turned the light off by reflex, but he called out and I went back and turned it on again. When I left this time he was staring at the bulb.

In the morning, after Marla had gone to work and Stan and I were still cranking up for the day, the mail came. Among the usual junk from supermarkets and electronics stores there was a single window-envelope. I opened it while Stan was upstairs in the bathroom cleaning his teeth and combing Brylcreem through his hair. It was a form letter from one of the banks in town, addressed to my father, and it said that payment on the mortgage for the house was overdue.

Two things went through my mind in quick succession. First, that it must be a mistake. My father, as far as I knew, owed nothing on the house. The small life insurance policy when my mother died had enabled him to get enough of a jump on it to close out the debt a year or so before I returned to Oakridge. He'd told me so in an e-mail while I was in London. The second was the realization, whether the threat to the house was real or not, that I was now solely responsible for Stan, for the place he lived in, the food he ate, the clothes he wore.... My father was no longer here to cover what it cost for him to survive in the world.

I called the bank and got an emergency slot with one of their customer service people that morning. Before Stan and I headed into town to keep the appointment I filled a cardboard folder with various papers - our copy of the missing persons report, my father's bank account details, his passport, a statement by Detective Patterson attesting to his disappearance....

The bank was air-conditioned and the cubicle we were shown into had a small octagonal aquarium of goldfish in one corner. Stan and I sat on padded vinyl chairs across a low table from a bank guy who had a name plate clipped to his shirt pocket that said he was a loan officer and that his name was Peter.

I showed him the contents of my folder to prove I had a right to the information I was asking for and after he'd called Patterson to confirm things he spent a couple of minutes checking records on his computer. Stan sat very straight in his chair. Every so often he glanced worriedly over at me. His hand rested against the top of his thigh and beneath it he held a matchbox. I saw that he'd pushed it open a crack.

Peter looked up from his computer and spoke earnestly. "It's true that at one point your father had paid off the house. But two months ago he remortgaged it in order to buy a piece of land at a place on the Swallow called Empty Mile. The house was the only collateral he had."

"How much?"

"Two hundred and fifty thousand."

"We owe two hundred and fifty thousand dollars?"

"Your father does."

"But he's disappeared, he might not even be alive anymore. How can you expect him to make payments on a loan?"

"We're a bank, that's what we do. We lend money on the expectation that it's going to be paid back."

"But that means we're going to lose the house."

"It's brutal, I know." He paused for a moment and softened a little. "In the final analysis all the bank cares about is that the debt gets serviced. It's immaterial to us whether your father makes the payments or someone else does. This might be an option for you. Though you should know that he took this mortgage out over a much shorter period than usual - ten years. Possibly because of his age. The payments are proportionally higher as a result."

"There is no way we can make payments whatever level they're at. No way at all. We've just started a small business, we have virtually no income."

"Do you have any assets?"

I was about to say no when I remembered that I was now technically the owner of the land at Empty Mile. I told Peter about the transfer of title.

He nodded and thought for a moment, then cleared his throat. "Okay. Given the situation with your father I'm sure we can put the payments on hold for a few weeks to give you some thinking room. But what it's going to come down to is one of four options. You make the mortgage payments; you don't make the payments and the bank forces a mortgagee sale of the house; you make payments until your father is officially declared dead and you can then legally sell the house yourself; or you sell the Empty Mile land and, if it realizes sufficient funds, you pay off the mortgage and keep the house."

"Jesus."

Stan reached over and tugged at my sleeve. "We gotta keep the house, Johnny."

Peter made an unhappy face. "It's a horrible situation. But unless your father reappears there really are only a set number of outcomes."

He walked us to the bank's front door. As it slid open he put his hand against the back of my shoulder.

"I'll see what we can do about that freeze."

And then Stan and I were outside on the sidewalk again in the sun and the heat with people passing by. Stan lifted the matchbox he was holding to his nose and breathed deeply.

"What's that?"

"We don't have enough power, Johnny."

"Let me see."

He handed over the box. I pushed it a little further open and saw two silvery-brown moths fluttering limply inside.

"Don't be mad, Johnny, okay? Please?"

I closed the box and gave it back to him and we worked through another day at our plant business.

CHAPTER FIFTEEN

If I hadn't been so worried about money I wouldn't have accepted Gareth's second offer of prostitute-driving work. Plantasaurus, though it was gathering momentum and gaining new customers every few days, was not yet covering costs and our expenses were being met out of what dwindling savings Stan and I had left.

On top of this, there was the fresh financial wound of the house mortgage. The bank had given us a one-month freeze on the loan, but after that I'd either have to start making payments or show that plans were underway to sell the Empty Mile land. So when Gareth called and offered his standard fifty dollars it seemed stupid to turn the money down.

Around nine p.m. I got into the pickup and headed for Gareth's place at Tunney Lake. I left Stan watching TV in the living room. He said it would creep him out to go to bed while there was no one else in the house so he was going to stay up till I got home.

At the lake only the office and the last cabin in the row showed any light. As I pulled up, the office door opened and Gareth stepped out onto the porch and stood there waiting while I walked over to him. By the light of the overhead bulb I could see that he was smiling.

"Thanks for helping out again, dude."

"No problem. End cabin?"

Gareth stayed smiling but he shook his head slowly. "Nope. I have her right here."

He reached for someone out of sight behind him in the office and pulled. Whoever it was seemed to be resisting him and he had to half turn to exert more strength before he could pull her out through the doorway.

When he did, I felt something run through me that I had not experienced since I'd seen Stan laid out at the edge of the lake twelve years before - a sensation of my insides draining in a rush, down through my body and out. For an instant I thought I might not be able to stay standing. Because the girl who now stood beside Gareth was Marla.

"What's going on?"

"Just what we talked about, dude. Easy money for you, even more easy money for me. Special request from a new customer."

Gareth let go of Marla's arm and gave her a small shove. She stepped down off the porch and walked quickly to my truck. She had her eyes on the ground and she didn't look up as she passed me. I heard her climb inside and close the door.

"Is this a joke?"

"It's business."

"You expect me to take Marla so some guy can fuck her?"

"What's the problem? It isn't the first time she's done it."

"What?"

Gareth looked suddenly aghast. He did a good job of it, but I knew he was putting it on.

"Oh, don't tell me you don't know! Please tell me you know."

"What?"

"That she hooks. I mean not all the time, man. But sometimes. Just now and then. I thought you two would have gone through all of that."

"I don't know what's going on here, but I'm not taking Marla anywhere."

Gareth looked somber. "Well, I'm sorry, Johnny, but you have to."

"I'll take one of your other girls."

"I wish I could, but this guy asked for her specifically. He doesn't want anyone else."

"What do you mean, asked for her specifically? If he's a new customer how would he even know about her?"

"Beats me, but he does, 'cause he asked for her by name."

"You're fucking insane."

"Johnny, listen. I'm sorry, but there's nothing I can do. I need the money to keep this place going. I start not giving people what they want and pretty soon they're going to stop calling me."

"So fucking what?"

Gareth didn't say anything else, he just stood there with his hands on his hips and no expression on his face. I stood there too. I had no intention of moving until he gave in. But then I heard Marla's voice behind me, calling sadly from the open window of the truck.

"Johnny."

I didn't turn and she called again.

"Johnny."

I looked over my shoulder then and she beckoned me with a small despairing movement of her hand.

"Get in. Please."

For a moment I hesitated, caught up in my anger, wanting to force Gareth to back down. But then it dawned on me that the simplest solution was to get in the pickup and just drive her home. So I told Gareth to get fucked, climbed into the truck, and drove down the hellish trail to the Oakridge Loop. I didn't speak on the way down, in the dark it took all my concentration to negotiate the broken surface of the trail, but when we hit the blacktop I pulled the pickup over.

"What the fuck is this all about?"

"Keep driving, Johnny, please."

"No, I want you to tell me what's going on."

"Start the truck and I'll explain."

I pulled out onto the road again and after a minute or two Marla began to speak.

"A couple of years ago, maybe a bit more, I was in a bad way. The kind of bad way where the world around you seems smashed to pieces and you feel smashed right along with it. I didn't have anything left to care about anymore. I didn't have a job, I didn't have you, I hadn't paid rent in months, and one day I got the final notice on the house. The night I decided to do it, it felt like everything left of me worth saving or protecting was so close to dying it didn't matter what I did. So I got in my car and drove over to Burton and I stood on a street corner where there were some other girls doing the same thing and... and I did it."

She took a cigarette from a pack in her purse. Her hands shook as she lit it. She blew smoke at the floor and kept her head bent and didn't look at me.

"Aren't you going to say anything?"

I looked out at the black road, at the wash of white light from my headlights, and wondered if there was anything I could say. I couldn't make it not have happened, the same as I couldn't not feel my anger. In the end I just shook my head.

Marla sighed, she sounded like a child that had cried itself out.

"I hated it. I did it for a year and I hated every second of it. Then finally I woke up and thought what the fuck am I doing? I was going to stop, I really was, but then Gareth found out."

"So you went to work for him instead. For what, old times sake?"

"Don't be a bastard. I didn't have a choice."

"Oh yeah, how's that?"

"I got arrested. And by some hideous coincidence Gareth was in Burton at the time. He saw me on the street and when I got into some guy's car and we parked in an alley he followed to watch. And while he was watching a patrol car came along and I got busted. He didn't use it at first. I guess when it happened I didn't have enough to lose to make me a blackmail target. But then I got my job and he realized he could make me do whatever he wanted. All it would take was one phone call from him and they'd fire me, they'd have to - you can't have a hooker working for the town council."

"You let him pimp you just so you could keep your job?"

"It's too important to me. That job makes me feel normal, like all the people who have proper houses and families and husbands. Without it, all I'll ever be is a waitress and an ex-hooker."

Marla put her cigarette out in the ashtray.

"I don't suppose it helps, but it wasn't like it was a fulltime thing. He'd make me do it once every couple of months. It was more about control than money."

"I feel like I'm in the Twilight Zone."

"I told you the first day you came around I wasn't the same person you left behind."

"You didn't tell me you were *that* different."

"How could I? All I'd dreamed of for eight years was that you'd come back to me. I wasn't going to risk losing that. You know, Johnny, everybody gets ruined by the past one way or another. You aren't the only one."

"Well, you're not doing it tonight."

"I am."

"What are you talking about? I'll see Gareth tomorrow and tell him to fuck off."

"No, you won't. If I don't do it he'll call the council, and I am not losing my job. I had it before you came back and I'm not giving it up just because you suddenly felt the need to come home and try to fix your past." She put her hand on my arm and her voice softened. "I'm not even there when it happens."

"Don't give me that shit. There aren't too many other places you can be when you're flat on your back with some guy on top of you."

Her tone changed abruptly and she pulled away. "You might want to consider that we wouldn't be having this conversation if you'd shown some fucking spine and hadn't run away to London. Do you think I would ever have started doing it then? Ever?"

We'd entered the town by then and the darkness of the forest had been replaced by the orange glow of streetlights. There were people walking around in the warm night and through the windows of restaurants and bars life gently ticked away the minutes and the hours.

And suddenly my anger faded and I wanted the dirt of this night to be gone. I wanted to stop the pickup and park and take Marla into a bar and forget everything that had ever happened in her past and in mine and just have a drink and some food and be alive in the present. For once. For one goddamned moment.

And I wanted Marla not to be right. But I knew what she said about me and what I'd done to her was true. And I knew I didn't have the right to force her to lose something she held dear. I'd taken too much away from her already.

So, on the other side of Back Town I didn't take the road up to my house, but turned instead onto the long dark grade of the forest road that led up to the Slopes.

"What's the address?"

Marla gripped my arm tightly and whispered, "I'm so sorry, Johnny."

She passed me a scrap of paper. I recognized the street name, but it wasn't until I turned into it ten minutes later that it finally dawned on me what our destination was.

Lights buried in the ground threw columns of gold against the white front of Jeremy Tripp's house. The plants in the garden and beside the driveway caught the light on the edges of their leaves so that they looked like ornaments placed for effect.

I should have stayed in the pickup, I should have let Marla climb out and go to the house by herself and do what she had to do. I should have waited for her out there on the dark street and tried not to think, or maybe gone driving in some attempt to distract myself until it was time to pick her up again. But I didn't. I couldn't bring myself to let go of her. So I walked with her to the front door and stood close as she rang the bell and waited.

Tripp opened the door holding his longbow. He was wearing knee-length shorts and an NYU T-shirt. When he saw me he looked a little surprised.

"John. This is a bonus. Doing a little moonlighting? Plants not working out?"

"I'm the driver."

His face changed nastily. "Not tonight, you're not." His eyes moved to Marla. They narrowed slightly as though the way she looked meant something to him.

I turned to her and nodded toward the pickup. "I guess I'll just wait, then."

Marla put her hand on my arm and leaned forward to kiss me quickly on the cheek. For a second her eyes held mine and I felt her hand tighten. I turned to go, but Jeremy Tripp stopped me.

"Oh, no, John. Now that you're here you're coming inside too."

Marla started to protest, but Tripp stopped her.

"Without John here I call your boss and tell him you wouldn't co-operate. He said all I had to do was pick up the phone if you gave me any trouble. Plus it might be safer. I could quite easily forget myself and become violent. It's up to you, though."

He looked blandly at Marla until she dropped her gaze. I saw her shoulders sag. I saw her press her hands against her thighs to stop them shaking. Then, after a long moment in which no one moved or spoke, she stepped forward and the three of us went into the house.

Out back the wooden deck was brightly lit by harsh white flood-lights that hurt my eyes. The long lawn shimmered in their light. The archery target had several arrows in it and behind it the forest made a smoky backdrop. At one end of the deck the jets of the Jacuzzi churned water and threw a halo of mist into the air.

Jeremy Tripp walked to the edge of the deck, took an arrow from a quiver, and set it in his bow. He drew the string and held it for several seconds before he loosed it. The arrow hit the target near its center.

He turned and leaned against the railing and pointed to a bench against the wall of the house. "You sit over there and don't move until we're finished." And then, to Marla, "Take your clothes off."

Marla looked uncertainly at me and then at Tripp.

"Can't he wait in the house?"

"No, he can't."

The bench was fifteen feet from where Marla stood and I saw her sigh and as the air left her she seemed to break, to be no longer something with free will but an object, resigned to whatever battering life had decided to dish out.

She dropped the purse she was carrying on the wooden planking and pulled the pieces of clothing from her body - her shirt, her sandals, her short skirt and her underwear.

Jeremy Tripp watched every second of it with an angry intensity. He told Marla to lie on her back, then took off his own clothes and peeled on a condom. He stepped over her and crouched and leaned forward and forced himself into her mouth.

I started to rise from my chair, desperate to leave, feeling sure that I would soon be physically sick, but Jeremy Tripp heard me move and called across to me: "Stay where you are, John. It'll be far safer for her."

Something moved out on the lawn. Several yards in front of the archery target a large brown rabbit took a few slow hops and then stopped to nibble grass. Jeremy Tripp saw it. He pulled himself out of Marla's mouth and retrieved his bow. He set an arrow and drew the string back. For a moment he was frozen in the hard light, then the arrow streaked across the lawn and into the rabbit's stomach, skewering the animal to the ground. It lay on its side with its legs running and blood darkening its fur and screamed like a child burning.

Jeremy Tripp went back to Marla and climbed on top and started to grind himself into her. Out on the lawn the rabbit kept on screaming and I covered my ears and closed my eyes and tried not to feel the world tearing itself open around me.

In the truck on the way down from the Slopes afterwards Marla smoked one cigarette after another. We didn't speak. What could we say to each other? By that point recriminations were as pointless as apologies.

I drove to my place. Stan was asleep on the couch in the living room. The TV was still on, tuned to Nickelodeon. There was a Coke can and an empty packet of potato chips on the floor. I woke him and walked him up the stairs to his bedroom. While I was getting him settled Marla showered, then she and I sat in the kitchen and drank bourbon until the alcohol blurred the images of the night enough for us to risk the darkness of the bedroom.

As Marla undressed she said, "You know Gareth hates both of us, don't you?"

"Well, he must hate you, that's for sure."

"And you. He loved it that he could involve you. You could have picked me up from my place. Instead he drove me up to the lake and made you come out there. Why? Because he wanted to be there when you found out. He wanted to see how much it hurt you."

Later, as we lingered at the edge of an alcohol-hazed sleep, she pressed her face against the base of my neck and whispered for me to tell her that nothing had changed between us. And I did, because although the horror of that night had been almost insupportable I knew that being without her, being unable to somehow make up for abandoning her, would be something I was far less able to bear.

CHAPTER SIXTEEN

The next morning, after Marla had gone to work, I went outside and sat in the back garden and forced myself not to replay images of her lying underneath Jeremy Tripp. I spent a long time doing this before I turned to one of my other problems - how the hell I was going to hold on to the house.

Leaving would traumatize Stan, and if there was any way to spare him the loss of his home I had to try and find it. The only solution I could see right then, and the one the bank seemed to favor, was to sell the Empty Mile land. But my father had made me promise not to do that under any circumstances. Why? What could be so important about a piece of land that he had plunged himself into debt again at the age of fifty-seven to buy it?

Stan and I had to meet a prospective customer at the warehouse that afternoon but everything else we had scheduled work-wise could be put off to another day. When I told Stan we were taking some time off he was dubious at first, but he came around pretty quickly when he realized it would involve seeing Rosie.

At Empty Mile the meadow had trapped the sun and crickets were singing in the long grass. On the porch of Millicent Jeffries's house the smell of warm wood and dust was sweetened by a sprig of jasmine that stood in a jar of water on a sill outside an open window. The screen door was closed and on the other side of it the old woman stood peering at us through the mesh.

"I wondered who it was."

"Stan and I thought we'd say hello."

"I figured we'd see you at some point. Rosie wanted to visit after we read about your father but I told her to let you be for a while. Come inside."

The front door opened directly onto a sitting room that occupied much of the front of the house. It was clean and smelled somehow as though everything in it had just been swept. The walls and the furnishings were pale and because the room was not large its surfaces were cluttered with the vases and knickknacks they held. But it was a pleasant place to be - the porch roof shielded its walls from the sun and there was a cooling movement to the air as it came in through the open windows.

Millicent sat in a chair with a creaking mechanism beneath its upholstery that allowed it to rock. She had been in the middle of some needlework and she picked up the hoop again and laid it on her lap and the dry ends of her fingers moved absently across a half-completed stitching of flowers. I sat on a couch but Stan stayed standing.

"Is Rosie here, Mrs. Jeffries?"

"She's in her room."

Stan looked uncertain.

"Go on, you can go through."

Stan walked through a square arch in the back wall and a moment later I heard him tapping on a door. Millicent smiled gently at me.

"We were both sorry to hear about your father. What a mystery. He seemed like a decent man."

"Yes, he was."

"The police don't expect to find him?"

"I don't think so."

Millicent nodded to herself. "Will you sell the land?"

"My father wanted me to keep it."

"Well, it's a pretty enough spot."

"It is, but I'm kind of puzzled about what he was planning to do with it."

Millicent shrugged. "First time I met him he was trying to get me to put my house on the market. Maybe when he saw the land he just fell in love with it. Maybe he didn't have any plans."

"When was that?"

"February. I remember because it seemed a silly time to be selling a house, but he said there were a lot of buyers in the market for vacation homes and he wanted to get it listed for spring when people started to buy. He said he could get me a good price. I told him to take a look and tell me where I could go on the kind of money I'd get for this place. Our water's that rain tank out there, toilet's another tank buried in the ground. He kept trying, of course, I suppose they have to, but he gave up when he saw I wasn't going to change my mind. We ended up talking about gold, of all things."

"Gold?"

"Yes, he and the young man he had with him were both amateur prospectors and it happens that one of my ancestors, an Englishman like your father, came to California in the Gold Rush and kept something of a journal about it. Your father asked to see it. He seemed very interested in the history of the area."

"Who was the guy with him?"

"I don't know, a friend, perhaps. He didn't appear to be involved in your father's business."

"Does the journal say anything about this land here?"

"A little, I think. It's been a long time since I even looked at it. It never interested me all that much."

Stan and Rosie came into the room then. Rosie had her eyes on the floor, as usual, but as she moved to the front door she turned her head slightly toward her grandmother.

"We're going for a walk."

She headed on out of the house without stopping. Stan followed her closely. I watched them pass through the doorway and when I looked back at Millicent I saw that she had been watching me.

"You don't have to worry, you know."

"What?"

"About him getting her pregnant. I could see it in your face."

"Stan hasn't had much experience with girls. Any, in fact."

"Rosie can't have children. She had her tubes tied when she was sixteen. She was in a home for disturbed adolescents at the time and she was very withdrawn. No one knew what was going to become of her and they said the operation would be for the best because sooner or later one of the boys there was sure to get at her. I had to say yes. What else could I do? She couldn't take care of a child." Millicent stared at the needlework in her lap and after a long pause said, "It was for the best."

She spoke the words firmly then shook herself.

"You wanted to know if the journal says anything about this place. You can read it yourself if you like. It's over there." She pointed to a small set of shelves beneath one of the windows. "The gray one on the end."

I took the book she indicated. Millicent started her needlework again and while she pushed and pulled the needle and its bright thread through the disk of cotton I sat in that quiet pale room and turned pages that had been written a hundred and thirty years before I was born.

The book was covered with coarse canvas. In places the depressions in the weave still held a residue of its original green color, but mostly the covers were faded to a grubby shale. Inside, the first two-thirds of the book had been damaged by water and were unreadable. The remaining pages were covered in a precise hand that gave little slope to its letters. The name Nathaniel Bletcher was printed on the inside of the back cover - Millicent's ancestor, I assumed.

The Gold Rush had had its start in January 1848 when James Marshall found traces of gold in a millrace he was building on the American River at Coloma for a would-be land baron named Joseph Sutter. California was relatively sparsely populated at the time but that all changed over the next year as news spread around the world that a man could get rich simply by scooping dirt out of a river. By 1849 fortune hunters were pouring into the state from every part of the world, most of them heading north for the streams and rivers on the western slopes of the Sierra Nevada. Nathaniel Bletcher had been one of them.

With so many men competing for claims it became less and less easy to earn a decent day's wage with each month that passed, let alone hit the big time. For some men the solution to this problem was to head further inland, beyond the already established diggings, in search of a river or creek that had not yet been discovered and worked by others.

From the journal it appeared Nathaniel Bletcher had been forced, eventually, to adopt this approach. He'd begun his quest for gold on the Feather River where he'd worked a claim for a month without success before selling it and moving on to the Yuba. He prospected this river for three months, moving steadily toward the junction with its south fork. Many of the diggings he passed through had been rich strikes, but he came on them too late to pan anything like the amount of gold he needed to make himself a wealthy man. And so, finally, he abandoned the Yuba, bought a mule and supplies, and walked north into the surrounding forest, determined to keep going until he found his own untouched river.

It took him nine days and even then what he first found was not what he had been hoping for. The bright line of water that guided him out of the forest was already named and known - the Swallow River. To his disappointment there were men there before him and they were panning rich deposits. But there were not many of them and from talking to them he learned that they were the first to reach so far up the Swallow.

He spent two nights on the periphery of this newborn mining encampment, but the lure of his own personal El Dorado was too strong and on the third morning he repacked his mule and struck off alone upriver.

Though California's population exploded as a result of the Gold Rush it was by no means entirely unsettled beforehand. Places had been named, some of the land had been mapped. Settlers who had known nothing of gold had hacked homesteads out of the wilds and, here and there, small hamlets had formed.

I turned the pages of the journal that charted Nathaniel's progress upriver, looking for a place name or the mention of a settlement in the hope that I might be able to pinpoint what part of the Swallow River he had journeyed along.

For several pages there was little, just the outline of four days' slow travel. Immediately beyond the encampment of miners the riverbed had lost its gold-bearing floor of sand and gravel and its water flowed instead over flat rock and jumbles of boulders, terrain poorly suited for the collection of gold dust. Nathaniel's entries on these days were weighted with despondency and he began to consider cutting his losses and returning to the encampment. On the fourth day, however, he made this entry:

March 15, 1849
At last! The river has grown a little wider and I am camped this evening beside a shoal of gravel that yields good color. From noon to dusk I took two ounces with my pan. The gold is not heavily concentrated, but it is here! It is here! The surrounding land provides good reason for optimism. Upriver, above the tops of the trees, I can see a tall formation of rock that is surely quartz-bearing. It is greatly eroded and can have shed its minerals nowhere else but into the river which it appears to border so closely. Ahead of me the river curves and I cannot see the lay of it but I feel that I am at the ragged end of a great deposit. And of the multitudes who scrabble over this country it is I alone who am here to mine it. What will tomorrow bring? I will journey further. If my luck is good I will find the belly of this lode. If my luck is good.

And the day after that:

March 16, 1849
Half a day's travel and the same of panning. The dirt is richer and I feel an excitement of the kind the hunter must feel as he closes with his prey. I am near. I know it. Tomorrow, perhaps, just a little further along the river, my

fortune will present itself. Though I was lucky enough tonight. As I prepared my supper a trapper happened across me. Praise God that I had stopped my work and that my equipment was stowed out of sight. He travels downriver with beaver pelts and dried meat and took me at my word, I think, when I lied that I was looking for land to homestead. I bought some meat from him and we shared the meal. I asked for a description of the river ahead. There is, he said, a landmark known to those who have traveled this way but a few hours from where I write - an unusual length of river, curved so roundly that it bears the name Cooper's Bend, as if it followed one side of a giant barrel. The river is quite broad and slow here, he said, with a bed of gravel and sand. Though I am lonely for company I was glad when our meal was over and he left to continue his journey downriver for I could not have much longer contained my euphoria. The place he speaks of can be no less than what I seek. All things point to it. The form of the land about, the slowness of the river, the composition of its bed. What treasure must lie trapped within it! I will leave at first light. He seeks to trade with the men I encountered five days previous and he may mention my presence here. Miners are suspicious men and some of them perhaps will not believe a tale of homesteading.

This entry finished at the bottom of the last page in the book. I had become caught up in the narrative and I felt a pang of disappointment that the outcome of his quest had not been recorded. I held the book open in my hands for a moment, wondering what had become of the man, and as I did so I noticed jagged lines of paper along the inside of its spine. It looked like three pages had been torn out.

I put the book back on its shelf.

"The last few pages are missing."

"Are they? I never noticed. But then, as I said, I haven't looked at it for years."

"What happened to him?"

She laughed. "What happened to your great-great-grandfather?"

"I don't even know who he was."

"Exactly. I know he was supposed to have been reasonably well off. Whether it came from gold or not I couldn't say." She looked tiredly about the room. "I know his money didn't stick around too long, though. Our family's been in this area since Nathaniel came up that river and I don't think a single one of us ever was what you would call even comfortable."

"Have you ever heard of a place called Cooper's Bend? He mentions it in the journal."

"Yes, though there aren't many people still alive who know it by that name."

"Where is it?"

"Right here. That piece of river at the bottom of your father's land. That's what used to be called Cooper's Bend till folks took to calling it Empty Mile - after all the gold was mined out, I guess."

I leaned back in my chair and closed my eyes for a moment. I'd come here hoping to find out why my father had bought the land. An old journal would have been an exciting place to discover the secret, but I had read nothing there that might explain the land's importance to him. The only whiff of meaning came from the mention of gold, but what of that? Any gold there might have been in the Swallow River at Empty Mile, along with all the gold in all the other Californian rivers, was long gone.

Millicent smiled patiently at me. "Does any of that help? A couple of months after his first visit, your father came back by himself and asked to read the journal again and then, not long after that, he and his friend showed up to dig some fence post holes."

"I didn't see a fence. Where did they dig?"

"Down in the trees at the bottom of the meadow. Made such a racket I went down to have a look. They had this thing like a big corkscrew with a gasoline engine that they held between them. Bored right into the ground. Looked like a crazy place to do it, right in the trees. I don't know how they thought they were going to string wire through all that brush. But then, your father didn't look too much like the practical type, and I don't think they drilled more than a handful of holes anyhow."

"When was this?"

"Three or four months ago."

"And you don't know who this friend was? You didn't hear a name?"

"No. He was a redhead, the sandy type. Tall, thin."

I took my cell phone out and brought up the photo Gareth had insisted I take of him. Millicent nodded.

"Yes, that's him."

"My father didn't buy the place until a month ago. Why would he be digging fence holes on land he didn't own?"

"Perhaps he was getting a jump on things."

"Who owned the land before?"

"I don't know."

"Can you show me where the holes are?"

Millicent went to the front door, pushed open the screen, and pointed to a spot in the trees at the bottom of the meadow.

"Go straight in from there, you should find them."

I thanked her and walked down across the meadow.

The first hole I found was about twenty yards in from the start of the trees and I'd seen it before. It was the hole my father had stood pondering over the day he brought Stan and me to Empty Mile for the first time. By walking parallel to the meadow from this point I found two others.

Although I'd never put up a fence I guessed the holes were about the right diameter but everything else about them looked wrong. They were too widely spaced, at least twenty-five feet between each, and they seemed overly deep, they went down about four feet. And what was the logic of erecting a fence on uncleared land?

I left the belt of trees and walked back up the slope to take a look at the log cabin. It was reasonably large for that type of building and had three bedrooms. Through the window of one of these I saw Stan and Rosie. They were standing in the middle of an empty room.

She had her arms around him and their faces were pressed together, kissing.

I knocked on the door of the cabin and waited. A few seconds later Stan and Rosie came out and I told him I had errands to run and that he could stay at Empty Mile while I took care of them if he wanted.

From Millicent's place I drove straight to Tunney Lake. Marla and I had reached an unspoken agreement to act as though the night with Jeremy Tripp had never happened, but that didn't mean I had the same agreement with Gareth.

He was sweeping the steps to one of the cabins when I pulled into the parking lot. He looked up from his broom as I approached.

"You took your time. I thought you'd be back last night."

"She told me what you have on her."

"Mmm...busted for hooking. Nasty."

"You prick. Why would you do something like that?"

"Um...money?"

"You've got the other girls for that."

"Johnny, I want to be friends with you. This thing with Marla, it's between me and her. It's part of our history."

"You haven't lived with her for ten years."

"You're pretty self-focused, you know that? So what if it's been ten years? She took my fucking future. I mean, honestly, Johnny, can you blame me if sometimes I treat her like a cunt?"

Gareth took a deep breath, sighed it out, and steadied himself.

"Look, you've been away a long time. And while you were away our lives went on without you, and maybe they got a bit twisted, I admit it. I know I shouldn't still hate her so much, but sometimes.... I don't know, I just get fixated."

"Blackmailing someone into prostitution is beyond fixated."

"She was hooking on her own way before I ever got involved."

"What difference does that make?"

For a moment I thought Gareth was going to puff himself up again but he nodded and seemed to let go of something.

"Okay, you and Marla are obviously back together. I wasn't sure before, but things are different now, I can see that. You shouldn't have your lover being forced to do other men. I actually thought about it a lot after you left and you're right, it can't go on."

"So you're saying, what?"

"I'll leave her alone. Call it my gift to you. I won't make her do it again. I promise."

I wasn't really sure what to say to this. I'd expected a prolonged argument, a screaming match, even a brawl. His about-face took the wind out me and I stood there just looking at him for a moment. Gareth laughed.

"Dude! I'm not a complete shit. What do you think, I'm going to be this evil force forever fucking up your life? Like every day it's gonna be, Sorry, Johnny, but Marla's got to work tonight? Come on!"

"He made me watch."

"You watched? Oh, man, I'm really sorry. That must have been shitty. I had no idea that would happen. Look, I'm finished here. You want to hang around and have a beer?"

What I wanted was to meet up with Marla and tell her how I'd convinced Gareth to set her free. But for Marla's sake, keeping Gareth friendly seemed like the smarter choice right then, so I said yes to the beer.

Gareth got the drinks from the kitchen in the bungalow and led me out to the barn. David, his father, was seated in his wheelchair in the far corner working on something with a drill press. He waved distractedly as we came in and kept on working. We sat in the large open doorway, facing back toward the house. At intervals, behind us, David's drill whined against metal.

Gareth nudged me and made his eyes wide. "Hey, you hear about Patricia Prentice?"

"Stan and I were the ones who found her."

"Really? Holy shit!"

"Stan was delivering some plants."

"What'd she look like?

"What do you mean?"

"I don't know. Was she wearing clothes? Was it, like, a total mess?"

"She looked dead, Gareth, okay? Just dead."

Gareth held up his hands. "Dude, just asking."

"Well, fuck...."

"Okay, okay...." Gareth leaned forward and dropped his voice. "I'm glad you came up today, Johnny. I need someone to talk to. Something's going on between that asshole Marla did last night and Vivian."

"Jeremy Tripp?"

"Yeah."

I knew damn well there was something going on - I'd caught her coming out of his shower - but there was no way I was going to get mixed up in it.

Gareth shook his head sadly. "I go around to see her and she's coming back across the road from his place. I call her on her cell and she doesn't answer, or she's around there practicing archery. Archery, for fucksake! I mean, Jesus, man, I love her."

He took a gulp of his beer.

"I can't believe it, you know? Two women in my life, the only two relationships that have ever meant anything, and both of them turn to shit."

"Why would Tripp pay for Marla if he's seeing Vivian?"

Gareth shrugged. "He's rich.... Fuck, all I need is a little time to turn this place around, to get some decent money together, and I'd be able to keep her. I know I would."

He looked away and cleared his throat, then changed the subject.

"How are you doing about your dad anyway?"

"We're coping."

"When I read the paper I felt bad. Ray was a neat guy. We got to be pretty good friends."

"Really?"

"Yeah, about a year ago I was panning up near Malakoff and he was there too, on the same stretch of river. We started talking, we had the gold thing in common and I was your old buddy so we got along pretty good."

"Oh? He never said."

"Yeah, we used to meet up and go panning. Or we'd go to Elephant Society meetings together. I tell you, I was freaked when he disappeared. The cops didn't find anything?"

"No. But I wanted to ask you something. Did you ever go out with him when he was working? When he was doing his real estate thing?"

"No."

"Not outside Oakridge, ever? Looking for properties to market?"

"Why would I?"

"I was out at a place called Empty Mile. The woman who lives there said that when my father went out to try and get her to put it on the market he had someone with him."

Gareth frowned and shook his head, then suddenly his face brightened.

"Oh yeah! I know what you're talking about. My Jeep broke down coming back from Burton. Ray was passing and gave me a ride, but first he had to go someplace for business. Empty Mile. But I wasn't working with him, dude."

"Did he have a particular interest in that land?"

"I don't know. The woman didn't want to sell, I remember that."

"I mean the land below her house."

"I don't think so, it's just a patch of land."

"Did you know he ended up buying it? For himself."

"Yeah, I heard something about that."

"The woman said you were interested in a journal she had."

"Oh yeah, that. It was pretty cool. We both spent, like, an hour reading it. Do you think you'll sell the land, after Ray's will and everything gets sorted?"

"I could sell it now if I wanted, he put it in my name before he disappeared."

"Really? How come?"

"Some tax dodge."

"Interesting.... You know, me and Dad have been thinking about getting a piece of land, something for the future. Maybe we could work something out."

"You want to buy Empty Mile?"

"If you're selling, why not? I've seen it, it's just the kind of thing we'd be interested in."

"I thought you guys were broke."

"We are, but I could still raise the money on the equity we have in this place."

"I'm not planning to sell."

He looked disappointed. "Okay, promise me one thing. If you change your mind, give me first crack at it, okay? I'll pay market value, I'm not asking for a discount or anything."

After we'd had another beer, Gareth walked me out to my truck. As I got into it I remembered something.

"What were the holes for?"

"What holes?"

"The ones you drilled with my father at Empty Mile."

"Fence posts."

"Really?"

"That's what Ray said."

"But they're too deep. And they're right in the middle of the trees."

"Dude, I was just labor. Your father wanted a hand, he said they were for fence posts. Who gives a fuck? Remember what I said about selling."

He turned and walked back into the bungalow. I drove to Empty Mile and picked Stan up and we headed to the warehouse for our appointment with what we hoped would be a new customer for Plantasaurus.

There was a high-sided rental van parked at the junction of the garden center driveway and the Oakridge Loop. Its engine wasn't running and I got the feeling that it had been there for a while. There was someone in the cab but the light was such that I couldn't make out more than a dim shape behind the wheel.

Stan and I passed it and went on up the driveway. We opened the warehouse and, as we had a little time before our prospective customer was due, Stan turned on the hose and started watering. We'd received our first shipment from the Sacramento wholesaler ten days before and it felt good to stand there and look at the plants, at the different greens of their leaves, shining under the spray of water, knowing that this miniature forest of trees and potted shrubs was ours, that we were in business and this was *our* stock.

When the watering was done we took several sample displays outside and placed them along the front of the warehouse. As we finished positioning the last of them a champagne Mercedes SUV pulled in from the road, crunched up the drive, and parked in front of us. Three well-dressed women got out, one of them was the customer we'd been waiting for - the owner of an expensive clothing boutique in Old Town. Her name was Cloris and she wanted plants for both her store and her house on the Slopes. The women gathered in front of the displays.

We all said hello and Cloris introduced her friends as fellow Slopes-dwellers who'd come along because they were interested in displays for their homes. Stan managed to shoot me a quick look without anyone seeing and I knew if he'd been able to get away with it he'd have made the sound of a cash register. I left it to him to explain about the various types of plants we used and the other options that were available if they didn't like what they saw today. The women nodded and made approving noises.

While Stan was speaking I heard an engine start a little way off and half a minute later the van that had been parked at the side of the road raced noisily up the drive and slid to a stop behind the

Mercedes. The women turned in surprise. Stan stopped his spiel and looked uncertainly at me.

Jeremy Tripp climbed out of the van and walked calmly around to the double doors at the rear of the vehicle. He paused there and nodded to the women.

Stan lifted his hand timidly. "Hello, Mr. Tripp."

Tripp ignored him and addressed the women. "You might want to look at this before you waste your money."

He opened the back of the van and began hauling out the planters we had installed in his house. He handled them with quick angry movements and let them fall heavily on the ground. When he was done he put his foot against one of the tub planters and tipped it over. The Yucca it contained broke rottenly, its trunk opening to show a center of soggy pulp. Its leaves, too, had shriveled from their usual tough greenness and were now empty skin, wet and darkly discolored. The other plants were the same, all blasted and dark and dead.

"Great service, guys."

The women made small, anxious comments to each other as they tried to figure out what was going on. Stan stammered that something must have gone wrong, that the plants must have caught a disease, that we would replace them immediately....

Tripp snorted in disgust and climbed back into his van. Before he closed the door he paused and took a long look around the garden center land.

"You know, this site would be perfect for a small hotel. Say about thirty rooms. You ever thought of that?"

He made a tight U-turn and drove leisurely down to the road and away. Stan dropped to his knees and started inspecting the plants, pulling their limp carcasses from the soil and holding them up to the light. The women looked briefly at each other then got into their Mercedes. Cloris thanked us then quickly made her own U-turn and drove away before I could say anything.

"They're not going to be customers, are they, Johnny?"

"Somehow, I don't think so."

"This is bad. They might tell someone else."

"What do you think happened?"

Stan shook his head. "I don't know. It's too quick to be a disease. The only thing it looks like is too much insect spray."

I prodded a couple of the plants with the toe of my shoe but it was pointless, I didn't know anything about the things plants died of. Some of the planters had fallen onto their sides and I bent down to right them, pushing the spilled soil back into them with the flat of my hand. As I did so I smelled something - an ammoniac, chemical tang. I lifted a handful of soil to my nose, then held it out for Stan to sniff.

"Smells like bleach, Johnny."

"Yeah."

I dug a sample from another of the planters. Same thing. The plants had been fed bleach.

Stan frowned. "Why would he kill his own plants?"

"Maybe someone spilled something when they were cleaning."

"Rosie's his cleaner. She'd never do anything like that, she's careful."

Stan was right of course. No one had accidentally done anything to these plants.

At the kitchen table that evening Stan seemed drained and serious. He ate quietly without any of his usual wise-cracking or horsing around. The matchbox in which he kept his moths lay next to his plate and occasionally he pushed it open and looked for a few moments at the insects inside. When he had finished eating he drank a glass of milk.

"Johnny, do you think Plantasaurus is going to work out?"

"Other than today, I think it's looking pretty good, don't you?"

"It's important now, Johnny. Really important." He was silent for a moment, then he added, "Because of Rosie. I've got to make sure she doesn't stop liking me."

Later, when he was in bed and I was saying goodnight to him, he reached across to the nightstand for his matchbox. He was wearing his pajamas but he had his Captain America mask on. He pushed the box open slightly and breathed deeply from the opening and then said seriously, "When things get hard you need more power. If you don't have enough everything starts to go wrong, like today. Maybe you should get a costume. You can have Superman if you want."

"I'm not wearing a costume, Stan."

"But we'll get more power."

"Listen to me, dude, this power thing is getting a bit tired."

"That's because you don't believe in anything. You're so upset all the time about things that have already happened you don't think there's anything good left in the world."

"That's not true."

"The world's a good place, Johnny, it is. Only sometimes you have to get extra power to help it along."

I could see the subject was important to him so I didn't push things any further.

"Okay, but you'll have to do it for both of us, 'cause I still ain't wearing no costume."

He smiled softly. "Okay, Johnny."

After I left Stan I called Marla to see if she wanted to come over and spend the night, but it was late by then and she told me she couldn't face the drive.

"I wouldn't be much company anyway, Johnny. I feel like a pig."

"You're not a pig."

"I'm disgusting."

"Don't talk like that. You're a good person."

On the other end of the line Marla's laughter sounded lost and a long way off. "Really?"

I thought about telling her of Gareth's promise not to pimp her anymore but the way she sounded right then I didn't think it would have much of an impact. Instead, I made a date to go to her place for lunch the next day. Then I told her I loved her and hung up.

CHAPTER SEVENTEEN

The next day was Saturday. I took Stan out to Empty Mile so he could spend it with Rosie, then I headed to the Channon.

Marla's road was quiet, as usual. I had the windows down and in the shade of the trees the air was cool. Ordinarily it would have been a pleasant scene, but it was marred for me that morning by the sight of a red Jaguar parked on the shoulder of the road opposite her driveway. Its top was down and as I turned into Marla's place, Jeremy Tripp waved at me from the driver's seat and smiled like we were old friends.

Marla opened her door as soon as I knocked and jerked me inside. "Did you see him?"

"Yeah, what's that about?"

"What's he doing?"

"Looks like he's watching the house."

"He's been there for half an hour."

We went through to the kitchen at the back of the house.

"Why would he come here?"

"I don't think it's too hard to guess, Johnny. He must have gotten my address from Gareth."

Marla looked pale and frightened and the skin under her eyes was dark. I put my hands on her shoulders.

"I don't think Gareth has anything to do with this."

"Don't be stupid."

"No, I mean it. I went to see him yesterday, about this pimping bullshit. He told me he was going to leave you alone now that he knows we're together. He even apologized."

"Doesn't sound like Gareth."

"I think he meant it. You're in the book, Tripp could have gotten your last name when he spoke to Gareth and found out where you live himself."

"So, what, he thinks now he can come around and fuck me whenever he wants? Jesus Christ!"

We made coffee and stood around expecting Tripp to knock on the door at any moment. As Marla raised her cup I noticed a long thin burn on the inside of her forearm.

"What happened?"

She shrugged and didn't say anything. I took hold of her arm and looked more closely at the burn. The blister was about four inches long and the skin that bordered it was singed a pale brown and looked dry and dead.

"What the fuck happened?"

She pulled her arm away. "I told you last night, I'm a pig. And people who act like pigs should be punished."

"You did that to yourself? Christ! How?"

"I heated up a knife on the stove."

"Marla, this is terrible."

"No, it's not. It's exactly right."

I was about to say more, but the bubble of toxic emotion that had formed around us was punctured then by a loud knocking on the front door. Marla looked stricken and groaned.

"I can't do it again. I can't...."

She trudged along the hall to the front of the house and tiredly pulled the door open.

On the porch, Jeremy Tripp stood beside a smaller man who wore a smooth dark suit and held a large manila envelope. Beyond them, in the driveway, a new-looking silver sedan sat under a pattern of leaf shadow. Jeremy Tripp lit his face up with a high-voltage expression.

"Time to fuck off and find somewhere else to live."

The man with Jeremy Tripp cleared his throat. He reached into his jacket pocket and held out a business card.

"Gerald Turnbull. I act as Mr. Tripp's lawyer in this matter."

Marla frowned. "What matter?"

"Slight change of landlord," Jeremy Tripp hissed.

The lawyer cleared his throat again. He opened the envelope he was carrying and drew out several pieces of paper which had been stapled together. He held the papers out to us and turned the sheets one by one so that we could see their contents. They looked like they formed some sort of contract.

Marla shrugged. "So?"

"So, today Mr. Tripp closed the sale of this property."

"What?"

"He owns this house now. Your previous landlord, Mr. Constantian, sold it to him."

"Bullshit." Marla snatched the papers from him and looked through them closely. A few moments later her arm dropped and the lawyer took his papers back. "He never said anything to me about selling."

"The sale was conducted somewhat more rapidly than usual."

Jeremy Tripp turned the palms of both hands up and grinned. "One of the happy consequences of having a lot of money."

"You are fucking kidding. You're my landlord?"

"Not for long."

The lawyer reached into his envelope again and took out another sheet of typewritten paper. "You rent this house on a month-by-month basis. You don't have a lease. Mr. Tripp would like you to quit the property as soon as possible, and in any case not later than six weeks."

He held out the sheet. Marla took it and looked at it so blankly the lawyer frowned.

"That means six weeks from today. Do you understand?"

Marla shook her head. "This is my house. I've lived here ten years." She turned to Jeremy Tripp. "Why are you doing this? You don't need this place. I can't leave here."

"Oh, I think you can probably do anything you put your mind to." He looked up at the sky and the trees around him and took a deep breath. "What a day."

He turned and walked down the porch steps. At the bottom he looked back at me.

"You know what? If you and your dumb-ass brother had a bit of competition you might raise your game. Might be good for you. What do you think?"

Then he turned and headed back along the drive and out to the road. The lawyer checked inside his envelope to see if he'd missed anything then nodded goodbye and went down and got into the silver sedan. Marla slammed the front door so hard the glass rattled.

We lay on her bed and I held her as the light outside the windows softened into late afternoon. I knew what this eviction meant to her. She had no family of her own, no hometown to go back to for Christmases and birthdays, no childhood repository of happy memories. This house had become all of these things for her and losing it would rob her of the largest piece of the life she had managed to create for herself.

She threw her head back and sighed.

"I thought I'd end up buying this place. It's the one thing, the *one thing* I've managed to hang on to."

"You don't know this Tripp guy outside of the other night, right?"

"I never saw him before in my life."

"Then this is getting weird."

I told Marla about his visit to the warehouse, how he'd poisoned the plants and driven our customers away. "He was obviously trying to hurt our business. Now, for some reason, he wants to hurt you too. I don't understand what's going on."

"Maybe it's a man thing, like he has to destroy the whore he slept with."

"But buying a house to do it?"

"Yeah, I'd have to be a monumentally bad lay."

Marla tried to smile at her own joke but just ended up looking sadder.

I stayed at her place as long as I could before I had to pick up Stan. When I left I asked her to come with me but by then she was so thoroughly depressed she'd curled into a ball on the bed and wouldn't move.

In the pickup, on the way back from Rosie's house, Stan had a smirk on his face and kept giving me sideways looks.

"Okay. What is it?"

He turned toward me and smiled painfully. "I did it."

"Did what?"

"With Rosie. We had sex."

I'd known it would happen at some point, but now that it had I didn't really know how to react.

"Wow.... That's pretty big."

Stan must have mistaken my hesitancy for disapproval because he spoke quickly. "It's all right, she can't have babies."

"I know. Her grandmother told me. It's okay, dude. I don't think it's wrong or anything, I'm just, you know, taking it in."

"It was my first time."

"I figured. How do you feel about it?"

"I feel good. I mean, gosh, Johnny, it makes your head spin round. It's good to be that close to someone."

"Yeah."

"Yeah...." Stan nodded softly to himself as though he was turning over the experience, running the truth of it between his fingers. "Yeah...it makes you feel different."

CHAPTER EIGHTEEN

onday was pretty much what most of our working days had become. A few hours servicing existing Plantasaurus customers and installing displays for new ones, the rest of the time back at the warehouse looking after our plants and doing whatever office work the business required. Including private houses, we had about fifty clients now. That was really only enough work to fill three and a half days a week but I spread it over five to create the illusion for Stan that Plantasaurus was a regular, full-time concern.

He was thriving in his new role of 'businessman', but he dealt with only one side of the operation - the making up of plant displays and the maintenance visits. What he wasn't involved in was the constant juggling of finances, the balancing of outgoings and income, paying invoices for plants and soil and containers, issues of tax and insurance. He knew about these things because I talked to him about them, but that kind of information was too complex for him to hold in his head long enough for it to become real.

In a way this was a blessing because it prevented him from seeing the real direction the business was taking. I'd done some calculating and though we were just about covering costs now, we were still a long way from the total number of customers we needed for the business to be financially stable.

This probably wasn't unusual for a new company, but the rate at which we were acquiring new clients was beginning to fall. If our rate of growth slowed further, or some catastrophe struck and we actually began to lose clients, long-term survival would not be possible - we couldn't go on indefinitely running an enterprise that didn't pay us a wage.

It was late afternoon when Bill Prentice pulled up outside the warehouse. The day was warm and we had the doors open a little for air. When Stan saw the car he jumped up from the planter he'd been working on and called out happily, "Hey, Johnny, it's Bill."

He went to the doors and yanked them apart. Bill stood in the opening, staring into the warehouse.

Stan gave him a mock salute and said, "Hiya, Bill, long time no see."

For a moment Bill didn't register him, his eyes were locked deeper inside the building, on me. I hadn't told Stan about the confrontation Marla and I had had with him outside the Black Cat café and Stan frowned as he followed Bill's gaze, trying to figure out what was going on. He turned back to Bill and waved a hand in front of his eyes.

"Hey, Earth to Bill."

Bill Prentice looked at Stan then and nodded tiredly.

"Hello, Stan."

If Stan had been a puppy he would have bounced. He grabbed Bill's sleeve and pulled him over the threshold. "Look at the place, Bill. Check out all the plants we've got."

Bill pulled his arm away and looked grimly around the warehouse. I could see Stan was hurt but he tried to hide it and ran over to where we'd stacked the empty planters and the sacks of potting mix.

"See how we have it organized? All neat. I told you I could do it."

Bill closed his eyes and pinched the bridge of his nose as though he was fighting off a headache. "Yes, Stan. I see what you've done."

The overhead lighting in the warehouse brought out the hollows of his cheeks and the bags around his eyes. He'd lost weight and the linen jacket he wore was loose on him, but there was more to the way he looked than just the loss of a few pounds. He seemed somehow to have fallen in on himself, as though some dreadful cancer or parasite was eating him from the inside out.

Stan cleared his throat and grinned nervously.

"Seen any more bears, Bill?"

But Bill was not there to reminisce. He pulled two sheets of folded paper from inside his jacket and held them out to me.

"I want you to leave. This will cancel the lease agreement. You can just go, you won't be liable for anything. You'll get back all the rent you've paid."

"What!" Stan screwed his eyes up and shook his head rapidly from side to side. "What? This is our place! You said it was. You said- You said- Johnny, what is he saying?"

I took the papers and skimmed them. Two copies of the same document, confirming that we agreed to cancel our lease on the warehouse. Bill had already signed in the space next to his name. While I was reading he turned to Stan and his face softened a little.

"I'm sorry, Stan, but I need the warehouse back."

"You said we could use it."

"That was before Pat died."

"But we need it. I'm a businessman now!"

Bill took a breath and let it out.

"Stan, things go on in this world that are complicated, things you can't understand."

Stan looked as though he'd been slapped. Bill saw it, started to speak again, then fell silent.

Stan put his hands on his head and looked at me. He was lost. He'd thought of Bill as his friend and now this friend wanted to wipe out his business. I handed back the papers. "You want to sell the property, right? Someone made you an offer but they don't want tenants."

"I want you out. That's all."

"We have this place for a year with right of renewal for two more if we want it. We're not leaving."

Stan stepped quickly to my side and held on to the sleeve of my shirt. He pointed toward the doorway and shouted, "This is our business! This is Plantasaurus! You better go."

Bill looked surprised at the outburst. For a moment he did nothing but blink, then his face flushed and his lips compressed. I didn't understand what was happening at first, it was so far beyond anything I might have expected, but as we stood there it became apparent he was struggling not to cry.

It only lasted a moment, then it was over and his face was still again. His eyes, though, glistened under the light. When he spoke it was to Stan.

"I just want to finish things. I want an end to it, that's all. It's not about you."

He turned and walked out to his car and drove away. Stan sat down on a sack of potting mix, put his hands on his knees, and started rocking back and forth.

"My head feels like it's going to burst open. Do you think that can happen, Johnny? Are there things that can make your head explode?"

"No, but I know what you mean."

"But your brain's strong, you can hold things in. My brain's not like that. What if one day something happens and I just can't stop it?"

"Stan, your head's not going to explode."

"I wish Bill hadn't come around. Why is he so upset?"

"It's a huge shock losing your wife. Sometimes people flip out."

Stan took a matchbox out of his jeans pocket and pushed it half open. The moths inside moved sluggishly about. He breathed warm air on them then lifted the box and pressed the open part of it against his forehead. He closed his eyes for a moment. When he opened them again he looked vaguely dissatisfied.

We finished up at the warehouse and went home. Stan was worn out from the scene with Bill and soon after dinner he went upstairs to his room. I sat in the kitchen and wondered if, rather than declining customer numbers, it was going to be me who destroyed Plantasaurus.

Unless Bill actually did have some sound business reason for wanting us out of the warehouse, the explanation for his visit that afternoon had to be his strange hatred of me. And if that was so, it wasn't a situation I could allow to continue. Plantasaurus was too important to Stan for me to be the cause of any threat to it.

I brooded on the problem until the sky outside started to darken. Stan had told me that when Bill closed down the garden center after his wife's death he had also moved out of the house he'd shared with her and relocated to a cabin in the mountains. At around 8:30 I went upstairs to Stan's room and asked him if he knew where the cabin was. Fortunately, the garden center staff had had a team lunch there at the beginning of summer and Stan was able to give me directions. I told him I'd be back in an hour or two and headed off in the pickup to find out what, exactly, Bill's problem with me was.

The cabin was in the hills northeast of Oakridge. The country there was higher and craggier than that closer to the Oakridge basin and in daytime the views could be spectacular. A single thin lane of black-top climbed through this area. Occasional trails twisted off it to small weekend homes built by those for whom the scenery nearer town was not quite overwhelming enough.

It was night now, but the sky was clear and a three-quarter moon made driving easy enough. The start of the trail that led to Bill's cabin was marked by a boulder that had been painted white. From there, Stan had said, it was a couple of hundred yards. Bill's cabin was the only one on the trail.

I made the turn and parked just past the white rock and killed the engine. I didn't want Bill to hear me coming and do anything that might prevent my planned visit - lock his door against me, pretend he wasn't home, arm himself with a weapon....

I walked quietly along the trail practicing my opening speech. It was going to be difficult enough to get a foot in the door and I want-ed to make the most of those first few seconds - *Listen, Bill, we need to sit down and talk things over man to man....*

When I reached the cabin, though, it was immediately apparent I wasn't going to get a chance to talk to him man to man or any other way. Parked carelessly in front of Bill's SUV at the side of the cabin, Jeremy Tripp's E-type Jaguar glimmered grayly in the moonlight. I could hear its engine ticking as it cooled.

Jeremy Tripp and Bill Prentice. *Click, click, click.* A series of incidents from the recent past stepped brightly forward from the dark background of memory. Things which, at the time, had seemed uncertain or inexplicable now gathered meaning to themselves. The way Jeremy Tripp had looked at the garden center on his first visit to it, as though measuring it against some plan in his head. His crack about how the place would make a good site for a hotel. His bleached plants, dumped so publicly. And Bill's weak attempt to move us out

Bill Prentice and Jeremy Tripp. What could it equal but one man wanting to sell and the other wanting to buy? And the buyer not wanting the inconvenience of tenants. That had to be what Jeremy Tripp's dead plants were about - a first step toward wrecking our ability to afford the business and, by so doing, remove our need for the warehouse. Bill's visit, with his absurdly unenforceable demand that we give up our tenancy, must have been the push from his side.

And at the end of this freight train of conclusions there followed one other, the possibility that even Jeremy Tripp's attacks on Marla - evicting her from her house, buying her as a prostitute - might be part of this same offensive. Was she perhaps just another way to strike at me, part of a war of attrition designed to force me to terminate Plantasaurus?

The threat that Stan and I might lose our business seemed suddenly very real. Our lease couldn't legally be terminated unless we failed to pay rent, but if two rich men wanted us out things could get very difficult indeed for our already fragile enterprise. And, the terrible thought occurred to me, they might not even have to get us out for Plantasaurus to suffer. If Tripp bought the place with us as sitting tenants, having a man who fucked Marla on his deck and shot rabbits with a longbow as our landlord would make running our business a living nightmare. What series of obstructions might he not place in our path?

Though speaking with Bill was out of the question, I couldn't leave without at least trying to learn something that might help me against these two men.

The cabin didn't reflect Bill's wealth. It was similar to many scattered throughout the mountains - made of logs with a stone chimney at one end, one or two bedrooms and a living area, a rainwater tank, electricity from a generator twenty yards back in the woods. The front windows were heavily curtained but on the side of the cabin where Bill's SUV was parked there was another window. It was small and uncovered and set at about shoulder height. I squeezed into the space between the cabin and the car and moved carefully along the wall until I reached the edge of the window. I crouched down, then slowly raised myself until I was able to see through the bottom corner of the glass.

My line of sight was at an angle to the interior of the room but I could see enough. I was looking into the living area of the cabin. The room was spartan, the walls undecorated and the floor without covering. There was a wooden kitchen table and some chairs and, in front of them, a couch and a coffee table. Bill Prentice and Jeremy Tripp sat at opposite ends of the couch and it was plain they were not whiling away the minutes in idle conversation.

A large sheet of paper was spread across the coffee table. It was a mottled white and had thin lines and rectangular shapes on it. I couldn't see it clearly, but it looked like a set of architectural plans. If the two men had been examining it earlier, though, they weren't now. Tripp had just said something and was waiting for a response, his face stony with anger. Bill was staring at the floor, immobile.

After a moment, Tripp spoke again and when Bill still didn't respond he made an abrupt, irritated movement and snatched a remote from the coffee table. He pointed it into a corner of the room I couldn't see and a thin wash of light spread back over the bare floorboards. Tripp's jaw muscles bunched as he watched whatever had just appeared on the screen. Bill slumped forward and covered his face with his hands.

I stayed there for maybe half a minute but the scene didn't change and soon the fear of getting caught forced me away from the window and back along the trail to my truck.

CHAPTER NINETEEN

A week later, as Stan and I were finishing breakfast, a guy with a beard and sunglasses rang our doorbell. He held out an envelope and a paper on a clipboard for me to sign. He wore a windbreaker that was frayed around the cuffs and the car I could see behind him out on the road was an old sedan with a bad paint job. I figured he must be a local guy UPS outsourced to.

When I signed for the envelope he nodded and said, "Served."

It dawned on me as he drove away that UPS probably didn't outsource.

I knew what the envelope held, I'd been expecting it. Plantasaurus hadn't magically unleashed an avalanche of money in the last few weeks and the mortgage on the house remained unpaid. I held the result of that failure in my hand now - a notice of eviction and a statement about the right of the bank to undertake a mortgagee sale. We had two weeks to vacate.

When things had started to look like they might reach this point I'd talked it over with Stan. He'd been more than horrified. In a way he was like a blind man, someone who could only survive the chaos of the world by sectioning off a small piece of it and progressively limiting its variables until it was ordered and repeatable enough to exist within. Losing the house would rob him of an environment that had not only been a safe and familiar refuge since childhood, but which was also a touchstone to that time before he changed, before the lack of oxygen took away part of him.

I stayed on the doorstep after the courier had gone. Around me the sounds of morning - birdsong, a car starting, a child shouting somewhere further up the street - made the small front garden seem suddenly precious, a place whose true importance had only just been revealed. I stood and listened for a while, then I went inside and told Stan.

He was very quiet for a long time afterwards and just looked around at the walls of the kitchen. Then he wrapped his arms around himself and folded forward a little.

"I won't be able to remember it all, Johnny. How can I store every-thing up inside me so it won't get lost? There's too much."

"You won't forget anything."

"But some of the things I don't even know I know. I can't think of them right now but sometimes I look at something and then suddenly I remember what happened or what someone said or who was there. Like a flash. How can I do that for everything before we go?"

It was technically possible for me to spare Stan this heartache, of course, all I had to do was pick up the phone and list Empty Mile with a realtor. If the land had had no mystery about it, if I could have been certain that it was a plot of grass and trees and nothing more, Stan's distress was such that I would have done so despite the promise I had made to my father. But I couldn't believe Empty Mile was only what it appeared to be. My father simply wouldn't have bought it if it was.

It was in an attempt, then, to find some justification for subjecting Stan to the loss of the house, for my decision not to sell the land, that I went upstairs.

My father's room was a dark, strange place to me. As children Stan and I had not been allowed into it without permission. Ours had not been a family where we could wander in and bounce on the bed and kick off a Saturday morning horsing around with just-woken parents. This had always been their room, and after my mother died, his room.

It was a dim place of adult secrets, of glimpsed-into cupboards that held things you never saw anywhere else - boxes for cuff links, a small stack of books that were never held in the bookcase downstairs, a rack of ties, shadowy ranks of clothes through wardrobe doors just ajar.... Stan and I had spent a silent ten minutes there after my father disappeared and then avoided it ever since.

There was a bed, an oak dresser with small belongings ordered neatly across its top, a looming wooden wardrobe with a mirror on its center panel, worn carpet, a bedside table. Everything old and dark. And against the foot of the bed the large wooden trunk he'd made as a schoolboy assignment in England and which he'd possessed longer than I'd been alive.

This had been his private storage space. In here he kept his photographs, his papers, his letters, private copies of his real estate deals, bits and pieces of his early life in England. As I lifted the lid and smelled the cool waft of old paper and the dry tang of wood long closed up, I felt as though I was trespassing.

And as I began searching through the trunk I found that I was reluctant to examine some of the things it contained, to have them cast their small illuminations across the shadowed terrain of his personality. A lifetime of being held at arm's length had made it difficult for me to take more than the crippled intimacy I was used to from him. I left many of his possessions alone for this reason - a pair of gold cuff links, a watch that did not work, a rugby trophy from his youth, a bag of old coins. But I spent an hour flicking through papers and documents and at the end of that time I'd found three things connected to Empty Mile.

I had seen one of them before, or at least a version of it - an eight-by-ten aerial photograph, a smaller print of the image my father had so excitedly hung on the wall of the living room. It looked like this smaller photo was the original. It was sharper and the paper had a heavy professional feel to it. I turned the print over. There was writing in a corner, done in my father's hand with a fountain pen - a short note: *The trees are different.*

I flipped the picture several times, looking first at the image and then reading again what my father had written. There were trees on either side of the Empty Mile curve of river, but there was nothing special in that. There were trees everywhere in this part of the country. What had my father seen in these particularly? I looked at the picture a little longer but I couldn't find an answer, so I put it aside and picked up the second of my finds - the papers for the original sale of the Empty Mile land to my father.

The date of the sale was recorded - just two weeks after my return to Oakridge. There was information that the owner possessed, along with freehold to the land, both mineral and water rights. There were references to the cabin and to boundaries and numbers of acres. And there were, of course, the details of the parties involved - my father as the new owner, and a company called Simba Inc. as the seller. The address for Simba Inc. was given as care of a law firm in Sacramento.

I called information on my cell phone, got the firm's number, and called them. After bouncing from a receptionist, to an assistant, to a lawyer, I was finally told that the reason the law firm's contact details were used for Simba Inc. was because Simba Inc. was a small investment concern whose principal valued privacy. The firm regretted, therefore, that it could provide no details whatsoever as to the identity of the previous owner of the Empty Mile land without a court order.

I hung up disappointed, but I figured that if there was some secret to Empty Mile the last owners wouldn't have known about it anyhow, otherwise they wouldn't have sold it to my father.

The final thing I'd found relating to Empty Mile was over a hundred and fifty years old and its presence in the trunk was as puzzling as the information it contained. Three sheets of discolored paper. Six pages of precise handwriting in ink. The missing pages from the gold-hunter's journal I'd read at Millicent Jeffries's place.

I could think of no explanation for them being there other than that my father had stolen them. But in all my life I had never known him to do anything remotely like that.

The room was gloomy. I turned on the lamp that stood beside my father's bed and started to read, hoping that in these final pages of the journal I would discover some reason for his purchase of Empty Mile.

March 17 1849

I rose at dawn and broke camp, determined to reach the stretch of river spoken of by the trapper before the sun was risen above the trees. The going was not difficult. The banks of the river, before I had gone very much more than half a mile, thinned of vegetation and I was able to proceed with relative ease. I was alert for indications of my longed for El Dorado and feared lest I passed by without recognizing it. The description the man had made possessed me - a broad curve of sandy bank, the water slow moving and shallow. From the panning at my last camp I knew that this part of the river was rich and I was conscious of the deposits that almost certainly lay within feet of me. But I want the best of the river and did not stop. At midmorning I found the place I was looking for. I need not have feared missing it. Cooper's Bend. It is well named. A sweep of river curving roundly about a swell of land on its right bank. It is a pretty place but I did not stand long admiring it. Whether or not the trapper has told the men at the diggings downstream about this place they will, by their natural progression through the country, arrive here soon. I might have a week or two. I might have but days. I have to make my advantage count.

A river that makes a pronounced curve will generally deposit its gold to-ward the outside bank at the apex of the curve. My desire was to rush for this point and begin panning but I have learned that with gold nothing is properly predictable and it seemed prudent that I sample the length of this curve, this Cooper's Bend, in order that I might be assured of the richest claim before the arrival of my competitors. And so I began where I was, at the downriver start of the bend on the left-hand bank. Today, though, I have had little luck. I have panned along one hundred yards of the bank, and I have panned in the body of the river for it runs shallow and affords no great difficulty. But I have found nothing. The faintest traces of color only, far less than in any other part of this river I have so far prospected. It is a disappointment and I worry, for even though I am only at the beginning of the bend I had high hopes. Still, there is much riverbed ahead of me.

March 19 1849

For two days I have worked methodically up the river, crossing from one bank to the other and working the bed carefully in between so that I should not miss any but the smallest accumulation of gold dust in the river's gravel no matter where it might lie. But does it lie anywhere? I have found nothing. Nothing! Some traces of dust, a sad thimbleful by the end of the day. I have not seen a stretch of river so poor. It is beyond my understanding. I could stop at random along the miles of Swallow River that wind behind me and, if there were space for a claim, pan a day's wages at least. But here it seems a man would starve before he could dig enough to buy a week's provisions. What unhappy luck it was that my path crossed that of the trapper's! The river is broad, the water is slow, dust should fall from it and settle, and there is sand and gravel aplenty to catch it, but it seems some giant hand has already scooped it up. Men have not mined here before, this stretch of the river bears none of their scars. It must be nature then, alone, who plays this cruel joke. I have another day ahead of me before I reach the middle of the bend. I dare not speculate what awaits

March 21, 1849

Cursed river! Yesterday I reached the repository of my greatest hopes - the middle of the bend - and that day and this I have worked until it was too dark to see. I am burned by the sun, the flesh of my hands is raw from shovel and pick and constant immersion in water, but I have not found my storehouse of wealth. The middle of the bend is as barren of gold as the stretch I have so far prospected. There are some hundreds of yards yet before Cooper's Bend becomes again the Swallow River, but I do not think now that they will make my fortune. How can they be any different from the yards I have already scrabbled over? There is a chance, it is true, and I must hold that hope close to me, but even if the river changes its nature ahead things will not be as I wished them. Men from the diggings downriver have begun to arrive this evening and are staking claims as the light fades. The dream of having a new strike to myself is gone. I am once again one among many and if any wealth is ever revealed here it cannot but be diminished by such division.

March 29, 1849

I must let it go. If Cooper's Bend had carried the amount of gold any sane man had a right to expect I would have succeeded in my goal, I would have returned to civilization a man to be remarked upon. But it is not to be. Cooper's Bend holds nothing. More than two hundred of us, for the influx from the diggings downriver has been swift, have worked the river here for a week and know this as a truth. Though the riverbed has been thoroughly turned, not a single man has panned more than an ounce and there is movement away from here, onwards up the river or back to the diggings downstream. Those who have not already left, though all will do so soon, have re-christened this wretched stretch of water. The name they call it by now is "Empty Mile." It seems fitting. I will move upriver with the others. I may yet find paying dirt, and though I am unlikely now to become a gold dust tycoon I may still pan myself a house, or perhaps, if I am lucky, a small ranch. If I am lucky....

April 2, 1849

The river is rich again! We are beyond "Empty Mile." Men, from where the bend finishes to as far upriver as it is possible to see, and more arriving by the hour. Each of us throwing himself at the small square of bank or bed we have claimed as our own. We are like some mad race of boring insects, our humanity temporarily suspended as we dash to secure a future for ourselves. How many of us will succeed? Will I be among them? Already I have four ounces safely stored and the river's golden heart beats steadily with each pan I lift. Let it beat this way tomorrow and all the days after. Let the gold never end.

There was nothing more. Nathaniel Bletcher had run out of paper and the end of his story was not recorded. I wondered what the Gold Rush had left him with. Millicent had said she thought he had become well off, so I guessed that at least he had not been one of the hordes of broken men who went home poorer than they had been when they started.

Whatever had eventually become of him, though, what he'd written was not what I needed. It did not clear up the mystery of Empty Mile. If anything, after reading the final pages of the journal, my

181

father's purchase of the land seemed stranger than ever. If there had once been gold in that part of the river I might have suspected that he'd had some sort of plan to find an overlooked pocket of dust. But the journal pages showed plainly that this could not have been the case, that there had never been any gold there to overlook in the first place.

I gathered the pages, the land document, and the aerial photo together and put them back in the trunk. As I was about to close the lid I noticed a photo that had slipped from a stack of Kodak packets which filled one corner of the box. I picked it up and looked at it. It was a shot of my father in front of the entrance gate to a large wooden roller coaster. He was standing overly upright and grinning broadly, as though he was clowning for whoever had taken the shot. There was a sign beside him on which I could read the words *San Diego* but nothing else. I put the picture back in its packet and closed the trunk.

In an effort to cheer Stan up I talked him into driving to town with me to have lunch in a diner. With money so tight we didn't eat out and it was something of a treat. Even so, he was reluctant and stayed silent for most of the journey. But that changed rather dramatically when we hit the edge of Old Town.

We were driving along a street of stores when a guy in his early twenties came out of a bookshop lugging a weeping fig in a cylindrical planter. Stan saw him first and yelped for me to look.

"Hey, Johnny, he's stealing our plants."

At first I thought Stan was right and I pulled quickly to the curb. Then I realized that the store the guy had come out of wasn't one of our customers.

"We don't do that place."

"What?"

"It's not our plant."

"But it's a rental. Look at the planter."

We watched the guy carry the plant a few yards along the sidewalk to a shiny new van that had the business name Plantagion and a phone number painted on each side under an orange sun and palm tree silhouette.

Stan let out a wail and started shaking his hands in front of him like he was trying to ward off some dreadful attack. "It's not fair! It's not fair! It was my idea."

"Stan, calm down. A lot of other people do it in a lot of other towns and cities. The idea's not ours."

"But I thought of it for Oakridge. So I could be a businessman." He dug frantically in his jeans pocket and pulled out the matchbox he kept his moths in. He pushed it open and held it to his mouth and started breathing rapidly in and out.

"What are you doing?"

"Moth essence. I gotta charge up."

"Stop it."

"I have to, Johnny. The connection's getting weak. The power isn't coming through. That's why this is happening."

"Jesus Christ, Stan!"

I pulled his hands away from his face. He looked suddenly frightened.

"Johnny.... Am I going crazy?"

I took a breath and forced myself to calm down. "You're not going crazy. But I don't think any power or anything not coming back from some other place has anything to do with that guy and his van."

"Why is he here, then? We checked and no one else did plants in Oakridge."

Stan was right. Before we'd kicked off Plantasaurus we'd done a search of the local business directory to make sure no one else in town was already leasing plants. We hadn't found anyone. Which meant Plantagion had only recently started operating.

"I don't know."

What I did know, though, was that we were in trouble - our business simply would not survive competition. And looking at Stan I could see he knew this just as well as I did.

As we sat in the pickup and watched the Plantagion guy move plants and sacks of potting mix around in the back of his van I wondered about the timing of this new company.

I used my cell and dialed the number on the side of the van. The call was answered by a female voice that sounded vaguely familiar. I told the woman I was interested in leasing plants and asked where the Plantagion office was. She gave me an address in the Oakridge commercial precinct. Stan and I put lunch on hold.

The Oakridge commercial precinct was an area of warehouses and workshops set in a couple of acres of tarmac five minutes drive from the eastern edge of Back Town. There'd been an outcry by environmentalists when it was built in the '80s, but it had given the town a solid base for its small manufacturing and service industries.

Plantagion occupied a pressed metal warehouse on the edge of a maze of similar buildings. A sliding glass door in the front wall opened directly onto a reception/office area and as soon as Stan and I stepped inside I understood why the voice on the phone had sounded familiar. Vivian, the woman Gareth was supposedly in love with, the woman I'd bumped into in Jeremy Tripp's bedroom, sat behind a desk with an Oakridge business directory open in front of her. I saw that a number of entries had been crossed through. It looked like she was working her way down the page. She was in the middle of dialing a number but she put down the phone when she saw us and waved us to a couple of chairs in front of the desk.

"You can't be here to lease plants."

"We wanted to check out the competition. You do know you're the competition?"

"Of course, but I don't like to think in terms of competition. Do you know Schumacher?"

"The car racing guy?"

"Economist. Buddhist economics. Came up with a model for a limited-growth economy. Very popular among us greenies."

"Er, anyway.... This is your business?"

"No. I was bored up there on the hill. Jeremy Tripp is the owner. You've met him I think." She looked archly at me as she said this. "He asked me to manage it. I'm very good at getting things started."

"When did you open?"

"A week ago."

"Got many customers?"

"Quite a few. But with the prices Jeremy's charging it's not surprising; they are far too low."

"Can I see a price list?"

"Of course."

She handed me a printed sheet that gave fees for various combinations of plants and the charges for maintaining them. What we offered customers was simpler, but wherever I could make a comparison, Plantagion was at least twenty-five percent cheaper than we were.

"We saw your van."

"We have two. Jeremy had them painted specially. He said he wanted them to be visible. To stand out."

"You've got *two* vans?"

"Two vans, two men working them, a warehouse man, and me."

I glanced at Stan. His face was pale and set. He looked as though he'd just been robbed.

"I am not trying to intimidate you. But Jeremy said that you would visit us and he wanted me to be quite open about how robust the business is."

"It's an odd business for someone like him to be involved in. I mean, there's not a whole lot of money in it."

"He's planning to grow it. Jeremy was quite the big shot out in the world, you know."

After that there was a moment of awkward silence. Stan broke it by clearing his throat and nodding toward a dracaena in the corner behind her. "Your plant is too wet. The ends of its leaves are dead."

Vivian glanced at it, then her phone rang and when she answered it I nudged Stan and we got up and headed out of the office.

Outside the warehouse the day seemed too hot and too bright. The right kind of climate for forests and rivers and mountains but wrong for this area of tarmac and bolted-together metal. The heat came off the steel walls of the buildings like it was trying to push us away.

As we passed the end corner of one of the adjacent warehouses someone called out to me. I turned and saw Gareth pressed close to the metal wall. He was partly covered by the shadow the building made and it looked like he had chosen the spot for the small measure of concealment it offered. He waved quickly for us to come over, then pulled us around the corner so that we were out of sight of the Plantagion warehouse.

"Is he in there?"

"Who?"

"Tripp."

"I don't think so. What are you doing?"

"I told you something was going on. She's fucking him."

"How do you know?"

"I can tell."

"So you're, what? Trying to get evidence?"

"Wouldn't you?"

"And then what?"

"Well, I'm not a hundred percent sure about that, Johnboy. Maybe I'll just walk away. Maybe I'll cut his balls off. That'd help you out, wouldn't it? Neutralize the competition, so to speak."

"We have to go."

"We should catch up sometime, it's been awhile."

Stan and I began to walk away. But before we'd gone more than a couple of steps I felt Gareth's hand on my arm.

"Did you think about the Empty Mile land? I'm still interested, you know."

"I'm not selling it."

"But you guys have got to need the money."

"Maybe so, but it's not for sale."

Gareth frowned at me for a moment, then turned away without saying anything else and went back to the corner of the warehouse.

Stan didn't want to go to lunch anymore and asked me to take him home. When we got there I sat with him in the back garden, watching the trees in the shimmering afternoon stillness while he slumped in his chair like the bones had been pulled from his body. When I stirred, about to get up and go into the cooler house, he roused himself and said, "Jeremy Tripp is trying to get us."

It was true. Any businessman would know that Oakridge couldn't support two plant companies. Even if they charged similar prices, one would eventually have to go. The fact that Plantagion was charging twenty-five percent less than us, a level of pricing that simply couldn't earn them a worthwhile return, said to me that Tripp had set the business up purely to compete us out of existence. And he'd wanted us to know it. He'd wanted us to see the vans, he'd wanted us to go to the office.

Stan stood up and headed into the house.

"I've got to get some more moths."

Toward the end of the afternoon I made Stan an early dinner. He didn't eat much of it and when I left to go visit Marla he was sitting in front of the TV in his Batman suit. He'd found some moths and added them to the ones he already had. The matchbox was stuck in his utility belt.

CHAPTER TWENTY

When I got to Marla's place she was just getting out of her car with an armful of the empty cardboard boxes she'd been scavenging in preparation for her forced move. We went inside and she dropped them on top of some others in a corner of the living room. I asked her if she'd started looking for a place. She shook her head.

"I haven't been able to face it."

"I've been thinking about something."

"Something about you and me?"

"Yeah."

"About us living together?"

"Makes sense to me...if you want to."

Marla buried her head in my chest and held me. "Thank you, Johnny. Thank you...."

"There's a problem, though. We got the eviction notice on the house today."

"So sell the land. It's in your name. Sell it, pay off the house, we can live there together."

"I can't."

"Why not? What does it matter what Ray wanted?"

"He must have had a reason for buying the place. Until I know what it was I can't sell it."

"Look, I had to research local Gold Rush history when I first started my job. Empty Mile's on the Swallow River and the Swallow River used to be a big gold river. Maybe Ray thought there was still something to be found."

"It's called Empty Mile for a reason."

"I'm not saying there *is* gold there, I'm saying Ray might have *thought* there was. He was in the Elephant Society. They're nice people, but all of them live for this idea that one day they're going to dig up a million dollars. I went to a lot of meetings for that research and I saw Ray there all the time. He was into it as much as any of them. He'd go on and on about how the Forty-Niners couldn't have found everything. If you feel like that, maybe you can make yourself believe something about a piece of land next to a river."

Marla went into her bedroom to change. When she came out she was looking at her watch.

"If you want to ask about Empty Mile we've still got time."

"What do you mean?"

"The Elephant Society. They meet tonight. They might be able to tell you something about it."

"We're not members."

"Like they'd care. Plus they know me from when I used to go."

The Elephant Society met in Back Town in a hall above a short row of stores that had been built in the '20s. The place was a couple of blocks before the town hall, on the other side of the road, and was rented out as a resource to various groups in the community. We went up a flight of wooden stairs to a long room with a cathedral ceiling that ran the length of two storefronts. Lights in glass globes were suspended from the ceiling in a line down the middle. The glass was opaque and had aged to a murky cream. The floorboards were bare and unpolished and dust rose from them so that the air in the place seemed dry and moved against the skin with a papery feel.

At the entrance a woman sitting behind a card table asked us to sign our names in an attendance register. The page she turned toward us bore what I assumed were the signatures and names of the members who had already arrived. The day's date was stamped at the top of the page and beside it the words *Magnetometers and their Role in*

Placer Gold Deposit Location were printed in red ink. The woman saw me reading and said helpfully, "Tonight's lecture."

Metal folding chairs had been set out in five rows at the opposite end of the hall. A few were occupied, but we were early for the meeting and most of the ten or so people in the hall stood around in twos and threes chatting. I recognized a couple of them from the Society picnic.

As Marla led me toward an office door behind the chairs she whispered, "Chris Reynolds is the chairman. He knows as much as anybody. It's good we're early, we can talk to him and then get out before the meeting starts."

"And miss the lecture?"

"Most of them don't exactly live up to that description. Someone stands up and drones on about his or her pet subject for half an hour. Different one each meeting. This diggings, that diggings, the journey across the country to the gold fields, where's the best place to look for gold now...."

"Not good?"

"Some of them are okay, but you come often enough and you start hearing the same thing again and again."

The upper half of the office door was frosted glass set in dark oak. Marla tapped on it and a voice told her to come in.

We entered a small room that was paneled to waist height in more oak. An old wooden desk that had lost its varnish filled most of the space. Chris Reynolds sat behind it poring over some sort of financial ledger. He had a tired, weathered face and the skin around his eyes looked bruised. I hadn't recognized the name, but I remembered the face. He owned a prospector supply store in town called the Nugget Shooter and we'd recently installed a couple of standing plants for him. Like anyone else who read the Oakridge paper he knew about my father's disappearance.

We all said hi. Marla and I sat on chairs in front of his desk and she told him I was interested in the history of Empty Mile. He looked happy to have the chance to hold forth on his area of expertise.

"Empty Mile. What do you want to know?"

"Anything you can tell me. My father bought some land there on the Swallow River and I'm trying to figure out why."

"You're here, so you must be thinking gold, one way or another."

"It's the only thing that stands out about the place."

He laughed. "You could say that about almost anywhere around here. Look, the Swallow was thoroughly prospected during the Rush. There's no gold left in that river, believe me. Not the sort you can take out with a pan. A lot of miners came this way. And a lot of miners means that all the gold got found. Even the name of the place bears it out. Empty Mile. Empty, nothing left. They came, they saw, they dug it all up. Did such a good job everyone who came later remarked on it. Started calling it...?" He raised his eyebrows.

"Empty Mile."

"Exactly. And your father would have known that the same as any other member of the Society. It's a nice thought, but I can't see him thinking he'd bought himself an undiscovered strike. He must have had another reason."

"That's the origin of the name? That it was mined so thoroughly it became...notorious? It couldn't have been that there just wasn't any gold there to start with?"

"The Swallow was rich pretty much all the way up to where Oakridge is today. It doesn't make sense that Empty Mile was barren. I know that stretch of river. The banks, the riverbed, slow water. There couldn't not have been gold there. And there's actually an account by a miner who passed through there complaining about the way it had been cleaned out. It's a pretty strong indication that there had to be something there in the first place."

He twisted in his chair and pulled open a drawer in a dented filing cabinet behind him. After a minute spent struggling with densely packed hanging folders he turned back to us and handed me a sheet of paper. It was a photocopy of a handwritten page. The creases where the original had been folded into eighths were visible in dark lines of toner.

"Copy of a letter sent back home by a miner to his wife. Part of a document collection they have at Berkeley. He mentions Empty Mile by name. Earliest reference to it anyone's found."

He nodded for me to read it.

The writing was rough, as though the man who'd written it had had only his knees to rest the paper against. It wasn't flowery or poetic, and it wasn't as carefully put together as Nathanial Bletcher's journal, but it must have meant more than gold to the woman it was written for - news from a husband thousands of miles away, perhaps the only confirmation he was still alive. As I read through the endearments, the report on his health, his hopes that he and his wife would be together again before another year passed, I couldn't help feeling how intensely lonely life must have been for so many of the men who went looking for gold.

I found the reference Reynolds had mentioned in the last third of the letter. Just a couple of lines at the end of a brief description of the man's most recent journeying.

I am camped this day at a place the miners have learned to call Empty Mile, so well has it been dug. The men here mutter that Chinese must have been the first to come upon this spot.

The letter was dated May 29, 1849, almost two months after Nathaniel Bletcher had reached the same stretch of river.

Bletcher's journal would be an important find for Chris Reynolds, I knew. But until I had either solved the mystery of Empty Mile or discounted the land as worthless I wasn't about to share the one thing I'd discovered about its history with anyone. I handed him back the miner's letter.

"Chinese?"

"The Chinese were known in those days for taking over claims that ostensibly had already been worked out and abandoned. Essentially, they reprocessed tailings. Tailings are what's thrown away at the end of the panning or washing process - soil, gravel, sand, etcetera. Poor in gold. But the Chinese were able to make it pay. They tended to work in larger groups, so they could get through more dirt in a given time. But also they were content to settle for earning a living rather than chasing the idea of a golden jackpot." Reynolds tapped the miner's letter. "What this guy is saying is that if a group of Chinese had been the first to get to Empty Mile they would have worked it with the same kind of thoroughness they applied to working tailings. Consequently, the river would have been left far emptier of gold than if anyone else had worked it."

"Do you think that's what happened?"

"I don't think it was more likely to be the Chinese than anyone else. The miners who got there too late were just pissed off." He looked at his watch. "You know, Ray asked me about Empty Mile too. Maybe four, five months ago."

"What did he want to know?"

"When it had first been prospected. He was really quite insistent about it, as though he absolutely had to tie down when the first miners got there. Came in here after a meeting one night with Gareth Rogers."

"Really? With Gareth?"

"I know what you mean, bit of a strange combination. Your father had been coming for years but Gareth was a rather short-lived member. I think he joined about six months ago, came for a while, then stopped. I haven't seen him here for about three months. Ray kept coming, though, until...." Chris looked embarrassed that he'd raised the issue of my father's disappearance and continued quickly. "They seemed to share an interest in Empty Mile. The Swallow River is, after all, Oakridge's claim to Gold Rush fame."

"What did you tell them?"

"Showed them that letter." Reynolds looked at his watch again and stood. "Time for the meeting. You're going to stay?"

I could tell Marla wanted to go, and I had no great desire to sit on a hard seat and listen to a bunch of eccentrics discuss how to find gold, so I made an excuse and said we had to leave. Reynolds looked a little disappointed, as though perhaps the Elephant Society was suffering a dwindling membership and he had hoped I might sign up.

As Marla and I were preparing to leave, Reynolds pulled open a draw in his desk and took out a diary with hard blue covers. He flipped pages for a moment and then made a sound as he came to what he was looking for.

"I don't know if it's of any use but the only other thing I remember Ray - and Gareth too - showing more interest in than usual was a particular lecture we had here around that time. We have it on again at next week's meeting if you're interested. 'Geological Reengineering Through Topographical Catastrophe.'"

I must have looked a somewhat disbelieving because he smiled a little.

"Randolph Morris, the man who gives the lecture, is, ah, serious about his subject. He repeats it every six months."

I couldn't see how a lecture with such a title would reveal anything to me about Empty Mile, but it was an opportunity to leave with a little grace, so I said I'd attend. Reynolds looked happier and shook my hand.

It was just after eight p.m. when Marla and I stepped out onto the street. The sky was a milky phosphorescence, not yet fully dark, and the air smelled of the still-warm bricks the buildings on that block were built from.

"Did you know my father and Gareth were friends?"

"Being interested in the same thing doesn't make them friends. I can't see Ray wanting to spend much time with Gareth."

"Gareth says they were. He told me they used to go panning together. Did my father ever say anything about that?"

"No."

"How about at the meetings you went to? Did you see them together?"

"I went for a few months about a year ago. According to Chris, Gareth didn't start going until six months later."

"But you saw my father there?"

"Yeah. And no, he didn't say anything about Empty Mile."

Marla came back to stay the night at my place. I was hoping I'd be able to turn off, to put Stan to bed then climb into my own with Marla and, for a few hours at least, not worry about Empty Mile, or losing the house, or Plantasaurus going down the drain. But when we got home, Stan was standing in the middle of the kitchen floor stripped to the waist, the front of his body dotted with moths. He was holding his arms straight out from his sides and staring intently at the black mirror of the kitchen window.

When he heard us enter the room he dropped his arms with a groan of relief, as though he'd been holding them that way a long time.

He'd used adhesive tape to attach the moths to his chest and stomach and arms. I counted sixteen of them. One or two moved a leg or wing where their bodies stuck out beyond the tape, but most were still. There were smudges of moth-down around some of the larger ones. Under the hard light of the kitchen Stan's body looked pale against the dark marks of the insects. He seemed dazed.

Marla sat down and just stared at him. I peeled a moth from his chest.

"These have to come off."

"I imagined the window was the barrier, the edge of the world. I tried to make the power come across. I used to be a super-brain."

"You're still a smart guy."

"Do you feel anything, Johnny? Do you think some power came across for Plantasaurus?"

"Come on, Stan, take them off."

I reached for another moth but Stan took a quick step away. "No, Johnny! I want to leave them on. I might have to be asleep for the power to come."

"Stan, we talked about this. A bunch of moths aren't going to make a damned bit of difference to Plantasaurus."

"That's what you think but you're not always right."

He stood and glared at me, clenching his jaw to stop his lips trembling. The silence dragged between us as I tried to figure out what to say next. Eventually I gave up.

"You look tired, you should go to bed."

After a moment he nodded and walked out of the room without saying anything else. As he passed Marla he kissed her goodnight on the cheek. I followed him upstairs and saw him into bed. He climbed in carefully and lay flat on his back under a light blanket with the moths still taped to him. He looked up at me and said, "Don't be frightened, Johnny. I'm not crazy. Sometimes I don't think like you, that's all."

Marla was already in bed when I got to my own room. I undressed and squeezed in beside her. The single bed made things tight but I didn't care. I wanted to press my body against hers, to push my face into her hair and pretend there was nothing beyond the smell and the warmth of her and the soft protection of the blankets around us. But of course that was impossible, so I lay with my arm around her and stared into the darkness and told her about the new plant company in town, about Bill Prentice's attempt to get us out of the warehouse, and how badly Stan had been affected by these things.

"Hence the moths?"

"He thinks they connect him to some other world that can send him power."

"I could do with some of that."

"You and me both."

"Was Chris Reynolds any help with Empty Mile?"

"I don't know. I still can't figure it out. But there's one thing my father seems to have known that no one else did. Chris said that Empty Mile got called that because someone came along, dug up all the gold, and then, when all the rest of the miners showed up, there was nothing left. And this is obviously what anyone else looking into Empty Mile would conclude as well. But my father got hold of an old journal from the Gold Rush where the guy says he's at the same part of the river that ended up getting called Empty Mile and that it looks like the river's never been mined before. He's the first guy to get a crack at it, right? Before anyone else even gets there. But he doesn't find any gold. He pans right along the bend and gets nothing. And this journal was written two months before that letter Chris showed us."

"So? Empty Mile's still Empty Mile."

"Yeah, but the difference is that while the general belief is that there was gold and it got panned out, my father knew that there was never any gold there in the first place. Empty Mile was just empty, end of story."

"And that would make him want to buy the land, why?"

I wanted to hit her with a great explanation, a cast-iron reason to support me hanging onto the land, but the fact that there had never been any gold was, if anything, more of an argument for selling it than keeping it. I sighed.

"I have no idea."

The other thing I had no idea about, as we lay there chasing sleep, was the connection between my father and Gareth. They'd both been to Millicent's house and read the journal, Chris Reynolds at the Elephant Society had said there seemed to have been some sort of relationship between them, and Gareth himself maintained that they'd been friends.

On the other hand my father, while he was drunk after hearing about Pat's death, had warned me against him. Given that, and the fact that Gareth had stopped attending Elephant Society meetings three months ago while my father kept going, it was beginning to look to me as though they may well have had a falling out at some point. This seemed perfectly reasonable to me. I just couldn't see a man like my father finding anything in Gareth he'd admire or respect. What I couldn't understand, however, was why he would ever have spent time with him in the first place.

For a long time I lay awake trying out imaginary conversations between the two of them. After that I started worrying about Stan. And then finally, finally I fell asleep.

CHAPTER TWENTY-ONE

I woke the next morning in despair. It seemed a certainty that all areas of my life were set to crash and burn. Stan was going to go mad, we were going to end up living someplace we didn't want to be, Bill Prentice and Jeremy Tripp were going to maneuver us out of the warehouse, and Plantasaurus was going to die a premature death.

Stan was already in the kitchen reading a comic book and eating cereal when I came downstairs. He was wearing fresh clothes - dark blue jeans and a yellow polo shirt - and his hair was combed and freshly Brylcreemed. It didn't look like he had any moths taped to himself under his shirt. He seemed serious but relaxed, as though sleep had eased the hold our current problems had on him.

"Know why I like comics, Johnny? They're about a different way of living. The comic world isn't the same as this one."

"Oakridge ain't Gotham City, that's for sure."

"I pretend that all the things in comics are really happening, it's just that they're in another dimension we can't see."

The depression I'd woken up with jumped another notch. Stan finished the last of his cereal. Outside, I heard the bleep of a small horn. Stan pushed himself up quickly and took his empty bowl to the sink.

"That's Rosie. The hall's open on weekends, we're going to practice our dancing."

"Did I just kind of forget this arrangement?"

"Johnny, you have Marla here. You're going to be doing stuff with her."

"All right, but tell me next time, okay?"

"Sure, Johnny. Can you pick me up from Rosie's later? We're going to go back there."

"Yeah, okay."

He winked and made pistols with his hands.

"See ya later, pardner."

He left the room and a moment later I heard Rosie's Datsun pull away.

By the time Marla came down for breakfast I'd decided I was going to try Bill Prentice at his cabin again and, one way or another, get him to tell me what he had planned for the warehouse. If he was selling it to Jeremy Tripp I could brace myself for it, maybe try to figure out some alternative way to house the business. And if he wasn't, I could at least cross something off my list of things to worry about.

It was a beautiful day, a few white clouds in a blue sky and a light breeze that up in the hills around the Oakridge basin made the air feel almost brisk. Marla and I drove to Bill Prentice's cabin without speaking much. After the scene outside the Black Cat café she hadn't wanted to put herself near him again and it had taken me half an hour of cajoling to get her to come along for support. She needn't have worried, though, because when we got to the cabin there was no one home.

We parked and got out and stood in front of the place. There were no cars in sight and the cabin itself had the hollow look of a house people have gone away from. I knocked on the door but no one answered. I knocked again, listening as each roll of sound lengthened into emptiness.

These cabins were not hard to get into. Doors shifted in their jambs, windows in their frames, locks were not fitted with the precision of those in the cities. So, as I stood there, I was aware of an opportunity. I had seen Jeremy Tripp in the cabin. It was possible there was something inside that might help explain what he and Bill were doing together. I went back to the pickup and got a screwdriver.

The window at the side of the cabin, which had been so useful to me before, opened easily after a little levering. I hoisted Marla up and climbed in after her. For a moment we stood motionless inside the room, waiting and listening. But no dog came snarling from under a table, no knife-wielding hillbilly came thundering through a doorway, so we stepped away from the window and started to search the place.

In daylight the cabin looked untidy and dirty. It smelled of old food and unwashed clothes. The sink at the end of the main room was filled with dirty dishes and opened cans and most of the surfaces around it held items that should have been in the trash or stored elsewhere.

We checked the bedroom first. It held nothing but a rumpled bed, a lamp on a side table, and a pile of clothes on top of a low dresser. The small bathroom off it was just as barren - a towel, a piece of soap, a toothbrush and shaving gear. If there was anything to be found it looked like it was going to be back in the main room.

The first thing I checked there was the large piece of paper I'd seen on my last visit to the cabin. It still lay on the coffee table and was indeed an architectural drawing, but it was for the garden center as it stood, not for any proposed hotel.

We spent the next twenty minutes hurriedly picking things up and putting them carefully back, listening all the time for the sound of an approaching car, but we found nothing that told me how Bill and Jeremy Tripp knew each other, or what plans Bill had, if any, for the warehouse.

We did, however, find something else.

A hip-high bookcase ran along a good part of the wall opposite the widow we'd entered through. It held paperback novels and a lot of coffee-table books about the scenery and the history of the area. It was also where Bill stored a small stack of DVDs. I rifled through them not expecting to find anything of interest, but near the top of the pile I came across one I'd seen before - at Patricia Prentice's house when Stan and I had waited with her body for Bill and the police. A burned disk with a smiley face sticker on its upper surface.

I showed it to Marla and told her how it had looked like Patricia was watching it before she killed herself. If it had been a set of papers or a contract I might have stolen it to examine in the safety of my own house. But I couldn't bring myself to take something so intimately connected with that day, something that Bill obviously felt strongly enough about to keep from the police and bring with him on his self-imposed exile in the mountains. Instead, Marla and I stood and watched it on the TV in the corner of the cabin.

When the disk started to play there were a few seconds of empty gray, then the screen cleared abruptly to show long grass, a shallow declivity, a surrounding wall of trees. Next to me Marla groaned and brought her hands to her mouth.

The scene stayed that way as I fast-forwarded through the first twenty minutes, unchanging except for the movement of a light breeze across the grass. Then three people walked into view. Marla, me, and Bill Prentice. The scene was shot from a foot or two above head height, as though the camera was in the branches of one of the surrounding trees, and the field of vision was narrow enough that the grassy hollow filled most of the frame.

After that there was ten minutes of action, ten minutes of Marla and me undressing, of the pale skin of my back and Marla's rocking legs. Of Bill watching us.

The camera had recorded sound as well, but the breeze and its movement through leaves had muffled most of what there might have been to hear. Bill's instruction to us to take our clothes off was barely audible and the few words Marla and I spoke were only a deeper muttering against the background rub of the air.

There was no camera wobble or change of angle, no panning or zooming. It seemed to me that the camera had been fixed in place rather than held by someone during the filming. And indeed, no one could have stood as close to us as the shot suggested without us spotting them.

It was sinister to see myself this way, to see how I looked when I had no idea I was being recorded. And it was strange, too, when the sex ended, to watch ourselves disappear simply by walking out of frame. First Bill, even before we had started to dress. And then Marla and me several minutes later, subdued, not speaking. I kept expecting the camera to swivel, to follow us, to supply some sort of cinematic closure, but it remained focused instead on the place where we had been and stayed that way as I fast-forwarded through the rest of the recording.

I put the disk back in its place on the bookshelf and turned off the TV. Marla and I left the cabin immediately. We drove to my house without saying anything to each other beyond a breathed "Jesus Christ...." or the occasional, disbelieving "Fuuuuck" - each of us silenced by the dreadful weight of the knowledge we had just acquired.

The kitchen had trapped the warmth of the afternoon and when we got back I opened the windows and the back door and poured cold soda into glasses and we sat at the table and stared out at the green-gold blur of the garden.

When Marla spoke her voice was flat and final. "It was our fault she killed herself."

"You don't kill yourself just because you see a video of your husband watching people have sex."

"But it obviously pushed her over the edge. If I'd said no to Bill she'd still be alive."

"She might not be."

"I shouldn't have done it."

"There were two of us there, it wasn't just you."

Marla shook her head sadly. "Yes, it was. You would have said yes to anything. And I knew it."

"So it was a stupid thing to do, but we didn't know it was going to be filmed. And we sure as hell didn't know Patricia would ever see it. You can't talk yourself into thinking we killed her. If anyone's to blame it's Bill."

"You think he shot it?"

"Who else? He chose the place. He could have easily put the camera in a tree beforehand and started it with a remote. Value for money. He gets to watch us and he gets the movie too."

"But to give it to Pat? He's not that far gone."

"Maybe she found it by accident."

"He'd have to be a complete moron to leave something like that lying around."

We were quiet for a while and I thought about Pat watching the video, lying there on her bed as her husband masturbated over two people squirming on the ground, waiting for the Halcion and the whiskey to take hold and end the dreadful knowledge of the distance that separated her from a man she must still have loved. And I thought about Bill too, of the sickening guilt he must have felt when he saw what she'd been watching.

And then it struck me. "Bill didn't make the video. He thinks *we* did."

"What?"

"That's why he freaked out in front of the Black Cat. Not because he felt guilty about watching us screw, but because he thinks we set him up to be filmed. And he probably thinks we gave the disk to Pat as well."

Marla groaned. "You are fucking kidding me."

"But if he didn't make the video, and we know it wasn't us, then who did?"

Marla looked blank and didn't say anything. Eventually, I said:

"I'm thinking Gareth,"

"Why?"

"He hates Bill because when they bought the cabins Bill told them a new road up to the lake was a done deal-"

"And it never happened. Yeah, I've heard the story."

"So he has a reason to want to hurt him. What I can't figure out, though, is how he would have known where to put the camera. And when to start it. I mean, it was Bill who took us to that place."

Marla was silent for a long time then she said, "You know what I'd like to do, Johnny? What I'd really, really like to do? I'd like to forget the whole thing in the forest ever happened."

She got up then and said she was tired and was going upstairs to lie down for a while. When she'd gone I sat by myself on the kitchen step and stared out at the garden and thought about how changed Marla was.

When I'd come back to Oakridge she had been older, of course. The loneliness and the life she'd suffered had taken its toll on her youth. But there had still been a spark to her, a feeling that she was still young, that life could begin again. Now, though, it seemed she had none of that left, that she was so worn down by living that it was beyond her to even care about the truth behind the death of a woman she'd been friendly with.

Toward the end of the day Marla and I went out to Empty Mile to pick up Stan. The clear brightness of the sky had softened by then and the curving blades of the long grass in the meadow were burnished where the late sun touched them.

Stan and Rosie lay on their backs in the middle of the meadow staring up at the sky, holding hands. Rosie had made a ring of field daisies and Stan wore it on his head like a crown. I stood with Marla beside the pickup watching them for a moment, reluctant to intrude on their time together.

That afternoon, in contrast to the hell that life back in town seemed bent on becoming, this land with its trees, its birdsong, and its protecting rock wall gave the illusion of somewhere to escape to. And as I looked over it, reveling in its peace, it occurred to me that the answer to at least one of my problems was staring me in the face.

The cabin that came with the property had three bedrooms, a large central room that was both kitchen and living room, a rainwater tank, a septic system in the ground, and electricity. Water, power, shelter. Room enough for the three of us, easily. And best of all, the money we would otherwise have had to spend on rent could be plowed back into Plantasaurus. It wouldn't be enough to save the business from the impact of Jeremy Tripp's rival company but it would keep Stan's dream alive a little longer.

And for Marla and me it was the right thing to do. Our relationship would not progress beyond the fragile reconnection we had so far established until we started living with each other again.

I raised the subject as the three of us drove back to Oakridge. Five days later Stan and I had sold the things we weren't taking with us in a yard sale and moved into the cabin. Marla would join us the following week.

CHAPTER TWENTY-TWO

The first few days we were at the cabin I kept Stan as busy as I could. There was Plantasaurus to take care of during the day and in the evenings we had our cleaning, unpacking, and arranging of furniture to occupy us. Although he was withdrawn and quiet early on, by the end of the three days it took us to get the cabin into some sort of shape it seemed that he was coming to terms with his new surroundings, something that was helped enormously by the fact that he was now so close to Rosie.

Shortly before we'd left the house on Taylor Street two items had been delivered to it. One was a small gift basket with a card identifying it as having been sent by Rolf Kortekas, my father's boss at the real estate office, expressing his regret at our "situation." The other, by regular mail, was a business envelope addressed to my father. I'd opened it expecting a bill of some sort but had found instead a letter from a company called Minco Inc. in Burton.

Dear Mr. Richardson,

We note that you have not collected the samples you submitted on May 11 to this laboratory. We thank you for your payment, which was received May 30, and trust our analysis was satisfactory. However, it is not our policy to hold samples longer than ninety days and we would be obliged if you could collect them at your earliest convenience. Alternatively, we would be happy to deliver them to you for a small charge.

Kind regards,

Reginald Singh, Compositional Analyst
Minco Inc.

I had no idea what samples Reginald Singh was referring to, or why my father might have submitted them to a "Compositional Analyst," but once we'd finished settling into the cabin I felt the need to follow up on the letter. The pattern of life around me had become so complex that I couldn't pass up an opportunity to unravel even the smallest part of it. So, on our fourth morning at Empty Mile I called the number on the letterhead and asked if I could collect the samples for my father. No problem as long as I brought some ID with me.

I rescheduled the maintenance visits we had booked for that day and arranged with Stan that I'd go to Burton in the afternoon while he worked at the warehouse. Before that, though, I planned to take the first step toward finding some proof for my theory that Gareth was responsible for the video of Marla and me in the forest.

When I suggested an early picnic lunch in the woods at Tunney Lake I was prepared for Stan to balk at the idea - it was the site of his drowning, after all - but he just nodded with his jaw held firm and said it sounded okay to him.

The lake was not yet fully out of the shadow of the hillside behind it when we got there and away from the beach the water looked flat and dark, like a cover thrown over secrets. As we walked along the sand Stan kept me between the water and himself, but when we reached the part of the beach where he'd been dragged out and brought back to life he stepped close to the water and stopped and looked around at the lake and the cliff and the trees.

"It's weird, Johnny. I felt so much...space around everything when I came back alive and I felt it all the time afterwards too. But now sometimes I don't feel anything except just what I can see."

"But that's how everyone feels, Stan. That's how I feel."

"I know, Johnny. I know."

Stan looked so bereft as he said this that the giant corkscrew of guilt on which it seemed I would be forever impaled made one more wrenching turn in my guts. I had made it plain to him that I thought his ideas of power, of something beyond the world we could see, were nonsense. I suppose some part of me had hoped that my reaction would school him toward a more socially palatable interpretation of the world around him. But I realized now that rather than guiding him toward some replica of normality, my selfishness of spirit had begun to rob him of something he found beautiful about life.

"Have you ever been swimming again?"

"No."

He put his head down and we started toward the trees. It was shadowy in the forest and in the denser, darker areas the undergrowth was finely beaded with dew. If I had brought Stan on this walk earlier, before Plantasaurus and Jeremy Tripp, before the loss of my father and our house, he would have stampeded through the damp clumps of ferns, barrel-rolled across open patches of grass, pretended he was an explorer. That day, though, he walked somberly beside me. He chatted responsively enough, but his usual bouncing energy was just not there.

I remembered the way easily enough and after a couple of minutes we found the rock with red paint and the dip in the ground behind it where two months ago I had had sex with Marla in front of another man, while somewhere close by the mechanism of a video camera had whirred silently away, recording everything we did.

Stan made a small sound of delight as we skirted the rock and stepped into the hidden depression behind it. After his staid performance through the forest it was heartening to see there was still enough wonder left in him to enjoy the discovery of a secret place. He sat down in the middle of the grassy bowl. I left him pulling things to eat out of the backpack we'd brought with us and went to see what evidence I could find.

It wasn't hard to figure out where the camera had been placed. The position in which Marla and I had lain that day was clear in my mind. Matching it to the image we'd watched on the TV in Bill's cabin indicated a group of trees at one end of the curving screen of foliage. About seven or eight feet off the ground the trees threw out lightly leaved branches that did little to obscure the trunks from which they grew. I found what I wanted almost as soon as I started looking for it.

A metal, L-shaped bracket had been fixed to the side of one of the trees immediately below the bough line. The horizontal part of it stuck out about four inches and had three holes drilled along its length. The screws that held the bracket in place, through another three holes in the vertical section, looked like they'd been hammered into the tree. There were pieces of brown packing tape stuck to the bracket and it was a fair guess that the camera had been taped into place.

I went back to where Stan had set out our food, got the Swiss Army knife that was part of our picnic kit, and spent five minutes struggling with the battered screws until I had the bracket loose. Stan came over to watch me work. As he knew nothing of the thing's significance, though, he lost interest after I explained I had no idea why it was there but that I didn't want it to damage the tree.

When I had it free I turned it in my hand but there wasn't much to be learned from it. It was steel. Its edges were smoothly ground and the holes for the screws were countersunk. It was well made and nicely finished but beyond that it was just a bracket. I put it in my jacket pocket and went to sit with Stan. We ate peanut butter sandwiches and potato chips. We told jokes and for a couple of brief minutes talked about my father.

Later, when we were done, we walked back out into the sunshine of the lake. My mission to the forest was over and I wanted to get the visit to Burton and the mineral laboratory out of the way and still have some of the day left. But as we approached the pickup in the parking lot near the cabins, the door to the bungalow/office opened and Gareth trotted over to us

"Dude. Hey, Stan. I saw the truck but I didn't know where you went. Come in the house and have a beer. Coke for you, buddy." He winked and cocked his finger at Stan.

"We've got things to do in Burton."

"Fuck that. Come inside. Ten minutes. We gotta catch up, man."

"I really have to get-"

"Haven't I kept my word about the Marla thing? I'm trying, dude. Come on. We'll sit, we'll chat, and then you'll go to Burton."

Stan tugged my sleeve. "I'm thirsty, Johnny, I need a Coke."

After that there didn't seem much chance of getting out of it without a scene and the three of us went into the office and on through to the living area at the back of the house. Gareth got a Coke and a couple of beers out of the fridge. As he handed Stan his drink he gestured to the open back door.

"Dad's working in the barn, Stan. You can go out and watch if you want."

"Cool."

Stan went outside and Gareth and I sat on the ratty lounge furniture. The room was dim and the light that came in through the doorway flared against the frame. Through it I could see some of the garden, and beyond that the barn with its doors swung wide and Gareth's father in his wheelchair at the bench inside, working on something with a machine that made a high whining noise. And Stan standing beside him, yakking away.

Gareth slugged his beer and burped. "I got rid of the hookers."

"Oh, yeah?"

"Yeah, I'm hearing noises that the council are thinking about the road again. Couple of whores on the premises isn't a good look. Man, if that road gets built...." Gareth shook his head in wonder.

I couldn't help spoiling his mood.

"How's Vivian?"

"Fucked. She's working for that prick, fucking him.... And she ended it with me. No more trips to the Slopes, no more visits to the big house. Old Gareth didn't have the money to make the grade."

I could see he was gearing up for a full-blown purge, so I cut him off quickly. "Marla took me to an Elephant Society meeting."

Gareth looked nonplussed for a moment, then his eyes shifted a little.

"Oh yeah?"

"You've heard of it, right?"

"You know I have, Johnny. I told you I used to go with your dad sometimes. Are you trying to catch me out?"

"A guy there said you and my father had the same interests."

"That's what the Society's for, isn't it? But I stopped going months ago."

"Anything particular you two were interested in?"

"Lots of things to be interested in, Johnboy. Lots and lots." He looked levelly at me for a long moment then his face brightened like he'd just remembered something. "Oh, I spoke to the bank and with the equity in this place I couldn't buy all of that land off you, but I can raise enough for half of it. No problem. I mean, that would solve everything for you, wouldn't it? You don't have to give up the whole thing but you get a bunch of dough to keep you going."

"I've told you twice I'm not selling. Besides, I'm living out there now."

"At Empty Mile? Really?"

"The bank sold the house."

"What are you doing with the land?"

"What do you mean?"

"What are you doing with it?"

Gareth was leaning forward in his chair and the bottle in his hand had tilted so that beer was spilling onto the floor by his foot. I pointed to it and he set the bottle down in the puddle and pressed his hands hard together and took a breath.

"Promise me that if you ever want to sell some of it you'll come to me first."

I made a move to stand up but Gareth held on to my arm.

"Hey, did I sound like a fucking idiot or something? Sorry, man. It just seems like such a good idea to me, that's all."

He let go of me and I yelled through the doorway for Stan. Gareth said goodbye as we left but he didn't come out of the house to see us off.

I made it down Lake Trail without incident and then turned left along the Loop to drop Stan off at the warehouse. He seemed chirpy after messing around in the barn and I asked him about his time with David.

"It's really neat how he makes stuff. He let me drill a hole. Here, look. He let me keep this one."

Stan dug inside his jacket and held something out so I could see it. I pulled immediately to the side of the road, a hot flush of triumph rising through me.

"Let me see that."

It was a steel bracket with three countersunk holes in each arm. I'd put the bracket I found that morning in the glove compartment. I took it out now and held it next to the one Stan had given me. Except for Stan's off-center drilling the two were identical.

"Wow, Johnny, they're the same. Why would David put one on a tree?"

"Maybe he was just testing it out. Can I keep this for a while?"

I dropped Stan at the warehouse then carried on to Burton. It was a nice day for the drive, but I didn't pay much attention to the scenery. I was too busy thinking about the brackets.

The Minco building in Burton had a utilitarian, '60s feel to it - all sharp angles, blank unadorned walls, and windows that were simply inset sheets of glass. The floor of the reception area was covered with gray linoleum that was mottled with shoe scuffings and pitted here and there where something too heavy had pressed against it for too long. There was a counter across one end and behind it a walk space and then a wall with a large shuttered hatch in the middle and a flat wooden door at one end. There was no one behind the counter and the room felt abandoned, as though I had turned up in the middle of a fire drill.

A button on the counter had a laminated plaque next to it that said customers should ring for assistance. I pressed it and somewhere way back behind the wall I heard a faint buzzing. A minute later a fat woman with oversize glasses opened the door and shuffled sideways along her side of the counter. I told her I had something to collect from Reginald Singh. She scribbled my name in pencil on a small pad and then shuffled back through the door.

After a while the door opened again and Reginald Singh came out. He was a slender Fijian Indian. He wore a white lab coat and spoke in a voice that sounded as though he'd worked hard to eradicate his accent. He placed a small clear plastic vial on the counter in front of me. It contained a thin wafer of gold-colored metal that had been bent into a half-circle to fit in the narrow tube.

"John Richardson?"

I nodded and showed him my driver's license.

"Ah, good. Nice to tie up loose ends. Would you mind signing?"

He opened a folder that had been wedged under his arm and took out a form for me to sign. When I handed it back he pushed the vial toward me and smiled. "Short and sweet."

"What is it?"

Reginald Singh looked confused. "You didn't read the report?"

"It's a long story. My father disappeared a couple of months ago. I'm sort of tying up some loose ends of my own. You can call the Oakridge police department if you need confirmation."

Reginald Singh looked mildly dismayed and shook his head. "Oh no, no, no. You have ID. Gold nine-thirty fine."

"Excuse me?"

He tapped the vial with his forefinger. "We received a sample of concentrates - the mixture of black sands and fine gold that most placer miners can easily reduce their pannings to. The work request was to determine the purity of the ore it contained. There are a number of ways to do this - ion probe analysis, fluorescence spectrometry

- but fire assay is simple, suitable for small samples, and more afford-able for an individual prospector. It is considered to be as accurate as any other method. We performed this type of assay on your father's sample. We determined the fineness - the purity - of this sample to be gold nine-thirty fine."

"Which means?"

"Gold is always alloyed with a certain amount of silver and other trace metals. Gold fineness is based on a scale of zero to one thou-sand. So, after we had separated the metal from the black sands we determined, through our assay, that its pure gold content was in the ratio of nine hundred and thirty parts to one thousand. About aver-age for California placer gold."

I picked up the vial and turned it so that the light caught the small wafer of gold. "So this actually has silver in it too?"

"No, that is pure gold. After we do the fire reduction we dissolve the silver content by immersion in a 50 percent solution of nitric acid. Weighing the sample before and after gives the percentage of non-gold metal. Is there anything else I can help you with?"

"Well, I was wondering if you remembered anything about when my father was here."

"What do you mean?"

"I don't know really. Did he say anything about the samples, where he got them? Did he make any sort of comment about anything that stood out?"

"Oh, I didn't meet your father, I performed the assay only. One of my colleagues took the work request. I can get him if you like."

I said that would be good and Reginald Singh went back into the building proper. A minute later a younger man with blond hair that hadn't been washed for a while came out and took his place behind the counter. Before he said anything he placed a large see-through plastic bag containing what looked like soil and gravel on the counter.

"This is yours too. I haven't been here too long and when your father...?" He raised his eyebrows and I nodded. "When your father came in he had the sample you already got, which he wanted tested for purity, and this one," he nodded at the bag, "which he wanted tested for content, like he wanted to know how much gold was in the whole thing. I accepted it by mistake. We don't work on samples that aren't at least refined down to concentrates. My fault, I'm sorry."

"Do you remember him saying where the samples came from?"

"Thing about prospectors - they don't say nothing about nothing. You find gold, you're not going to tell anyone where it is. No, he didn't say where he got it. That one," he pointed at the bag, "looks like river gravel to me."

"Did he say anything else...about anything?"

"All I remember is that he was with another guy, about your age. And I remember because a week or so after your father submitted the samples this guy came back and wanted to pick them up and get the report. But the only name on the work request was your father's so legally we couldn't tell him anything and we sure couldn't give him the samples. He was pretty pissed off about it."

I showed him the photo of Gareth on my cell phone.

"This the guy?"

"That's him."

Out in the pickup I put the vial in my pocket and tossed the bag of dirt on the passenger seat. I made it back to Oakridge toward the end of the afternoon and picked Stan up from the warehouse. When he saw the bag of river gravel he was full of questions. I showed him the wafer of gold and spent the rest of the drive telling him about the sample and the gravel and trying to contain his immediate assumption that my father had discovered a gold mine.

We were staying the night at Marla's place, to have dinner and help her with the last of her packing before she moved to Empty Mile, but first I wanted to drop by the real estate office where my father had worked to thank them for the gift basket they'd sent. During the drive Stan sat with the larger sample on his lap and at one point he shifted it a little and smoothed the plastic against its contents. I heard him make a small sound of happy surprise and turned to see him pointing at several small faded pink petals mixed with the dirt.

The real estate office, like most of the other businesses in Old Town, was housed in a converted two-story wooden building that had probably been a private residence or some sort of store back in the 1800s. A large plate-glass window had been cut into the front and was filled with rows of photographs advertising properties in the Oakridge area. I knew Rolf Kortekas, the guy who owned the business, well enough to say hello to. He was a Dutchman who'd come to the States as a kid - an immigrant like my father. But unlike my father he had achieved a reasonable level of financial success. I left Stan in the truck while I went inside.

Rolf was the only one in the office that afternoon and when I walked in he stood up behind his desk and spread his arms.

"Johnny. My God, what can I say? Do you need something? Sit down, sit down."

I told him I'd just dropped in to say thanks for the gift. We talked for a few minutes about my father and his disappearance and after that I asked Rolf if he had any idea why my father had bought the Empty Mile land.

"He was a good man, your father, I think. But I can't say that I knew him well, even after all this time. I know he bought the land, but I have no idea why. Your father wasn't a man who confided in others."

The office was decorated to mimic a turn-of-the-century land office. The plank walls had been painted a muddy cream and hung with antique land documents. It had a nostalgic, comfortable feel and I gazed idly at its old-fashioned decorations wondering if there was anything else Rolf could tell me.

I'd been staring at a set of three pictures on the wall behind him for several seconds before I realized what they were. Black-and-white aerial photographs. Different part of the landscape, but the same size, the same gray toning as the one my father had so proudly shown Stan and me. Rolf saw me looking at them.

"Bureau of Land Management. Part of a project to photograph some of the land around here. Aerial cataloging. Helps them decide if they should move more land into government ownership, or if they have any they can get rid of because it isn't of environmental significance. One of their surveyors was based in Oakridge for a while. We helped him out a little with local land knowledge, he gave us some prints in return."

"When was that?"

"April. Your father was fascinated with them. I think he even went to see the man to talk about them."

"Is he still in Oakridge?"

"No, he moves around, but he's in Burton sometimes, I think. I have his card if you'd like it."

Rolf rummaged through a drawer in his desk and passed me a business card for a surveyor named Howard Webb. I stood up to go. Rolf stood as well and leaned across his desk to shake my hand and tell me if he could help me out with anything to just let him know.

At the office door, before I went out, I thought of something and stopped. "Do you know who my father's accountant was?"

Rolf laughed pleasantly. "You won't get mad at me if I tell you your father was not so very smart when it came to money? If any man should have had an accountant it was him. But he didn't. Again, as far as I know. But you work with someone, you get to know these kinds of things. He didn't have an accountant."

CHAPTER TWENTY-THREE

In the street outside Marla's house there was a small rented dumpster half full of the things she was throwing away. Inside, the house had taken on a feeling of desolation. The living room was piled with the furniture she was going to get rid of in her own yard sale, the bedroom my father and Pat had used was crammed with the things she wanted to keep, and all over the house there were open cartons in various stages of being filled. Everywhere was sad and too bright and devoid of the welcoming comfort that for ten years had made the place a home.

While Stan watched superhero cartoons on a TV Marla hadn't yet disconnected, she and I sat in the small garden behind the house with bottles of beer and caught the last of the afternoon sun.

I told her about going to Burton and up to the lake, and I showed her the two metal brackets - one from the tree, one from David's workshop. She took them from me and sat with one in each hand, staring dully at them, her head bowed as though the metal's touch had somehow drained her energy. I explained what I thought they meant.

"You can't buy them anywhere, Gareth's father is the only person who makes them. Gareth must have taken one, hammered it onto the tree, and attached the camera to it before we got there. Then he probably just turned it on and left. Those things run for like two hours. What I can't figure out is how the hell he knew where we were going to be. Would Bill have told him? He picked the spot, after all."

Marla didn't say anything. I was so preoccupied with trying to solve the puzzle that I hardly noticed.

"But that doesn't make sense. Bill and Gareth don't even speak, and Bill would never let Gareth get that sort of power over him. But then we come back to how Gareth could possibly have known where to put the camera."

I groaned and ran my hands over my face.

"It has to be Gareth, but how? How the fuck did he know where we'd be?"

Finally Marla raised her head and I saw that there were tears on her cheeks. When she spoke, her first words were so quiet I could hardly hear them.

"Gareth knew because he was the one who chose the place. He told me I had to take Bill there."

"What are you talking about? Bill led us there."

Marla shook her head.

"I told him it had to be that place behind the rock or we wouldn't do it. He knew where to go because back when I was hooking, when I first started, before Gareth or anything, we'd both been there. Together. I just let it look like he was leading the way."

"You fucked Bill Prentice?"

Marla stood abruptly, took two steps away from me, bent at the waist, and threw up on the grass. She stayed like that for a while, clearing her throat and wiping her mouth, then she straightened and turned back to me.

"It was a long time ago. You know I have this stuff in my past. Please don't be a bastard about it."

Her hands were shaking and her crying, which had been interrupted by her throwing up, started again. I took a deep breath and tried to force the image of Bill on top of Marla out of my head. Then the deeper meaning of what she'd said hit me.

"Gareth picked the place? So the whole thing was a setup?"

"I didn't know anything about the camera, I swear. I swear, Johnny."

"Well, what the fuck, then?"

She took a breath and tried to calm herself.

"During the time I was hooking in Burton I went with Bill a couple of times. Once over there and once at that place at the lake. That was it. I didn't want to be doing it with somebody from where I lived so I cut him off. A long time later, when I had my job and Gareth was pimping me in Oakridge, I mentioned having been with Bill to him. No reason, it was just conversation, but it meant he knew about our connection. And one day, a little while after you got back, he told me I had to get Bill to watch you and me having sex. And he told me it had to be at that place up at the lake and that he had to know beforehand when it was going to happen. And I couldn't mention anything about him to Bill. I had no idea why. I mean, it was fucking weird, but in the end it was just one more installment of Gareth's madness. There was nothing I could do about it anyhow. You didn't know about my past then and Gareth said if I didn't do it he'd tell you I'd been a hooker. I was so scared of you finding out. I thought you'd never want anything to do with me again and I couldn't take that. I couldn't take losing you a second time. So I did what he said and I didn't ask questions. But I promise you, I absolutely promise, I didn't know it was going to be filmed."

"How do you get some guy to want to watch you having sex with someone else?"

"It wasn't hard, you know what he's like. I'd never bumped into him at work before because our offices are in different buildings, but it wasn't hard for me to find an excuse to take a file over to him. He recognized me right away and started offering me money for sex. I told him I didn't do that anymore but if he wanted just to watch I could arrange something. He jumped at it. And I.... I made it all look like a chance meeting so you wouldn't know."

"If Gareth wanted something incriminating on video why didn't he just get you to fuck him?"

"Because Gareth's a sick bastard and whatever he was up to, it would have tickled him to have you involved somehow. He hates you just as much as he hates me."

"But I might not have wanted to do it."

"Then it wouldn't have happened. But I knew you would. And so did Gareth. I'm so sorry, Johnny. I could cut my heart out."

Marla had stopped crying but her face was swollen and she looked tired and incredibly sad. She stood in front of me as though she was waiting to be executed.

I could have hated her for dragging me into something so sordid, I suppose. But I didn't. I was angry that I'd been used in someone else's plan. I was angry with Gareth for making Marla do it. But I wasn't angry with her. How could I be? As she'd said, I knew she had these things in her past. And I knew that I had played a role in creating that past. But even if I had not felt some measure of responsibility for how life had turned out for her, I could not have hated her the way she looked then. The need for this relationship with me, the utter necessity of it for her, was just too plain on her face.

So instead of shouting and accusing, I held her in the sunlight of that fading afternoon, in the small garden of the house she loved so much and was soon to leave, and tried somehow to absorb back into myself the seeds of damage my selfishness had sown eight years before. Later, we sat down again and finished our beer and talked about Gareth and the video.

"So the question now is why? Why did he do it?"

Marla shrugged. "It can't be anything related to us. What do we have to lose? We don't have reputations to worry about and we were hardly being unfaithful to anyone. I do know that there was bad blood between Pat and Gareth, though."

"I didn't know they knew each other."

"She used to have this dog, this big Lab that went everywhere with her, never on a leash, a bit old and dopey. She *loved* that dog. About a year ago Gareth was pushing his father around Old Town and it started barking at the wheelchair, really frightened the old man. Which was a big mistake, because a couple of days later Gareth ran it over with his Jeep. It was an 'accident,' of course, but...." Marla shrugged. "Pat knew he did it on purpose and she hated him for it."

"A year ago? That's a long time for Gareth to wait around. Plus he doesn't get anything material out of it. What if the video was a blackmail attempt that went wrong? Gareth might have thought he could pressure Bill into pushing the road through with the council."

"I don't think Bill has that sort of power. The Resource and Development Committee has to vote on things like that."

"Which he's on."

"He's the head of it but there are six other members."

"Surely he could influence them to some extent."

"Maybe."

Marla didn't sound convinced.

"Well, whatever the deal is, Gareth's up to something. And it's more than just Bill or Pat. All these connections between him and my father keep cropping up. Like at the Elephant Society - Chris Reynolds, the first thing he remembers about them is their interest in the history of Empty Mile. But Gareth's never said a thing about it, and I gave him plenty of opportunity today. The sample thing too - if he and my father had panned gold somewhere and were excited enough about it to get it assayed, wouldn't you think he'd have mentioned it by now? And on top of that he won't shut up about wanting to buy Empty Mile."

We sat outside for a while longer, then we went in and dragged Stan away from the TV and had dinner.

The rest of that evening was spent lugging furniture around, wrapping things in newspaper, and packing cardboard cartons with Marla's possessions. Marla was throwing away a lot of stuff and at one point after it got dark I made a few trips out to the dumpster with black plastic bags filled with papers and junk she no longer wanted.

The sides of the dumpster were high enough that I had to heave the bags up and half throw them into it. I misjudged my swing on one of them and caught it on a corner. The bag split open and a small avalanche of papers spilled out onto the grass next to the road. I was tired and for a moment I felt like just walking away from the mess, but I knew that any small breeze in the night would blow the papers into the road. So I bent and gathered up armfuls of old brochures, magazines, bills and credit card statements and stuffed them back into what was left of the bag. Halfway through the pile I saw, poking from between the pages of an old computer manual, the corner of a photograph.

I was vaguely interested to see what sort of picture Marla might be throwing away so I pulled it out to look at it. I got a whole lot less vague when I saw what the photo was of - Marla, posing in front of the entrance to a wooden roller coaster, beside a sign with San Diego painted on it. A quick-fire vacation snap on a standard-size print. Nothing remarkable about it. Except that it was a duplicate of the photo I'd found in my father's trunk a few weeks back. Marla was posing instead of him but the place and the framing were the same. And from what I could remember even the light and the color of the sky behind the wooden framework matched.

In the photo Marla looked a couple of years younger than she was now. She was laughing as though the person behind the camera had just made a joke.

It could have been a coincidence. By some amazing twist of fate they might both, at different times, have gone to San Diego. They might both have had a photo taken on the same spot. But they hadn't. It wasn't a coincidence. I knew it as I looked at the picture. The photos were too similar.

So, what, then? A vacation together? Perhaps my father had had a real estate convention to go to and had taken Marla along as a thank you for her occasional help with Stan. If it had been anyone other than him I might have suspected the photo was evidence of an affair, a dirty weekend away from the eyes of Oakridge. But not with my father. It couldn't have happened.

Yet as I stared at the photo in the spill of light from the porch, I couldn't help feeling the small cold feet of suspicion patter along some dark and deep-buried corridor within me. Why had neither my father nor Marla ever mentioned taking a trip so far from Oakridge? Surely it should have come up in conversation at some point. Unless there was a reason to hide it.

I could ask Marla, of course. But what if there *was* something there? Back in the years when I was away. It dawned on me that if there was, I didn't want to know anything about it. That kind of emotional mother lode was something I just wasn't equipped to handle. And, too, after her role in the forest sex session with Bill, which I knew she already felt terrible about, divulging an affair with my father might be more than she could safely bear.

So I folded the photo and put it in my wallet and cleaned up the rest of the spilled papers. In bed that night, Marla curled herself against my back, her arms tight around my chest, as though she could not stand to have even an inch of space between us.

Before work the next day Stan and I drove over to Empty Mile. I wanted to compare the soil in the sample the assayer had given me with that around the supposed fence post holes my father and Gareth had dug.

We stopped at the cabin to pick up a spade then headed on down the meadow and into the trees until we came to one of the holes. Stan stood over it and frowned.

"That's a really neat hole. It's too thin for a spade."

"He did it with a fence post digger."

Stan crouched down and peered into it.

"There's no water."

He lay on the ground and reached into the hole.

"I can just touch the bottom."

He brought up several handfuls of earth and piled them next to the hole - a loose mixture of sand and gravel. I opened the plastic sample bag and took a handful out and dropped it next to the mixture on the ground. There seemed to be no difference between the two.

As I was closing the bag I felt Stan tug my sleeve. He pointed to a small bush a few feet from the hole. It had dull gray-green leaves and I didn't know what sort it was but on the dusty earth around it there was a scattering of small pink petals; some of them had drifted to the edge of the hole. Stan prodded the sample bag.

"Same flowers, Johnny."

When we pulled up at the Plantasaurus warehouse later in the morning it looked the same as it always did. The day was fine and the sky was clear and we were all set for a solid day's work. As we got out of the pickup, though, we saw that the corrugated metal of the sliding door was buckled around the lock and that the door itself was open a couple of inches. We had always been very careful about locking up because of our plant stock and it was immediately obvious to both of us that we had had an intruder. Inside, it was more obvious still.

Our stock of large plants - the weeping figs, dracaenas, yuccas, etc. - had all been perfectly healthy the day before. Now, they were either dead or very rapidly dying and the air in the warehouse smelled strongly of bleach.

When Stan saw the sad ranks of trees he started running on the spot, pumping his arms and making a high whining noise through his nose. I felt an overwhelming tiredness. And anger. But mostly I just wanted to sit down and cover my face and not think about Plantasaurus ever again. I knew I couldn't do that, though, not while Stan still had such a heavy emotional investment in the business, so I held him and calmed him instead, and then we got down to the task of figuring out what had happened. It wasn't particularly difficult.

We traced the smell of bleach to the plastic-wrapped cylinders of soil in which each of the affected plants stood. It was something we'd seen before, of course, the day Jeremy Tripp had so angrily returned the plants we'd installed in his house, and it didn't take a genius to figure out he was responsible this time too.

It was a bad blow. We had Plantagion competing against us, and now we'd lost the stock that should have seen us through to the end of the month. I thought about sitting Stan down and explaining how bad our chances of keeping Plantasaurus going were in the face of such opposition. But before I could muster the nerve, he looked across at me from where he'd been poking at a dead kentia palm and said we'd have to order a new shipment of plants right away. After that, I knew he wasn't going to listen to anything I might say about winding down the business.

We spent the next couple of hours clearing the dead plants out of the warehouse. At one point I noticed that Stan had disappeared. I found him outside at the rear of the building, lying flat on his back in the dirt. He'd tipped the contents of his moth matchbox onto his face and the insects, dull from so long in the box, moved sluggishly in the depressions beside his nose and over his closed eyelids.

"What are you doing?"

"Recharging."

I stood there for a moment, but he didn't open his eyes, so I went back to work and a few minutes later he joined me and we didn't talk about the moths.

After the cleaning up was done, we began our maintenance visits for that day. At each store or office, after we'd watered, trimmed, and cleaned the displays, we asked if the customers were satisfied with our service. No one had any complaints, and most of them were openly complimentary, but at three of the places they also said they had been approached by a representative of another plant company offering to provide the same level of service at a lower cost.

One of the customers had a card the rep had left - a tropical palm against a setting sun, the name Plantagion in orange letters. Another customer quoted the name from memory, said he remembered it because it sounded like a disease.

We'd signed all our customers to either six- or twelve-month agreements and none of the three we spoke to that day wanted to pay the fee that early cancellation incurred. But I felt compelled to promise that we'd meet the competing offer when the agreements came up for renewal. Stan nodded seriously and stepped forward to shake their hands as we left.

At the end of the day, back at Empty Mile, Stan went over to see Rosie and I spent a long time sitting on the stoop, wondering what it was I had done that had pissed Jeremy Tripp off so badly.

CHAPTER TWENTY-FOUR

The next time I saw Gareth was the day before Marla moved into Empty Mile. Stan and I only had half a day's work and after we'd finished I dropped him at Empty Mile and went back into town alone. Since my return to Oakridge there hadn't been much of my time that wasn't fraught with the stresses of trying to understand what was going on with my father, or Gareth, or Marla, or the Empty Mile land. And on this last day before Marla and I began living together I wanted an hour or two to myself, to grab a coffee, to gaze out of a café window.

I went to the Mother Lode in Old Town and was doing a pretty good job of not thinking about much when Gareth wandered in. He saw me right away and without bothering to order anything came quickly over and sat down across the table from me.

"Dude, you won't believe it, we actually had a bunch of council assholes up at the lake today scoping things out. Wanted to discuss how we'd feel about restricted access on Lake Trail while they worked on the road! They still have to do what they call 'canvassing the community' - some bullshit the eco-liberals stuck in to make sure the tree huggers are happy. But it's movement, man, it's movement!"

He clapped his hands and sat back grinning. It was only then that he noticed the stony look I was giving him.

"What's the matter?"

"Wait here. I have to get something."

I went outside to my pickup and got the two L-shaped brackets I'd stored in the glove compartment. Back in the café I dropped them on the table in front of Gareth.

"One's from a tree in the forest at the lake, the other one your father gave to Stan when we were up at your place. They're the same. The one I found on the tree was the one you fixed a camera to so you could film Marla and me while we fucked for Bill Prentice. I've seen the video."

Gareth folded his arms. "Oh really? And where did you happen to stumble across that little piece of cinema?"

"Bill's cabin."

"I wouldn't have thought Bill would be showing it around."

"He wasn't home at the time."

"You naughty boy."

"I know you set the whole thing up."

"Courtesy of Marla, no doubt."

"I figured it out myself."

"Bullshit."

"She told me you forced her into it, you prick."

"Oh, come on, Johnny, we had all this out before. Don't call me a prick. You abandoned her, she wouldn't have started hooking otherwise. Just like you abandoned your father, just like you abandoned your brother. Call me a prick? Fuck, man, I'm an amateur next to you. I'd never walk out on my father."

"But you'd destroy some guy's life. Why? Because of the fucking road?"

Gareth smiled slyly, though he tried to hide it.

"You know how important that road is to us. And you know how it affected my dad when it didn't get built."

"Bill's wife killed herself watching that video."

"That sounds a bit farfetched."

"I saw the disk in her bedroom when we found her. It was in the machine."

"Careless old Bill."

"You really are a fucking psycho."

"Look, I made the vid to get some leverage on the road. I gave Bill a copy to show him I could fuck him up if he didn't play ball. And seeing how the council guys came around today, maybe he took the hint. If his wife found it, it isn't my fault. She was going to kill herself one day, anyhow."

"But you made it happen."

"You wanted to fuck Marla, Bill wanted to watch. Marla's dumb enough to be exploitable. Bill thinks with his dick. Everyone made it happen, man. I just filmed it."

Gareth stood up.

"I don't know why you don't want to be friends, Johnny. I'm trying my hardest."

After he left I ordered another coffee and sat trying to figure out why I had the feeling something didn't quite add up. In the end the closest I got was that the idea of Bill leaving such a disk where anyone could find it was ludicrous.

So much for turning off for a couple of hours.

Marla moved into Empty Mile on a Friday. She took a day off work and we ferried her things over in the pickup starting early that morning. We were finished by noon. We spent another few hours distributing her stuff around the cabin and when that was done we were all set to begin life as a newly created family.

In the early evening, too tired from moving furniture to be bothered with cooking, Marla and I decided to go into town for dinner. Stan had invited himself to eat at Rosie's and didn't come with us.

We went to a cheap place in Back Town and ordered steaks and a bottle of red wine. Marla talked about things we could do to the cabin and it seemed that the activity of the day, perhaps some notion of a fresh start, had lifted her spirits a little. I told her about my conversation with Gareth at the Mother Lode, how he'd admitted to making the video, but she asked me not to spoil the evening and steered the conversation back to ideas for a vegetable garden and whether or not it would be too expensive to build a deck.

We finished our food and stayed to drink the last of the wine and by the time we left the restaurant we were both relaxed and a little drunk. So when we bumped into Chris Reynolds on the street, hurrying to that night's Elephant Society meeting, and he reminded us that we'd promised to attend, trying to talk our way out of it seemed not only rude, but also too much effort.

We signed the attendance log at the door of the hall. There were only five names before us and the lecture heading printed in red at the top of the page read: *Geological Re-engineering through Topographical Catastrophe - Randolph Morris.* Chris, who hovered around us for a few moments digging membership forms out of the desk where the door woman sat, "just in case you want to consider it," sighed in resignation as he looked about the mostly empty hall.

"Might not be the most exciting of meetings, I'm afraid."

He wandered off to sit in the first row of a block of chairs that had been set up in front of a movable whiteboard. I looked at the woman behind the desk. She smiled and shrugged apologetically.

"Randolph's already given his talk once this year. It's his only subject. A lot of the members tend to skip it."

Marla and I sat in the back row. With so few people the hall seemed overly quiet and a little sad, like something that had been passed by and was now only a place for people too out of touch to know better.

Chris Reynolds stood up in front of the whiteboard and began to go through the minutes of the last meeting. I listened for a while and tried to stay interested in the state of the Society's finances, the plans for the next outing, some sort of communication from a sister society in Australia.... But the wine and the tiredness from moving Marla's furniture began to catch up with me, and in the dim hall I found my attention drifting so that periodically I had to drag myself back from some hazy other-world where I had been aimlessly turning over the trivia of daily life - groceries to buy, wondering if I had enough gas to get home....

On one of these returns I saw that Chris Reynolds had been re-placed in front of the whiteboard by a grizzled old guy who was point-ing to parts of a diagram thrown against the board by an overhead projector. The diagram was a topographical map of some area and appeared to show a number of rivers winding between blobs of con-centric altitude lines.

I guessed the guy was Randolph Morris and that we were now in the middle of the lecture so many of the Elephant Society's members had stayed away from. He spoke without pause in a zealot-like tone, grinding out figures on the history of seismic upheaval, erosion and the localized collapse of geological features in area after area around the world and throughout the United States.

His point seemed to be that occurrences like earthquakes and landslides had in some cases been responsible for altering the course of ancient rivers and that the riverbeds they'd left behind - what he called "tertiary rivers" - could still be found through geomagnetic surveys, aerial photography, and something known as "cesium vapor analysis." Where a river that existed nowadays cut through one of these tertiary rivers there was a good chance that it would contain rich deposits of gold. In fact, Randolph asserted, many of the larger strikes during the Gold Rush could be explained in this manner.

I'd never heard of tertiary rivers before and the idea was inter-esting, but Randolph spoke in such a torrent of words and repeated himself so often that after a couple of minutes I found myself again wondering about what to buy at the store

In the end I dozed off. When Marla nudged me awake Randolph and the other Society members were already filing out of the hall and Chris Reynolds was pushing the whiteboard into a corner. The lady at the door was gone. Marla and I went over to Chris and said goodbye. He smiled a little sheepishly and shook my hand.

"You're welcome if you ever want to come back some other night."

Marla and I were halfway across the hall when he called after us.

"Hey, Johnny, I don't know if you're aware of it, but there's an-other plant company making the rounds, looking for business."

"Yeah, Plantagion. I know about them."

"The owner came into the Nugget Shooter a couple of days ago, tried to talk me into going with them. I told him I was happy with Plantasaurus."

"Thanks. We'd really hate to lose anyone."

"I figured. Funny thing, though, this guy - we talked for a bit, and because I hadn't seen him around before I asked him how long he'd been in Oakridge. Turns out not long, moved here after his sister died." Chris paused for a moment. "Guess who his sister was."

I shrugged.

"Patricia Prentice. Bill Prentice's wife. Funny who you meet, huh?"

He gave a small wave and headed off toward the office at the back of the hall.

I asked Marla to drive us home. I sat in the passenger seat of the pick-up with a rushing in my ears, as though some angry autumn storm blew privately around me. Everything suddenly made sense. The scene with Jeremy Tripp in front of our customers, the break-in at the warehouse and the destruction of our stock, the rival firm setting up in competition to us, even Marla's enforced prostitution episode and eviction from her house.

These things hadn't happened randomly. They weren't un-planned. They hadn't even happened, or at least not primarily, be-cause Jeremy Tripp wanted to build a hotel on the warehouse land. These things had happened for an old-fashioned reason that you saw in movies and read about in books but never thought could possibly be part of your own life. These things had happened because of a desire for revenge.

Jeremy Tripp's sister was dead, pushed to suicide by a video. And because Marla and I were the star performers he blamed us for her death. I was certain of it. Of course, that meant he had to know about the video. But being Pat's brother meant he was also Bill's brother-in-law, close enough for Bill to swallow whatever guilt he felt and share that piece of amateur pornography with someone who had the personality to seek retribution for what it had caused. I remembered the night I'd seen them through the window of Bill's cabin watching something on the TV. I remembered the look of desolation on Bill's face and the way the muscles about Jeremy Tripp's jaw had clenched.

Jeremy Tripp believed we killed his sister and he was going to make us pay. But he wasn't a hit man. He wasn't a thug with a baseball bat. He was a corporate executive with a lot of money. When I first met him he'd talked about destroying someone, not physically hurting them, but destroying their entire life. And that was exactly what he had begun to do to us. Get at Marla by kicking her out of her house. Get at both of us by hiring her as a prostitute and making me watch. Get at me again by attacking Plantasaurus, not because he cared if I suffered financially, but because he knew it would destroy Stan and by doing so hurt me worst of all.

Plantasaurus had not gone under yet. We had enough money, just, to buy replacements for the plants that had been bleached to death, but I knew we couldn't take another hit like that without the business folding.

But there would be another hit. And another, and another after that, until Plantasaurus no longer existed. I'd seen the way Jeremy Tripp had fucked Marla, I'd seen him shoot the rabbit with his bow and arrow and leave it to scream through the night without a second thought, and I knew that he was a man who would not stop until he got the revenge he wanted. And I couldn't let that happen to Stan. I couldn't let something I'd done destroy his dream.

There was no point in telling Stan that Jeremy Tripp was Patricia's brother, no need to make him even more worried about the future of Plantasaurus, so I didn't mention the evening's discovery to him when we got back to the cabin. But Marla and I discussed it as we lay in bed. Or rather I talked about it and she made noises in the right places - cursed when I suggested it was the reason she had lost her house, shook her head in disgust at the threat to Plantasaurus. But there was an underlying current of disinterest to her responses, as though she didn't really want to engage. Eventually I called her on it.

"You don't seem very worried."

"I'm worried."

"Come on. You're lying there like I'm talking about football."

"Johnny, it happened. Knowing he's Pat's brother doesn't change anything."

"It changes what's going to happen. He's going to keep at us until we're completely fucked."

Marla took a breath and said quietly, "Maybe it's what we deserve. I do, anyhow."

"We didn't make the video. We don't deserve anything. And Stan sure as shit doesn't deserve to be punished. We have to stop Tripp doing anything else."

Marla snorted. "He's going to do whatever he wants."

"Not if we take away his reason for doing it."

"We can't make him un-see the video, Johnny. We can't make Pat be alive again."

"I know that. But we can tell him we didn't have anything to do with it.

"Good luck."

"I have the brackets."

"Like that'll convince him."

"It will if you tell him Gareth made you set the whole thing up."

"I really don't want to do that."

"Why the hell not? We tell him about Gareth and Gareth becomes his target, not us."

"Gareth'll go psycho."

"Gareth's already psycho."

"And he can tell the council about me whenever he wants. I'm not going to risk my job, Johnny. It's the only thing of my own I have left."

"Gareth told me all that blackmail shit was over."

Marla looked at me sadly and shook her head. "Nothing'll ever be over with Gareth until someone kills him."

"Well, you saw what happened to that rabbit. Maybe we'll get lucky."

"It's not a joke, Johnny."

I saw in her eyes how frightened she was and for a moment I had a flash of something inside her, as though behind her face there stretched a huge dark sea of experience, an expanse of past events that I knew absolutely nothing about.

"I know it's not a joke. But unless you're going to go out and buy a gun this is the only hope we have of getting Jeremy Tripp off our backs. Who knows what he'll do next? We have to give him Gareth. I don't understand why you wouldn't want to."

Marla looked at me for a while without saying anything, then she turned over and pulled the covers up around her.

"Marla?"

"I'm going to sleep."

I tried a couple more times to get her to respond, but she stayed silent and kept her back to me.

In the morning I got up early. The sun was coming in through the window and I was still tense from trying to figure out what was going on with Marla, why she wouldn't support me about Gareth and Jeremy Tripp.

The door to Stan's room was open and his bed was empty. I went outside and stood on the stoop and looked across the meadow. The sun had been up for a little while but the air was still cool from the night. From Rosie and Millicent's house the almost subliminal sound of a radio threaded its way through an open window. It was tuned to a classical station and swelled or diminished as currents of air moved across the long grass.

Movement down at the bottom of the meadow caught my eye. Stan and Rosie were just disappearing into the corridor of trees that separated the land from the river. I would have left them alone to pursue whatever adventure Stan had dreamed up for them, or whatever lovemaking they might be snatching at the start of the day, but before the branches closed around them I saw that they were both carrying towels.

I stood there for several minutes wondering what this might mean. Water, a towel, Stan.... In the end I stepped off the stoop and started down the meadow.

I entered the trees at the same point as Stan and Rosie and walked toward the river. As I neared it the stronger light beyond the trees made it possible to see through to the bright glitter of water. The shapes of two people moved there but they were hazed against the backlight and I could not make out what they were doing. I walked the last few yards softly and stopped, hidden by a bush where the riverbank began.

Stan and Rosie stood holding hands on a large flat rock that jutted out into the slow-moving water. They were both naked and in the morning light their bodies were luminous against the dark green of the leaves on the far bank. His, smooth and full and rounded, standing on solidly planted feet. Hers, very thin, back curving so that her chest and stomach seemed to be what was left after a larger body had been hollowed out. Both of them were very pale, though their arms and necks were brown from the summer.

There was a small sound of water moving, but along the whole length of Empty Mile the river was too broad to move quickly and I could easily hear what my brother and Rosie said to each other.

Rosie stood with her arms straight down by her sides and stared at the light on the water. After a while she said, "You don't have to."

"Johnny will keep feeling bad if I don't."

Stan inched forward until his toes curled over the edge of the rock. Rosie let go of his hand, took a step forward, pivoted on one foot, and fell backwards into the river. She rose spluttering a second later, wet and shining, rubbing her dark hair. The river was just below her waist.

"I hit my head."

Stan started running on the spot, breathing heavily through his mouth. Rosie lifted her hand toward him. Stan stopped running and bent his knees. He took a breath and squeezed his eyes shut and froze. From the water Rosie said,

"It's okay."

And Stan leapt from the rock into the river.

He sank to his chest and immediately pushed himself upright, eyes and mouth wide open as though the water was so cold he couldn't get his breath. He stayed that way for a moment, shocked into immobility, then his body relaxed and he smiled and smiled and smiled and ran the flat of his hand over the surface of the water.

"Wow."

He looked at Rosie.

"Wow."

Rosie looked down at herself and stroked drops of water from her breasts and said with her head bent, "The water rushing by takes your thoughts away with it." She lowered herself until the water was up to her neck. "Your hair's not wet."

Stan moved so that he was in front of her and crouched down until he too had only his head above the water. He took a deep breath and pinched his nose and with his cheeks puffed out went under completely. Rosie did the same and for several seconds I could see only a patch of disturbed, coiling water where they had been. When they came up again I thought they might start laughing but they did not. They crouched in the river with the water moving about their shoulders, saying nothing, their eyes on each other. Then Stan reached out and touched the side of Rosie's face.

I crept backwards until I was safely out of sight, and when I'd gone far enough I started to run, driving myself forward so that the branches of the trees tore my clothes and scratched my skin. When I was in the meadow again I stopped, panting, and in the sunlight and the open space did the best I could to hold myself together.

What I had witnessed had been a monumental leap forward for Stan, of course, and I felt good that he had carved this achievement from the granite face of life. But there had been a terrible side to it too. Because he had not leapt into the water to overcome some damaged part of himself, but to overcome me and the guilt I felt, a guilt, it seemed, which was beginning to infect him with my own unhappiness.

I trudged back up the slope of the meadow. It wasn't until I was almost at the cabin that I noticed Gareth's Jeep parked beside my pickup.

In the house Marla sat stiffly on a hard wooden chair in the middle of the living area. Across the floor from her Gareth sprawled on the sofa. When he saw me he straightened impatiently as though I'd kept him waiting.

"You're up early, Johnboy. Tendin' them hogs?" He clapped his hands and sat forward. "Right. I've been thinking about our conversation in the Mother Lode. I think we need to clarify where we all stand."

As he said this he shot a look at Marla and I saw her sag. Then he looked at me and winked.

"Shouldn't take long. Stand up, Marla."

I'd been poised just inside the front door and I took a step into the room. "What the fuck are you doing? Don't order her around."

Marla stood up. She stared emptily at the floor and wouldn't look at me. I tried to catch her eye.

"Marla, sit down."

She didn't move.

"Marla."

She spoke then, tiredly and without looking up.

"Let's just get it over with."

"Get what over with?"

From the couch Gareth said matter-of-factly, "Marla has a very good idea of the way things are supposed to operate. And what I'm hoping is, that she'll be able to convey some of that to you, Johnny. Take your top off, Marla."

"You fucker!" I charged across the room, grabbed Gareth by the front of his shirt, and hauled him upright. Before I could hit him, though, I felt Marla's hands on my shoulders, pulling me away.

"Johnny, stop. Stop it!" She jammed herself between me and Gareth and pushed me back a few paces. She kept her hands on me until she was satisfied I wasn't going to move, then she turned around to face Gareth and pulled the T-shirt she was wearing quickly up over her head and dropped it on the floor.

She wasn't wearing a bra and her small breasts looked pale and vulnerable. I could feel how much she wanted to cross her arms over them. Gareth looked levelly at me and shook his head like I had let him down.

"You two brought this on yourselves, you know. Take off the pants."

"I don't have anything on underneath."

"We'll be finished quicker then, won't we? Take them off."

Marla undid her sweat pants angrily and stepped out of them. "Are we done?"

"Lie on your back and spread your legs."

"What?" There was a small tremor in Marla's voice.

I took a step toward her, but she held up her hand. I turned my attention to Gareth.

"You fucking prick. Why are you doing this?"

"You ask too many questions and Marla talks too much."

"This is about Bill? About the video? Jesus, I found the disk - what do you think, I'm not going to ask her if she knows anything about it?"

"What I think, Johnny, is that she can make her own choices."

Marla started to cry, but there was anger under the tears. "You pig. You fucking pig!"

She lay down on the floor and spread her legs in front of him. For a moment he stared at her and something like sadness passed over his face, then he crossed the room and left the cabin and a moment later I heard his Jeep start and drive away. On the floor Marla had her hands over her face. I picked her up and carried her into our bedroom and put her on the bed with the covers over her. She held both my hands to her face and rubbed at her tears with my knuckles. The burn on her forearm was beginning to flake.

"You won't leave me, Johnny, will you?"

"Why would I do that?"

"I'm so disgusting. There's nothing good left in me."

"Why did you let him do that to you?"

"You know why."

"Because of your job? Because of your fucking job?"

"They'll fire me if they know I've been a whore."

"This is crazy. He completely degraded you. You do admin work for a bunch of small-town politicians, for Christ's sake. It's not worth it! How long is this going to go on, this random fucking exploitation?"

"It wasn't random. It was because you hassled him about Pat and because he figured out I told you about setting up Bill. It was a warning."

"I get that. But we can't live life endlessly being his victims."

Marla shuddered and took a breath and said quietly, "I know...." Her crying had stopped but her face was still wet and her hands were trembling. "I know we can't."

"Well let's fucking do something about it. Let's hit back. We've got the weapon. All we have to do is tell Jeremy Tripp about him making the video. It's got to stop, Marla."

She nodded and reached for a tissue on the nightstand and blew her nose. "All right...all right."

A few minutes later Stan came home with Rosie in tow. He stood in the doorway of the bedroom beaming at us, holding her hand.

"Hey, Johnny, look, my hair's wet."

They were wearing only their towels and their skin still shone from the water of the river. Stan stepped forward and put his arms around me and pressed the side of his damp head against my chest.

"You know what, Johnny? I feel like if I wasn't holding on to you I'd float away. Come on."

He took my hand and led me out of the cabin and he and I and Rosie walked down the meadow to the river.

At the edge of the water Stan didn't waste any time. He positioned me carefully on the bank and told me not to move. Then he walked out onto the rock. Rosie made to follow him but he stopped her, so she stood near me and the two of us watched as he dropped his towel and started swinging his arms out in front of him, bending his knees as though he was preparing to dive.

"You watching, Johnny?"

"I'm watching, man."

"You know how long it is?"

"Since you went swimming? Twelve years."

"You think I'm going to do it?"

"I think you're going to do it."

"You bet I am. And you know what it means, don't you?"

"That you're the bravest guy in the world."

"It means you can't feel sad about me anymore. You have to be happy. All the time."

And then he whooped and launched himself out over the water and plunged feet-first into it through a shining crown that rose above him and came apart high in the air so that he surfaced in a rain of droplets that caught the sun and broke it into rainbows.

As I watched him I understood a little better what Marla meant about deserving punishment.

CHAPTER TWENTY-FIVE

Jeremy Tripp opened the front door of his house holding a magazine about sports cars. He motioned Marla and me inside without speaking and led us through to the deck at the back.

The sky was a high clear blue and there were small clouds in a line to the east. The archery target still stood at the end of the property but I could see no sign of the rabbit.

Jeremy Tripp sat down at a large round table and drank from a glass of sparkling water. He didn't offer us a seat, but after standing uncertainly for a moment I took one anyway and Marla followed and held my hand under the table. Jeremy Tripp put his glass down and scanned the sky.

"You can feel autumn in the air. I can, anyway - a slight edge. Easier to notice here in the mountains."

"You're Patricia Prentice's brother."

"Until she killed herself."

"And you think we had something to do with it."

"I think you had everything to do with it."

"Because of the video."

Jeremy Tripp frowned.

"I would have denied knowledge of that if I were you. That way you could have done the whole 'It wasn't us, we didn't know anything about it' routine. But yes, because of the video. You made it, Patty watched it, and then she killed herself."

"We didn't even know there *was* a video until two weeks ago."

"And then it came to you in a dream?"

"I broke into Bill's cabin. I wanted to see if he was planning to sell our warehouse. I saw the disk. I'd seen it in Patricia's room the day she died-"

"Killed herself."

"We watched it. Before that we didn't know it existed."

"I thought your brother was the retarded one."

"He's not retarded. And we didn't know, I promise you. We didn't know anything about the camera. We were just...performing for Bill."

"And you're telling me this...because?"

"Because you're attacking us. You broke in and bleached all my plants-"

"Oh, I wouldn't be silly enough to do something like that."

"-you've set up your own company to compete against us, and you kicked Marla out of her house. And we're not the right people. We didn't do anything."

"Please don't tell me Bill made the video. He's a degenerate but he loved his wife, in his own way. And he's not stupid enough to put himself on film."

"It wasn't Bill. It was the guy who pimped Marla to you - Gareth Rogers. Everyone knows about Bill, what he's like. Gareth used his... tastes to manipulate him."

Jeremy Tripp looked at me like he didn't expect anything but lies. "Go on."

I took the two brackets out of my jacket and put them on the table in front of him. "Once I knew about the video I did some looking around. I found one of these on a tree where we did it. I'm pretty sure it's what the camera was attached to. The other one I got from Gareth's father's workshop."

Jeremy Tripp looked at it and snorted. "Does it have his name on it?"

"It's custom made. You can't buy them anywhere. His father does piecework for a fittings company. They're part of a batch he made. Plus he and Gareth live at the lake, they own the cabins there."

"Could have been the father by that logic."

"He's in a wheelchair."

"Still doesn't mean it was Gareth. Someone else could have got hold of one. You, for instance."

"There's more."

I nudged Marla. She cleared her throat and tried to look him in the eye, but failed and dropped her gaze to the surface of the table.

"It was supposed to be just another trick. Gareth wanted me to get Bill to watch me having sex with someone. He said it had to be in a certain part of the forest and his name wasn't to be mentioned. I'd tricked with Bill once or twice a long time ago and when I put it to him he jumped at it. But I didn't know it was going to be filmed. Gareth never said anything about that."

"Of course he didn't."

"I was Pat's friend. She used to come to my house. Why would I make a video of myself screwing in front of her husband?"

"I don't know. What I do know is that my sister killed herself because of a video of you two. Therefore, you had a hand in killing her, and that's a little wrinkle I just have to iron out."

Marla leaned back in her chair. There was nothing else she could offer. I spoke again.

"You're not fixing anything if you have the wrong people. What about motivation? What do we gain from it? I've been out of town for eight years. All I care about is scraping a life together-"

"Bill owns the warehouse you use - perhaps you wanted a rent reduction."

"We hadn't even started the business when the video was made. Jesus Christ! Look, Gareth made it because he needs a proper road built up to the lake and he was going to use the video to blackmail Bill into lobbying it through with the council. He told me this himself three days ago. And believe me, he's more than capable of blackmail. He hates Bill's guts because when Bill sold him the cabins he told him that the council was just about to put the road in. That would have meant a ton of business and Gareth and his father would have ended up rich. But the road never happened, Gareth's father tried to kill himself and got crippled instead, and Gareth's blamed Bill ever since. He thinks the road was just some bullshit Bill concocted to offload the cabins. If anyone has a reason to make the video it's Gareth."

For several moments Jeremy Tripp stared off across his garden. Then he started flipping through the pages of his magazine. "I'll talk to Bill."

After that he ignored us and Marla and I left.

Two days later, in the early afternoon, Stan and I were back at Empty Mile after our Plantasaurus day had finished. Marla was at her job in town and Rosie was out cleaning houses. The weather was still warm enough for it to be pleasant outside, so I sat with my brother on the stoop and we drank cans of soda and ate corn chips.

Stan had made himself a small pouch out of the end of a sock and fixed it around his neck with the gold chain my father had given him. He kept his moths in it now and several times a day he'd tip them out onto his palm to "reconnect." He did this once while we were sitting on the stoop, turning out the insects like an addict with a drug, self-conscious but unable to stop himself.

We chatted idly for a while and crunched chips and took swigs of our drinks, then Stan, who had been staring for several minutes at the line of trees that hid the river, frowned. "Johnny, don't you think it's weird how when you get inside the trees there's that part where they're scrawnier than everywhere else? I think it's weird how the trees are different there."

Maybe some buried part of my brain had recognized the same thing and been turning it over beneath the threshold of consciousness. Maybe it was just that I was relaxed enough at that moment for some particular synapse to fire and connect the dots. Whatever it was, Stan's phrase, the particular words he'd used, made me suddenly wonder if I possessed the key to the puzzle of my father's purchase of Empty Mile after all. *The trees are different....*

I got up and went around to the shed at the back of the cabin where we stored firewood and the things we didn't need inside. My father's wooden trunk was there in a corner under a tarp. I opened it and found the folder in which I kept everything that had anything to do with the Empty Mile land. In it, among other things, were the journal pages, the land deed, the papers transferring ownership to me...and the original of the black-and-white aerial photograph my father had had framed.

I took the photo out and turned it over. On the back, in my father's handwriting, I read the words Stan had so closely mimicked: *The trees are different.* I looked closely at the front of the photo and found the tiny rectangle that was the roof of our cabin. From there I could trace the sweep of the meadow across to the edge of the trees that filled the semicircle the Swallow River made as it bent around Empty Mile.

After squinting at these trees for several moments I saw something I hadn't noticed before, something running horizontally through the semicircle. A shadow, a ghost, an impression...stretching from the end of the rock spur to where the curve of the river straightened again downstream - something that looked like the memory of a pathway or a channel. This was what the inscription on the back of the photo referred to. This was where the trees were different.

For a long moment this smudge on the landscape held my eyes and a sharp fizz of excitement rose within me. I could see a reason for the land now. I could see why my father had mortgaged his house to buy it. It was a crazy *Hardy Boys* adventure reason, so far beyond the run of ordinary life that it was hard to take seriously. But it worked. It made sense.

I found an envelope in the trunk and slipped the aerial photograph inside it. I put the rest of the papers back in their folder and closed the trunk. I was about to leave the shed when I changed my mind and went back and opened the trunk again. After a minute of rummaging I found what I was looking for - the photo of my father in front of the roller coaster in San Diego. I'd been carrying the one of

Marla around with me since I'd found it. I took it out now and compared the two. There was no doubt. Everything about them indicated they'd been taken on the same day - the color of the sky, the light.... Even the poses looked like a quick change between photographer and subject. I folded the two pictures together and put them in my wallet and went back outside.

I didn't tell Stan what I thought I'd found on the aerial photograph, but asked him instead if he wanted to go exploring. He jumped to his feet immediately and he and I spent the next hour walking alongside the rock wall that formed the northern boundary of the meadow. We moved away from the river, back into the forest behind the cabin. When we'd gone about half a mile the edge of the wall began to soften and turn from a sheer face to a steep slope that was broken here and there with runnels and ledges. Another half mile later the slope, though still steep, became climbable and Stan and I sweated and scrambled and hauled our way up it. At the top, when we could breathe normally again, we turned and headed back along the ridge of the spur in the direction we'd just come.

Where we'd climbed it, the spur was a couple of hundred yards wide, but it narrowed steadily as it approached the meadow and the river. Very little vegetation grew up there. A few low shrubs had found a hold in the hard ground and there were some clumps of dry stringy grass, but that was about it. There was a light breeze and Stan and I cooled quickly from the exertion of our climb.

We were about sixty or seventy feet above the surrounding land and below us the forest rolled away in green waves. Looking straight out over it, scanning the mid-distance, there was very little sign of man - a segment of Rural Route 12, the occasional power-line pole, a few isolated dwellings, a thin column of smoke way off to the west....

We passed the meadow on our left. I could see our cabin, and Rosie and Millicent's house. Washing hung on a line behind it but the breeze we felt did not reach the meadow and the clothes were still.

The end of the spur was not a vertical drop but a series of ragged steps that formed a steep broken slope, as though at some time in the past this leading edge had grown tired of holding itself erect and had fallen to its knees, exhausted.

Here, there was nothing to block our view on three sides. Ahead of us the forest stretched out to a spine of hills, and beyond these hills there were more in ragged lines. The trees were mostly evergreen but there was a scattering, too, of those that autumn had colored.

From our right, on the other side of the spur to the meadow, the Swallow River came toward us in a long straight line. Miles away it would have boiled through Oakridge, broken by low rapids as it passed under the road bridge that led into town, but here it flowed smoothly. The river was aimed directly at the sloping edge of the spur, but fifty yards out it twisted from this course and began the pronounced curve that skirted the spur and became the Empty Mile bend.

I tracked it from right to left, turning slowly on my feet, running my eyes along the trail of water. The river might always have run this course. The troughs and hollows of the land and whatever else makes rivers run as they do might naturally have made it bend this way. But it was not difficult to imagine another scenario - that the slope of the spur was a newer addition to the landscape, one that had thrust itself into the river's original path, forcing it to swing out and around and become the curve that now existed.

I had brought the aerial photo with me and I compared it with the landscape around us. Stan looked over my shoulder, then shrugged disinterestedly and went off to stand at the very tip of the spur, shading his eyes like an explorer scanning the distance.

Empty Mile and our land were on the left of where I stood. I looked down at the trees that separated the meadow from the water. From this moderate height they seemed at first to be a solid mass, without much to differentiate one area from another. By using the photo as a guide, though, I was just able to see a lighter pathway running through them, continuing the straight line of the river from the other side of the spur.

I thought about the lecture Marla and I had endured at the Elephant Society on what sometimes happened to rivers, the lecture Chris Reynolds had said my father and Gareth had been so interested in. And I wondered if what I was thinking could possibly be true.

Stan and I left the spur and tramped our way back down to the meadow and our cabin. I didn't say anything to him about the photo or the river or the trees. I didn't say anything to Marla about them either when she came home that evening. Because although I would have liked nothing better than to give them something to hope for, I did not want to be responsible for snatching it back again if it turned out that I was wrong.

But while I avoided that particular pitfall, while I did not set them up for disappointment, that night, as so many days and nights during that time seemed to, brought its own unique portion of unhappiness nevertheless.

It is a strange thing to cause physical pain to someone you love, to watch as your arm sweeps down and welts appear on the body before you, to see the muscles clench and the spine twist as the reflex to escape is bitten down on by some greater imperative, some dark need for atonement that will not be ignored. But that was what Marla made me do to her for the first time that night.

She had found a slim bamboo rod somewhere in town and hidden it behind the dresser. When we went to bed she took it out and begged me to use it on her. I refused, of course, but she walked out to the kitchen and came back with a knife and said she'd start cutting her arms if I didn't do it.

How had such emotional horror come to be part of my life? How was it that a woman could feel so bad about herself? I'd known since my return to Oakridge that she was a long way from happy. I had stolen eight years from her, she felt terribly responsible for the death of Patricia Prentice, and she lived in daily fear of Gareth's pimping. But needing to be caned? None of it seemed a basis for such an extravagant act of penance.

Yet I did what she wanted. She was so insistent, so crazy with need, so determined to self-harm if I did not play this role that it seemed a safer option than leaving her to punish herself.

It wasn't until it was over and we were in bed together that I hit upon a possible motivation for her behavior.

The roller coaster photo.

My father and Marla together in San Diego.

Had there indeed been something between them? Was it this that drove her to fits of depression so black that her only escape was the distraction of physical pain?

It sounded like something from a daytime soap opera. But it was possible. My father was a handsome man. He was in his mid-fifties in the photo, not too old for a fling with a girl at the end of her twenties. And Marla? Could she have done something like that? I figured if she could be a hooker she could probably do pretty much anything.

I turned on the light and lifted my wallet from the nightstand. I took out the photograph of Marla and dropped it on the covers in front of her.

"Maybe it's time to stop feeling guilty."

She pushed herself up from her pillow, wincing as her back pressed against the wall, and picked up the photo with an expression of puzzled query on her face. Her eyes, though, I saw, carried a sheen of fear.

"It fell out of one of the trash bags when we were cleaning out your place."

"Oh. Yeah, I went to San Diego once. I didn't tell you, did I?"

"No."

I took the second photo from my wallet, the one of my father, and showed it to her.

"My father had one too, in his things. Just like yours."

Marla put a brittle smile on her face. "Well, yeah. It was kind of a coincidence. It was…. It was…."

She stopped and swallowed and tried again, and then her face crumpled and she began to cry, huge wracking sobs that tore through her chest as though they carried small pieces of her soul with them. For a long time she could do nothing else and I held her and felt her body shaking. Eventually, though, there was nothing left in her and she was able to force words into her broken voice.

"Three years ago we had an affair. It lasted six months. Sometime in the middle of it we went away for a few days, not even a week. Ray paid someone to take care of Stan."

Marla wiped her eyes with the palms of her hands. She didn't look at me.

"I thought you were never coming back. I'd waited so long. I'd waited for years. And then I just gave up and it seemed like it didn't matter what I did anymore. There wasn't any right or any wrong, there was just...nothing. I didn't have anything left to lose. But even then I knew it would turn to shit. You can't do something like that and get away with it. It doesn't change anything, I know, but we both felt terribly guilty about it. In the end the guilt was all Ray talked about. And I knew you'd find out. I didn't know how, but I knew you would. The only good thing was that no one else ever did, we were very careful. Stan never knew."

"How did it end?"

"Ray finished it. But I was glad he did. There was never any love there. We were just company for each other. You must be disgusted."

"I'm not disgusted."

"I'm such a pig. It was an insane thing to do."

Marla cast her eyes wildly about the bedroom. They came to rest on a small pair of nail scissors on her nightstand. I knew what was going through her mind.

"Don't you fucking dare." I reached past her and threw the scissors across the room.

Marla folded her arms over her chest.

"When it was over I felt so sick with myself. That's when I started hooking. I figured if I was such a pig I might as well act like one." She shook her head and laughed sadly. "All I wanted was to live in Oakridge and be quiet and to just get by. If you can do that anywhere it should be here. But you can't, you can't do it anywhere, not if you're the wrong sort of person. Are you going to leave me now?"

"Leave you? It was three years ago. I wasn't even here, I hadn't been for five years before that."

"It doesn't matter to you?"

"Of course it matters. I particularly don't want to visualize the bedroom scenes. But I'm not going to leave you over it."

I thought I would see some kind of relief in her face. Some great weight rising from her, freeing her of at least some of the hell she lived under, but it didn't happen. She closed her eyes and hung her head, slowly turning it from side to side like a blind woman listening to something in the distance.

It was disturbing to watch, but not as disturbing as when, a moment later, she threw back her head and opened her mouth, tears streaming from the corners of her eyes, and laughed at the ceiling - long, mad peals of noise as though she had just been told something so crushing that the only possible response was an insane, deformed humor.

I let it go on for as long as I could bear. She'd been caned, she'd been forced to confess to an affair with my father, some purging of emotion was understandable. But it was too raw and I became frightened that she was heading toward some sort of fit, so I held her and kissed her hair and at my touch she stopped her howling and buried her head in the hollow of my shoulder and sobbed quietly as I rocked her and made quiet noises to her until she fell asleep.

CHAPTER TWENTY-SIX

I was buying vegetables in an open-fronted store in Back Town the next day when Gareth accosted me. He'd just turned away from something he'd been watching out on the street and when he saw me he came right over. When he said hello I just stared at him.

Gareth waved away my anger as though I had made a blunder that was too embarrassing to address. "Jesus, Johnny, you're always focusing on the surface of things. Lighten up. The other day was just something that had to happen."

"What you made Marla do was disgusting."

"Forget that shit. You gotta see what's happening. You won't believe it."

He grabbed my arm and pulled me out onto the sidewalk.

"Look! Look what that fucking bitch is doing."

A small van was rolling slowly along the street. It had posters taped to its sides and the front of a handheld loudspeaker stuck through the open driver's window. It looked like something a small-town politician might use for electioneering. And it was being put to a similar use now.

The posters displayed several different slogans, but they all boiled down to the same thing - that the proposed road to Tunney Lake should be stopped on environmental grounds. And backing the posters up, the loudspeaker demanded that we save one of our natural beauty spots, that we preserve it from the overexploitation that would certainly come with easier access

"Look at her. I mean, am I insane? Did the world just take a vote and decide to fuck me in the ass? This is unbelievable."

I followed his outstretched arm as it tracked the van. In the shadows of the cab, past the bullhorn, I saw the reason for his rage. Vivian was speaking into the microphone and driving one-handed.

"She's been doing this for three days. And that's not all. Come here."

He pulled me along the street to a lamppost. Stapled to the dusty gray wood there was a flier outlining in more detail just what the negative effects of a blacktop road to the lake would be - from the destruction of forest to the death of wildlife to the erosion of the lake's foreshore.

Gareth tore it from the pole and ripped it to pieces. "She's putting them everywhere. She's even stuck them to trees on the Loop. Where's your car?"

"Around the block. Why?"

"I have something to show you."

"Not interested."

Gareth looked at me with dead eyes. "Your chum Jeremy Tripp's involved."

And so I found myself back at Tunney Lake, sitting in front of a blank TV in Gareth's bedroom. Out in some other part of the bungalow I could hear David rolling around in his wheelchair and muttering to himself.

Gareth took a DVD from his nightstand and slid it into a player.

"Tripp sent me this in the mail yesterday."

He hit the remote and the disk started to play. I recognized the setting immediately. Jeremy Tripp's house - the bedroom where I'd found Vivian wrapped in a towel. She was there again now, only she wasn't by herself this time.

Jeremy Tripp had her on all fours in front of him on the bed. She was naked and he plowed into her as though he was working out. On the screen I could see the bed inching across the floor with each of his thrusts. Vivian seemed unaware of the camera but Jeremy Tripp grinned straight at it from time to time and later, as he was finishing, he winked and gave it the finger.

After he was done with Vivian they lay on the bed together for a minute or two, then she got up and walked into the bathroom. After she'd gone, Jeremy Tripp rolled off the bed, picked up the camera from wherever it had been resting, and panned it around to a dresser in a corner of the room. On top of this there were several neatly stacked reams of paper. He lifted a sheet from one of them and held it in front of the camera.

For a moment the image blurred, then it sharpened again and the screen was filled with a close-up of a flier identical to the one Gareth had ripped from the telegraph pole in Back Town. Then the screen went black as the camera was turned off.

Gareth looked at me with his mouth open and his hands turned up.

"What sort of fucking psycho is he? It explains her sudden interest in the road, though."

"You think he put her up to it?"

"Of course he did. Jesus, Johnny. Vivian's one of these cunts who live to find excuses to rant at the world. All you have to do is point her and pull the trigger. I used to tell her how much we needed the road when I was seeing her and she moaned about it even then. Now this asshole's wound her up to the point where she thinks it's her duty to save the community from it. The fucking eco-liberals on the council are going to eat it up with a spoon."

"Well, thanks for sharing...."

I stood up and started to leave but Gareth stopped me.

"Johnny, wait a minute. Let me ask you something. You hate this guy as well, right? Two plant businesses in one town? He's gotta be fucking you up. If he wasn't around, both of us would be a whole lot better off. I might even get Vivian back. What would you say to us making him not be around anymore?"

"And how would we do that?"

Gareth held my gaze. "How do you think?"

The idea was appalling, but at the same time I couldn't help feeling a rush of desire to see Jeremy Tripp dead. When I didn't say anything, Gareth stood up.

"You owe me, Johnny. You'd be a dead man now if I hadn't stopped those jocks from cutting you open."

"That was ten years ago."

"You wouldn't be any less dead if it happened yesterday."

"I don't owe you that much."

For a moment Gareth looked closely at me, then, as though he had lost interest in the subject, he lifted his hands and smiled.

"Hey, just thought I'd say it, you know? I thought maybe you were thinking along the same lines. Forget about it. I tell you one thing that puzzles me, though. Vivian's Vivian and that's bad enough, but why the fuck should Tripp care if the road gets built or not?"

I shrugged and didn't answer. But of course I knew. Jeremy Tripp had begun to move against Gareth, the same way he'd moved against me and Marla, attacking from a distance through something each of us held dear.

As far as I was concerned Gareth deserved everything he got. But it was still strangely frightening to know that I had begun something which might well destroy the only hope he had for the future.

CHAPTER TWENTY-SEVEN

Jeremy Tripp called first thing next morning and spoke without preamble.

"Bill Prentice has confirmed what you said about Gareth Rogers, that he believes he was swindled over the proposed road to the lake."

"Does that mean you'll leave us alone now?"

"It means more than that. This shift of focus has made Plantagion redundant. As a gesture of recompense I'd like to hand over our customers to you. And our stock of plants. Gratis, of course."

I couldn't believe what I was hearing. This was an offer that would save Plantasaurus, that would raise it from certain failure and catapult it into the ranks of stable and sustainable businesses.

"Well, of course, we'd be happy-"

"Good. I'll have the plants delivered to your warehouse tomorrow. And I'll call you in a day or so about the customer agreements. How is your brother, by the way?"

"He's good."

"His girlfriend cleans my house, I think. Rosie. It must be profoundly affecting for someone in his condition to have an adult relationship."

"It's very important to him, yes."

There was a brief silence on the line while Jeremy Tripp digested this. Then he hung up.

It seemed that in the space of five minutes Plantasaurus had gone from certain ruin to potentially being more successful than we could have dreamed. That was, of course, if Jeremy Tripp was genuine.

Looking at it logically, I saw no reason for him not to be. He'd attacked us because he believed we'd made the video that drove his sister to suicide. Now that he knew someone else had made it he had no reason to continue persecuting us.

I went outside. Stan was dancing with Rosie on a flat patch of ground in front of the cabin. He had a radio balanced on the porch railing. It was tuned to a station that played jazz and swing.

Despite the illusion their dancing created, that Stan was happy and without care, I knew there was another, much larger part of him that was troubled and frightened - the moths and his increasing reliance on Rosie's company were clear evidence of that. So it was good to be able to tell him that Jeremy Tripp and Plantagion were no longer a threat to us, that the success of Plantasaurus was virtually guaranteed.

Stan hugged Rosie and let out a whoop.

"I told you, Johnny! I told you! I knew power was going to come across."

He lifted his moth pouch from the throat of his shirt, opened it, and held it to his nose. He inhaled deeply and his eyelids fluttered.

"I can feel it coming into me. I'm breathing it in, Johnny. Wow, what a great day!"

It was in the spirit of this newfound optimism that I decided to see if I could make the day even better. It had been two days since Stan and I had climbed to the top of the spur, two days since I'd discovered what I thought was the secret of Empty Mile, and the need to know if I was right had now reached a point where I could no longer put off doing something about it. So, around midday, after we'd finished what little Plantasaurus work we had, I used my phone and made an appointment and took Stan on a drive.

The Bureau of Land Management office in Burton was a storefront conversion that ran back through the ground floor of a '50s building made from shiny, burnt-purple bricks. There were two women behind computers in the room that opened off the street and one of them pointed us down a short corridor when I asked to see

Howard Webb, the man whose name was on the business card Rolf Kortekas had given me.

We passed a couple of doors as we made our way to the rear of the building. They had frosted glass panels in their upper halves and the light that came through them made me think there was no one in the rooms behind them.

The door at the end of the corridor was the same as the others except that the blurred nimbus of an electric light showed through the frosting. We knocked and went in.

Howard Webb was a small man with dark hair. He sat behind a wooden desk that looked like it had been thrown away by the local school years ago. There were windows behind him and it was bright in the room, but still he had a lamp burning on his desk. It was angled over a spread of black-and-white photographs.

At his direction, Stan and I dragged two hard chairs away from a wall and as we set them in front of his desk I saw that the photographs he was looking at had been taken from a plane. We made our introductions and he reached over the desk and shook our hands. Stan coughed nervously when it was his turn. Howard Webb leaned back in his chair.

"You're lucky to catch me. This office is mainly an administrative station - permits for land use, that sort of thing. I'm only really here when there's a survey in the area. You said on the phone that you have a picture you want me to look at?"

I handed him my father's aerial photograph. "I was wondering what you could tell us about it."

He looked at the picture for a moment, then set it down and typed the serial number in its bottom right-hand corner into a laptop that stood on a small table beside the desk. He read the screen for a moment then turned back to us.

"It's a place outside Oakridge. We did an aerial survey of the area a year ago. How'd you come across it?"

Stan shifted in his seat. "Uh-oh, Johnny."

Howard Webb glanced at him uncertainly. "There's nothing wrong with you having it. I just meant that they don't really find their way out into the world with any sort of prevalence...."

His voice tailed off on the last word, as though he was uncertain Stan would understand its meaning.

Stan looked embarrassed and said quietly, "My dad had it."

"Oh. Was he developing land in the area?"

"He was a real estate agent."

Howard Webb frowned and looked at the photo again. Then he turned it over and read out what was written there.

"*The trees are different....*"

He repeated it to himself and smiled.

"I remember this picture. Your father sold real estate in Oakridge. Yes, I remember him. We met at his office back in the middle of April when I was researching the area. He asked if I had any photos he could have for his office. And I remember particularly because, a few days after I'd given him some, he asked me exactly that - why the trees were different." Howard Webb looked at me and squinted. "How is he?"

"Well, we're not really sure right now. He may be off on a midlife crisis."

The surveyor was momentarily confused, but evidently decided it would be indelicate to probe further.

"Oh, well, he seemed like a nice man. Do you know what he meant, about the trees?"

"I can see something in the photo, but I'm not sure what it is."

"Okay, look here."

Stan and I stood up and leaned over the desk as Webb pointed at the photo with the tip of a pencil.

"So, most of what you can see is typical topography for the area - forest, river, a collapsed spur. But there's something else a little more interesting here too. The trees we're talking about are here."

Webb traced the faintly differentiated channel of trees on the picture with his pencil.

"You can see how this area of forest appears very slightly lighter on the photograph. That's because the vegetation here - the trees - is less dense and of lesser stature than the forest on either side of it. And it's like that because it's growing in ground that is poorer in nutrients. You see the course of the river? How it curves around this spur? That's not its original course. I think what we're looking at here is the result of a landslip. At some point the face of the spur fell away into the path of the river and forced it into this curve, here. The line of sparser vegetation on the other side of the bluff follows the original path of the river. The trees are, in effect, growing on top of the original riverbed. In some cases a riverbed will be sediment rich and we would see the opposite effect on vegetation - that it would grow more strongly - but in others the riverbed is composed of gravel and sand and plants have a harder time because they only have a shallow layer of topsoil from which to source nutrients. That's probably the case here."

"But we own that land and where those trees are doesn't look like a riverbed. I mean, it doesn't dip down or anything."

"The Swallow River is very shallow in that part of the country even now. There's no reason to suppose it was any deeper along this old, original stretch. The slip might have happened several hundred years ago. Over that time whatever depression there was could easily have been filled with windborne debris, matter washed in by rain, accumulated dead vegetation...."

Stan made two quick popping noises with his lips.

"Yikes, Johnny, a secret river and we didn't even know it was there!"

Howard Webb looked slightly nonplussed, but recovered quickly and smiled at Stan.

"A lot of these things are only visible from the air."

I had what I needed. Stan and I thanked Howard Webb for his time and headed out of the office. At the door, though, something occurred to me and I turned back to him.

"When my father was here asking about the picture, was there anyone else with him?"

"Yes, a kind of redheaded guy, about your age."

On the way home Stan was agog with the idea of a hidden river

"I bet we're the only people in the whole world who know about it, Johnny. It's right there, in the trees, and anyone else would just walk over it, but we know. I told you it was weird how the trees were like that. And I was right."

"That you were, dude."

"I wonder what it would look like if we dug it up."

For a moment he was silent, then he startled me with a sharp intake of breath.

"Johnny! That must be why Dad dug those holes there. Where he got that sample from. The hidden river must be full of gold!"

"Calm down, dude."

"But why would he dig samples if he didn't think it was? Hey, you know what? We should go exploring there."

"Don't worry, we'll be exploring it all right."

"We should make an equipment list. Like a flashlight and an axe. And some rope."

"What are you going to use rope for?"

"You coil it up and put it over your shoulder. So it goes across your chest."

"And you look totally cool."

"Yeah.... We gotta do it when Rosie's around so she can see."

He gazed out the window for a couple of minutes, then he turned back to me and said quietly, "You think we should get married, Johnny?"

"Can't, we're brothers."

"Me and Rosie, stupid."

That Stan and Rosie might get married was an idea so bizarre I'd never contemplated it, and caught unawares as I was now I couldn't help but react negatively.

"I don't know, Stan, Marla and I aren't married."

"Yeah, but Johnny," Stan looked uncomfortable, "you're you."

"Okay, even so, do you think it's a good idea? I mean, Rosie's a lovely girl but I think she had a pretty rough life in the past. Being married is kind of different than just going out, you have to deal with more of each other's problems."

"But Rosie and I don't have problems. We're happy."

"Yeah, but what I'm saying is you might have problems if you got married."

"That doesn't make sense, Johnny."

"Look, Stan, I know you love her, but you live right next door, you see her whenever you want. What's the difference?"

Stan was silent for a mile or so and I knew I'd made him unhappy. Eventually, he said, "But if we did get married you wouldn't be angry, would you, Johnny?"

"No, I wouldn't be angry."

Stan smiled to himself and wriggled comfortably deeper into his seat. And I drove on, wondering just how complicated life could get.

Marla was later than usual and it was dark when she got home from work. She dropped her things over the back of a chair and collapsed on the couch. Her cheeks were flushed from the cool air outside, but under the color she looked the same sort of tired she always did nowadays.

Stan was in his room watching TV and came out when he heard her arrive. He was bursting to tell her about our buried river but before he could start Marla sighed and launched into an explanation of why she was late.

"They called an unscheduled meeting at the town hall about the road to Tunney Lake. I had to go up and take minutes." She smiled grimly. "Things don't look good for Gareth. They took an informal vote; there wasn't enough of a majority to veto the project, but it could easily end up that way given time. You won't believe who was there - Jeremy Tripp. He was with that woman who's been campaigning around town."

"Vivian Gelhardt."

"You know her?"

"Gareth used to go out with her. He introduced us awhile ago, before she left him for Tripp."

"What a shame. Well, they've got this petition with a ton of signatures. Tripp said he was going to keep collecting them until he had enough to force the council to abandon the road."

"Could they really do that?"

"They see that van around town and enough people sign a piece of paper, they can't just ignore it. Plus a couple of the councilors don't want to spend the money anyhow."

Stan, who had been jigging from foot to foot while she spoke, couldn't contain himself any longer and blurted, "We've got a hidden river and it's full of gold!"

Marla looked confused and I could tell she was trying to figure out if his comment was another behavioral anomaly like his moths. I held my hand up to stop him saying any more and he sat down on a chair facing the couch, grinning at me, waiting for me to explain our discovery to Marla.

"Stan and I found out something today that makes me pretty sure I know why my father bought this land."

Stan leaned forward excitedly and said, "Because there's a river full of gold!"

Marla rolled her eyes. "Oh God, Johnny, he was always digging around in one place or another. He never found anything worth more than a couple hundred dollars, you know that."

"Well, listen to this - Millicent told me he was out here in February trying to get her to put her house on the market. While he was there she showed him a journal her great-great-grandfather or someone had written early in the Gold Rush. I've read it too, and this guy came up the Swallow and panned the whole length of Empty Mile. Didn't find a thing, got pissed off, and moved on up the river. Okay, no big deal. Empty Mile's called Empty Mile because no one found gold here. Everyone's always assumed it was because some early party of miners got to the bend before the Rush really got going and mined it clean. Thing is, Millicent's great-great-grandfather said in his journal that the bend had *never* been mined before he got to it. There were no piles of dirt, the riverbed wasn't disturbed, etcetera, etcetera. So the reason there was no gold at Empty Mile couldn't have been because it was mined out. Now, my father, being interested in gold forever, would have found this an interesting fact, and he would have remembered it, particularly because the rest of the Swallow River was so rich. Then, Chris Reynolds told us, he attended a lecture in March at the Elephant Society - the same subject you and I sat through - about how changes in the landscape, things like landslides and so on, can change the course of a river. I think it was at that point he started speculating about Empty Mile. But the breakthrough came with this."

I had the aerial photo ready at the side of the couch. I passed it to Marla. She looked at it blankly.

"I don't see anything."

Stan laughed. "That's because it's a secret river."

Marla looked levelly at me.

"A secret river?"

"It's true. He was all excited about this photo a couple of weeks after I got back to Oakridge. He had it blown up and he hung it on the wall in the living room. It's part of a Bureau of Land Management survey. He wouldn't say what the big deal was, but it was obviously important to him. This is the original print. He wrote something on the back."

Marla turned the photo so she could read my father's cryptic: *The trees are different.*

"Today, Stan and I took it to the guy my father got it from. He's a BLM surveyor."

Marla squinted closely at the front of the photo again.

"I still don't see anything."

"Look here."

I traced the pale line through the trees for her and continued it to the river on the other side of the spur.

"You can see the trees don't grow quite as strongly. The BLM guy said this is the original course of the river. It used to run pretty much straight, see? Then the front of this spur here, which is the cliff that runs down the side of the meadow, collapsed and forced the river into the curve it makes now. The part that got cut off gradually filled in over the years and things started to grow on it. If you go up high enough, though, you can still see it."

Stan nodded enthusiastically.

"See, Marla? A secret river. It's been like that for hundreds of years and nobody knew 'cause they never went high enough to see it."

"And Ray thought it was full of gold?" Marla's voice was droll.

"Well, it makes sense. The gold they found in the Gold Rush had built up over thousands and thousands of years. If just a few hundred years ago a river changed course, the new part of it probably wouldn't have time to build up much gold at all. Once my father read Millicent's journal he knew Empty Mile wasn't empty from having been mined out. And that meant there was a possibility the gold was somewhere else. You heard Chris Reynolds say how rich the Swallow River was. Some people made fortunes, and they were competing with thousands of other men wherever they went on the river. So imagine if you own a whole stretch of it and you're the only person who gets to mine it. I mean, gold's like over nine hundred dollars an ounce now. And my father did actually do a bit of testing before he bought the land. I told you about the assayer in Burton, about how he took some samples there. They came from this buried riverbed. Plus it explains why he was so adamant about me not selling the land after he put it in my name. It didn't have anything to do with something his accountant told him, because Rolf Kortekas told me he never had an accountant."

"And what about you? Do you think there's gold there?"

Marla's question made me pause. I'd been so focused on figuring out what was going on with the land that I hadn't really thought about whether or not I actually believed there was gold on it. I had my father's faith in what he thought he'd found - but he didn't have a great track record when it came to making money - and I had the small sample of gold from the assayer in Burton. It wasn't much.

"I guess the only way to know is to dig some more holes."

"And if you find something, then what? You can't dig up a whole river with a spade."

Stan chimed in, "I'll help you, Johnny. I could dig a whole bunch of holes."

To Marla I said, "Doing it on any sort of scale is obviously going to cost money - clearing the land, digging out the riverbed, processing the pay dirt, if there is any. And right now I don't see how we could finance it. Maybe if Plantasaurus picks up with these new customers we're supposed to be getting from Jeremy Tripp we could try and raise a small loan for some exploratory work. Until then it's just us and a spade."

Stan opened the pouch of moths around his neck, put the opening over his mouth and nose and took a few deep breaths. Then he closed it and blinked rapidly.

"We could all be millionaires. This is the power working. Hey, Johnny, do you think we could buy Bill's garden center and open it up again? That'd be so cool. And me and Rosie could have a big wedding out there and everyone would see how great we are."

"Right now we don't know anything for sure. Don't get too worked up about it just yet."

"I need to get some more moths. I gotta get more power to make it come true."

"Stan!"

"Okay, Johnny. Shutting down." Stan pretended he was turning a key on the side of his head. "Brain off.... But it would be cool, wouldn't it? A secret river full of gold, and we're the only ones who knew about it!"

Stan went off to his room. Marla stood up tiredly.

"It sounds a bit farfetched, Johnny."

She went into the kitchen area and while she fixed herself something to eat I sat by myself turning Stan's last words over in my head. Were we really the only people who knew about the possibility of gold on the land?

At every major turn along my father's path of discovery Gareth seemed to have been hovering in the shadows like some dark ghost. He'd been at Millicent's when my father first saw the journal and at the Elephant Society with my father when the lecture on how a river can change course was given. He'd even been with my father when the BLM guy explained what the aerial photo showed. And he'd been at the assayer's, as well. It wasn't a huge leap, then, to figure he knew just as much as my father had.

But he'd never mentioned anything more than that he'd been friends with my father, that they sometimes went to Elephant Society meetings together, and that one day he'd helped him drill a few "fence post holes." Nothing about any gold. Why was that? Did he figure it would make it easier for him to buy the share of Empty Mile he seemed so anxious to acquire? Or was it something else, something about his connection with my father, something tangled up in all those steps they'd taken together, that he didn't want me to know about?

CHAPTER TWENTY-EIGHT

Any moves we might have made to mine ourselves some physical proof of a million-dollar mother lode at the bottom of the meadow were forgotten during the following week, as it became increasingly apparent that Jeremy Tripp had lied, and I had made a dreadful mistake.

I'd been so desperate to eke out the existence of Plantasaurus for Stan's sake that, despite Tripp's past history of antagonism toward us, I'd acted on his promise of free plants before it had actually been fulfilled. I'd canceled our scheduled plant shipment and used the money instead to pay the quarterly insurance premiums that had fallen due on the business - warehouse contents, pickup, and the personal liability we had to carry in case we dropped a planter on someone.

It was only after I had committed the money to these areas, of course, that the first bubbles of suspicion began to surface. Our own stock of plants was depleted, and when two days had passed and the shipment from Jeremy Tripp still hadn't arrived I was forced to call him. He was immediately apologetic and cursed himself for forgetting. He asked if we could wait another day while he arranged a truck. I didn't really have a choice, so I told him we could, but when I hung up I couldn't shake the feeling that we were never going to see those plants. Jeremy Tripp was not a man to be apologetic.

Later, in town that day, while Stan and I were doing maintenance on a couple of our contracts, we saw both Plantagion vans making their rounds. It didn't look at all like Jeremy Tripp was winding his business down.

The next day came, and the one after that, and neither the plants nor any papers to do with the handover of Plantagion customers showed up. I called Jeremy Tripp several times that week but he didn't answer, so I called the Plantagion warehouse and spoke to Vivian. She didn't know anything about sending us any plants and in fact said they were too busy right then to spare any. It was at that point I realized Jeremy Tripp had never had any intention of stopping his attacks against us. The promise of customers and plants had just been his twisted way of inflicting even more damage.

Plantasaurus was in serious trouble. We couldn't sign up any new customers, something we desperately needed, because we had nothing left to build their displays out of. And, for the same reason, we couldn't properly service the customers we already had. It was more than three weeks to the end of the month when our customers made their payments and we'd have some cash again to buy plants. We might get lucky and ride it out, but it seemed pretty much inevitable to me that people were going to start canceling contracts

Stan and I did the best we could, but by the end of the second week we were starting to get complaints about the scruffiness of our displays, and at the beginning of the third, despite our promises of impending improvement and offers of reduced fees, six of our best customers in Old Town canceled and told us to remove our displays.

Carrying their planters out to the pickup felt like a public humiliation. After we'd finished at one of the places Stan sat in the cab and broke down crying. Whatever the truth of the situation, whether I could have managed the business better or whether it had been doomed from the start, I felt an overwhelming sense of failure. Not only had I not been able to stop this happening, but I was, in a sense, its cause.

As bad as the loss of customers was, though, it was not the worst thing life decided to throw at my brother that week.

That Friday he and I stayed longer than usual at our warehouse, sweeping the place out and washing down empty planters. It was a futile exercise. No amount of tidying up was going to save the business from its downward slide. Our reputation was damaged beyond repair, the number of clients canceling was increasing each day, and inquiries from possible future customers had stopped entirely. We worked on the warehouse out of some notion of pride and affection for the business - a desire not to let it die without a measure of respect.

By the time we got back to the cabin at Empty Mile Marla was already home. She was sitting beside Rosie on the couch, rubbing her back with one hand, as though she wanted to comfort her but knew a full embrace was out of the question. Rosie had her knees pressed together. Her hands were laced tightly in her lap.

As soon as he saw her, Stan began to shake. "Rosie, what's wrong!"

Rosie didn't look at him.

"Johnny, something's wrong."

Marla reached out with her free hand and passed me a large brown envelope. "She was waiting for me when I got home. She had these with her."

Stan sat down on the other side of Rosie and put his arm around her. She pressed herself stiffly against him.

The envelope was unsealed. I reached into it and took out a set of five photos which, from the look of the finish, had been printed on a home computer. As soon as I saw what was on them I knew I should have opened them somewhere away from Stan. But it was too late. He'd caught a glimpse of what they showed and he leapt from the couch to stand beside me. I tried to put them back in the envelope but he grabbed my wrist.

"No, Johnny, show me!"

I gave him the photos. Rosie was the lone subject of each one - naked, her body white, the soft tuft of pubic hair sharply dark between her legs. She stood as though frozen in the center of a large room with a polished wooden floor and white walls. A room both Stan and I knew.

"That's Jeremy Tripp's house!" Stan started to wave his arms rapidly back and forth in front of his face. "That's Jeremy Tripp's house! What's happening? Rosie, what happened?"

He stumbled back to her, clumsily taking her hands. Rosie stared at her knees and spoke in a voice that was empty of emotion.

"I was cleaning the house for him, in the big room that always seems so quiet. I never see him there, but he was today. He told me to take my clothes off and then he took pictures. Then he went away, then he came back and gave them to me. I didn't want Granny to know so I came here instead."

Stan was aghast. "He shouldn't have done that!"

Rosie turned her head toward him but didn't lift her eyes.

"He said if I didn't, he'd make it so you couldn't keep doing Plantasaurus. He said I had to show you the pictures."

Stan balled his fists and let out a bellow. His neck constricted and his entire head turned red. Another man might have punched holes in the walls but Stan had no experience with this level of rage and it bound him like a straightjacket.

There was no saving the situation, but Stan was so upset I had to try to at least eliminate the possibility that anything worse had happened.

"Did he do anything else besides take the pictures? Did he touch you?"

"No."

"Did he say he was going to hurt you?"

She shook her head. "Just Stanley's business."

"I think I should go get Millicent."

Rosie's head snapped up. "I don't want her to know. She'd be upset."

"But will you be all right?"

She nodded, then got up and went out to the stoop and through the windows at the front of the cabin we saw her stand for several minutes looking out at the meadow then sit on the bench against the front wall.

Stan looked confused to the point of fear.

"Johnny, this is bad."

"I know."

"What am I supposed to do?"

"You don't have to do anything."

"I do, Johnny, I have to make sure I act the right way. For Rosie. I don't want her to be disappointed. If I don't say the right things or if I don't do what I'm supposed to do it might be something she always thinks about."

Marla spoke from the couch. "All Rosie wants is for you to be with her."

Stan looked uncertain, as though he was sure a lot more than that was required, but after a moment he went outside and sat next to Rosie. A little while later they left the porch and headed to Millicent's house. Marla shook her head in disgust.

"What an asshole. What does Rosie have to do with anything?"

"He didn't do it to hurt Rosie."

"Not Stan, surely?"

"Me. Hurt Rosie you hurt Stan, hurt Stan you hurt me. Telling Tripp that Gareth made the video hasn't changed anything."

Marla slumped into the couch. "Fucking great."

Marla and I went to bed early. Around midnight I was woken by Millicent banging on the front door. She was carrying a flashlight and she had a shawl around her shoulders. She looked frail and worried.

"Stan and my Rosie have gone off in the car. I heard them talking. He wanted her to drive him someplace."

"Where did they go?"

"I don't know. I tried to ask him but he wouldn't say. I've never seen him like that before. He was angry. I think you should go after him."

"I will."

"Because he took the can of the kerosene we use for the heater and I don't know why he would want that."

Marla and I left Millicent making her way back up the slope to her house. We took Marla's car. I drove. I knew where Stan had gone. Kerosene and anger made a pretty obvious sum.

I made it to the Oakridge commercial precinct in under twenty minutes. By that time the fire had just started.

Rosie's Datsun was parked in front of the Plantagion warehouse. The glass reception door had been forced open and inside, through another open door behind Vivian's desk, I could see the warm orange of reflected fire softly hazing the air back in the warehouse proper.

Marla and I went inside. I was hoping against hope that the fire would be small, something that could be handled, that I could put out before it caused any significant damage. But as we went through the doorway it was obvious I was out of luck.

The warehouse was bigger than ours, and where ours was now bare of almost everything a plant business needed, this one was stuffed with it. Down one wall a shelving unit held stacks of planters, neatly arranged sacks of potting mix, and trays of the smaller plants that were used to dress displays. Along the opposite wall rows of weeping figs and dracaena and kentia palms stood ten and twelve deep.

Rosie was not far from the doorway, a yard or two along the corridor of concrete floor that ran between the plants and the shelving unit. She turned to us as we came in and pointed mutely toward the far end of the building. Stan was down there, frozen in front of a section of the larger plants, watching in horror as fire tore backwards through them.

I shouted but he didn't move, so I ran the length of the warehouse. Stan stayed transfixed until I reached him, but when I hauled him back against the shelving unit he turned toward me and wailed. The sound went on and on as though it was something beyond physical, beyond lungs and vocal chords, was instead a wind of terror and sadness direct from his soul. The sheer uncontrollability of it frightened me and I shook him to make him stop. At the entrance to the warehouse Marla and Rosie screamed for us to get out.

The temperature was now too high to bear and the smoke that the green leaves of the plants threw off had begun to choke us. I took a handful of Stan's shirt and dragged him toward the doorway.

Burning plants fell into our path and as the smoke became too thick to see through I felt a jolt of fear that we might not make it out. But then the sprinkler system kicked in and water fell from the roof in a solid curtain of mist, flattening the smoke, hissing against the burning plants.

We made it to the doorway and I turned to look back. The fire was already dying. Some of the plants had burned themselves out and the rest had too little fuel left on them to fight the water for long. The wall on the plant side of the warehouse was scorched black to the height of the roof and the stock of plants was completely destroyed, but there was little chance that anything was going to reignite.

The four of us ran from the building. Marla drove her own car and I drove Rosie's with Stan and Rosie in the back. As we pulled away I took a last look at the warehouse. The only sign of the fire that had blazed inside it so recently was a halo of smoke around the roof. We left there quickly. If the building had a sprinkler system it probably also had some sort of alarm. I led our two-car convoy around the perimeter of the precinct and then out, away from Oakridge.

The road we took cut through virgin countryside in a long series of twists that eventually connected with the Oakridge Loop a few miles north of our own Plantasaurus warehouse. I turned south there and headed for home. It was about the longest way you could take to Empty Mile but it meant we'd miss the Oakridge volunteer fire brigade if they were responding. And the police too, if it was that kind of alarm.

We didn't talk much in the car. Stan sat against Rosie, leaning forward with his elbows on his knees, glasses off and the heels of his hands pressed against his eyes. He rocked back and forth as much as the space in the small car would allow. He kept his eyes covered until we got back to Empty Mile.

In the cabin we all sat around the table. I made hot chocolate but Stan wouldn't touch his and Rosie said she didn't like milk. I tried to talk to Stan, to somehow break the shell of guilt that was so obviously hardening about him. But he was too horrified at what he'd done.

"Those photos made me go crazy."

"I don't want you to freak out about this, Stan. No one got hurt. The sprinklers put it out. A few plants got burned, so what? The warehouse was fine - other than the smoke it wasn't damaged at all."

"What would you have done, Johnny?"

"If the photos were of Marla I would have gone crazy too."

"I must be out of control." Stan lifted his hands and slapped the sides of his head rapidly and groaned. "What's going to happen to me?"

"No one saw us. No one's going to know who lit the fire. They'll just think something blew out in the building and started it."

"But if you do something that terrible how can something not happen to you?"

"I told you, no one saw us."

"I don't mean that, Johnny. I mean the world. Something in it sees what we do. Maybe it doesn't see normal stuff, but something as huge as this...."

Stan looked wide-eyed around the room. He was overtired and emotionally battered. Marla had some sleeping pills and I gave him one and put him to bed. Rosie got in with him, I was glad she was staying. Her warm body next to him would be a better comfort than any words or drug I could give him.

When they were settled I drove Millicent's car across the meadow to her house. She was sitting in the front room wrapped in her shawl, a small kerosene stove burning across the floor from her. The stove's wick needed trimming and the air in the room smelled of fumes.

I told her where Stan and Rosie had gone in the car and what had happened when they got there. And I told her as well about the photographs that had sparked it off.

"I suppose you haven't called the police about the son of a bitch."

"I can't really do that now."

"Might have been a better idea than letting Stanley run off."

"It wouldn't have made any difference. I know this guy. He'd say Rosie agreed to do it. Even Rosie says he didn't force her, she did it to protect Stan's business. Stan and Rosie aren't the type of people who can go up against someone like Jeremy Tripp. Believe me."

Millicent shook her head to herself. "That poor girl."

"She's sleeping now. She's going to be okay. She was more upset about Stan than she was about herself."

"You'd think if you were like Rosie or Stan life would go a little easier on you. But it doesn't. Mostly it seems to go the other way."

I gave her back the keys to the Datsun and left her staring at the blue flame of the heater, her fingers playing restlessly across the material of her shawl.

CHAPTER TWENTY-NINE

I spent the night listening for cars, expecting a cavalcade of them to come thundering across the meadow at any moment, carrying cops and a warrant for our arrest. But the night passed undisturbed and when I woke the next morning I lay for a while daring to hope that we might have escaped the warehouse fire undetected.

It was a Saturday. Marla at home and no Plantasaurus work - what little we had left of it. I thought I was the first one up but when I went out onto the stoop Stan was sitting in a patch of sunshine wearing his Batman costume. He had his eyes closed behind the mask and didn't realize I was there. His face was turned to the sun and his right hand was closed in a loose fist on his knee. Slowly, as I watched, he brought his hand up and I saw that his fingers were wrapped around a large brown moth. He pushed it into his mouth and started chewing, scrunching his face as he forced himself to eat the insect.

"What are you doing!"

He swallowed and shuddered, then opened his eyes and blinked and looked emptily at me.

"I don't know, Johnny."

"Jesus, Stan.... Look, dude, don't worry about last night. Jeremy Tripp deserved it. It's not something you have to feel bad about."

"I used to be happy, then all of this bad stuff happened. I don't understand it, Johnny."

I could have told him it was just the way life was, that the bad came along with the good, but that wouldn't have been the truth. Everything bad that was happening to Stan could be traced back to one event - Marla and me fucking in the forest for Bill Prentice. I couldn't have foreseen that it would have such disastrous consequences, I hadn't done it with the thought of hurting anyone at all, but still....

"Everything is going to be okay, Stan, I promise. I don't want you to be frightened or upset about anything."

"But there's nothing behind things anymore, not like there used to be." He looked at me then as though he had suddenly realized something. "Is this how you feel, Johnny? Am I like you now?"

By the middle of the morning Stan had changed out of his costume but he still had about him the air of someone who had been profoundly stunned. Rosie joined him on the stoop and the two of them spent a long time staring vacantly at the meadow.

In an attempt to distract him from his misery I reminded him that we hadn't investigated our secret river yet. He seemed to have lost all interest in it, but after I'd talked for a while about gold and how much money we could make and how the whole thing would be a huge adventure, he roused himself a little and agreed to accompany me on an expedition to find out what the buried riverbed held.

"And maybe, Johnny, if there's a lot of gold, maybe I could pay Jeremy Tripp back for his warehouse."

Over the years my father had accumulated all the basics necessary for amateur prospecting: shovels, wire-mesh graders for sieving out stones, even a modern aluminum sluice. We'd brought this gear with us from the old house and kept it now in the shed behind the cabin. Stan and I loaded ourselves with a couple of pans, a shovel, a mattock and a grader and were just coming back around to the front of the cabin when I realized that my plans for the day would have to be radically rethought.

Marla and Rosie were standing close together on the stoop looking up the slope of the meadow in alarm. I followed their gaze and saw, at the top of the track that led down to our cabin, a red E-type Jaguar sitting motionless against a background of trees.

Stan made a small whimpering sound and dropped the pan he was carrying.

"Johnny...."

"It's okay. He's probably just here to see if we can lend him some plants."

"No, he isn't."

"Why don't you take Rosie and show her how to pan for gold? We really need to find out what's in that riverbed."

I handed my pan to Rosie. Stan stayed staring worriedly at Jeremy Tripp's car.

"Go on, Stan. It'll be better if it's just me who talks to him. I'll come and get you when he's gone. Don't worry about anything, it's going to be all right."

Stan picked up his pan and tugged unhappily at Rosie and the two of them set off down the meadow. I went and stood beside Marla on the stoop. A minute later the E-type rolled down the track.

When Jeremy Tripp got out of the car I felt Marla flinch. He stepped onto the ground in front of the cabin as though he were taking ownership of everything around him, us included.

"Log cabin.... Very rustic, but don't you worry about fire?"

"Not especially."

"Really? I have to tell you, it's of some concern to me. You really don't worry about it?" He gazed off down the meadow. Stan and Rosie were just entering the trees. "Smart move sending your brother away. I expect he doesn't cope well with stress. Shall we go inside?"

Without waiting for an answer he climbed the steps and walked past us into the cabin. Marla looked dull and white and I felt a cold hand close about my stomach. For a moment neither of us moved, then we turned and went inside.

Jeremy Tripp sprawled on the couch. Marla took a chair as far away from him as possible and I stayed standing. Jeremy Tripp smirked when I didn't sit down.

"Standing won't do you any good, John. All that stuff about sitting with your back to a window, having your chair higher than the other guy? It's all pointless if you don't have the goods. There are only a few things that really allow you to dominate an exchange. Money is one of them. Knowledge is another. Strutting around the room usually means you don't have either."

"What do you want?"

"There was a fire at my warehouse last night."

"Oh?"

"Surprised? So was I. Fire department says it was arson. That got me thinking, as you might imagine. The target's a warehouse full of plants. There's another plant company in town whose business I've pretty much annihilated, run by someone less than kindly disposed toward me."

"Just because I have a plant company doesn't mean I started the fire."

"I'm not saying it does. You're probably not stupid enough to do something so obvious."

"Okay. Good. So what's this about?"

"You're not stupid enough...but your brother is."

I felt the cold hand around my stomach tighten. "Stan's not capable of doing anything like that."

"Anyone can do anything if the circumstances are right, and it's been a tough old time for Stanley. Business going down the toilet, losing your house.... If you don't have a strong mind these things can push you over the edge. It's just a guess, of course, but I'd say Stan's mind is a long way from strong. Finding out his girlfriend likes to pose for nude photos can't have helped, either."

"That was a fucking evil thing to do."

"Was that what happened? He saw the photos and lost it? Went on a rampage with a can of gas?"

"You're insane."

"But close enough to the mark."

"You don't have any proof at all that that's what happened."

"Do you really think I need any?"

"Get the fuck out of my house."

"John, when I go to the police and tell them I believe Stan set fire to my warehouse they'll take him in for questioning. Proof won't come into it because two minutes after they sit him down he'll have told them everything himself. You know he will, there's no way he could stand up to being questioned."

"What do you want?"

"To make the community a safer place. We can't have people running around setting things on fire."

"You mean prison? Are you fucking joking? We're talking about Stan here. It would destroy him."

"Do you think I care about that?"

"This is about you and me and Marla and Gareth and that fucking video. Don't bring Stan into it."

"Maybe you could persuade me not to."

"I already asked you what you want."

"Cancel your lease on Bill's warehouse and move out. I want to buy the land."

"But we won't be able to run our business."

"You're hardly doing that now. And I want this land, as well."

"What land?"

"This land, here."

"Are you joking? Why?"

Jeremy Tripp shrugged. "Because you have it. You've got to understand, I'm honor-bound to take everything you have. You and that Gareth twerp and your slut here." He pointed his chin at Marla.

"The fire was just what you wanted, wasn't it?"

"You made a mistake. You should have looked after your brother better."

"How do I know you won't go to the police even if I do what you want?"

"You don't. But what choice do you have? I'm saying I won't tell anyone. What are you going to do, fail your brother again by not even trying to save him?"

Giving up the warehouse didn't bother me much, Plantasaurus was on its last legs anyhow. But Empty Mile was a whole other matter.

"I'm waiting, John."

"The warehouse lease I can cancel as soon as I can get hold of Bill. But the land will involve a lawyer. I'll need a few days to arrange it."

"Just as long as you don't dilly-dally." Jeremy Tripp stood up. "And now, to seal the bargain, I'd like your girlfriend to take care of me."

"Take care of you?"

"Blowjob."

"Fuck off. She doesn't work for Gareth anymore and she's not whoring herself to you."

Jeremy Tripp looked at me like I was insane. "Your brother will go to prison. At the very least a psychiatric institution. Do you think he'll ever be the same again? Do you think you will, knowing you could have saved him from it?"

I hated the idea of Marla going down on Jeremy Tripp, but it was the lesser of two evils. She would be a little more damaged because of it but she would still be Marla after it was over. Stan, though, most definitely would not be Stan if he was locked up for any length of time.

Of course she knew what I was thinking, or saw it in my face. She sighed and dropped to her knees in front of him and unzipped his fly. Over her head, Jeremy Tripp winked at me

"Someone's got some sense."

I couldn't watch. I went to stand at the end of the room where the sink and the counter ran across the rear wall. When I got there, I glanced over my shoulder. Jeremy Tripp's back was toward me, buttocks clenching, hands wrapped in Marla's hair. I turned away and braced myself against the counter, wishing the earth would open up.

When Jeremy Tripp started to make grunting noises my gaze wandered across the counter to the sink. To a large kitchen knife lying there waiting to be washed. I reached out and closed my hand around the brown wood of its handle. And then I turned and started quietly back across the floor.

Tripp had been taking his time but he wasn't far away now and his hips were driving at Marla in hard thrusts, making her gag. I held the knife out in front of me. The distance between its blade and Tripp's back was not great, maybe fifteen feet. I watched it narrow as I moved forward, this space that was all there was between the life and death of a man I hated.

Part of Marla's face was visible past his right hip and she watched me with one eye.

I wanted to plunge the knife into his back and twist it. I wanted revenge for what he was doing to Marla, for what he had done to her in the past. I wanted revenge for the destruction of my brother's hopes. I wanted this threat to our lives gone forever.

But I couldn't do it. Halfway across the floor I stopped. For a moment I just stood there, pointing the knife at him. Then I turned around and walked back to the sink and stood looking blankly out of the window above it.

Later, when he had gone, Marla brushed her teeth and stood at the sink and stared out the window with me.

She had done things like this before. She had been a hooker and had sex with men she didn't know, she had been made to service Jeremy Tripp by Gareth, and she and I had performed in the forest for Bill Prentice. So going down on Jeremy Tripp that day wasn't the worst thing she'd ever done. But it had happened in her home, and it had happened soon after Gareth had forced a similar experience on her.

I knew she didn't want to talk about it but I felt I had to say something.

"Thank you."

It was inadequate, I knew, but I thought anything else would sound self-serving.

Marla lit a cigarette and slowly pinched the flame of the match out between her thumb and forefinger. She didn't flinch or make a sound. When she had smoked the cigarette she turned to me and said in an overly controlled voice, "Are you going to give him what he wants?"

"It won't make any difference. He wants to destroy us, asking for the warehouse and the land is just another step along the way, but it's not the end. All his attacks so far have been personal. He throws you out of your house, he fucks you in front of me, he poisons our plants, he sets up a competing firm, and for Gareth he's wrecking the chances of a road to the lake. None of this is about getting anything material, it's about revenge for Pat. And it's not going to stop while any of us are still functioning. He's going to tell the police about Stan whether I give him the land or not."

"So?"

"Fuck, I don't know...."

"You do, Johnny. I can see you thinking it."

"You mean kill him?"

"What do you want me to tell you? That I'd be all right with it? Is that what you're waiting for?"

"I'm not waiting for anything."

"Because I am okay with it, Johnny. I am."

"I couldn't do it. I tried-"

"I'm okay with it, but you have to know it'll always be with you. You'll never get rid of it."

"I said I couldn't do it!"

"But you've thought of a way, haven't you?"

Marla's voice was worn through with sadness. She ran her fingers over the back of my neck and without feeling it my legs buckled and I hit the floor with my knees and stayed there, holding her to me, my face pressed against her stomach, crying into the rough cotton of her shirt.

Later, I made a phone call to Gareth and then I went down to the river to tell Stan and Rosie it was safe to come out. In the corridor of less strongly growing trees that we now knew to be the course of the old riverbed I found that one of the holes my father had dug to take his samples had been enlarged to a small crater about five feet wide and waist-height deep. The walls of the hole were dark brown soil but its floor was made of something else, paler and more granular, a mixture of sand and gravel - unmistakably riverbed material.

There was nothing about it to indicate that it was laced with gold. But it was there, the bed of an old river, visible, touchable. Real. Until now it had been a blur on a photograph, the dream of a desperate man. But not any longer. I felt something tugging at me, skirting my reasoning mind, going straight for whatever part of me it was that wanted to believe in miracles.

I continued through the trees to the river. Stan and Rosie were sitting on the bank beside a pile of excavated dirt. They were holding hands and their backs were toward me. They seemed to be doing nothing but staring at the bright water that moved in front of them. Stan's shovel lay on the ground near him, next to the gold pans.

When they heard me approaching they turned and for a moment I wasn't sure what I was seeing. Both of them had something smeared on their faces. Against the glare of the water it looked dull and dark and I thought at first that it must be mud. But as I stepped closer I saw it was something else. Stan and Rosie had covered their faces with a slurry of water, crushed moths, and concentrates.

The mixture was almost dry and as their faces moved small pieces of it fell away. One of Stan's hands lay closed in his lap. He raised it toward me and opened his fingers. A damp mound of concentrates lay creased in the center of his palm.

"Dad was right, Johnny. We only had to do five pans to get this." He scraped the mix of black sand and gold dust off his hand into one of the pans beside him. "Dad never found so much in just five pans."

I knelt and examined the concentrates. Without refining them properly it was impossible to tell exactly what proportion of gold they contained, but there was so much color there, so much dull yellow in the black sand, that it looked to me like Stan had panned at least an ounce of gold. It might be that not all of the buried river was so impregnated with wealth, but it showed that at least where Stan had dug it was very rich indeed.

"What do you have on your face?"

"I didn't want anything to go wrong with getting the gold. I don't want it to be like Plantasaurus. Rosie was helping me. Has Jeremy Tripp gone?"

"Yes, he's gone."

"He knows it was me, doesn't he?"

"He was just asking questions."

"Johnny!"

"Yes, okay, he knows, but it's going to be all right."

"How can it be all right?"

"I fixed things."

"How?"

"I just explained how it was all a bad mistake and you didn't mean to do it. He understood."

Stan looked at me for a long moment. "You promise, Johnny?"

"I promise."

He glanced at Rosie and let out a heavy breath.

Gareth and I met at the Black Cat café in Back Town. It was the middle of the afternoon and the place was empty. We took a booth on the other side of the room from the counter. Gareth looked across the table at me measuringly.

"I'd like to think this means we're going to be friends. You asking me out for coffee and all. But I wonder if there isn't a little more to it."

"How are things going with the road to the lake?"

"Oh, I think me first, Johnny. I saw a thing this morning that for some reason made me think immediately of you. Swinging by the Plantagion warehouse on my usual pathetic route to get a glimpse of Viv, I happened to notice there'd been a fire. I bet Jeremy Tripp isn't too happy with you."

"What's that got to do with me?"

"Fires don't start themselves."

I drank some coffee, looked at Gareth for a while, then figured there was no point in delaying things.

"Marla was at a meeting at the town hall where Tripp and Vivian petitioned the council against building the road. They said they weren't going to stop until they had enough signatures to shut it down."

"That cunt." Garth shook his head. "Why doesn't it surprise me?"

"Do you have any idea who Jeremy Tripp is?"

"A rich asshole who stole my woman and who's busy fucking up what's left of my life."

"He's Patricia Prentice's brother."

Gareth blinked and looked blankly at me as though he hadn't understood.

"He's Patricia Prentice's brother. He's seen the video and he knows you shot it. He thinks all three of us are responsible for her death and he's not going to let up on any of us till he gets his revenge. The way he's going after me is by attacking Plantasaurus. He bought Marla's house and kicked her out of it. And he's working against the road to get at you. And he took Vivian, of course."

"And there's the fire, of course."

"What about the fire?"

"Johnny, if we're leading up to what I think we're leading up to, there's no room for bullshitting each other. You've got him on your ass about that fire. It's too fucking coincidental that we're here the morning after it happened."

"Okay, the fire."

"And he's right?"

I didn't want to tell Gareth any more than I had to, but I needed his help to do something I wasn't capable of doing alone. "Stan made an error of judgment."

"There you go, wasn't too hard. Now we can move forward. How do you know he's her brother?"

"I heard it from one of our clients. And later he told me himself."

"You talked to him?"

"I was trying to get him to leave us alone."

"Johnny, it's just you and Marla on that tape. Why does he think I made it?"

I'd known I was going to have to cover this unfortunate detail and I tried now to make it sound as matter of fact and unavoidable as possible.

"I told him. It was all I had, man. He was destroying our business. I mean, you set up the video, it didn't have anything to do with us. If anyone should have been taking the heat it was you."

"Ah...." Gareth smiled tightly to himself. "That explains something. I had Bill on the phone yesterday screaming all kinds of insanity. I do believe he mentioned the video. I denied all knowledge, of course. Not very nice using me like that, Johnboy."

"Like I said, it was all I had. Anyway, it didn't work. Tripp just added you to the list and kept right on attacking us. Now, because of the fire, he's demanding that I give him Empty Mile. If I don't he's going to send Stan to prison."

I watched Gareth carefully as I said this. His face went hard and he shook his head violently.

"Your land? No fucking way. That is not happening."

I shook my own head and sighed. "I don't see any way around it."

"Yes you do, Johnny. That's why we're here. You want me to kill him for you."

"You told me already that you wanted to do it."

"What I said was that *we* should do it. Together."

"I don't have it in me."

"But you think I do."

I shrugged. Gareth looked at me for a long time without speaking, tapping his forefinger on the table beside his coffee cup.

"Okay, I'll do it, but you have to help. I'll take care of the nasty stuff, don't worry. But you have to be there."

"Okay."

"And I want a third of Empty Mile. I told you I was interested in the land and it seems like fair payment for what you want done. Especially as Tripp wants all of it."

The thought of being connected to Gareth through the land made my blood run cold, but we were going to be connected anyway if we killed Jeremy Tripp, so I said yes. I didn't really have a choice.

"Okay, a third."

"And we're talking a full one-third share, right?"

"What do you mean?"

"Water rights, a share in the timber if we cut any trees down, mineral rights...that sort of thing."

"If you want."

"Cool. We're going to be partners, Johnny!"

"Tripp is only going to hold off a day or two before he goes to the police on the fire thing."

"That won't be a problem. I've been thinking about this for a while now."

"It'll take me a week or so to get the ownership papers for the land changed."

"We've got a deal, dude. I trust you. Shake my hand and it's done. Just do the papers when you can. You know, a partnership like this could really benefit you, Johnny. If we ever need to put any money into the place I could leverage the cabins."

He held out his hand and as I shook it I felt like I was being pulled into a long dark tunnel from which there was no exit except some dreadful future where everything was dangerous and irrevocably changed from the way it was now.

A little while later Gareth left, saying he'd call me the next day when things were set. I deliberately didn't ask him how he planned to do it. I didn't want to know any sooner than I had to.

I sat by myself in the Black Cat for another half hour, thinking about how easy it was for humans to do things that changed them forever. One decision. One action. That was all it took. I was poised between two versions of myself - innocent and killer. In moving from one to the other I knew I would lose part of who I was and I wondered, that afternoon, if there would be enough of me left to recognize when it was all over.

Back at the cabin, when I told Marla things were in motion, she seemed to accept it until I came to the part about the price Gareth had exacted.

"Are you fucking joking?"

"What was I going to say? I can't do it by myself. And he *wants* to do it. It's only a third, we'll still have the rest."

"It means he'll be here all the time. Don't you understand that? It gives him an excuse. Are you blind? Have you just kind of missed that I can't stand him anywhere near me? He hates you, Johnny. And he hates me. And he's not going to waste a fucking minute of this."

"What was I supposed to do?"

Marla looked at me and shook her head. For a moment her mouth worked, but whatever it was she wanted to say was strangled by her despair.

CHAPTER THIRTY

The morning of the next day started with Gareth calling and asking about the garden at the back of Jeremy Tripp's house.

"Can other houses see into it?"

"No, it's cut straight into the forest."

"Does it have a fence?"

"No."

Gareth seemed pleased with this and told me to keep my phone on me and to be ready to go sometime in the afternoon. He called again around three and told me to get over to Old Town as fast as I could.

He was parked a hundred yards back from Oakridge's only movie theater. I pulled up behind him and got into his Jeep. As I slid into the seat he reached across and I was forced to clasp hands with him.

"You ready, Johnboy? This is where the tough get going."

"I guess."

"I've been following him around all day. He's been in town with Vivian getting more signatures for his fucking petition." Gareth nodded down the street at the theater. "Now they're watching a movie. They just went in - that gives us a couple of hours."

"To do what?"

"They're using Vivian's van - she's been driving, like the good little pig she is. Which means Tripp's car is back at his place."

Gareth took his cell phone out and turned it off. "Yours too, dude. Don't want them tracked."

He started the Jeep and made a U-turn and we drove north out of Old Town, out of Oakridge, and into the belt of forest that separated the Slopes from the town. It was BLM land here and there were no houses among the trees. The only traffic that used the road was either tourists or people who lived in, or worked for, the big houses higher up. But it was late in the year now and there were few tourists visiting Oakridge and we didn't see a single other car.

We didn't speak until Gareth pulled the Jeep off the road, into a fire trail a half mile short of where the houses of the Slopes began. The land here was steep and as the car made the turn I looked back over my shoulder, down the stretch of road we'd just traveled up, and saw a long narrow straight that made a right-hand turn at the bottom so tight it looked like the road dead-ended in a solid wall of trees. We bounced along the trail for several hundred yards then Gareth stopped the Jeep and got out. He took a backpack from the rear seat and slung it over his shoulder.

"End of the line, Johnny. We have to walk from here, I don't want anyone seeing the car."

"Through the forest?"

"Yeah. Tripp's on Eyrie. That's off the road we just came up, another half mile or so. And his place is about five hundred yards along it. So all we have to do is head uphill from here and we should hit his backyard."

Gareth took a compass from his pocket, checked the direction, and stepped off the trail into the trees. The forest here felt threatening. It was a place men did not usually come and it seemed to me that our presence violated the way things were supposed to be.

Whatever Gareth had in his backpack made a metallic clinking, and that and the forest and what we were going to do started to work on me. I began to picture one horrific bludgeoning scene after another.

Gareth must have seen the fear on my face.

"Relax, dude, we're not going to chop him into pieces or anything. All we're going to do is make a little alteration to that fancy car of his and then he's going to have an accident." Gareth held up his hands. "Totally hands-off."

We continued our way through the forest. The ground was steep and covered with a thick carpet of dry brown pine needles that slipped under our feet. We made slow progress. I kept my eyes on the ground as much as I could and tried to convince myself that killing someone by engineering an accident wasn't quite as bad as stabbing the life out of them.

It took us half an hour to get level with the properties on the downhill side of Eyrie Street. Gareth's navigation was slightly off and because we couldn't see more than twenty yards on either side of us we unknowingly walked through a corridor of forest between two properties and almost blundered out onto the road. From there, though, we got our bearings and it only took us another couple of minutes to backtrack and find the rear border of Jeremy Tripp's garden.

We stood hidden at the edge of the trees looking out at the bright expanse of lawn. The archery target was there, and on a table on the deck the pages of a magazine lifted lazily as a light breeze caught them. The house was still and quiet.

Gareth nodded toward the carport at the side of the house. The top on Jeremy Tripp's V12 E-type Jaguar roadster was down and the heavy chrome frame along the upper edge of its windshield caught a stray shaft of sun and made a single bright highlight in the shade.

"That's going to make things easier, I thought we'd have to break into a garage. We better hurry up, though. If they come back right after the movie we only have an hour or so."

We stepped out into the light of the garden and although neither it nor the house was overlooked by any of the neighboring properties I felt immediately that we were on show to the world. We walked quickly along the left edge of the garden and into the carport. The open structure was shielded from view on one side by the forest, and on the other by the house. The hedge out front covered us from the road.

Gareth took a flashlight from his backpack, then lay down on the concrete floor so that, by angling his head, he could see behind one of the car's chrome-wire front wheels. He pulled his head back and sat up.

"Good."

He took a fine metal file out of the pack and leaned back under the car. For the next couple of minutes he filed gently at something on the other side of the wheel. He stopped regularly and checked his work with the flashlight. When he was satisfied he reached out toward me with one hand.

"There's a bottle in there. Be careful with it."

I opened the backpack. Inside was a small collection of loose tools, a pair of industrial rubber gloves, a three-foot length of steel pipe about an inch in diameter, a wad of something that looked like cotton wool, and a small bottle covered with bubble wrap. The bottle looked like something from an old-fashioned drug store. It had a ground-glass stopper and it was half full of a colorless liquid. I pulled the bubble wrap off it and handed it to Gareth.

"What is it?"

"Nitric acid. Give me the gloves and that wool stuff."

I passed over what he wanted and as he pulled on the gloves he outlined what he was going to do.

"The brake lines carry brake fluid from a master cylinder to the brakes on each wheel. When you put your foot on the brake pedal it increases the pressure on the fluid and this transfers to sets of calipers which squeeze the brake pads against the discs and slow the car. Of course, if there's a hole in the brake lines then brake fluid squirts out when you put the brakes on and your brakes, they don't work so good no more. We could just cut the brake line, but that would look a tad suspicious. What I want to do is make them just thin enough so that when he brakes hard they rupture. The acid removes the file marks and eats through more of the metal. You do it right, it looks just like a faulty part. It's pretty hard to judge with this stuff, though, but if I use too much his brakes will still be fucked and we'll just have to hope he doesn't notice the leak till it's too late."

Gareth pulled a piece of the cotton-like material off the main wad and held it up to me.

"Glass wool. They use it in fish tank filters. It's the only thing you can use as a sponge with acid."

He twisted the stopper out of the bottle and carefully wet the glass wool with several drops of acid. Then he lay down and reached behind the wheel again. I lay head-on to the front of the car and watched as he stroked an angled metal pipe about a quarter-inch diameter with the acid. Thin white fumes hazed the outline of the pipe after each pass.

When he'd finished with that wheel, Gareth did the same to the one on the other side. Then he went back and checked the first.

"Okay, I guess. Take a look."

He moved away and I took his place. The brake line was still intact but it now appeared to be sweating beads of reddish-brown liquid along three or four inches of its length.

Gareth stuffed the used glass wool into the acid bottle, stoppered it again, and returned everything to the backpack.

"It'll go for sure the first time he hits the brakes."

"What about the back ones?"

"This car's got what's called split diagonals - one circuit feeds the left front and right rear brakes, the other does vice versa. You put a hole anywhere in the circuit and both ends are fucked. And even if he slams the rears on with the emergency it's only going to help us. The car will either spin or flip."

"You don't think anyone will figure it out?"

"Depends how suspicious they are, how deeply they investigate, whether or not the car gets fucked up enough to hide certain things. It's thirty-five years old. It's not beyond the realm of possibility that something on it could fail. Those brake lines are just going to look like they were corroded. Even if someone does suspect something, why would they connect it to us? We're just a couple of small-town slobs, and you're the nice guy looking after his challenged brother. As far as anyone knows we had peripheral contact with Tripp at most."

Gareth started away from the carport.

"What do we do now?"

"Wait for them to come home."

We went into the corridor of forest at the side of the garden and cut right toward the road. Staying so close to the scene of our crime seemed to me to be a monumentally stupid thing to do. I tugged at Gareth's sleeve.

"Wouldn't it be better to get out of here?"

"We can't just leave things for whenever that prick feels like going for a drive again. We have to know when he gets home and we have to know when Vivian's not with him anymore. So, we're going to stay hidden in these trees and watch the road and Vivian's house. When she's safely back at her own place we'll trigger Jerry-boy into taking the Jag for a late night spin."

"How?"

"I'll make a phone call. Only problem will be if he takes Vivian back to his place for a bit of sausage action."

We crouched in the trees a few yards back from the edge of the road. We were hidden from view but we could see a stretch of tarmac and the front of Vivian's house. Jeremy Tripp and Vivian must have stayed in town for dinner after their movie because they didn't come home for close to three hours. I was cold and I had my eyes closed in an uncomfortable doze when we heard the sound of a car, faint at first, then louder as it moved up the long slope toward the intersection with Eyrie. It had started to get dark by then and when the car made the turn, the road in front of us was suddenly washed in the yellow-white of headlights.

Vivian's van pulled into her driveway. The security lights at the front of the house popped on. The van idled for a moment, then the engine shut off and the headlights went dark. Jeremy Tripp and Vivian got out and stood talking for a couple of minutes. At the end of this he took her hand and made a show of trying to pull her down the driveway. Vivian laughed and shook her head and waved him off. After a little more talk they embraced and kissed, then Tripp walked diagonally across the road toward his house and out of our line of sight. Vivian went into her own house and Gareth muttered under his breath: "Goodnight, bitch."

I went to stand up but he held me down and whispered, "I want to make sure he doesn't come back."

We waited another five minutes but there was no further movement on the road, so we moved back through the forest and started down toward Gareth's Jeep. The journey was more difficult in the dark and both of us slipped and fell more than once on the pine needles. We couldn't risk using the flashlight. Luckily, the fire trail cut right across that part of the mountain and all we had to do was keep stumbling downhill till we hit it. We veered off course quite a way and when we finally came out of the forest we were a couple of hundred yards further along the trail than where we'd left the Jeep.

There was no moon but there were stars and the dry flattened grass of the trail was silver as we walked back along it not talking and rubbing at the scratches the forest had left on our arms.

When we got to the car we climbed inside and closed the doors. I was exhausted and it seemed to me that we had done more than enough for this thing to be over with.

Gareth looked at me as he started the Jeep. "That was the easy part. It's going to get nastier now, Johnny. You're not going to fuck up, are you?"

I shook my head, though truthfully I was now so scared I felt outside my body, felt that I observed and acted, but had no ability whatsoever to influence events around me.

"Good."

We drove slowly back along the fire trail to the road with our lights out. Just before we emerged Gareth stopped and rolled his window down and listened for other cars. When he was satisfied there was no other traffic he pulled out and we rolled down the long straight slope of tarmac with the engine in neutral to make as little noise as possible.

Half a mile on, Gareth slowed to a crawl as we reached the part of the road where it made a sharp bend to the right. I assumed he was just being cautious in case there was oncoming traffic that we couldn't yet see. But rather than rounding the bend and kicking the car into drive, Gareth stopped completely.

The Jeep was still fully on the tarmac, blocking the right lane, and I glanced nervously back up the road, wondering if this was where fate had decreed we should be caught.

Gareth dropped the backpack in my lap.

"This is where you get out."

"What!"

"Hurry up before someone comes."

"What the fuck are you talking about?"

The world slipped sideways and for a moment I felt I had become the night's victim, that Gareth was now finally taking revenge on me for having stolen Marla from him.

He put his hand on my knee. "Dude, get a grip. We have to get Tripp to drive down the hill. When he tries to take this corner his brakes will fail and he'll go straight into the trees. Bingo, one dead asshole. But it has to happen tonight. And it has to happen where we want it to happen. It's no good if he just drives his car to Vivian's or something, he'll know the brakes are fucked up and he'll get them fixed. So I'm going to Back Town to call him from a pay phone, anonymously, and tell him to come meet me. It's a ten- to fifteen-minute drive. I'll tell him not to come for forty-five minutes, so I will definitely be back here before he comes down the hill. But just in case, you have to be here to make sure everything works."

"Why don't you call him on your cell?"

"Phone records, dumb-ass."

"What are you going to say to him?"

Gareth smiled a little. "I'm going to tell him I have evidence that Patricia Prentice's death wasn't a suicide."

"Do you?"

"How would I have something like that, you idiot? Come on, get out. We get seen here, we're fucked."

He gave me a shove and I opened the door and got out.

"What do I need the backpack for?"

"I don't want it in the car if I get stopped by a cop. Just hide in the trees there and stay out of sight till I get back. There's another fire trail about twenty yards past the bend. I'll park there and walk up. Look out for me."

He put the car in gear and drove away before I could say anything else, and I was left alone in the sudden silence of the night. Gareth's explanation for what he was doing sounded plausible, but just the same I felt terribly vulnerable and very, very lonely.

I ran across the tarmac and into the trees. The starshine fell away almost immediately and I only had to go a few yards to find a place where I was invisible from the road but could still see its long silvered sweep running uphill.

I didn't want to sit down. The situation was so grave, so electric with deadly potential, that making myself comfortable seemed wrong. For long minutes I stood motionless, one hand pressed against the trunk of a tree, straining my eyes against the road, listening as hard as I could for the sound of a car coming down from the Slopes. And all the time praying that I would never see or hear it, that Jeremy Tripp's car would never leave its carport.

He had to die. I knew that. Stan and Marla and I would never be safe if he didn't. But in that dark, lonely time at the edge of the forest all I wanted was for this plan never to have been hatched, for me never to have approached Gareth, and for him never to have accepted.

Twenty minutes passed and I was still alone. I sank into a crouch. I had the backpack between my knees, the piece of pipe it held stuck up through the opening. By Gareth's projected schedule there was still plenty of time for him to get back before anything happened but I was so frightened I had already convinced myself that he wouldn't.

And he didn't. I'd been crouching for five minutes when I heard the throb of a large engine being pushed hard. I wanted it to come from my left, for it to be Gareth racing uphill to park on the fire trail and take over from me. I tried to fool my hearing, but it was no use. Though I couldn't see it yet, the car was unmistakably further up the mountain, coming down.

I stood and leaned out around my tree. For a moment the road was as dark and empty as it had been since I got there, but then, far back at the top of the slope, the trees on either side bloomed yellow. For a moment there was nothing else, just the light against the trees, as though it were caught there and could not come any further, as though the howling engine noise pressed against it, squeezing it against the night, thickening it with some horrible pressure.

And then the light burst and the car was there on the hill, rocketing down the long strip of tarmac. At first the distance made it impossible to see anything behind the hard bright fan of the headlights, but I knew it was the E-type by the sound of the engine. And because there wasn't anyone else it could be.

Jeremy Tripp was driving fast and it was only a matter of seconds before I could see the faint gleam of bodywork and chrome behind the headlights. And then the outline of the car itself. And then the star-mirrored glass of the windshield in its metal frame.

I stood frozen, watching through the trees as the car's rear wheels locked and smoked against the asphalt. Its front wheels, though, kept turning and the back of the car slid out to the left until the whole vehicle was drifting diagonally across the road, across the beginning of the bend, going far too fast to ever have any hope of escaping the forest.

I was directly back from the apex of the bend and Jeremy Tripp passed me by twenty yards before plowing into the trees, but still I felt the impact beneath my feet and in all the trees around me. And the sound of metal slamming against living wood, like the discharge of some monstrous piece of artillery, echoed in the forest and rolled back up the hill and away, and after it had gone there seemed to be a vacuum about me, as though all the forest sounds, its smells, the quality of its light, had been blown away, leaving me in a silent and alien dream world where things could be seen but not understood.

Gradually, a sound made its way through this new world, a faint hissing and, behind it, the creaking of hot metal settling. I picked up the backpack and crept through the trees until I came to the wreck of Jeremy Tripp's car.

He could have been fortunate, perhaps, and hit a stand of thin saplings that might have drained his speed as he crashed through them, reducing the destruction of whatever final impact brought him to a halt. But Jeremy Tripp had not been fortunate. He had hit a tree with a trunk three feet wide and there had been no gradual slowing.

The long hood of the E-type had jack-knifed upwards as though some giant had tried to fold the vehicle in two, and what was left of the front of the car was so badly disintegrated that I could not see one of its wheels. The windshield had shattered and granules of safety glass glinted on the floor of the forest. A thin rill of steam escaped from somewhere under the chassis and in the air there was a smell of gasoline and hot water.

Jeremy Tripp was slumped forward in his seat, chin resting almost on his chest, his head a few inches from the windshield frame. If he had not been held in place by his seat belt he would have collapsed against the steering wheel. He was wearing a white windbreaker and his left arm hung outside the car. His hand had been half torn from his wrist and there was blood over most of his sleeve and in great smears across the car door. There was blood on the side of his head as well, running from his ear and from his scalp, and though I could not see his face clearly it looked as though Gareth's brake tampering had done everything it was supposed to do.

As I approached the car I felt a visceral revulsion at the sight of so much blood and human damage, but there was a sense of resignation, too, that was almost peaceful. The thing was done. Questions of whether to go through with it or not, issues of right and wrong, opportunities to change my mind, had all been settled. It occurred to me that it might still be possible to resuscitate him. But I wasn't going to try. Despite all the sickening fear I'd felt in the lead up to this moment I was glad he was dead.

The car had traveled several yards through the forest's fringe before it hit the tree but it would still be visible from the road if anyone in a passing car happened to look the right way at the right moment. There had been no other traffic so far that night but that wouldn't last forever. I decided to hike through the forest until I reached the fire trail where Gareth had said he'd park when he came back. I didn't let myself think about what I'd do if he hadn't turned up by the time I got there.

I was about to skirt the car when Jeremy Tripp made a sound and the blood in my body turned to ice. The noise from his throat was wet and ragged, like a long, gulping breath through something too thick to swallow. For a moment I thought I might scream, but then my explanation-seeking mind kicked in and I told myself it was a death rattle, just the lungs letting go of the last of their air. Yet I knew I was wrong even before he sank back into his seat and turned his head and looked at me.

I don't know what other kind of injuries he might have had, but Jeremy Tripp had hit the top edge of the windshield frame, that much was obvious. His forehead had a deep trough running horizontally across it. It was not just a split in the skin. The skull had actually been pushed back into itself in a furrow about an inch deep. Below the wound Jeremy Tripp's eyebrows bulged grotesquely.

One of his eyes had burst but the other one held mine and blinked as his mouth twisted into a lopsided grin and he tried to speak.

"Johnny...."

The word came out slurred and malformed but it was unmistakable. He'd recognized me. I knew right then he wasn't going to die as a result of this car wreck. He would live and he would tell people I was there and I would spend the rest of my life in jail and Stan would end up ruined in some state-run institution

I stared at him for more than a minute as he grinned back at me and repeated my name. Then I dropped the backpack on the ground and took the length of pipe out of it.

His head had begun to droop forward again and was lolling toward his right shoulder. I pushed it back against the headrest and straightened it and when I had it set so that it would not move I lifted the pipe and lay it along the trench in his forehead. It fit snugly into the wound. I made a few slow practice passes with it. The windshield frame got in the way and it was difficult swinging from the left, so I had to turn his head toward me and then shift a little to the side to get a clear enough shot.

When I was ready I drew the pipe back one last time and took a breath. I'd planned to just breathe out and swing, to slam the pipe across his forehead, but my lungs would not release their air and my muscles would not perform the task my brain so desperately wanted to be finished with. I stood, like a batter frozen at the plate, fighting against myself to make this last dreadful commitment.

For a moment there was only the silent pounding of this struggle within me. Then, faintly, another sound started high up on the hill. At first I didn't realize what it was, but it grew louder and I breathed out and turned my head. Through the trees, already a quarter of the way down the hill, the headlights of a car were moving toward me.

When it got to the bend its driver would only have to glace to his left and he would see the short corridor the E-type had ploughed through the forest, and at the end of that corridor the car itself. And if he saw that he'd stop and get out and find Jeremy Tripp alive and sometime after that Jeremy Tripp would tell everyone about me.

I turned back to the E-type and tightened my grip on the pipe. But still I hesitated, paralyzed by my fear of becoming a killer.

Then Gareth was there. I hadn't heard him arrive but I saw him now, a few yards away on the other side of the car, raking his eyes across Jeremy Tripp, instantly taking in the fact that he wasn't dead, knowing what had to be done.

The car on the road was seconds away. There was no time for Gareth to cross to my side of the Jaguar and relieve me of this hideous task.

"Do it, Johnny! Do it!"

His words severed whatever shred of decency it was that had been holding me in check and I brought the pipe across in a clean, flat arc as hard as I could. It slammed perfectly into Jeremy Tripp's wound. His head bounced off the headrest and the arm hanging over the door flapped into the air. He made a loud sneezing noise and a spray of blood shot from his nostrils. Then he slumped forward against his seat belt and was still.

"Move! We have to go!"

Gareth waved urgently at me then ran back into the forest the way he'd come. I grabbed the backpack, skirted the car, and followed. A second later I almost fell over him. He was crouched behind a bush, peering intently toward the road. He pulled me down and put a finger to his lips and together we watched the headlights approach. They came down the last yards of the hill, slowing as they made the bend, then accelerating again as they passed where Jeremy Tripp's Jaguar had entered the trees. The car did not stop. It kept on downhill, passing where we hid, moving on into the night until its light was gone. Whoever was driving it had not seen what had happened to Jeremy Tripp.

Gareth grinned and put his hand up for a high-five. When I didn't respond he took the backpack from me, got a plastic garbage bag out of it, and held it open for me to drop the pipe into. He carefully rolled it up and returned it to the backpack. We waited another minute to make sure the car wasn't coming back, then we got up and walked as quickly as we could along the edge of the forest, far enough in from the road not to be seen, but close enough to use it as a guide to the fire trail where Gareth had parked.

We didn't speak until we were in the Jeep driving toward Back Town.

"Where were you?"

"It wasn't my fault, Johnny. I called him, I told him not to come for an hour. I can't help it if he got straight into his fucking car. Anyhow, it worked out okay."

"Except I had to do what you were supposed to."

"And you fucking held up good, man."

He gave me a solid, sincere look - there was even a trace of sympathy in it - but I couldn't help wondering just how long he'd been standing there on the other side of Jeremy Tripp's car before I noticed him. Or exactly what time he'd told Jeremy Tripp to get to the bogus meeting.

Back in Old Town Gareth parked behind my pickup. As I started to get out of the Jeep he stopped me.

"Johnny, we got a result tonight. He's not going to be fucking either of us up ever again and no one's going to think it was anything but an accident. Did you see the front of the car? There won't be enough of the brake lines left to examine properly even if anyone gets suspicious. He crashed, he banged his head, and he died. Don't think anything else, even to yourself. In a month or two it'll be like it never happened. Game plan now, dude, is we don't contact each other for the next two weeks, just to be on the safe side, okay? After that it's you, me, and Empty Mile, baby."

It wasn't until I was out of the Jeep that I remembered the backpack lying on the backseat. I felt my stomach twist inside me, but it was too late. Gareth had already pulled the door closed and locked it. I wrenched at the handle and hammered on the roof. Inside the car Gareth smiled and wound the window down an inch.

"You don't need to worry about a thing, Johnny. I'll take care of that stuff."

"I want the pipe."

He made an expression like he couldn't hear me and pulled away from the curb.

"Be cool, dude."

I watched him U-turn and drive along the street. Then I got into my pickup and sat without moving for a long time, cursing myself. My

313

fingerprints and Jeremy Tripp's blood. I couldn't have given Gareth a bigger threat to hold over me if I'd tried.

Marla was awake in bed when I got home, she sat with her back against the wall and her knees drawn up to her chest, as though preparing to receive some dreadful assault. I'd picked up a bottle of bourbon on my way through the kitchen and I sat next to her and drank and closed my eyes and then opened them again when I could no longer stand what I saw there.

For a long time Marla clung mutely to me and I felt how frightened she was that Jeremy Tripp's murder would reach into our future and destroy what little hope we had left for a normal life together. If we could have stayed silent forever, never speaking, never admitting or acknowledging what I had done, we would have - but horror demands its say and so, around mouthfuls of the coarse, burning whiskey, I told her about the night.

I told her how Jeremy Tripp had died and how Gareth now had a piece of pipe with my fingerprints on it. And as I spoke, as the bloody events were plucked from the fog of terror and made solid with words, a realization which had been born within me the moment Gareth lay down against Jeremy Tripp's car, but which I had been too fear-struck to face at the time, began to surface.

"My father's crash."

"What?" Marla, bound by thoughts of murder, was thrown by the change of subject.

"My father's crash was caused by a faulty brake line."

"So?"

"A *corroded* brake line."

"And Gareth put acid on Tripp's brakes."

"Exactly."

"But Ray's car was just old, there wasn't any acid on it. At least, you never said."

"They thought it was a faulty part. No one was looking for anything like that. Why would they? But two crashes? Two corroded brake lines? It's too similar not to be connected, don't you think?"

"But Ray didn't die. The crash didn't even hurt him. Stop it, Johnny. You've got to hold on to yourself. Tonight was enough. It's enough to deal with. Drink. Stop thinking."

Though Marla held me tightly to her, I was cold. Too cold to ever get warm again. What Gareth had said about the killing eventually being like it never happened would be true for him, I knew, but not for me. There was no hope of ever forgetting the weight of the pipe in my hands, the heft of it as it traveled through the air, the dull impact of it against Jeremy Tripp's skull. These things would never leave me.

Some sort of shivering physical reaction set in and I knew I had to bury it or be overwhelmed by it. So I drank faster, filling my glass by the harsh light of the overhead bulb, a light that seemed to flay everything it touched. I had one, then another, and another. It took a long time for the alcohol to take hold and when it did, when its warm tide finally started to blur the edges of thought, my tired mind drifted not to a blank oblivion, but to images of another road, of another car hurtling down a different hill. My father and I escaping unhurt, laughing. And later, as I finally fell asleep, a mechanic, holding out a corroded piece of brake line for inspection....

CHAPTER THIRTY-ONE

For the next two weeks I bought every newspaper I could get my hands on - the Oakridge Banner, the local Burton paper, even the day-old San Francisco Chronicle one of the shops in Oakridge sold.

The Banner carried a piece on Jeremy Tripp's death in one edition, the Burton paper had two articles over the course of the first week outlining the crash and later identifying the victim, but nothing afterwards. Neither of the papers called it anything but an accident - just another fatality on a difficult country road. The San Francisco Chronicle, of course, didn't mention it at all.

No police came to Empty Mile to question or arrest me. No rumors of foul play were raised on the local radio station, no one in town muttered that there was something odd about the crash. But I was so scared of being caught that I couldn't stop myself from grasping after a more concrete reassurance.

I figured that if the police had made anyone aware there was something suspicious about Tripp's death it would be his lover, Vivian. So, on the Monday of the second week after the crash, I drove into Oakridge and spoke to her at the Plantagion warehouse on the pretext of needing to borrow a few sacks of potting mix for Plantasaurus.

They'd cleaned up the warehouse after Stan's fire but there was still a damp burnt smell in the air and here and there, high up on the walls, I could see smears of soot they'd missed. Vivian was sitting behind the desk in the reception area and she looked bored. We made conversation and she told me she was finishing as manager at the end of the week.

One of the installation guys was going to take over and run the business until whoever inherited the estate decided otherwise.

"I was really only doing Jeremy a favor. Without him I have no reason to be here. I need my energy for other things."

"I read about the accident. What happened?"

She shrugged. "The usual story. He was driving too fast and lost control. Smashed his head to smithereens on the windshield. It would have been quick, at least."

"I'm sorry for your loss."

She turned down the corners of her mouth and shrugged. "Ach, it was an affair." After a pause she said, "Gareth called me as soon as he heard. He thought it might mean we would get back together. The child."

"You won't?"

"Good God, no. We have a conflict of interest in the road. I am close to convincing the council not to go ahead with it, you know. I have a lot of signatures."

I took several sacks of potting mix to justify my visit and left.

And that was it. The night in the forest, which I had been so sure would bring the world down around me, slid into the past without a ripple. It seemed impossible that the consequences of something as monstrous as killing a human being could be escaped, but that was just what happened, and Stan and Marla and I remained free to pursue our unhappy lives at Empty Mile.

Besides allaying my fear of arrest, my visit to the Plantagion warehouse prompted me to put Plantasaurus out of its misery. The business had failed beyond the point of recovery. We had lost too many customers, our savings were gone - eaten up covering living expenses and subsidizing the last throes of the business - and we still had not been able to afford to replenish our stock of plants. Now that I knew Plantagion was set to stay in business, at least for the foreseeable future, it would have been an idiocy to continue the struggle.

I sat Stan down and explained that we had to let it go. He'd known it was coming and just nodded and kept his eyes on the ground. Later that week we met Vivian at her warehouse and signed over our re-maining customers to Plantagion. They had been our enemy, one of the reasons our business had failed, and it was galling to have them bail us out of responsibilities we could no longer meet. But this way at least we avoided letting down those customers who'd stayed with us.

Stan was quiet as we sat with the lawyer Vivian had arranged and signed our names to various papers. He was silent, too, in the pickup on the way home and all I could think of to try and make him feel better was to talk up how the gold we were going to mine out of our riverbed would eclipse anything he'd dreamed of earning as a businessman.

It didn't seem to help much. Just before he got out of the pickup at Empty Mile he turned to me and said, "I know that, Johnny, but I *thought* of Plantasaurus. It was my idea. It came out of my brain."

Later that morning I called Bill Prentice and told him we would cancel our lease on the warehouse if he still wanted us to. With Jeremy Tripp gone he didn't have an immediate buyer for the garden cen-ter property anymore, but I guess he figured he was going to sell it sooner or later and that it would be easier to do so without tenants be-cause he sent a cancellation agreement over in a taxi that afternoon. I signed it and sent it back with the driver and the next day, Saturday, Stan and I went around to the warehouse and cleared out what little stuff we still had there. We left the keys inside the building and never went back.

With Plantasaurus closed down, Stan and I were free to concentrate on our buried river. On Sunday we took our pans and shovels and went down to the trees at the bottom of the meadow to see if we really were going to get rich.

We spent the first couple of hours digging dirt from the hole Stan had started previously and carting it to the edge of the river in buckets. The weather was cool but we were sweating by the time we'd accumulated a pile large enough to last the day and for a short time, before our shoulders and backs started to ache, it was a pleasant change to crouch with our pans at the edge of running water.

An experienced panner can get through a bit less than a cubic yard of dirt a day. By midday Stan and I together hadn't done anywhere near that, but we'd still liberated half a peanut butter jar of concentrates. It seemed we were indeed on the kind of untouched land that could make fairytale changes in lives. Like stories of lottery wins, or tourists picking up alluvial diamonds on a beach in Africa, we had one of those crazy, unearned chances at wealth. All we had to do was put dirt in a pan and wash it in the river.

The excitement of watching our jar fill steadily with black sand and gold dust began to rub off on Stan despite the emotional battering he'd taken over the last week. Though work on the river would never match the satisfaction a successful Plantasaurus might have brought him, the possibilities gold held for providing some sort of standing in society became more real to him as he held the jar and felt its weight and saw the swirls of yellow dust.

We broke for a lunch of sandwiches and Coke, sitting on the bank of the river with the sun in bright cool patches on the rocky ground about us. I ate and watched the river pass. It was a beautiful place on a beautiful day and it looked like we had money for the taking. I should have been able to rejoice in such good fortune, but I could not.

Three days after Tripp's crash I'd visited a lawyer in town and signed the papers that gave Gareth a one-third share of the Empty Mile land. This, the fact that the two-week no-contact period he'd imposed was going to expire the following day, and my feeling that he knew just as much about the gold at Empty Mile as I did, made it a safe bet that everything good which might have come from the buried river would soon be polluted by his presence.

Stan knew Jeremy Tripp was dead but he didn't know Gareth or I had had anything to do with it. As far as he was concerned it had been a road accident, pure and simple. To prepare him for the fact that Gareth would soon be a dark constant in our lives, though, I'd had to explain his share of the land - so I'd told Stan that it was the only way we could get the capital we needed to fully exploit the gold. He hadn't seemed too bothered and just shrugged and nodded as though what I'd said held little meaning for him.

We were panning again after lunch when the day's grace I thought we had suddenly evaporated and Gareth appeared at the edge of the trees.

"Hey, Johnboy, I figured you might be down here. Marvelous day for a spot of panning, what? I saw the hole you guys dug back there. Is that what you're working?" He moved down the bank to the water's edge. "What are you getting?"

Stan looked at me questioningly. I nodded and he held up the jar. "This is just one day."

Gareth took the jar and rolled it in his hands so that the concentrates separated and the grains of gold caught the light.

"One day? Jesus!"

Gareth threw a couple of handfuls of dirt into a pan and spent the next few minutes washing it intently at the edge of the river. When he was done he stood up and rubbed the tip of his finger through what he'd collected. He looked at me and smiled.

"Looks like I made a smart investment for a change."

I told Stan to keep panning and drew Gareth away from the river. We went into the trees, out of Stan's hearing. Gareth looked like he was about to start congratulating himself again but I cut him off before he could start.

"Let me ask you something. When, exactly, did you find out about the gold here?"

Gareth's happy face became deliberately dumb. "What, the stuff you guys are panning? Just then, when Stan showed it to me, of course."

"Bullshit!"

Gareth frowned and put his hands on his hips. "We're in bed together now, Johnny, so to speak. It's not going to do either of us any good to be antagonistic."

"What did you do with the pipe?"

"That dirty old thing all covered with blood? Not something you can just drop by the side of the road. I put it somewhere safe, don't worry."

"I want it."

"I bet you do. But I'm going to hang on to it for a while. You know what they say, money and friendship travel different paths. And it looks like there's going to be a whole shitload of money around here soon. We need something to make sure we stay together."

Stan and Gareth and I spent the next few hours panning. By the end of the afternoon our jar was full. Gareth said he had some mercury at his place and though we were tired from our work all of us wanted to find out how much gold we'd panned. We went up to the cabin and dumped our gear on the stoop. Marla was inside and must have heard us, but she didn't come out. As we drove away, Gareth in his Jeep, Stan and I in my pickup, I saw her behind the front window, her face haunted and pale, watching Gareth leave.

The lake at that time of day was softly lit by the tiring sun, and the shadows of trees back from the beach had begun their first dark tappings at the edge of the water. The scent of pine was strong as we walked along the path from the parking lot, as though the air, in cooling, was squeezing from itself essences that earlier in the day had been diluted by warmth and sunshine and blue sky.

I could hear David singing before Gareth opened the door of the bungalow, an unhappy drunken yodel against a background of the Eagles blasting from a stereo. Gareth looked at me ruefully.

"The council told us on Friday that the road isn't happening. Any further action on it has been 'postponed indefinitely.' Dad's pretty fucked up about it."

We went into the living room and found Gareth's father sitting in his wheelchair, head thrown back, howling the words to "Hotel California." He was unshaven and there was an open bottle on the floor beside him. His back was turned to us and Gareth had to grab the handles of his wheelchair and shake it before he realized we were there. The singing stopped abruptly and David reached out toward his son, his hands trembled and there was spilled liquor on the front of his shirt. Gareth bent and hugged him and turned off the stereo. David reached for the bottle but Gareth beat him to it and held it out of reach.

"Party's over."

"You're right about that!"

Stan stepped nervously closer to me. The movement caught David's eye.

"I'll tell you something, young fella, life'll fuck you in the ass as soon as look at you. You remember that. In fact it *likes* to fuck you in the ass."

Gareth put his hand on his father's shoulder.

"Dad, I told you it's going to be okay. We've got this other thing now, this land at Empty Mile, and you, me, Johnny, and Stan here, we're all going to be rich. You want to watch us mercury what we got today?"

David closed his eyes and shook his head slowly.

"No."

"Okay. I won't be long. Just try and relax, okay?"

Gareth headed out of the room for the barn. Stan followed him, glad to get away from the frightening drunk man. I was the last out. As I passed David he caught hold of my arm

"It's good you and Gareth are friends. He's always been a good son, a good boy.... But people don't seem to take to him too well. It's good that you like each other. Especially after your father and all."

"My father?"

"When he cut him out of that land of yours. Boy, that deal was all Gareth could talk about for weeks. The land, and how if they could somehow get it they were going to be rich, rich, rich. And then, boom, your father decides to up and go it alone. I've never seen Gareth so upset. Maybe things are turning out okay now, I don't know, but he almost went crazy back then."

I wanted to question David more about the relationship between my father and his son, but Gareth stuck his head through the doorway and asked if I was coming or what and I was forced to bite down on the explosion of understanding David's words had ignited within me and instead put on the expression of a man whose only thoughts were of gold and the money it could bring.

Placer gold, gold you can just dig out of a river, comes in particles of various size - sometimes flakes, sometimes grains, sometimes so fine the gold is known as flour gold. The smaller the particles of gold, the more difficult it is, using a pan alone, to fully separate them from the dirt in which they are found. The gold we'd dug out of Empty Mile was what would generally be called fine gold - grains a little smaller than grains of beach sand.

Panning works on the principle of specific gravity - the weight of something compared with the weight of water. Gold has a very high specific gravity and so in a pan of water it sinks to the bottom, allowing lighter material like soil and silica to be washed away. Black sand, though, which is made up of metallic minerals, also has a high specific gravity and tends to collect with the gold, making it difficult to separate the two with water alone.

One of the easiest ways to get down to pure gold from concentrates is mercury amalgamation. The chemicals needed can be bought from most prospector stores and the process is simple enough that it was used by miners during the Gold Rush.

When I entered the barn behind the bungalow Gareth had already dumped the contents of our jar into a steel pan and was drying them out over a portable electric hot plate. Stan was standing beside him watching intently, absently stroking the moth bag around his neck. He looked up as I walked in.

"Showtime, Johnny."

When the concentrates were dry Gareth spread them out on a large sheet of paper. From a drawer in the bench he took a cylinder-shaped magnet, covered it in Saran Wrap, and began dragging one end of it back and forth through the dark powder. Grains of black sand collected against it. Twice Gareth removed the plastic film and replaced it with a new piece.

Using a magnet to remove the magnetic elements of the black sand is a quick and easy first step, but black sand also contains non-magnetic elements which a magnet can't pick up.

Gareth tipped the remaining concentrates into a wide glass beaker. He put on clear plastic safety goggles and a pair of heavy rubber gloves, then he reached under the bench and brought up a half gallon ceramic flagon. He motioned Stan to move back.

"You don't want to get any of this on you."

Gareth unstoppered the flagon and slowly poured a clear liquid into the glass beaker until the concentrates were covered to a depth of about half an inch. Stan, made a little nervous by the intensity of the situation, looked over at me wide-eyed.

"We're in a mad scientist movie, Johnny."

Gareth chuckled as he carefully agitated the beaker. "Nitric acid, dude. Spill it on the floor, it'll eat a hole to China."

"Yikes!" Stan moved another step away.

"The grains of gold in here are covered with all sorts of shit - pine oil from the trees, magnesium, iron sulfide.... I'm just cleaning them up before we use the mercury."

Gareth rocked the beaker gently a little while longer then drained the acid into an empty glass bottle and rinsed the concentrates several times with water from a sink in the corner of the barn. He filled a plastic milk jug with water and brought it back with the beaker to the bench.

"Stage two. Mercury, please, nurse."

He nodded at a stoppered glass container under the bench. Stan handed it to him like it was a bomb. Gareth opened it and poured the shiny liquid metal onto the concentrates in the beaker. Then he poured in water from the milk jug and began swirling the beaker around, using the motion of the water to mix the mercury and the concentrates together.

I'd seen my father go through this process several times and I knew that one of the properties of mercury is that it will absorb gold. The blob of mercury/gold compound that results is called amalgam and can be easily lifted from the remaining non-gold concentrates.

When he was done, Gareth used an old spoon to remove the amalgam from the beaker. Without thinking, Stan and I both moved a little closer. This was magic. This was alchemy. We were now looking at a firm, dull gray lump that would soon release a pure metal we could sell for money

The next step had to be conducted outside because of the toxic fumes it would generate. We used a long extension cord and set the hot plate up on a stool several yards beyond the barn's entrance. Gareth placed a Pyrex dish about two-thirds full of nitric acid on the hot plate and into this lowered the lump of amalgam. Almost immediately fumes began to rise from the surface of the acid and I had to shoo Stan back so that he didn't inhale them. Gareth turned the hot plate on and all three of us retreated to the entrance of the barn to let the solution boil away the mercury.

After five minutes, Gareth pulled the extension cord out of its wall socket and once the acid had cooled a little we went back out and watched as he used a pair of tongs to lift out our gold.

It would have fit the occasion, our first reduction of dirt to precious metal, if the gold Gareth held before us had been bright and solid and shiny, but mercury amalgamation yields what is known as sponge gold, gold that is the color of rust and honeycombed with holes where the mercury has been dissolved by the acid. It would take heat from a blowtorch or gas burner to bring out its true color and luster.

Inside the barn again, we rinsed the gold and weighed it. When the needle of the scales came to rest we were suddenly silent. It took almost a minute before Gareth uttered a bemused "Jesus." The needle of the scales had stopped a little past the six-ounce mark. At the current price of over nine hundred dollars an ounce we'd made more than five thousand dollars for one day's work.

We spent a little while passing the lump between ourselves, feeling its weight, holding it up to the light. But now that it had been refined and there was nothing more to distract us, the day's labor began to take its toll. I was shattered and Stan looked dead on his feet. We went out to the pickup, leaving Gareth in the barn with the gold. He wanted to keep it to show his father and I couldn't be bothered arguing. We had the whole river to dig up, after all.

Stan dozed most of the way back to Empty Mile and when we got there I had to shake him to get him out of the pickup. He muttered something about going over to see Rosie, but instead plodded into the cabin still only half awake.

It was after nine o'clock but Marla had waited to eat with us. I told her about our day, about the five thousand dollars we'd panned, how it looked like the buried river was going to make us rich. Her responses didn't rise above the noncommittal and try as I might to infect her with some enthusiasm for a gold-dusted future she did little more than nod occasionally. Stan shoveled in his food, head down, too tired to speak. He got up when he was done, gave both of us a kiss, and stumbled off to his room.

When he'd gone, Marla put her fork down and said tiredly, "This is the start, isn't it?"

"Of Gareth? Yeah."

"I don't know how long I can take it, Johnny."

"Can't you just focus on the money?"

"I don't give a shit about the money. There isn't enough of it on the planet to make Gareth bearable. Don't you understand what hell this is going to be for me?"

"What do you want me to do? He owns a third of the land now, I can't stop him from coming here. And he's got that fucking pipe."

"We could move away."

"Marla, we need that money. I have nothing left. Stan has nothing left. I'm not saying we have to dig up every last ounce, but we need something at least."

Marla was quiet for a long time. Her hands were together in front of her on the table and her fingers twined anxiously. She watched them as though they were something she had no control over. Eventually she spoke.

"You know what I dream about, Johnny? I dream about going somewhere far away. To the East Coast, maybe. Somewhere we can just live and be together and start again and nothing can spoil it. Sometimes I think that's the only way we'll ever have a chance."

Later we moved to sit on the couch, and as we watched the fire burn I told her what I'd learned from David that evening - that Gareth and my father had planned to buy Empty Mile together, that for some reason they'd fallen out, and that my father had then bought the land by himself.

Marla shrugged, unimpressed. "Small town intrigue - gotta love it."

"It's more than that. Way more. Think how Gareth would have reacted. He'd done all this investigating, he was expecting a big payoff, then my father snatches it away from him. He would have freaked. He would have wanted revenge. What if he decided to get that revenge by making Pat kill herself? What if that was his reason for making the video? It makes sense. After Patricia and Bill, the only other person who could possibly be hurt by it was my father."

"Pretty horrific revenge."

"Gareth's a pretty horrific person."

"But he already told you he made it to blackmail Bill. To force him to do something about the road to the lake."

"That was just smoke. He wanted me to sell him Empty Mile, for Christ's sake. He's not going to tell me he made it to attack my father."

"This is about Ray's crash again, isn't it? The whole brakes thing. They were fucked up on Ray's car, they were fucked up on Tripp's car. Now you've got an argument between Ray and Gareth over land."

"Well, fuck, if we accept that Gareth made a video designed to get Pat to kill herself, it's not much of a stretch to figure he could have tampered with my father's brakes. And if he did that, then maybe he tried again some other way and actually ended up killing him."

Marla rolled her eyes. "This is getting a bit much, Johnny."

"What do you mean?"

"Maybe the cars are connected, maybe they're not, I don't know. But I can't see why Gareth would kill Ray. You said he made the video to punish Ray for cutting him out of the land. Okay. Pat killed herself, Ray's punished big time - Gareth's successful. He's *successful*, he's achieved his goal. He wouldn't need to kill him. There's no reason for it. And whatever else he is, Gareth's a guy who usually has a reason for what he does."

Marla's logic was sound and I had nothing to contradict it with. Why would Gareth kill my father? If he'd had his revenge with Pat, why would he bother? I had no answer.

That night, however, the question of who was right and who was wrong didn't bother me nearly as much as the quality of Marla's dismissal. She had been so immediate, so adamant in her rejection of my theory, that although we sat pressed against each other on a comfortable couch in front of a fire, I felt suddenly very much alone.

Given her feelings toward Gareth, I'd expected her to be more than receptive to the idea that he had been the cause of my father's disappearance. Hating him so much, any halfway logical explanation should have provoked a knee-jerk reaction of support, and I couldn't shake the feeling that there was something less than genuine about her refusal to agree with me.

CHAPTER THIRTY-TWO

O ur gold mining operation moved ahead swiftly. Gareth raised
a loan against his cabins and we hired a contractor in Burton
to bring in bulldozers and a gang of men. When they were done, we
were left with a strip of torn earth twenty yards wide and two hundred
yards long. On each side of this the stronger, older trees that bordered the course of our hidden river had been left untouched and
their dark trunks formed walls which made the space feel like a vast
natural cathedral.

The debris from the ground-clearing was stacked in house-sized
piles along the bottom of the meadow. Looking down from the
cabin, these mounds seemed ominous and ragged, as though they
were the result of preparations for some primitive battle soon to be
commenced.

We had a backhoe delivered and Gareth, who had used one before to dig drainage ditches around his cabins, trundled it through a
space in the trees and parked it in the center of the cleared ground.
It seemed as good a place as any to begin the process of making ourselves rich.

Throughout these preparations Gareth left Marla alone, coming
to Empty Mile only to check on the progress of the contractors, entering our cabin only when she was out at work. The first day we started
mining, though, this hands-off approach changed.

He arrived shortly after the sun had cleared the surrounding hills
and the dew in the meadow was beginning to turn to a thin low-cling-
ing mist. Marla had not yet left for the day, so when I heard Gareth's

Jeep pull up I went outside with Stan and our equipment in the hope that we'd be able to head him off and go straight down to the river.

But Gareth had other ideas. He wanted to have breakfast with us. When I told him it was out of the question he smiled at me and mimed swinging a piece of pipe. There was nothing I could do. We went back into the cabin and sat around the table. Stan ate a second bowl of cereal. Gareth drank coffee and ate toast with exaggerated relish.

As Marla moved from one part of the cabin to another in her preparations for work, he followed her closely with his eyes, trying to engage her in conversation whenever he could. She refused to answer him and did her best to pretend he wasn't there, but I could tell by the tight lines of her face and the high color in her cheeks that it was a struggle for her. She left without eating anything or saying goodbye. As she went through the front door I saw something in Gareth's eyes. It was only there a moment, but I caught it nevertheless - a wounded tenderness, a longing for something that had been lost forever.

A little while later Stan, Gareth, and I walked down the meadow and through the screen of trees to where the backhoe waited, cold and dewy from its night outdoors. Gareth slapped the engine cowling then put his hands on his hips and turned to us like we were all part of a gang.

"This is it, guys. Let's make it happen."

Our plan was to use the backhoe to clear the three or four feet of soil that had built up over the old riverbed and then to excavate the material beneath it. We had two sluices, one from my father's cache of equipment, one supplied by Gareth; these were to be our primary means of processing the gold-bearing sand and gravel.

A sluice is basically a long rectangular box open at both ends. On its floor, running horizontally across it, are a series of inch-high bars called riffles. The sluice is placed deep enough at the edge of a river so that the base of it is submerged but its walls rise a couple of inches above the water. Dirt is fed into the upstream end and the current of the water washes it along the length of the sluice. As it passes from one end to the other, the heavier material settles to the bottom of the box where it is caught by the riffles, while the mud and sand are washed out of the other end and into the river.

Every so often the sluice is taken out of the water and whatever has collected against the riffles is knocked off into a bucket. This material is then further refined by panning. The result is concentrates - the same mixture of black sand and grains of gold we had refined by mercury amalgamation in Gareth's barn.

Running a sluice requires a certain amount of skill and a lot of attention. Dirt has to be fed in at just the right rate or the sluice becomes overloaded, and stones and other larger pieces of debris have to be constantly picked out by hand. But the amount of dirt that can be processed is exponentially larger than by using a pan alone, and if there is more than one person operating the sluice - one to feed it and one to pick out debris - the process goes even faster.

Because of his experience, Gareth was going to run the backhoe and build up a stock of riverbed material while Stan and I concentrated on the sluicing. That first morning, though, Gareth was too anxious to see what results we'd get to pile up more than a couple of hundred pounds of gravel and sand on the riverbank before stopping and joining us at the sluices.

We worked without speaking. Carrying dirt in large plastic buckets, using shovels to sift it into the sluices, watching carefully as the water turned muddy, letting it clear again so we could see the black sand building against the riffles, moving the sluice a little side to side to let the light catch flecks of gold, reaching beneath the water to touch them with a fingertip....

Toward the end of the afternoon, while it was still fully light, we put the concentrates we'd collected in a plastic container. For a while the three of us just stood around and looked at it, ticking off in our minds all the future purchases this grubby metallic sand represented. Then we carried it up the meadow and put it in the shed at the back of the cabin. Our first day was over.

Stan went off to see Rosie. Gareth climbed into his Jeep and spoke to me through the window before he drove away.

"Some things can make everything else all right, just wipe the slate clean, don't you think? All my shit with the road to the lake, all your shit with Tripp - doesn't mean much now, huh?"

"Maybe we should split what we get each day. I don't want you accusing us of stealing."

"I trust you, Johnboy. Why wouldn't I?" He winked and started his car. "See you tomorrow. I'm looking forward to breakfast. Maybe Marla will join us this time."

Life quickly fell into a routine for Stan and Gareth and me - digging dirt and sluicing it, panning it down and then, every few days, amalgamating it with mercury. It was boring, tiring, backbreaking work that raised blisters on our hands and waterlogged our feet, but the richness of the dirt we were mining overrode our fatigue so that we worked in an avaricious trance where the filling of our bucket each day with black sand did not calm us with its promise of certain wealth but drove us on to want more and more and more. It was as though we became lost each morning and only regained ourselves when we threw down our tools at the end of the afternoon and walked away from the earth we had torn up and the river we had muddied.

Being wet every day forced Stan to change his approach to his moths. Instead of keeping them in a pouch around his neck he put them, while he was working, in a large glass jar which he stood on a nearby rock. The moths were always dying but Stan didn't seem to care. He called the jar his power generator and often during the day would touch it and hold it up and breathe deeply with the glass pressed against his forehead.

All three of us stopped shaving, and as any clothes became soaked and filthy after five minutes of work, we tended, at the river, to wear the same things day after day without washing them. Sometimes Stan would bring his cassette player with him and run it on batteries and we would work to the sound of his mellow dance music, but mostly there was just the sound of water splashing, shovels going into dirt, and at intervals through the day the grind of the backhoe's diesel engine.

Most days we took at least five ounces of gold from our hidden river. There were times when the content of the dirt dropped, when we found ourselves with nothing in our sluices after several hours work, but then all that was needed was for Gareth to direct his backhoe more to the left or the right and the gold always returned. Gradually, in this way, we were able to define the banks of the old river and get some idea of the distribution of gold along its length. And the better our picture of the river became, the more consistent our returns were.

We worked the first ten days straight through. After that we were exhausted and we took a day off to melt down the gold we had so far acquired in a crucible at Gareth's place and take it to the assayer in Burton. We walked out of the Minco office with a check for a little more than forty thousand dollars. We'd sold them around fifty-five ounces, but there was a commission fee plus our gold contained a small percentage of silver. This brought the per-ounce price down a little and we also incurred a charge for the further refining that would be necessary to turn it into gold that fell into the standard purity range of between .995 and .999.

None of this was unexpected and we rode back to Oakridge with Gareth smugly proclaiming that at this rate each of us would earn a quarter of a million dollars in a year. While he was on this high I got him to agree to confining our workdays to Monday to Friday, with the weekends off. This was necessary anyhow if we were going to last the distance, but it also meant Marla would at least be spared him two days a week.

But two days a week for Marla was, by then, nowhere near enough. Since we'd started mining she'd descended rapidly into a state of outright distress. When Gareth was anywhere on the property she withdrew completely, sequestering herself in our bedroom, coming out only for brief dashes to the kitchen or bathroom or to run for her car.

In fact, during the same period, the stresses at play on all elements of life at Empty Mile had grown greater and more destructive and it seemed now only a matter of time before everything must surely fall to pieces - before Marla went berserk, or Stan became lost to a world of moths and power, or I could no longer hold myself back from confronting Gareth over my father's disappearance.

The first cracks began to show on a Sunday in November when Marla and I were sitting on the couch in front of the fire drinking coffee and Bill Prentice picked up his phone and called me.

I hadn't heard from him since I'd canceled the lease on the Plantasaurus warehouse, and the time during which we'd had no contact seemed to have drained some of the burning anger he had previously directed toward me. Perhaps he now believed Gareth was to blame for the video. I had no way of knowing. But his voice over the phone was measured and tiredly business-like, as though he had become resigned to a life he knew could never be set back on course. He began without small talk.

"The lawyers who administered my wife's investments have recently supplied me with her financial records."

"Okay."

"They show a payment to her from your father. Do you know anything about it?"

"No."

"That's hard to believe. He wasn't a rich man and this is a lot of money. A quarter of a million dollars."

"Must be a mistake, he didn't have anywhere near that much."

As I spoke, however, it dawned on me that he had indeed had that much money. The remortgaging of our house had given him exactly that amount. And I knew what he'd spent that money on. When I spoke again I had to work to stop my voice from shaking.

"Can I ask you a question? Does the name Simba Inc. mean anything to you?"

"Patricia had family wealth, she administered her assets through a business entity of that name. What about it?"

"Do you know what assets she had, exactly?"

"Some of them, not all. Her money was always very much her own. She didn't discuss it with me. Her will left whatever she had under that company to her brother. I had no visibility of it. I have no idea where it's gone now that he's dead too. How do you know about Simba?"

"You know that I live outside Oakridge now?"

"I don't know anything about you."

"I have some land at a place called Empty Mile. My father bought it just before he disappeared. Before Pat died. The seller is listed on the papers as Simba Inc. It's the only thing the payment could be for."

"Oh...." There was a long pause and a heavy, slowly let out breath, and then, quietly, "Lovers *and* business partners."

"As far as I know there was just that one deal."

Bill made a small choking noise.

"Bill, I'm sorry, but there's something else I have to ask you."

He didn't say anything, but he stayed on the line.

"The video, the one Patricia was watching. Was that sent to you, like addressed to you, and Pat somehow found it?"

Bill spoke with a furious exactness. "The first time I saw that disk, Patricia was lying dead in our bedroom. I don't know how she got it, but it wasn't through me."

He hung up and in the dark, empty silence of the phone against my ear I heard another piece of Bill Prentice's soul scream and die. For me, though, there was a sunburst of sudden understanding.

"I know what the fucking video's about!"

Marla sighed. "Oh Christ...."

"It wasn't just to hurt my father. There's more to it than that. Gareth made it to try and stop my father from getting this land."

I told Marla what I had just learned, that Patricia Prentice had been Empty Mile's previous owner and that the video had to have been sent straight to her, not to Bill.

"You told me that Pat hated Gareth because he ran her dog over, right? That means after my father severed his relationship with him, Gareth didn't have a hope in hell of buying Empty Mile and getting his hands on the gold, even if he had the money. Pat wouldn't have given him the time of day, let alone sold him anything. So what would he do? His first thought would be, if he couldn't have it, then he was going to make damn sure my father couldn't either. So he makes a video which he knows has a good chance of pushing an already suicidal woman over the edge. If she's dead she can't sell the land."

"But Ray still bought it."

"Yeah, but only because he closed the deal before Gareth could get the video together."

"Jesus, I'm so tired of this."

"What are you talking about? This isn't something you can be tired of. It's not just Pat and the video and the fact that we got sucked into some failed plan of Gareth's. This gives Gareth a reason for killing my father."

"Johnny, please-"

"Listen to me. If Pat was just a way to hurt my father for cutting Gareth out of the land deal, some kind of revenge after the fact, then, like you said, when she died Gareth had achieved his objective and he had no reason to do anything else. But if the aim was to stop my father getting the land in the first place, to fuck up the deal before it happened, then Gareth had failed. And if that was the case, then the only way to make things right, to stop my father from benefiting from the gold even though he now had the land, would have been to kill him. And you know what? I think my father knew. He'd spent enough time with Gareth to know what he was capable of, and after we had that crash I think he saw the writing on the wall. That's why he put the land in my name, not because of any bogus accountant. He knew Gareth was after him."

Marla leaned forward, put her elbows on her knees, and ran her fingers through her hair. She let out a long breath.

"I can't do this anymore. I can't go through this endless rehashing of why Gareth did this, or why Gareth did that. We either accept that he's an animal and try to live with what he did to Pat and what he maybe did to Ray, or...." She lifted her head and fixed her eyes on me. "Or we talk about killing him."

We were both silent for a long time. Eventually she spoke again.

"Well, are we going to?"

"Going to what?"

"Talk about killing him."

"Jesus, Marla, please...."

"It would be for the best, Johnny. It really would."

CHAPTER THIRTY-THREE

For the rest of that Sunday the idea that Gareth had killed my father grew inside me like a vicious pearl. It seemed to fit everything I knew. It made sense of my father's disappearance, something I had always felt was completely out of character for the kind of man he'd been. And, knowing the violence that lay hidden in Gareth, it was certainly a possible response to the loss of what he must have seen as a way to save his father and himself from their failing cabins at the lake.

He'd had no compunction about pushing Patricia Prentice to suicide and he'd arranged Jeremy Tripp's death. What was to say he hadn't done the same with my father? But of course I had no proof, no indisputable item or event that could settle the matter one way or the other. And it was this lack of confirmation, this knowing but not knowing, that haunted me and ruined my sleep so that when Monday came I was primed and set to explode.

The weather was bad that morning and Stan had a cold and did not come down to the river. A fine misting rain hung in the air, collecting on the leaves of the trees, dripping, turning the surface of the river milky. Gareth and I were soaked in the first five minutes and we worked with our heads down, cold, saying little to each other.

He was beside me at the sluice and seeing him there, so close, with what I assumed was a dreadful knowledge hidden inside his head, but acting as though he had nothing more on his mind than soldiering through an honest day's work, the rage within me boiled over and I threw a shovel of dirt in his face.

Gareth recoiled, spluttering and blinking, trying to clear his eyes, calling me an idiot. I grabbed him by the front of his jacket and threw him backwards into the river. He went under and came up and for a moment just sat there in the shallows, face now washed clean, staring up at me, his mouth working with the effort of figuring out what was going on. I thought I might jump on him, lock my hands around his throat and force him under the water until he was limp and dead, but then he moved and the grip of my rage loosened.

He climbed out of the river and we faced each other on the bank. I expected to see anger in his face, perhaps a quickly rising threat to go running to the police about Jeremy Tripp. But there was only shock and a hurt confusion, as though I had broken some unspoken code that existed between us.

"Jesus, dude, why did you do that?"

"The video."

"The video?"

"The disk of me and Marla, you asshole. You didn't send it to Bill. You sent it straight to Pat. And it didn't have anything at all to do with the road to the lake."

"If you say so."

"Don't fuck with me. I know it was Pat who sold the land to my father. The video was supposed to stop the sale, wasn't it? It was supposed to take her out before he had a chance to buy it."

Gareth looked consideringly at me, then seemed to come to some decision.

"You want to know about the video? All right. The whole thing was a fucking waste of time anyway."

He turned and walked to the screen of trees that bordered the river. I followed him and we found partial shelter under the branches of a fir. Gareth squatted on the wet ground, he motioned for me to do the same but I stayed standing.

"Jesus, come on, Johnny, I'll tell you whatever you want to know."

For a moment I didn't move, then I gave up and squatted facing him.

Gareth nodded. "Good. Okay. Let me ask you first, how did you find out about the gold here? Did Ray tell you?"

"I figured it out after he disappeared."

"The journal at that old lady's house, the aerial photo-"

"The lecture at the Elephant Society about rivers changing course.... Pretty much the way you and he did."

"The difference being that Ray and I were together every step of the way. We got friendly because we were both into prospecting. We came across the journal together and then the photo. We took it from there. The thing you have to understand is that right from the start discovering the gold was something Ray and I did together. He didn't have dibs on it. The plan was we were going to buy the place together and both get rich. Only Daddy didn't stick to the plan."

"Probably when he realized what a psycho you are."

Gareth swallowed and, shockingly, just for an instant, his eyes filled with tears. "Do you want the story or not?"

I nodded. Gareth blinked and cleared his throat.

"Once we'd figured out about the land, we had to find out who owned it so we could make them an offer. We went to the deed office at the town hall - turns out the land's owned by some holding company who won't even discuss it with us. We think we're fucked. But then, guess what? Ray's been banging Patricia Prentice for months. He happens to mention he's interested in the land at Empty Mile and, bingo, turns out Pattycake owns it. Instantly, instead of *us* being fucked, *I'm* the one who's fucked. One, because Ray suddenly has all the power. He's obviously going to get preferential treatment - I mean, he's fucking her, right? And two, she hates my guts because - how pathetic is this? - I ran her dog over like a year ago, so I can't be part of any deal he arranges. At this point Ray's all, yeah, yeah, don't worry, I'll do the deal and then we'll split it afterwards. But I knew right then he couldn't stop thinking about what it would be like to have all that money for himself. I could see it on his face. What brought things to a head, or at least the way your father played it, was Marla. While we'd been getting to know each other I'd told him about my hookers, Marla included. And you know, it was weird, but he didn't say shit about it then. Just when he held all the cards on the land deal, though, he started getting all pissy and moral and told me I had to leave her alone. His story was that he didn't want you to come home and find out your old girlfriend was a whore. I told him to fuck off, of course. Stupid in a way because it gave him just the excuse he needed to cut me out of the Empty Mile deal. But you know what? Even without Marla he would have done it. He smelled that money and he was hooked."

The air was still full of rain. It dripped from the branches above us, tapping out a rhythm that made a wall against the rest of the world. Gareth picked up a twig and began poking it into the muddy ground.

"When I saw the way things were going, I decided if Ray was going to treat me like that then I was going to fuck the deal up for him. And it was kind of fitting that Marla gave me the idea of how to do it. She was friends with Patty and poor Patty was having trouble sleeping. Marla wanted me to get some weed for her, but I figured she had to be on antidepressants so I gave her a whole shitload of Halcion instead. As you know, I'm no stranger to what can happen when you mix benzodiazepines with acute depression. A few weeks later you and Marla were kind enough to star in my video. On top of Pat already having tried to kill herself a bunch of times it seemed to me that a little extra medication and watching her husband doing something nice and disgusting might very well be the final straw she needed to make a proper job of it."

"But you couldn't have known for sure."

Gareth shrugged. "Nothing's ever for sure, Johnny, but it was worth trying. By the time I got things together, though, Ray had already closed the deal. Of course I didn't know that when I sent Pattycake the disk because Ray and I weren't speaking a whole lot by then."

"So Pat dies and Bill is fucked forever and it was all for nothing."

"Like I said, big waste of time."

"That must have made you pretty mad. I bet after that, you couldn't stand the sight of Ray."

Gareth narrowed his eyes.

"Careful there, Johnboy. That sounds a little bit like an accusation."

"You know my father had a car crash just a couple of days after Pat died?"

Gareth shook his head and frowned. "Didn't hear about that."

"No? You know what caused it? A corroded brake line."

"Oh, Jesus, Johnny, come on! Because I did Tripp that way?"

"And it wasn't long after that, that he disappeared."

"Why would I do anything to Ray? What would I get out of it? It wasn't like the land would pass to me. Don't go looking for skeletons where there aren't any. We're sitting pretty. We've got the land, we're going to be rich. Just stay in line while we get the gold, and a couple of years from now it's sayonara, dude - we all go our separate ways."

Gareth looked out through the trees at the rain-stippled river. He threw the twig he'd been playing with away and stood up.

"Might as well forget it for today, this isn't going to let up."

After Gareth had gone I went up to the cabin and lit a fire. Stan came out of his bedroom wearing his Captain America suit and we sat in front of the fire and listened to the rain on the roof.

Stan sprawled in his chair and tipped moths out of the pouch around his neck and watched them crawl jerkily over the surface of his belly. They were too damaged to fly and one or two of them weren't moving at all. He touched them with his finger and sighed.

"Keeping the power coming across makes me tired out."

After a while he pushed the moths back into the pouch and sat up straighter.

"I have to marry Rosie soon."

He had a small notebook with him in which he kept a tally of the gold money he'd deposited in his bank account. He leaned forward over it now, running his thumb down the column of pencil-written figures, staring at them morosely, as though they somehow failed to convey the meaning he expected to find in them.

"You have a lot of money, Stan. You're going to have a lot more."

"I know."

"More than you'd ever have made from Plantasaurus."

"Yeah."

Though he had worked hard at the river throughout our mining, and though his spirits had lifted enough to share in the reflex enthusiasm any person would feel at acquiring wealth, I knew that the money didn't mean much to him. He had more in the bank than many families ever saved, but nothing else had really changed. He was still Stan, he was still the fat guy with heavy glasses who was treated in town with the overly careful attention usually reserved for children. Gold had not brought about the kind of magical transformation he had hoped for from Plantasaurus.

The only thing he had left now, the only thing of any real emotional worth, was Rosie. It seemed to me that he felt marrying her was his last chance to participate in at least some part of the mainstream world. I had previously seen such a move as fraught with potential sadness, but there wasn't much else I could give him - Plantasaurus had failed, and the gold, of itself, was meaningless to him. So now I embraced the idea of his marriage. It was the only thing I could contribute to that might claw back some happiness for him.

For half an hour we talked about it and Stan came alive. The cold he'd had that morning was already clearing and he stood up and moved around the room, chattering about all the things he and Rosie would do together, elated now that he had my support. And because I wanted my support to be real for him, because I really did want his world to change, I took him into Oakridge that afternoon and helped him buy an engagement ring and two wedding rings from a jewelry store in Old Town.

That evening was a happy affair. Stan went over to Rosie's with the engagement ring held tightly in his hand and when he came back he had Rosie and Millicent with him and Rosie was wearing the ring. Marla fussed over Rosie and made her hold her hand out so the diamond would flash in the light. Rosie tolerated the attention with her head bent as always and her arms limp and straight at her sides, but every now and then a small wondering smile played at the corners of her mouth and it was hard not to think that on this day, at least, she felt herself to be lucky.

Millicent drank wine with Marla and me, and later we all had dinner together. Stan and Rosie held hands under the table and we had the fire and candles, and the lights were off so that the night became a series of glowing frescoes. And I was there at last, after so many years away. I was with my brother when something important and good was happening to him. Across the plates and glasses his face was luminous with happiness and I saw that he had, if only for those fire-lit hours, reached a point where he felt as good as everyone else, where the concept of difference had ceased to exist.

Around ten o'clock Millicent and Rosie went home. It wasn't unusual for Stan to spend the night at Rosie's, but now that marriage was certain he took himself off to his own bed full of high-minded notions of chivalry.

Marla and I sat near the fire and watched it burn down to a bed of coals. Though she had engaged in the evening I knew it had been a struggle for her and now, with everyone gone, a bleak unhappiness claimed her again and she felt dull and lethargic in my arms. I told her about my confrontation with Gareth earlier that day, about how he'd admitted that Pat's suicide was an attempt to stop my father acquiring the Empty Mile land.

"But he wouldn't admit to killing him."

"Did you expect him to?"

"I guess not."

"Did he say anything about it at all?"

"No. What do you mean? What would he say?"

Marla shook her head and didn't answer. After a moment she stood up and pulled me into our bedroom. She opened a drawer in her dresser, pushed aside a pile of her underwear, and took out something wrapped in a cloth. She laid the bundle on the bed and opened it carefully.

The gun was an ugly black thing. It lay against its cloth like some deadly reptile, a dangerous presence that drew too much of the room's light to itself.

Marla waited for my reaction, looking eager and frightened at the same time.

"I got it today."

"A gun? Jesus, Marla, what were you thinking?"

The tense energy of a second before drained from her and she was suddenly overcome with despair.

"I can't stand it anymore, Johnny. Gareth being here every day, in our world, coming into our fucking house for Christ's sake. Looking at me all the time.... I can't live with it. I can't!"

She cast her eyes about the room as though searching for help, then picked up the gun and held it out to me with both hands.

"We can use this, Johnny. For Ray. For ourselves. He deserves it."

"Marla, come on! What do you think we are? We're not fucking killers."

"Isn't that just what we are? Jeremy Tripp didn't pass away in his sleep. You did it. And I know about it. Pretty hard not to call that murder."

"Walking up to someone and shooting them is a bit different."

"How?"

"Fuck, Marla, this is insane. I can't believe we're even talking about it."

"Johnny, he has to go."

"So we shoot him and spend the rest of our lives in jail. Great plan."

"You got away with Jeremy Tripp."

"Jesus Christ, stop it!"

From the open doorway behind us there was a shuffling of slippered feet and then Stan's drowsy voice.

"Why are you guys yelling? Oh-"

I turned to see him standing there, transfixed, staring at the gun Marla was now holding loosely in front of her.

"Wow, you got a gun! Can I see?"

Marla turned quickly and thrust the gun back into her underwear drawer. Stan's eyes tracked the weapon as it moved.

I took him by the arm and steered him out of the room, back along the short corridor to his own bedroom. He'd used his Superman costume as pajamas and the cape was twisted over his shoulder and hung down across the top of his belly.

"How come you got a gun, Johnny?"

"Marla thought we should have one, living all the way out here. She made a mistake."

"Tomorrow, can I shoot it?"

"No one's going to be using that gun, Stan. Just forget you saw it."

"But it would be so awesome. We could pretend we were cops. We could shoot cans and stuff."

"I'm not joking, Stan. Forget about it."

Stan groaned and trundled into his room. I shut the door behind him and went back to Marla. She had undressed and was lying beneath the covers of the bed.

"I meant it when I said he has to go, Johnny."

"I figured that from the gun."

Marla threw her arm across her face. "I can't stand it...."

She moaned the phrase to herself several times, then stopped abruptly, flung off the covers, and reached under the bed for her cane. She held it out to me. When I didn't move, she shook it violently.

"Do it."

"Marla, I-"

"Do it! Do it, Johnny!"

"Marla, why do you feel so bad? I don't understand-"

But Marla wasn't in the mood to help me understand anything that night and screamed at me from the bed, "Just fucking do it!"

So I took the cane and raised it up and brought it down across her naked back. Her body clenched. One of her fingernails broke against the fabric of the mattress. Almost immediately a red welt rose on her pale skin. She grunted through clenched teeth. And I raised the cane again.

Later, next to her in bed as she slept, I knew that she was slipping away from me. If Gareth wasn't dealt with soon she would be gone, her own survival would demand it. But if I couldn't kill him there was only one way to save our relationship - leave Empty Mile. We could do it now. I had enough money to travel across the country, to rent a house in the East as Marla had said she wanted, to start looking for work, to rebuild our lives.

But there was Stan. The trauma of moving again would be more than he could bear, and something he would refuse to do now any-way because of Rosie. And if I could not take him with us then how could I possibly leave?

In the darkness of the bedroom there seemed to be no solution, and in the end my tired mind gave up and turned instead to some-thing Gareth had told me earlier that day - that my father had de-manded he stop pimping Marla so that I would not be hurt on my return to Oakridge.

It would have better fit the picture I had of my father if this had been nothing more than an excuse, a step in his process of cutting Gareth out of the Empty Mile land. But by that time he already had everything he needed to go it alone. He had enough money from remortgaging our house, he knew about the possibility of gold on the land, and, most importantly, he had exclusive access to Patricia Prentice. Why would he need to manufacture a reason for falling out with Gareth?

It seemed unavoidable, then, that he had acted simply out of love for me, that he really had just been trying to spare me some pain. It was a startling notion that at the very end of his life he had left me something to balance against all those dark, wanting years when I had been so sure that he did not like me. And this isolated expression of affection was made all the more poignant because it seemed that in trying to help me this way he had, in effect, signed his own death warrant.

CHAPTER THIRTY-FOUR

We held Stan's wedding on a weekend so that Gareth would not be at Empty Mile. I had a lot of flowers delivered and Marla and I covered the front of the cabin with them. A celebrant came over from Burton. Marla, Rosie and Millicent all bought matching dresses and Stan and I each rented a tux. On the day we looked like any other wedding party, freshly washed, dressed up, and smiling.

The three women had spent the night at Millicent's place and as Stan and I waited for them early that morning in front of our cabin he asked me over and over if he looked okay, until finally I put my arms around him and hugged him till he quieted. When I let go he shook his hands in front of his face and grinned at me.

"Boy, Johnny. Boy, oh boy, oh boy. I'm going to burst. You know what I feel like? I feel like when I woke up from drowning. Like everything that happened before is on one side and all the new stuff is just about to start."

For a moment he stood there, beaming at me, but then he frowned.

"What's going to happen to me, Johnny? I don't know how to be married. What if I mess it up? What if I can't do it?"

"You won't mess it up."

The celebrant was standing several yards off to one side, cradling the folder from which he was going to read the service. Stan looked over at him.

"I'm freaking out!"

The man chuckled.

A few minutes later the sun cleared the mountains and Stan's eyes went round.

"Look, Johnny, there's sun everywhere. Look!"

It was true. The angle of the light caught the dew that coated the long grass of the meadow and for several minutes the whole field was incandescent. The door to Millicent's house opened and the three women began a small wedding procession. We watched them come toward us, wading knee deep through a field of light. Stan made small squeaks of delight and shifted his weight from foot to foot.

The ceremony was not long. Stan and Rosie stood together holding hands while the celebrant read some passages Marla and I had picked from a poetry book. Stan kept glancing at Rosie and smiling and though Rosie usually held her head down, she raised it for the reading and kept her eyes fixed on him, as though it was only by this connection that she could survive the event.

Though the sun was climbing, the celebrant's breath steamed and this and the sharp edge to the air made the scene seem festive and somehow entrenched, a ritual that would not only join Stan and Rosie to each other, but also make them part of all those other people across the world who had performed the same rite, who had shared the same hopes for a future together.

After the poetry, though no one there was at all religious, the celebrant read something from the Bible. He finished with the passages that formalized the marriage and Stan and Rosie exchanged rings and kissed each other self-consciously. And then it was over.

Millicent, Marla, and I shared a couple of bottles of champagne with the celebrant and we all watched as Stan put on some music and danced with Rosie in front of the cabin. And in watching them, the worry I'd had since Stan first told me he wanted to get married, that it could only ever result in some flawed approximation of the real thing, disappeared. Together, dancing, Stan and Rosie removed themselves from comparison with the world at large. They became graceful and self-sufficient, buttressed by each other against the storm of life that raged around them.

In the days that followed Stan used some of his gold money to lease a trailer. We had it placed at a right angle to our cabin and ran electricity in from there. The same firm of contractors who had cleared the ground over the buried river spent a day linking the trailer to the cabin's plumbing.

In this prefab home Stan and Rosie built around themselves a fragile independence. As withdrawn as Rosie was, she could still drive a car, buy groceries, cook meals, clean house - all the things that Stan either could not do, or could not with any consistency schedule for himself. Being married to her allowed him to participate by proxy, and the disillusionment he'd suffered when he realized how money alone had failed him was replaced now by a new sense of his ability to contribute. He might not have been able to perform all the tasks daily life demanded, but he could certainly fund them.

He was happier in the weeks after his marriage than he had been since the early days of Plantasaurus. He and Rosie danced each day in front of their trailer and, most heartening of all, the pouch of moths disappeared from around his neck.

It was a joy for me to see him like this. It did not expunge the guilt I felt about his drowning. It did not make up for the damage his brain had suffered or the wound I had torn in his emotions by leaving Oakridge, but it was as close as I was going to get to fixing that part of my past. He was happy. He had a wife and his own place to live. These were things I had not dreamed possible when I'd rolled back into Oakridge six months earlier.

On the downside, a few days after Stan's wedding, Marla's desperation reached a point where she could no longer cope at work and she quit her job at the town hall. The job had previously been of such importance to her that I was surprised at her decision, and I took it as a measure of her unhappiness that she would give up something which until now she'd been willing to prostitute herself to keep.

Through all this time the gold mining continued, and every minute Gareth was at Empty Mile I was conscious that I was in the presence of my father's killer. We spoke only when our work demanded it, and at the end of each day I left the river with Stan before Gareth was quite ready so that we would not have to walk back across the meadow together.

It was bad enough being near him, but what galled me more was that I knew I was too weak and too scared to do anything about it. Despite Marla's urging, and the eye-for-an-eye appropriateness of it, I knew I didn't have it in me to pull out a gun and murder him. The best I could do was make barbed references to my father's death, to wonder aloud as we worked on the river exactly how he had died. Gareth ignored me for a while. Eventually, though, I did it one too many times.

Gareth was loading dirt into the sluice at the time. When I spoke, he stopped working and stood glaring at me, clenching his fists so hard his arms shook. Stan was sitting close to us on the riverbank, resting, but he stood when he saw what was happening.

I was glad to see Gareth so angry, but the pleasure didn't last long. Because Gareth killed it by beginning the process which would eventually destroy my brother.

"You're an ungrateful prick, Johnny. I wanted to be your friend. I saved your life when those assholes were going to cut you, I saved your whole fucking world when Jeremy Tripp wanted to tear it down. I could have said no when you wanted help with him. I could have made you give me *all* of this land. What did I ask for? A third. And now I have to suffer this? Even though I fucking told you I didn't do anything to Ray I have to put up with, '*Oh, I wonder how he died,*' and '*Gee, I wish we knew where the body was.*' Get it through your head, whatever happened to Ray, it wasn't me."

This seemed to me such an obvious lie that I spoke without thinking.

"You tried to stop him getting this land. I'm supposed to believe you just gave up after your video didn't work? Bullshit. You killed him."

Stan screamed and my stomach turned cold as I realized what I'd done.

"What? Johnny! What!" He grabbed his head with both hands and turned it rapidly from side to side. "My brain's going to burst!"

I tried to calm him, but he was too far gone to respond. He stopped shaking his head and started to paw the ground with one of his feet like a bull getting ready to charge. His fists were balled and spit flew across his lips.

"You're a bad man, Gareth. You fucking shit bastard!"

Stan raised both fists above his head. Gareth lifted his shovel and held its blade out in front of him.

"Careful there, Einstein."

Stan shrieked: "Don't call me Einstein! I'm going to smash you!"

"No you're not, *Einstein*, you're going to stand there and calm down. I told your brother and I'm telling you, I didn't kill your father. But there's a killer here all right."

Gareth looked at me and his eyes glittered and I felt the world fall away from me. I knew what was coming. I took a step forward but Gareth pointed the shovel at me and shook his head.

"You can't win this one, Johnboy."

Stan shouted at him, "I hate you!"

"Stanley, you remember Jeremy Tripp? You remember how you burned his warehouse down?"

Stan was thrown by this sudden change of subject and shame-faced puzzlement replaced his anger. "Yes...?"

I tried to stop Gareth, to talk over him and drown him out, to beg him not to do this. But he just waited until I stopped, then carried on.

"Why do you think you never got in trouble for that?"

Stan looked uncertainly at me and I felt my heart breaking. I knew that nothing could ever be saved after this.

"Because I didn't mean to do it. Then he had a car crash and died."

Gareth nodded. "Yes, he did have a crash, didn't he? But you know what? It didn't kill him. He still died, though, because Johnny was waiting where he had the crash and when he saw that Jeremy was alive, Johnny got a big hunk of metal pipe and smashed his head in with it."

"No!"

"Yeah, he did. Maybe one day I'll show you the pipe. It has blood all over it."

Stan moaned and started crying. "Johnny...."

He reached out for me like a small child and I held him and he cried against me. And though nothing more needed to be said, Gareth said it anyway.

"And you know why he had to do that? He had to do that to stop Jeremy Tripp telling the police you burned his warehouse down."

Stan lifted his head, blinking through his tears like a man trying to see through smoke, his face twisted by the horror that had this moment taken root in his soul.

"What? What, Johnny? Because of me? You had to do it because of me?"

His large body sagged against me and I stumbled and caught him under the arms and lowered him so that he lay on the ground.

Gareth threw down his shovel then and left the river. As he passed me he said quietly, "Why the fuck couldn't you leave things alone?"

After he'd gone the only sound in the world was that of Stan sobbing. He shook against the ground and curled into himself as though some dreadful physical pain clawed at his guts. I lay beside him and tried to hold him still, tried to quiet him with words that sounded meaningless even to myself. But Stan cried on and on until eventually exhaustion claimed him and it seemed that I felt his body cool and stiffen against me.

A long time after that, with nothing left inside either of us, Stan and I sat at the edge of the river and watched blankly as the water passed by, and I did what I could to sew up the terrible hole in my brother.

"Listen, Stan. Listen to me. What I did to Jeremy Tripp had to be done. He was an evil man. That doesn't make it right but it means it's not such a bad thing. And it didn't have anything to do with you."

"But if I hadn't lit the fire, everything would still be all right."

"No, it wouldn't. He was never going to stop attacking us. Sooner or later I would have to have done it. You lighting the fire doesn't mean anything."

"But you feel bad about everything, Johnny. Even small things. And I made you kill someone. That's the biggest thing that could ever happen to anyone."

"Stan, honestly, I don't even think about it."

He didn't believe me, of course. He sat with his shoulders slumped so that his belly ballooned below his ribs and his misery was so great I thought he might sink into the riverbank beneath its weight. He was silent for several moments and then, without turning his head to look at me, asked what I'd meant when I'd accused Gareth of killing our father.

I told him everything I'd found out, everything I suspected. He listened without interrupting and when I'd finished he didn't speak again that day.

I walked him back up the meadow to his trailer. He moved like his limbs were frozen. He seemed to see nothing around him and several times he stumbled against a rock or a twist of grass. Rosie took him from me when I opened their door. She led him into the trailer's dim interior and when the door closed behind them I stood staring at it for several minutes. Then I went into my cabin and sat at the table in the kitchen with Marla and told her about the latest horror I had visited on someone I loved.

Gareth had the good sense not to turn up at Empty Mile for a week. I spent the time sitting on the stoop staring at the meadow or walking the few yards to Stan's trailer to check on him. At these times I would find him either staring blankly at some children's show on his TV or half asleep in bed. If I tried to rouse him he would look sleepily at me and ask if I was all right before turning over and closing his eyes again.

I began to think that I would have to get him psychiatric help. How I could do this, though, without the whole Jeremy Tripp issue coming to light, I had no idea. I was in a state of despair. I knew how badly Stan must feel. Anyone would bow under the weight of knowing they were responsible for driving a loved one to kill another human being. But Stan, who had so little experience with these dreadful adult emotions, who had so little ability to intellectualize justifications for action, would be crushed.

That he was in pain was terrible enough, but it was made infinitely worse for me by knowing that if I had not provoked Gareth, if I had not lost my head, Stan would still be basking in the honeymoon glow of his marriage. But I *had* lost my head, and in so doing I had infected Stan with my own personal disease. I had passed on to him the dreadful contagion of guilt.

When Gareth returned to Empty Mile, early one morning, he didn't bang on the door and push his way in for breakfast as he had done in the past, but yelled from outside that he was going to start sluicing again and headed off across the meadow without waiting for an answer.

Stan had begun to reemerge by this time and would sit in the afternoons outside his trailer, wrapped against the cooling weather, or walk with Rosie through the long grass, talking quietly and holding hands. Neither he nor I had been down to the river since Stan had learned about Jeremy Tripp, and there was now such a distance between him and the workings of the world around him that I knew his time digging gold out of the ground was over.

And for my part, there was no way I could ever work alongside Gareth again. We had reached a point where the dreadful partnership could not continue.

Toward the end of the morning I put on a heavy coat and went down to the river. I found Gareth working one of the sluices, his face set and angry.

"Johnny. Glad you could finally get off your ass."

"I'm not here to work."

Gareth leaned on his shovel. "What?"

"I want to move on. I don't care about the gold anymore. I want to sell the land to a mining company. You can have half of what we get for it."

"No fucking way. We are *not* selling. Those guys'll pay us a fraction of what it's worth, you know that. They'll see us coming and fuck us in the ass without even thinking about it. No, we're going to keep on mining just like we've been doing. And you're going to behave yourself, and Marla's going to come out of the fucking cabin and say hello to me once in a while. In fact, Johnny, while we're on the subject, there's a whole lot more Marla could be doing."

"What are you talking about?"

"Given our history, how we all started off together and how we're all together again-"

"We're not 'all together again.'"

"-how we're all together again, I think we should share Marla. I have a share in the land, dude. I should have a share in the woman."

"Are you fucking insane?"

"Gosh, I hope you haven't forgotten that piece of pipe."

"Gareth, we are not sharing Marla. You're not getting anywhere near her."

"Well, you're angry now, you're not thinking clearly. But I'm telling you, Johnboy, tomorrow I'm coming a-courtin'."

Gareth smirked at me and lifted a shovel of dirt and began sifting it into the sluice.

On my way back to the cabin I collected Stan and Rosie from their trailer. If it had been anything else I would have tried to keep Stan out of it. There was no need, after all, to load him with worries that he could do nothing about. But I knew we could not give in to Gareth and opposing him would have serious consequences for all of us. It seemed only fair, then, that Stan should be included if his future was at stake as well.

Marla, Stan, and Rosie sat across from me in the living room. Marla and Stan looked worried. Rosie stared at her lap.

I told them what Gareth wanted and explained that his leverage to make it happen was the threat of having me arrested for the death of Jeremy Tripp. Stan looked ashen and began squeezing his knees with his hands, trying not to cry. It occurred to me then, too late of course, that he would now feel not only responsible for making me kill Jeremy Tripp, but also for the fact that Gareth might send me to jail for it.

"Don't worry, Stan, we're not giving in this time. We have to stand up to him or this will go on forever."

Stan spoke in a kind of croaking whisper: "But Johnny, I don't want you to go to jail."

"I'm not going to jail. I don't think Gareth will really tell the police."

Marla snorted incredulously. "What makes you think that?"

"He'll have to explain how he got the pipe and that'll make him almost as guilty as me."

"He'll send it in anonymously, you idiot."

"Then I'll tell the police about him, same thing. And anyway, I think there's more to it. I think in a weird way he doesn't want to be without me, without you. He needs his toys to play with."

"What if you're wrong?"

"I don't know, but we have to at least try to get out from under him. If we don't, this kind of shit is going to keep on happening."

Marla made a gun with her thumb and forefinger and fired it at the side of her head. "My way would be better, Johnny."

Even though, if my planned opposition to Gareth failed and we were forced to capitulate, Marla would be the one suffering most at his hands, I was more worried right then about Stan. I felt powerless to do anything for him, to get past his unhappiness and help him in some way. Out of desperation, I asked him to camp out with me that night. We had often gone camping as kids and I was hoping that memories of those times and the closeness of just the two of us together outdoors would help him shed a little of his guilt.

It was no great expedition, just a tent and some food and a hike in the afternoon, up to the top of the spur that bordered the meadow - the same hike we'd made when I'd checked my father's aerial photograph against the landscape.

We pitched our tent twenty yards back from the collapsed end of the spur. There was still an hour of daylight left when we were done and we prepared a fire for later then sat wearing sweaters and coats, gazing at the view. The hills ran off to the distance in broken ranks, their upper slopes copper-gold in the lowering sun, the valleys between them in shadow, filling with mist as the air cooled.

It got cold enough for us to start our fire pretty soon, and while there was a little light left in the air we made a dinner of sausages, beans and bread rolls. Stan became quiet as evening fell and when we were finished eating we sat close to the fire and there were long periods of silence between us. I was hoping he would open up, that the hard shell of his depression might crack a little. But between our sparse bursts of small-talk he stared into the fire and said nothing.

We had a gas light set a couple of yards out from the fire and moths battered themselves against its bright frosted glass. I went over and caught a few and gave them to him in the plastic bag our bread rolls had come in.

"If you don't have any moths, how are you going to bring the power across?"

Stan took the bag from me and held it up to the fire. For a moment he watched the moths crawl around, then he handed the bag back to me.

"I don't want them. I don't want to bring any more power across."

"Why not?"

"Everything's too wrong."

"Won't the power fix it?"

Stan breathed in and out and shook his head.

"Look, Stan, you lit a fire when you were angry. And you did it because Jeremy Tripp did something bad to Rosie. That's all. Everything else has nothing to do with you."

"You're going to go to jail."

"I'm not going to jail, I told you. Nothing bad is going to happen."

Stan turned away from me and stared into the fire.

"It is, Johnny."

"Stan-"

"It is."

We were cold that night in the tent. We lay in our sleeping bags fully clothed and breathed steam against the close nylon walls and I told Stan all the stories I remembered from our childhood, all the tiny, normal events we had shared as brothers growing up in the same family. I wanted him to laugh, I wanted to bring back to him the memory of how it felt to be carefree. But rather than remind him of the good things in his past my stories seemed only to make him more aware of what he no longer had.

In the morning there was frost on the ground and Stan and I stood beside the remains of our fire as the sun picked out the land around us in clear yellows and blues. For a short time, after the interruption of sleep, Stan was able to watch the scene about him without reference to the sadnesses which were currently undoing his world. He stood and looked and breathed and he was still and I saw the soft bravery which I so much associated with him return to his eyes

"Johnny, don't you think it would be better if you could just live like this? If all you had to do was cook your dinner and sleep and be in the forest and you didn't have to do anything with other people?"

"Yeah, I do."

Stan nodded. "Yeah...."

He walked off to the end of the spur and sat there, knees hunched up to his chin, staring out at the landscape. I relit the fire and made coffee and cooked pancakes. I expected Stan to come when he smelled the food but he didn't move and when I called to him he turned his head and smiled and called back, "I'm just going to sit here, okay?"

He sat for a long time. So long that I had to busy myself packing up the tent and the rest of our things. I knew this time was good for him and I left him alone with himself as long as I could, but we had no more food with us and I was getting anxious about being away from Marla, so eventually, around midday, I had to tell him it was time to go.

He came back from the edge of the spur and looked at the packed-up camping gear.

"We should run away, Johnny. Get Marla and Rosie and another tent and just disappear in the forest where Gareth can't find us."

For a moment he stood looking about him, then he sighed and reached down and started picking up pieces of our gear

When we got home Rosie was sitting in front of the trailer, listening to the soft music they liked to dance to. She had been waiting for Stan's return and stood when she saw him, her head down as always but her hand out for his. Stan took it and kissed her and led her into the trailer. As he passed the portable stereo he turned the music off.

After they had gone I stood looking at my cabin, at the space in front of it, at my pickup and Marla's car, at the track that led up to the road.... And I couldn't help feeling that Stan's desire to run away from it all made an awful lot of sense.

CHAPTER THIRTY-FIVE

The next day, in the morning, the world for the four of us at Empty Mile started to fall apart. Five, if you count Gareth.

Marla and I were on the stoop, waiting for him to arrive and begin work on the river. Stan and Rosie had come over for breakfast and were sitting inside the cabin at the kitchen table. Stan was picking at a plate of fried eggs and Rosie, who didn't eat breakfast, was drinking black coffee.

I felt frightened and resigned and energized all at the same time. I don't know if I thought there was any chance that the morning would end successfully for us, but I knew that what I was about to do was something that had to be done, something it would have been wrong not to do.

When Gareth climbed out of his Jeep and saw Marla a smile broke across his face and he made a pistol with his hand and cocked it at me.

"Dude, what can I say? This means so much, that you two would do this for me. I can't tell you how fucking relieved I am that we're not going to have any trouble about it."

He held his arms out for Marla to come to him. She looked at him tiredly and shook her head.

"Jesus, Gareth...."

Gareth frowned and glanced uncertainly at me. "Dude?"

"It's not going to happen."

"Johnny, come on, man. Don't fuck around."

"You're not getting Marla."

"We were clear on the consequences?"

"Go tell the cops. Do whatever the fuck you want. I'm not putting up with this insanity any longer. This is the end of it."

Gareth looked at Marla. I saw that she was staring at him, her eyes dark and hard, as though willing him to leave us alone. Gareth held her gaze for a long moment, then turned back to me.

"Know what I think? I think you're bluffing. You don't think I'll go through with it, do you? But I have to tell you, Johnny, Marla was mine before she was yours and this is where things get made right."

"You don't share people, you fucking psycho. Just go down to the river and mine your gold."

"You took away the only chance I had to be happy. My one fucking chance! Why didn't you find someone else?"

Gareth was shouting now, almost crying, his face straining and red.

I heard Millicent's front door open. She waved at us as she came down her front steps, but by the time she reached the bottom some of the tension surrounding Gareth and me must have communicated itself to her because she paused and stood watching us.

"Do you know what you do to the people around you, Johnny? You fucking destroy them. Marla, your brother.... Well, you're not going to do it to me. I'm going to get what I want. And if it means taking you out, that's what I'm going to do. You fucking asshole."

Gareth turned and reached for the door of his Jeep. I heard footsteps behind me, someone coming out of the cabin and onto the stoop. Out of the corner of my eye I saw a flash of gray and black as Stan, in full Batman suit, rocketed past me, down onto the bare earth in front of the cabin. In his hand I saw the ugly black shape of Marla's revolver. It was so incongruous a sight that for a second I was unable to process what I was seeing. Unfortunately, a second was all it took for Stan to raise his arm and pull the trigger.

He'd moved so quickly that no one had had a chance to call out or say anything and when the gun fired, it fired in a place where no other noise existed. Our small world was split by the gargantuan sound of gunpowder igniting, of explosive gasses jetting from the barrel's opening, of a bullet moving across a few short yards, from the gun's chamber to the middle of Gareth's back.

For a moment it seemed that the intensity of the sound would freeze the scene, that we would be forever left staring at a three-quarter view of Stan with his arm extended, at Gareth thrown against the door of his Jeep, at the smoke in the cold air and the fine spray of blood on the car's side windows.

But then the sound was gone and Stan lowered his arm and dropped the gun and Gareth slid down the side of his car and fell backwards onto the ground. There was a long smear of blood on the Jeep's door. In it, a few inches below the window, a small round hole marked the bullet's exit from Gareth's body. Across the meadow Millicent wailed weakly.

Stan stood staring at what he had done, his body rooted to the ground, a rapid tremor playing over his arms and chest and head. I went to him and put my hand on his arm.

"Stan...."

"You can't go to jail, Johnny. You just can't."

I felt so complicit, so responsible for what had happened, that I could think of nothing to say to him and we stood there in silence until Rosie, who had seen the shooting from the doorway of our cabin, came down and took Stan's hand and led him across the meadow to Millicent. When they got there all three of them went quickly up the steps and into the house.

Marla came to me long before Stan and Rosie had finished crossing the meadow and she and I stepped close to Gareth and looked down at him. The front of his shirt was soaked with blood and more of it welled steadily from a torn cavity in the center of his chest. His bladder had let go and the crotch of his jeans was dark.

Marla slid her hand into mine and I heard her breathe quietly to herself, "At last...."

But Gareth wasn't dead yet. His eyes had been half closed but they opened fully now and he coughed a mouthful of blood over his chin and spoke in a wet choking voice that made me think of a room filling with water.

"Looks like Einstein's fucked himself up again."

"Not as much as he's fucked you up."

Gareth laughed and choked and spat out more blood. "He's going to go to jail for killing me to protect you from something you did to stop him from going to jail in the first place. I think you call that irony."

He stopped for a moment and fought for breath. I noticed there were small bubbles forming in the pool of blood that had collected on his chest.

"Aren't you going to call 911?"

"No."

"They might be able to save me."

"Honestly? I don't think so."

"And that's okay because I killed your father, right? Well, I'm going to leave you with a little present. You too, Marla - you most of all. And if you're smart, Johnny, you'll do the right thing with it."

Marla squatted so that her face was only a foot from his and hissed, "Don't!"

"It'll always be there between you if I don't."

"You promised."

"Dying's kind of a free pass. Johnny, get down here too, it hurts to talk."

I squatted next to Marla. For a moment Gareth closed his eyes and gathered his strength. On the other side of the meadow I heard an engine start and a car pull away. When Gareth opened his eyes again the light had gone out of them.

"Okay.... I did fix the brakes on Ray's car, same as Tripp's. But I didn't kill him. I'm not saying I wouldn't have tried again, I just didn't have to-"

I glanced at Marla and saw that she was watching me and crying.

"-because Marla did it for me. But you have to know, Johnny, it was an accident. It wasn't her fault...." He paused and blinked rapidly several times. "And that pipe, I got rid of it weeks ago. Kiss my dad for me."

Gareth tried twice to take another breath but couldn't do it. The wound in his chest fizzed nastily. And then he was dead.

I stood slowly and looked down at him, at the now-cooling body of a man I had known for more than ten years - a friend I had robbed of the woman he loved, a friend I had made my enemy. So many years ago....

How could I have foreseen that his desire for Marla would one day lead my poor damaged brother to commit murder? There was no way, of course. Even so...even so, it seemed to me that I should have known.

Marla had her head in her hands; she wasn't crying for Gareth, though. There was now a fresh horror in our lives demanding to be dug from its grave and examined. But I was terribly conscious that I had to go to Stan. Killing Jeremy Tripp had been something I could only just support. For someone like Stan, the most innocent of people, the act of murder would tear his soul to shreds.

I lifted Marla to her feet and began to pull her across the meadow toward Millicent's house but she hung back and took her hand away from me.

"Johnny.... Johnny...."

Her face was blotchy from crying and she stood in front of me unable to speak, her mouth twisting.

"Marla, come on. I need you with me."

For a moment she didn't move, then the briefest flicker of hope crossed her face and she held my hand again and ran with me, up the meadow to Millicent's house.

When we got there I saw that the Datsun was gone. Millicent came to the door when she heard us on her stoop and the sight of her chilled me. That she was there meant someone else had driven the car away.

"What happened? Why did Stanley shoot that man? Is he dead?"

"Where did they go?"

"I don't know. They went into the bedroom for a minute, then Rosie got the keys and they took the car."

"Didn't they say anything?"

"Not a thing. Except Rosie stopped on her way out, just here by the door, and put her arms around me and told me, 'Thank you.' What for, I don't know, but she hasn't hugged me like that more than three or four times in her life."

I called Stan's cell phone from Millicent's stoop but he didn't answer. Marla and I ran back down the slope and got into the pickup and charged out of Empty Mile.

We went straight to Old Town first and then, when we didn't find them there, doubled back to Back Town. With each street we checked I felt an increasing sense of foreboding. Marla tried Stan's phone constantly but it went straight to voice mail.

Near the town hall a thought struck me and I accelerated past the remaining stores and headed out to the Oakridge commercial precinct. If Stan was being eaten alive with guilt he might go to the place he most closely associated with the beginning of that guilt.

But when we got to the Plantagion warehouse there was no sign of the orange Datsun. I got out of the pickup to look around just in case. The warehouse was locked up and deserted. Through the window I could see all the office furniture was gone. It seemed that whoever had inherited Jeremy Tripp's estate had closed the business down. I made a circuit of the building but there was no sign Stan had broken in anywhere. When I got back to the pickup my cell phone was ringing. Stan - his voice dreamlike, as though while he was speaking to me he was looking at something of beauty.

"Hi, Johnny-"

"Where are you?"

"It's okay."

"What do you mean? Stan? I want you to go back to the cabin right now."

"Rosie and me talked about it. And you mustn't be sad, Johnny, okay? You mustn't be sad."

"Stan! Get back to the cabin now. Put Rosie on the phone."

"I had to shoot Gareth."

"I know you did, and it's okay. I'm not angry with you."

"I know that, Johnny. You're never angry with me. You're the best brother in the world."

"Stan, please. Where are you? What are you going to do?"

I heard my voice break and though I knew I was crying I couldn't feel the tears on my face or the tightness in my throat. My perception had narrowed to only the voice against my ear and the dreadful visions flying through my head.

"I love you, Johnny, and I know how you tried to make things good for me with Plantasaurus and the gold and you let me marry Rosie and you took care of me. And I remember all the times we had together, since you came back and before that when I was a kid. I remember them all and I'm going to take them with me. Just like when I drowned and came awake again. The first thing I saw was the sky and it was so deep and blue, and then I saw you looking down at me and you were so worried and I thought how much I loved you and even when you were gone I never stopped feeling that way. Don't forget, Johnny. Don't think anything else."

"Stan, I'm not going to think anything. We'll talk about it at home."

"You should wear my costumes, Johnny. Sometimes when you put them on it feels like things can't hurt you so much."

"Stan, please.... You're not going to hurt yourself, are you? I couldn't bear it if anything happened to you. Promise me."

"I'm going to take you with me in my heart. I love you, Johnny."

The line went dead. I dialed him back immediately but there was no answer. Marla put her hand on my thigh.

"Where is he?"

I shook my head and was about to tell her I didn't know, but then it hit me - the only place it would make sense for him to be.

"The lake."

I threw the pickup into gear and began the race to get to Stan before he did anything to himself.

I drove fast. I took the shortest route I knew - out the other side of the precinct and along the narrow road we'd taken the night Stan set fire to the Plantagion warehouse. It took me fifteen minutes at high speed to reach the Loop and another two from there to get to the start of Lake Trail.

I had to take it slower then because of the road. Everything in me screamed to go faster, but the one time I tried it the rear wheels lost traction and the pickup slid dangerously on a bend.

Two hundred yards from the end of the trail we found the Datsun. It had gone off the road, fortunately on the uphill side, and ploughed sideways into a tree. The passenger side was heavily dented. I stopped the pickup and ran to it, but it was empty. There was a small amount of blood on the dash in front of the passenger seat, but nothing that suggested serious injury.

We raced up the last short stretch of trail and flew out into the sunlight going way too fast. I had to wrench the pickup into a hard left turn and hit the brakes to avoid careening over the grass and onto the beach. Marla and I jumped out and scanned the lake and the land surrounding it.

I didn't know where to look, what part of the place to scour for a sign that Stan still existed. The world around me was a frantic series of snapshots, shuddering as I turned my head, impossible to assimilate. I felt as though some dazzling light shone into my eyes, allowing me to see only the edges of what I looked at. But then my brain caught up and all the images smashing at the air around me slammed into place and I was able to see what was happening at the lake that day.

So late in the year the weather was too cold for people to be swimming and there were only two vehicles in the parking lot. Gareth and David's bungalow looked closed and without movement, though a weak column of smoke rose vertically into the air from its chimney. Beyond the bungalow and the cabins the wooden jetty caught my eye. The small rowboat that usually lay upturned at its end was missing.

I looked across the water and saw the boat empty and drifting, about as far from the beach as it was possible to get - out near the sheer rock wall that held back the land on the opposite side of the lake. There was nothing around it, no desperately flailing swimmers, no churned and broken water.

I moved my gaze quickly back to the beach, wanting to find Stan and Rosie sitting cuddled together, waiting for me to find them and solve the problem of their crashed car. But they weren't there. The beach was deserted except for two elderly couples standing at the edge of the water. I started to look beyond them, further up the beach, but there was something wrong. The old people were not admiring the stillness of the water or enjoying the thin autumn sun. They were pointing and shouting and looking desperately about them. I knew then where Stan was and I ran across the grass and the coarse sand to the lake.

One of the women spoke to me first. She looked to be in her seventies. The weathered skin of her face was drawn tight with worry.

"Two people just drowned."

"A man and a woman?"

"Yes, yes! We saw them out there and they were rowing and then both of them just stood up and jumped in the water. They didn't even try to swim."

The man standing next to her interjected, "They were holding hands when they jumped."

The woman nodded rapidly. "They were on the surface for maybe a minute, then they went under and they didn't come back up. We couldn't do anything. We're old. We couldn't do anything."

The two men nodded and made noises of agreement. The other woman was crying.

"How long?"

One of the men shook his head gravely. "They went under at least ten minutes ago. We called the police. There was no one else here." He gestured uselessly with the cell phone he was holding.

I did the only thing I could do, a thing I couldn't stop myself doing. I took off my clothes and swam out to the rowboat. It was a distance of almost two hundred yards and I was not a strong swimmer and when I got there I was gasping and had to hold on to the side of the boat to rest.

What I was doing was futile. The boat would have drifted and there was little chance I was close enough to where they entered the water to make an effective search. And even if I was, the lake here was more than fifty feet deep and they had been under far, far too long. But when I had my breath back I dove beneath the surface of the cold water and swam down as far as I could, stretching my eyes wide to see, groping about me as the light grew dimmer. I found nothing, touched no trailing limb, no waterlogged torso. I surfaced and dove down again, and again, and again, until the world became a tumbling storm of white bubbles and dark water and a terrible hunger for air.

I was so weakened that I would certainly have run into trouble, but at some point the police arrived and two officers swam out and dragged me back to shore.

There were three police cruisers there, pulled up on the grass at the edge of the beach, and while my rescuers dried themselves, their colleagues took statements from the elderly couples and then from Marla and me. When they were finished with us they went over to the bungalow and questioned David, but he had been in the barn out back and had no idea anything had even happened.

The Oakridge police had no resources to make a search of the lake themselves, and because there was no question that Stan and Rosie could still be alive, they shut the scene down until a dive team could be brought up from Sacramento the following morning. The couples were allowed to go, crime scene tape was strung across the entrance to Lake Trail to close it to the public, and a cruiser was posted there as backup.

Marla and I, however, were far from finished for the day. We had to take the police out to Empty Mile and explain why a dead body with a bullet hole in it was lying on the ground in front of our cabin. And how it connected to Stan and Rosie's drowning.

One of the detectives who joined the uniforms at Empty Mile was Patterson, the lead officer on my father's disappearance. There was, I think, some cynicism in his surprise that I was now part of a murder investigation, but the fact that Millicent confirmed she'd seen Stan shoot Gareth and that Marla and I had had nothing to do with it didn't leave him much option but to accept the version of events we gave him.

The business of the crime scene - the recording of evidence, the videoing of the surrounding area, the photographing of the body, the repeated questioning - took until the middle of the afternoon. Then, around three p.m., Marla and I and Millicent, so shattered by the loss of her grand-daughter that she had to be helped to stand by one of the officers, were taken to the Oakridge police station to give formal statements.

The police had a confirmed culprit, or at least they would have when they could raise him from the bottom of the lake, and we weren't treated as suspects. The only finessing Marla and I had to do concerned Stan's motivation for the shooting, but this was simple enough. In a private moment at the lake before we told them about the shooting, we'd agreed to say that Gareth had sexually proposi-tioned Rosie a number of times and that it had finally pushed Stan over the edge. We said nothing at all about Jeremy Tripp.

The statements took about an hour and a half and when they were done we were driven back to Empty Mile. The cruiser dropped us at Millicent's house and Marla and I helped her up the steps and put her to bed where she lay staring at nothing, her hands loose and forgot-ten on top of the covers. Marla made tea but Millicent didn't want it and after a while it seemed that we were out of place there, intruders on her misery, and so we excused ourselves and left her alone in the slowly darkening room, without family now in the whole of the world.

Gareth's body was gone from in front of the cabin. In its place there were small traces of police activity - strips of marker tape, empty evidence bags, some small yellow plastic stakes hammered into the ground to show where the body had lain. There was birdsong in the air with the approach of evening, but rather than soften the scene about us it made the place seem forlorn and abandoned as though, along with the corpse, the police had taken away with them whatever it was that had made the cabin and the land around it feel welcoming and lived in.

Marla went through the door with her head bowed. She walked straight to the couch and sat down and started talking before I'd finished taking my coat off. Her voice was flat, but there was relief in it as well, as though her words carried from her some poison that had been progressively corroding her system.

"When you came back to Oakridge, Ray wanted to start fresh with you, to build a better relationship. But he thought the affair he'd had with me was something so terrible he wouldn't be able to do this if he kept it hidden from you. The evening it happened, he came to my house and told me he was going to tell you what we'd done."

Marla looked desperately at me. She had a small handkerchief in her lap and was shredding the thin material with her fingernails.

"I thought if you knew, we'd be finished. All I wanted was to be with you. It was all I ever wanted. And you'd just come back and I saw everything I thought I was going to have with you being taken away again. I begged him not to say anything, to just let it stay in the past. But he wouldn't. He kept saying he had to tell you. Over and over. And I was going crazy. I was begging. But he wouldn't change his mind. And then I pushed him. That's all. I just pushed him on the chest, just to make him stop. Just a push.... I didn't mean to kill him. I didn't even want to hurt him. I just wanted him not to tell you."

Marla paused and sobbed and then with an effort gathered herself and spoke again.

"We were in the kitchen and he fell. I don't know why. It shouldn't have happened, he should have just stepped backwards. But he didn't. He fell and hit the back of his head on the edge of the counter. I tried to revive him. I did CPR.... I'm so sorry, Johnny. I'm so sorry."

"But his car was found out at Jerry's Gas. I don't understand."

"When I saw he was dead I panicked. I didn't know what to do. So I called Gareth. He was the only person I could think of who'd help me. He came around and we waited till two in the morning then we drove Ray's car out to Jerry's to make it look like he'd run out and hopped a bus somewhere. It was a stupid idea but it was the only thing we could think of to lead the police away from Oakridge."

Marla stopped again. She looked drained and utterly exhausted.

I said, "What did you do with his body?"

She shook her head. "I don't know. Gareth said it would be safer if I didn't know."

"You don't know where his body is?"

"Gareth took it away. I don't know what he did with it." Marla started to cry again. "And you know what the crazy thing is? The most fucking insane thing of all time? It didn't need to happen. Ray's death, the things I had to let Gareth make me do afterwards.... None of it had to happen. Because when you found out about the affair you didn't leave me. You didn't even stop loving me. What I'd been so frightened of turned out to be...nothing."

For a long time I sat there and watched Marla and tried to muster some sort of anger toward her, but the plain truth was that I couldn't make my father's death more important to me than keeping her.

My father had been a good man, a man who knew right from wrong and lived according to this knowledge. He had been, perhaps, just as lost as I was, just as bewildered by the world and uncertain of his path through it. And in the terrible face of the universe he had been as innocent as all good men are. But he had not loved me. Or, if he had, his emotional distance, his stifling of all tender expression, had made it seem that he did not. Throughout my life he had been a cipher, an acquaintance, someone who bore me none of the forgiveness of true affection.

It seemed, toward the end, that he had wanted to change this. There had been the expensive presents he'd given Stan and me, the trust he'd shown by putting Empty Mile in my name, the need to come clean about his affair with Marla and, finally, his attempt at persuading Gareth to stop pimping her.

He must have seen even the smallest of these moves, even the shallow intimacies he attempted on the evenings after dinner as we sat at the kitchen table, as monumental efforts of engagement. To me, though, looking back across them now, they were small sad beacons in the gloom of our relationship, flickerings of what might have been if he had only cared more and sooner. And while I would treasure them, they were too few for a lifetime and they had come too late to change my belief that he was essentially someone I did not belong to.

But Marla loved me. We were free now of Gareth and my father and Jeremy Tripp. We could be free, even, of Empty Mile if we wanted. We had a chance to build a life together, a chance for Marla to make real her aching dreams of emotional security. I believed her when she said my father's death had been an accident. I had no doubt about it at all. But I think even if she had killed him with malice and planning my decision would have been the same.

What were we after all? Two killers who weren't killers. Two guilty people who had never planned for guilt. In a way, perhaps, we canceled each other out. Neither of us, given what each of us had separately done, was fit ever to find or want another partner. So love was enough and forgiveness a concept that did not apply. We were as we had become, two people whose lives could no longer be matched against the usual measures of what the world considered right.

And if nothing else, she was alive and my father was dead. There was nothing I could do for him, but I still had a chance to make up for the unhappiness I had sentenced Marla to when I left Oakridge eight years ago.

So, that sad, dreadful evening I told her I loved her and we went to bed and clung to each other as the darkness came. I understood now so many of the things that had puzzled me about her - how Gareth was able to manipulate her, to make her strip naked for him in our cabin, to prostitute herself to Jeremy Tripp. She had said it was because she was frightened he would tell her employers about her hooking past, but the real threat he held over her, what gave him the power to make her do anything he wanted, was the fact that he knew she was responsible for my father's death.

Her terrible depression and her need for physical punishment made sense. She had been living not only with the guilt of having killed the father of the man she loved, but also with the daily fear that she would be exposed for it. Gareth's presence at Empty Mile must have made her life a living hell, knowing as she did that at any moment he might choose to drop that one fatal comment. It was no wonder that she had protested so strongly about him being there, or that she had been initially so reluctant to tell Jeremy Tripp that Gareth had made the video that drove Patricia Prentice to suicide. She must have thought it would provoke him to retaliate against her by revealing the truth about my father's disappearance.

That it had not, made me realize how much Gareth must still have loved her. It had been a twisted, cruel love, but he had kept the secret of my father's death for her even though he must have longed to use it to break us up. And his revelation of it as he died had not been a last vindictive twisting of the knife but, as he had said, a gift to Marla. He knew that I had to be given the opportunity to forgive her, because without this forgiveness she would never be able to live beyond her guilt.

I could not sleep that night. My grief for Stan lay over me like a thousand miles of stone. Around two in the morning I got up and went outside.

Stan and Rosie's bedroom occupied one whole end of their trailer and when I entered it I felt, at first, cheated. The brown Formica walls, the concertina door, the aluminum window frames...none of this was Stan to me. This was not where he had grown up, this was not where he had lived with me. This was Stan's new life, a life which had existed independently of me.

But as I stood longer in the room Stan's imprint on the place began to show. Like a photograph developing, his things rose one by one out of a background of unfamiliar furniture and a thin scattering of Rosie's possessions - a comic book on the floor beside the bed that he must have been reading the night before, pairs of sneakers slung haphazardly against a wall, sketches of superheroes, an open can of Coke and a packet of potato chips.... These glimpses of the everyday moments in his life, these small, mundane, intimate times when he was most himself, cut me so deeply I had to steady myself against the doorframe.

There was a closet beside the door. I opened it and ran my hands across Stan's clothes. The leather jacket I'd given him when I left Oakridge was at the head of the row, and beside it the pale blue bowling shirt he'd been wearing on my first day back. I took the shirt from its hanger and sat at the foot of the bed and buried my face in it, breathing in the scent of my brother - perspiration and the perfume of Brylcreem - trying to breathe into existence a world around myself which still contained him. But of course I could not, and in the end the shirt served only to drive home how utterly and permanently gone he was. I sat and cried into it until I felt empty of anything worthwhile, empty of anything I might have held up as evidence that I was, if only in the smallest of ways, a good man.

When, finally, I put the shirt back in its place, I saw Stan's two remaining superhero costumes and remembered his words to me about how I should wear them sometimes. I took them out of the closet and draped them over my arm. I spent another minute in the bedroom trying to absorb as much of him as I could, to parcel up and carry away with me forever these last, fading traces of his life, but I had come to my limit and did not have the strength to stay longer. The only other thing I took from the room was the leather jacket.

Outside, it was very cold. I walked quietly back to the cabin and sat on the steps out front. I put the leather jacket on and zipped it up and sat breathing steam into the air with my hands in its pockets, thinking about how I had destroyed Stan's faith in life.

He had seen the world as a place of hope, as something that looked after the people who lived within it. There had been a magic to it for him. It was a place where you could hold a tree and be energized, where moths could somehow draw power to you. But six months in my presence had taken every last piece of this magic away from him.

My guilt was a condition of the soul that lay about me like a gray tubercular cloud, and Stan had breathed it in every day that he was with me. He had recognized it for what it was. He had told me to stop feeling bad, to leave the horrors of the past in the past. But it had made no difference. My self-loathing had sustained me for so long that I could not give it up. And Stan, who had never had the chance to build resistance to this most adult of afflictions, was unable to withstand its unremitting onslaught, unable to prevent his own trusting view of life becoming terminally infected with it.

He had worshipped me, he had looked to me for a model of how to live, and I had shown him only regret and hopelessness and a barren future where happiness was impossible. And it had been this, more than any attack by Jeremy Tripp or Gareth, that had changed him into a person capable of picking up a handgun, pointing it at another human being, and pulling the trigger.

Later, as it was starting to get light, Marla came out with coffee and sat next to me. I put my head on her shoulder and she stroked my hair and I wanted to stay like that forever, sitting there with the feel of her fingers taking away thought, never having to address anything or deal with anything or think about myself ever again.

Around 6:30 a.m. we got into the pickup and drove out to Tunney Lake to watch the police dive team from Sacramento search for Stan and Rosie's bodies. On the way past Millicent's house we stopped and knocked on her door. It took her a long time to answer, when she did she was wrapped in a quilt from her bed and her face looked gray and immobile. We asked her if she wanted to come with us, but she shuddered and said she couldn't bear it and went back into her house.

The officer stationed at the entrance to Lake Trail recognized us and rolled his car back so we could pass. At the lake there was an ambulance and an Oakridge police cruiser in the parking lot. On the beach three large black SUVs with crests on their sides and long metal trailers behind them were backed up to the water's edge. Three gray semi-inflatable boats had just launched. Two of them each held a driver and a pair of wet-suited divers, the third appeared to be some sort of coordinating vessel and carried a pod of electronic equipment and three men in dark fatigues and peaked caps.

Two Oakridge police officers were on the beach talking to a guy with a mustache who looked like he was the head of the dive team. One of the officers saw us and came over and told us it might take most of the day for the divers to find anything. He pointed to the rocks at the far end of the beach and said that the most private place to watch from would probably be there. The man with the mustache nodded at us and tugged the bill of his cap.

Marla and I sat huddled in our coats on the sand where the rocks started. The divers were in the water now and the boats idled behind them, following their bubble trails. The cold air was still and sound traveled easily and around us the morning filled with the noise of outboard motors, the calls of the men in the boats, and the burble of two-way radios. The dive team had begun working near the shore and was only slowly making its way out toward the deeper water by the cliff face.

As I watched them, blankly waiting for the inevitable, I realized that Oakridge and all it had ever held for me was finished, that I would sell Empty Mile as soon as I could find a buyer. Gareth's share would go to his father and I would give Stan's to Millicent. Marla and I would take the rest and travel east across the country until there was no more land to travel across. We would find a place to live and hope that the three thousand miles of land between us and Oakridge would be enough to keep us safe from the people we had been.

By midday the divers had moved across the lake and were within fifteen yards of the cliff face. They found Stan first. We heard one of the men in the boats shout, then all three boats quickly converged on a pair of divers who had surfaced and were supporting something between them. I couldn't see much at first from where we were, but when the body was lifted into one of the boats I saw that it was dressed in gray and black.

The boat came into shore and the police and the dive team members on the beach jumped to meet it. They lifted Stan's body out and lay it face up on the sand.

When Marla and I got there, the men fell silent and made way for us. I stood close to Stan, staring down at him. He'd lost his mask and his glasses and the wet Batman costume stuck tightly to his rounded body. His eyes were closed and the dark lashes against the white skin made him look very young, as though death had stripped away the attempts he had made to disguise himself as an adult, leaving behind instead the soft brave boy he had always really been.

It was an impossible thing to accept that those eyes would never open again. The lids were not damaged, his face, though swollen a little, was unmarked. There seemed no reason why, if I shook him hard enough or breathed into him long enough, those eyes should not flutter open, that he should not smile and say to me, "Hiya, Johnny. Don't worry, I'm fine."

It had happened once before.

But it wouldn't happen this time.

I bent and put my hand against the side of his face. I was not prepared for how cold he felt, how hard the bone of his skull seemed beneath his skin, but I kept my hand where it was. He was my beautiful brother, the man I had come back to Oakridge to fix. My last, lost hope for absolution.

This was the last time I would see him outside a coffin, this was the last shred of connection between us before formal process took over. I wanted to stop this headlong race, this rocketing of him away from me. I wanted to hold on to him, to not let him go, and believe that by doing so I could keep some essential part of him alive. But he was already gone and there was nothing, not a thing in the entire universe, I could do to bring him back.

When I stepped away from the body, two of the dive team picked him up carefully and placed him in a black vinyl body bag. As they were zipping it up one of them asked me if I wanted them to leave his face showing. I shook my head and they closed the bag and then all of the men on the beach gathered about it and lifted it in silence and carried it gently and slowly over to the ambulance in the parking lot.

Fifteen minutes later the same pair of divers who had found Stan found Rosie. When she was laid out on the sand we went over and stood beside her. She had been a quiet, closed presence and only Stan had really passed beyond the locked façade she held against the world, but she had been a part of our lives for six months and I was as responsible for her death as I was for Stan's. Before they closed the body bag Marla stepped forward and smoothed Rosie's hair away from her face and arranged the collar of her dress more closely about her throat.

After that there was nothing more for us at the lake. The police would pack up, the bodies would be transported to the coroner in Burton, there would be an autopsy, and sometime later Stan and Rosie would be released for burial. I wanted to get home as fast as I could, to close the door behind me and shut out the world, but as Marla and I were walking across the grass bank to the pickup there was a shout from the two divers who were still in the water. We turned to see them waving to their command boat. They were a long way out across the lake, almost at the cliff face, and it was impossible to see what they were holding just below the surface of the water. But I had a sickening feeling I knew exactly what it was they had found.

Marla clutched my arm and we stood there on that low grassy bank, unable to move, unable to look away as a third body was pulled from the water and ferried to shore. The police, having no reason to associate us with this one, paid no attention to us and unloaded the body and laid it out with less ceremony than they had previously.

This new body was in far worse condition than Stan or Rosie. If it hadn't been for the remains of the business suit that clung to it, it would have been difficult to identify it as human at all from where we stood. It was a white, bloated thing that curved from head to toe like the back of a whale. Where the flesh was exposed the skin was tattered and peeling. The head was bigger than it should have been and most of its hair was gone.

But Marla and I both knew who it was.

I took a step forward but Marla pulled me back. Her eyes were wide and frightened. She whispered, "I can't do it. I'll give myself away."

"If they knew anything about you and him they would have come to you when it happened."

"I know, but I can't do it, Johnny. I can't."

"Okay, go home and wait for me. I'll get a ride back."

I gave her the keys to the pickup and kissed her quickly. She nodded but her face was ashen and I wasn't sure she was registering anything other than the fear of being connected to Ray's death. She walked to the pickup, doing her best to look like what was happening on the beach meant nothing to her, and drove away without looking back.

All the boats were beached now and the police and the dive team were standing in a loose circle around the body. Several of them were talking on their radios, reporting this unexpected find to their various superiors. As I approached them the Oakridge officer who had earlier suggested we wait by the rocks held up his hand and blocked my path.

"I'm sorry, you'll have to stay back."

But I had a clear view of the body now. I lifted my hand to my mouth and gasped, "That's my father!"

And so a day which I'd known would be long became longer. Patterson had to be called out. I had to explain to him why I was certain it was my father - how I could tell by his watch and his clothes - that I had nothing new to add to the case, that him being found there was pure coincidence as far as I was concerned and, when the question was put to me, that I did not think the fact Stan had killed Gareth meant that either one of them had killed my father.

Patterson said they'd take my father's body to the lab in Burton to determine the cause of death and to see if there was any forensic evidence. But he told me I shouldn't be too optimistic they'd find anything that would further their original investigation, given the length of time he'd been underwater.

They gave me a few moments alone with the body. The months underwater had erased the features from its face and left it a pulpy ball on which it was hard to define any trace of personality at all. It was a shocking sight, but I was shocked more by my own ambivalence. The sight of my father's dead body should have broken me with grief. But it did not. As I looked at the soggy mass I felt only a puzzled emptiness, as though this body was not that of my father, but of some unknown person I had once passed in the street long ago. I wondered how it was possible for a son to feel this way about his father. But I knew. I knew.

By four o'clock it was all over at the lake. The ambulance had taken the bodies away, the dive team had packed up and gone, and Patterson had headed back to town to deal with his paperwork. The two uniformed officers were the last to leave. They walked up and down the beach for several minutes picking up small pieces of trash the other men had left behind, then one of them came over and asked where they should drive me. All day long I had wanted to be gone, away from this place, but now I felt I could not leave without a last, solitary goodbye to a site that was both the start of the guilt I carried for my brother and the end of all the attempts I had made to fix it.

I told the cop I'd make my own way home. He looked dubious for a moment, then reached into the rear of the cruiser and handed me a folded survival blanket.

"Don't stay too long, it'll be cold tonight."

He gave a small salute and the cruiser pulled away.

I looked across at the bungalow where Gareth had lived. There was smoke coming from the chimney and I knew David would be inside, alone with the loss of his son. I thought about going to see him, but I had enough pain of my own. I sat on the grass bank and wrapped the foil blanket around me.

There was less than an hour till the sun dropped below the mountains and the light on the lake was softening and small insects had come out to stand trembling on the surface of the water near the shore. It seemed to me suddenly that I had been cold forever, and I was cold still, even with the blanket. I drew it up so that it covered my head and I looked out from under it at the lake.

Eight years ago I had left Oakridge hoping to outrun the guilt I felt at Stan's drowning. But far from distancing myself from it, I had compounded it, because by leaving I had added the guilt of abandonment, of sentencing Stan to the exclusive care of my emotionally arid father. Later, too, there had been more guilt as I realized better what my departure must also have meant to Marla.

I should have learned over those eight years that guilt can neither be worked off nor outdistanced. But I did not, and in the end my desperation to be rid of it had driven me back to my hometown. I worked hard there, with Stan and with Marla, trying to force the present to compensate the past. I did the best I could. But it didn't make any difference.

Stan had believed that life would take care of him. And though his mind was less capable than mine he had been smarter than me. He had understood that you cannot hang on to guilt so desperately, so tenaciously, and hope to live a life that is either bearable or worthwhile.

Now, with my utter failure staring me in the face, I saw, finally, that he had been right. It was not the fixing of guilt that was important, but learning to find a way to come to terms with it, to understand that the past must be lived with, not forever battled against.

My guilt had become the structure of my world, but that day, as I watched the waters of the lake darken, the sheer weight of regret I carried finally pushed me beyond itself and somehow, by overload, cauterized that part of me which made such an ongoing agony of my mistakes. I'd simply had too much to take any more and I knew that if I kept feeding my guilt, kept it alive at such a level, I would certainly destroy what little there was left in the world that I still held dear. There would be no chance at all for Marla and me.

I was not absolved, I was not free of everything I had ever done. My past would always be with me and I would always regret so much of it, but there was now a curtain drawn across it, through which it could still be seen but which muted its sounds and colors and filtered it just enough that its incandescent horror could no longer scorch the present so deeply.

Perhaps it would not last. Perhaps my guilt would again catch me and begin anew the process of tearing the lives of those around me to pieces. But for now I was beyond it, and I would use this respite from it to build a life with Marla in which she and I would at last be able to find some measure of joy in each other. Sometime in the future. Sometime, if we were lucky.

I left the lake as the light was fading. There were clouds now in the sky and a breeze had started. Millicent's Datsun had been towed from the trail and there was nothing where it had been but torn earth and the trunk of a tree from which the bark had been scraped. When I reached the Oakridge Loop I called Marla on my cell phone. Half an hour later she met me in the pickup, and we drove home pressed against each other with the heater not working and whatever thoughts we were thinking kept silent inside ourselves.

Patterson called in the middle of the following week to tell me my father's body had yielded nothing conclusive. The fact that he'd been found in the lake dressed in business clothes seemed to support a theory of foul play, but neither the wound they had discovered on the back of his head, nor anything on his person, gave any indication as to who might have been involved. Similarly, questioning David, the lake's only permanent resident, had provided no useful information. Patterson told me he was sorry, but finding the body was probably as good as it was going to get.

Two days later, in the morning, we buried Stan and Rosie and my father.

The next day there was snow on the ground at Empty Mile.

And the day after that, Marla and I locked up the cabin and got into the pickup and drove out of Oakridge toward the East.

THE END

ABOUT THE AUTHOR

Matthew Stokoe was born in England. He currently lives with his wife in Sydney, Australia. In 2014 *Empty Mile* was nominated for France's most prestigious crime fiction prize – the Grand Prix de Littérature Policière. His latest novel, *Colony of Whores*, is available through Amazon.

Printed in Great Britain
by Amazon

33033395R00227